GOLIATH TREMBLED

CONFRONTING THE CABAL

A Novel by

CHRISTOPHER MURPHY

ISBN-13: 978-1530268795
ISBN-10: 1530268796

Portrait of author on the book cover, from an oil painting by Keith Evans Q.C.
Cover picture conceived by Patti Blair
Cover Design, Book Interior Design & eBook Conversion by manuscript2ebook.com

Advance professional reviews

I loved it! How can I not? It is a powerhouse! The content, the writing... the characters... I can't say enough good about it. What a wonderful vision and we know that sooner or later in some way similar to this novel, IT WILL BE. The novel holds your interest right through, even though there are many characters to follow. Thanks for an absolutely fabulous story. I have just finished reading it for the second time

—**Shanna MacLean,**
M.A., Freelance editor and writer

Christopher Murphy takes up where Dan Brown left off in the Da Vinci Code in taking on the "illuminati," in this case the world's plutocratic overlords (and yes, he names names). His protagonist, a sensual, McGyveresque yachtsman/writer with a wry sense of humor and preternaturally deep spirituality finds danger and romance in the most extraordinary of venues, spilling across continents and infiltrating the highest echelons of those very powers seeking to use and dispose of him. If you love page-turner thrillers, exceedingly sensual romances, or new age spirituality, this book is for you!

—**Terra Pressler, J.D., Ph.D.,**
author of Creative Juice: 8 Weeks to Authentic Writing and Callie's Turn, a novel of recovery

"To my beloved sons and grandchildren,
may we all make a difference!"

Acknowledgements

My sincere thanks to:

Nana Tilley
Dave Weininger
Pauli Murphy
John Tilley
Michael Bunnell
Terra Pressler
Ashley Margetson
Virginia Gilstrap
Patti Blair
Larry Salganek
Lillie Veon
Peter Grose
Shanna MacLean

"All quotes from A Course in Miracles © are from the Third Edition, published in 2007 year. They are used with permission from the copyright holder and publisher, the Foundation for Inner Peace, P.O. Box 598, Mill Valley, CA 94942-0598, www.acim.org and info@acim.org."

* "Lyrics of Spirits (Having Flown) by the BeeGees quoted by permission of Hal Leonard."

Spirits Having Flown

Words and Music by Barry Gibb, Robin Gibb and Maurice Gibb
Copyright (c) 1978 by Yvonne Gibb, The Estate of Robin Gibb, Warner-Tameerlane Publishing Corp and Crompton Songs LLC
All rights for Yvonne Gibb and the Estate of Robin Gibb administered in the USA and Canada by Universal Music-Careers
International Copyright Secured. All Rights Reserved
Reprinted by Permission of Hal Leonard Corporation

Forewarning: There are revelations in this story which are factual and very alarming. If one believes the 'official' versions about JFK, 9/11, Flt 800 etc, it is suggested to pause and take another look. The evidence is out there, extensive, damning and proven, but not of course in the mainstream media. Which is controlled by the Corporate Goliath...

CHAPTER 1

One group, one collective, one unified species---consider the tonnage of propaganda that has been poured into that formula, in order to convince populations that elites want the Good, rather than what they really want: Control.

Jon Rappoport

CIA office, Los Alamos National Laboratory, New Mexico, USA

Even well before noon, the sun blazed with terrible power in the rarified air. The hilltop town which housed the "laboratory" had been chosen during World War 2 for its remoteness and limited access, so the trucks which hauled away the nuclear waste to Carlsbad had to travel a perilous escarpment. The security was as tight as Cheyenne Mountain.

The two men had no idea what they were setting in motion, but neither did their new quarry. Furious, the Russian glanced out of the window to see crisscross trails in the sky over the Jemez mountains, but decided not to mention them again. The CIA itself had invented the term "Conspiracy Theory" to mock any exposés by the truth seekers, and being assigned to the birthplace of the atomic bomb was a hideous irony for one who fancied himself an ambassador of peace.

He and the American watched each other with guarded malevolence. One despised the other and the other loathed him for it. Both had recently shaven heads with graying stubble. Frank Uren was overweight, straining the arms of his chair. His look was pugnacious, his eyes sly and suspicious. With several books under his arm, Igor

Knyazev stood facing him across the desk. He was gaunt, lean and edgy.

The American watched with sadistic amusement as the Russian struggled to tamp down his rage, finally saying with icy control, "Frank, you asked me to meet and befriend him and now to betray him. I believe he's harmless, just a fiction writer."

"C'mon, Igor, you betrayed your country. What's one expatriate Anglo? Just take it from the beginning, the whole scoop."

The Russian exhaled his impatience and placed the books on the desk. He tried to clear his throat but 20-odd years of unfiltered Kazbeks had lined it with protective gravel.

"I thought you fully briefed."

Uren pointedly pressed Record on his desk-phone and looked up, his open palm inviting.

Igor shrugged resignedly. "OK, so the Englishman is meeting a guy at a drinks party, not knowing this guy was one of yours, and tells some background on Cold War story he had written. This background stuff turned out highly classified and your guy just clammed up and moved away. He was shocked and scared. He wondered if it was loyalty test. So he reports it and we are sent down to tail the Englishman. The watchers, I never saw them, directed me to a bridge in Santa Fe. They said, 'See that guy eating sandwich, strike up conversation'. So I did and he looked astonished, almost laughing, when he heard my accent. He said, 'Do you know this is the exact spot where Klaus Fuchs handed over the A-bomb secrets to his Soviet courier, back in `47?' He said something about a hinge-point of history."

"*That* it surely was!"

"Yes. It was the start of the Cold War." Igor tapped one of the books. "Now he says he's found out how it ended."

"Like we don't *know* how it ended? Kennedy cold-cocked Kruschev and I kinda thought Ronnie busted down your frickin' Wall!"

The Russian inflated his cheeks and placed the books on the corner of the desk. "Frank," he said patiently, "I'm talking about subtle level. In here he reveals how old Soviet Union discovered that Cruise missiles which America was pouring into England and West Germany did not have nuclear warheads. Late Seventies. Can you imagine what this information was *worth?*"

Uren nodded eagerly. "Yeah. It's still classified. That was the bit that alerted our guy."

"But you see, back then Moscow went monkey-poop, they thought they had Europe by the prunes, all their lethal SS22's lined up in Czechoslovakia and East Germany, dominating the theater, loaded with nukies and the USA was impotent."

The American made no attempt to hide a sneer. "It's nukes, and it's *ape-shit*, Igor, and you better believe me, if one single Comrade had even glanced at an arming panel, we'd have - "

Igor swung his arm in agitation and the topmost book sailed off. Jet-pilot reaction snapped it up in mid-fall. Uren looked surprised, but Igor didn't notice. "Frank, you don't seem to get this. It was worth many fortunes. The truth is they were *not armed*. It was considered too dangerous, too expensive and also pointless."

"*Pointless?* Why? And how the hell do you *know?*"

"Excuse, please, it would help for this conversation efficiently if you would not play bulldog. It was pointless because of what was sold to Moscow in the next book, a sequel. Moscow wanted to know *why* you hadn't armed them."

Uren uncurled his hands, feigning a reduction in skepticism. "I don't follow. Is this for real or in the fiction?"

Igor sat and tried to clear his throat again. "Well, that's the whole point. Who knows? Why don't *you* decide? See, the next thing he tells or sells the Soviets, is that you Americans didn't arm Tomahawk and Pershing Cruise missiles with nukie warheads *because* you had found out that we in USSR hadn't armed our own SS22's, at least the ones in East Germany and Czechoslovakia."

Frank Uren's face seemed to change outline, softening into an expression of satisfaction. "And you hadn't." It wasn't a question.

Slightly gratified, Igor shook his head and went on, "See, what is happening then? Both sides realized there was no way absolutely to find truth, unless actually setting bombs off. You could not just walk up to strategic ICBM and tell by looking or asking politely if it's got nuclear warhead or conventional, and that's just with your friendly ones! At this point it dawned at last on everybody, starting with USSR because of lack of money, that if they ever had to do it, we'd all be up, how you say, crapping creek anyway, so what's the point? *That* was the beginning of the end."

"Huh. But it wasn't the end itself." The American shifted in his seat as if about to stand.

"No, Frank, but wait, there's more, how the impasse was broken. He got this from the Brits. He claims that Mikhail Gorbachev himself engineered the fall of the Wall."

Uren's face resumed its disbelief as he sat back in the broad leather chair, then turned to adjust the window blind, shutting out all the activity in the sky. The searing New Mexico sunlight cut sharp gridlines on the wall, before the gathering haze made everything opaque. "Go on," he said darkly

"Gorbachev, according to this Moncrieffe, was Master Statesman of all time, rivaling even Solon of Athens, 500 BC."

"What did he do?" Uren's response seemed to convey suspicion or scorn for education.

"He set up the Athenian constitution and then exiled himself. He understood the danger, the seduction of power."

"I meant Gorbachev!" Uren snarled.

"Ah. Well, in his case, Gorbachev really wanted *Glasnost*, the opening-up, it was the only way to avoid national bankruptcy, but he had some hard-liners in the Politburo not shifting, so *Glasnost* was at stall. According to this "proof", Gorbachev, not himself of course but through channels and cut-offs, got German student called Matthias Rust to fly single-engine Cessna from Sweden over 700 miles into Soviet territory and there to land right in Red Square, remember? Club planes *never* have long-range tanks, but this one did. Why? So also it was Border Guards' Day and the watchers were all gargling vodka and the stunt was harmless but it indeed penetrated our radar and gave Gorbachev crucial excuse to sack Defense Chief and Air Force Chief, hardliners both. The rest is history. Rust got ridiculous short sentence in easy billet, and of course he denies the whole connection, even now. Says it was just prank. That must have been part of the deal."

Uren leaned forward. "Igor, I remember all that but now you're stretching my credence." He pointed to the books. "You say Moncrieffe has proof?"

"No, I'm saying he *says* he has proof. He is not telling his sources. He also said that something is coming for to turn everything we know downside up."

The two men faced each other grimly. Uren didn't bother to correct but drummed his fingers for half a minute and then leaned forward even more earnestly, like a bloodhound on scent.

"Igor, it's my job, it's our goddamn *duty* to find out what it is, and to unearth those sources. We may have to twist his nuts off to do it, but do it we gotta. Homeland Security, get it?" Uren raised his eyes in private disdain.

Igor shook his head. "Supposing Moncrieffe is just storyteller and that's all. Or if Langley set it up, testing....?"

Uren wasn't letting a chance slip. He held up his hand firmly. "Testing who? Us? Anyway, forget that angle. We gotta cover our asses. We're talkin' *sources* here. He must be making money out of it. He stuck his frickin' neck out, so now he can take his frickin' lumps. We bring him in, OK?"

Igor waved away with both palms. "Hold on, Frank, there's one more. Remember at the end of the '91 Gulf War, Saddam was threatening to destroy the Gulf, turn it into a sea of oil? Apparently someone had sold him the means to do this, the arming panel and the codes - explosives fixed to trees, that's what they call the well-heads on the sea-floor. Saddam would have done it, our KGB already knew this for sure, but he was sold a puppy, isn't that what you say? Pushed plunger and nothing happened. He got so pissed about it, he started 500 oil-well fires in Kuwait instead."

"The big dud," Uren's heavy brows turned ferocious. "You're saying Moncrieffe got hold of that too? How?"

"You mean you knew also?" Getting no response, Igor shrugged again and then held up his hand. "Frank, before we do anything, I have to tell you he's working on new book. He just made trip to Europe. There's the Russian-Jewish ex-wife. He's a Resident, not a US citizen."

Uren had turned business-like, bristling and eager, reminding the Russian of others in the department who felt they had lost their life's purpose with the end of the Cold War.

"Even better," he growled, "We did some background. For a while he was yacht-broking or yacht delivery, and then he disappeared. Did he go to sea? There's several years unaccounted for. We need to find out what he was doing. What else ya got?"

Sneering at Igor's martyred expression, Uren started punching his keyboard aggressively. "See if Plots at Langley came up with anything," he muttered.

"What?" Igor tried to sound disinterested.

"Plots. Section there, they feed novel plots into computers. They reckon some novelists are really inventors who come up with bizarre scenarios, prophetic sometimes. Remember what happened to Clancy after *Red October*? They took him away and grilled the guts out of him for knowing all sorts of classified stuff. He said he either made it up or got it off the Internet. Yeah, right. Trouble was, he thought he was too famous to get whacked, as they say."

Igor chuckled dutifully with some relief that Uren seemed to be lightening up, but after a pause, Uren added matter-of-factly, "So they whacked him. And his pathologist too, after the autopsy."

Igor gulped visibly. "There is no end to this stuff…Moncrieffe also said he had evidence about Philby, remember him? Famous British defector, back in the '70's. The Soviets believed they scored victorious coup with Philby but then later got to doubting, maybe it was all a plant. Now Moncrieffe says he was actually a Triple-agent, a loyal Brit to the day he died in Moscow."

"Huh. That's gotta be total bullshit. Any confirmation from your goons over there?"

"They never could find out. The egg would all be on dead or retired faces anyway."

"I guess. Point is, where'd Moncrieffe get his stuff from?"

"He does not say. He must have sources. Or is it, how you say, artistic license?"

"Chew my ass, comrade. I meant, what's new, what we got now?"

"He says there is maxim: 'Never discuss work-in-progress'. It takes away from energy required for the work."

Uren thrust his jaw with decision. "Neat evasion…Right. Phone-tap. Mail and trash. Email, ISP's. Computer history. Bank accounts. Credit cards. Travel agents. See if there's anything on the missing years. You can borrow the Nasty Wojer to get started." He chuckled, staccato. "Y'know, something about that woman gives me a head o' steam."

Igor put his hands on the desk and leaned forward earnestly. "Frank, you do know about Fuchs' reasoning? He was deep thinker—"

"Yeah, for a goddam Commie!"

"—and he believed it would be a catastrophe if only the West had the Bomb and there was no deterrent. From my conversations, this Moncrieffe is just story-teller and maybe something of philosopher but no way dangerous. He's now like a friend of me. The stuff is seeming harmless anyway."

"I don't care. He's gotta source and we gotta ream it out of him. With the Chinese fiasco and all these recent breaches, this department's gotta kill something with meat on it. And I mean *kill*, Igor. We're not going public just to look like idiots."

"Frank, he's really a good fellow. I wish I had not ever—"

"Yeah, be careful Comrade. Spare me the KY jelly. We *are* the system, and this is business. Look, I gotta go lunch. Catch ya later."

An hour afterward Igor was languidly drawing up his agenda when Frank Uren strode in without knocking, sat heavily in the single chair and burped from his heavy lunch.

"Listen, Ig, so he won't discuss work-in-progress – how's about you tickle him with some outdated stuff that might feed into his current story - get you involved, see? He'll open up then, if you're part of the plot. Could save you a lotta time. Just forget about friendship, `kay?"

"Frank, I have to say, I do not like sound of this."

"Yeah, well, I was only thinking of you, Igor. Like it's still winter up there, and sifting through trash in Alaska at 60 below ain't no picnic, get me?"

"I get you. Tell me, Frank, what happened with the 9/11 satellite pictures that I brought with me, the proof?"

Uren looked suspiciously blank as if he'd heard nothing. He walked out, closing the door softly. Igor put his head in his hands and sighed at the futility of his entire defection.

Igor was surprised by a message on his voicemail. "Igor, something rang a bell so I searched for it. There was an article which tickled me, late Nineties, I found it at the *New Mexican*. Came out long before you got here. Would this still work, ha hah? And have you decided whose side you're on? I gmailed it to you."

The message ended with only a snicker but the accent was unmistakably English.

With bleak feelings of guilt and regret about his new assignment, Igor went downstairs and across the grounds to the library where he opened up one of the computers. In his inbox he read a pasted article from the newspaper.

Traitor Hotline Draws Chuckles

MOSCOW - *An appeal by Russia's espionage chief to prospective double agents doesn't seem to have turned up any new traitors. But it did inspire a burst of front-page humor in Russian newspapers.*
Several dailies couldn't help guffawing Thursday in response to the unusual offer this week by the Chief of the Federal Security Bureau, Gen Nikolai Kovalyov.
Kovalyov said Russians working for foreign intelligence services would be granted immunity from prosecution and could retain the money paid by their foreign masters if they offered to switch sides again and work as double agents for Moscow. In a television broadcast Thursday, he repeated a special number for would-be turncoats to call.

"And then I found another, this is hysterical. Igor, you could go triple and stay right where you are, heh heh!"

On Tuesday the grandsons of Iron Felix (Dzerzhinski) struck a deadly blow to espionage services worldwide. Director of FSB, Nikolai Kovalyov appealed to Russian citizens engaged by foreign intelligence services to get in touch with FSB via telephone number 224-35-00 and become double agents. It is specially emphasized in the appeal that remuneration received by Russian citizens for betraying the Motherland can be retained. Our correspondent, the agent of Sûreté Générale since 1916, tried to get in touch with Nikolai Kovalyov at the above number and to give out the whole network but was unable to get through. FSB press office explained to him that there is only one telephone line and an inordinate number of spies, and further warned him that due to the staff's inability to handle massive response and particularly heavy traffic on the telephone line preference will be given to triple agents.
!!!!

Igor felt his eyebrows tenting in astonishment, since this was something he'd never heard about when on active duty. He shook his head in wry disbelief and amusement, his cynicism reinforced daily. One of his chores in Los Alamos was to scan the main Russian newspapers, a task he'd omitted that morning because he'd been late to work, the result of a fierce and demanding tryst with a dancer from the strip club happily named ABunDance. Such attempts to relieve his loneliness had merely deepened it while the dizzying promise of physical beauty now felt like a barbed lure, another sidetrack from the truth.

Heading back to his tiny office, he wondered if the Brit would turn out to be just a thorn in the foot. The man seemed to laugh at everything, switching unpredictably from scathing to sardonic to pure delight, eyes a-twinkle and reveling in human foibles and frailty. He also seemed very devious. Igor had been neatly deflected whenever he brought up the question of sources, Moncrieffe in sparkling innocence pointing skyward and saying simply "Inspiration." Igor tried to look past the sparkle into faraway eyes, finding nothing to feed suspicion, but logic told him that so much accuracy couldn't spring from pure imagination.

He'd meant to discover more in his own leisurely time but instead that obnoxious, blustering, burger-and-Coke receptacle that called itself Frank Uren had made it an assignment. He foresaw some confusion between his reluctance for the job and his relief to be spending time in the field, or at least away from Uren and Los Alamos Lab. Santa Fe had some mysterious pull, but the downside would be trying to maintain a friendship with Moncrieffe whilst delving into every aspect of his private life. The friendship was threatened at a time when his loneliness and disorientation weighed most heavily. If the probe produced any fruit, Moncrieffe would certainly be made to drive into a tree or just disappear without trace.

Igor felt in his inner pocket for the printout of his last message to Elena in Zaporozhye. He had composed it on his own machine, in English because of the keyboard and he didn't want to raise any alert by switching to Cyrillic. He got a translation program to change it to Russian, corrected the stilted language on a separate keyboard and then taken the flash-drive to Moncrieffe's computer to send it, a risky compromise in itself. He took out the paper and read it one more time before shredding it.

My Dearest Elena,

It feels like a big mistake. Moncrieffe talks about things I want to understand but I am resisting. He has much suspicious information that I'm now thinking they put me onto him deliberately - if so, was that to check on him or on me? Is this my old Soviet mentality, the notion that I was being tested through him, and if I did not report his activities then I would lose my neck? How they used the terror tricks to make us betray friends!

Lena, I would love for you to meet Moncrieffe! He writes stories with action and intrigue. Also he pretends to treat me so pityingly, the other day he was playing a typical mournful Russian tune on keyboard, the Volga Bargemen, then he brought in distant strings and hung so poignantly on certain notes, kept glancing at me to see if I was getting tearful and sentimental, which of course I did, then he roars with laughter and says "Gotcha" and goes off into something called Ragtime.

And he tells me of the parties they have, my little dancer, you would go crazy! He asks: What do you think is the most enviable personal quality? What do you think?

My position here is still very fragile. No question that I'm really on trial every day, and just like in Soviet times it looks like I am supposed to inform on a friend in order to survive. I have no idea how long I need to do this to get permanent papers so I can send for you and Ilya, meanwhile I cannot move with no passport. And of course the notion fights with my homesickness, which is a complete mystery. Homesick for what? Unfeeling authority, cold, poverty, terror, the feeling of being in a gulag of soullessness, yet here I am now afraid of finding my soul! I need your help, sweet angel, so I hope I can help you to bring it to me. You will like Moncrieffe if they let him stay free or even live..... I wish I knew whose side I am on. One of these days he will accidentally see your photograph. Meanwhile, love to you and Ilya. Say nothing to Mama yet. Dasvidania.

Feeding it into the shredder, Igor reflected that his relationship to his sister Elena was close enough to threaten both of them. He'd several times considered the extinction of Leonid, her ex-husband, yet in truth the man was to be pitied for losing such a jewel. Suspicion being so endemic all over the old Union, the *apparatchik* Leonid couldn't believe she was real, that her truthfulness and passion did not have to threaten him or harbor sinister meaning. An easterly transfer of 3000 miles to Vladivostok and minus-50° winters was one solution but then Leonid had spitefully lapsed his connection with his ten year old son. For the child, emotional and learning difficulties had followed, testing Elena's buoyant nature to the limit.

He wondered if she would really thrive in the West, perhaps with someone chosen for and not by her. Typically he fudged the answer and turned to his new task, creating a top-security file for Moncrieffe, code-name, what? After a few moments the name "Enigma" popped into mind, and then he hesitated over the Category even though Uren had effectively given him no choice. The order had a number of automatic follow-throughs, not least being his own appointment to a team of shifty sifters.

Without the Cold War, people like Uren had been forced to invent daily more strained reasons for existence. The Chinese crisis had been timely, but so overblown that the big boys in Washington had jumped on it, leaving the local team scratching for leftovers. The biggest nonsense was the indictment of a Taiwanese on charges of spying *for* China, made public and going nowhere. Then came 9/11, Afghanistan, Iraq, Homeland Security, paranoia, colored scare alerts, and the hounds fresh-pumped with adrenalin. Meanwhile the overwhelming and damning evidence he'd brought all the way from Russia seemed to have disappeared without trace or comment.

Nic Moncrieffe sat puzzled in his office, a small section partitioned from the wood-shop. On-screen, his Inbox contained an item from one *Elemosk@cs.ru.com*. When he pulled it up, there appeared a lengthy script in Cyrillic letters. He shook his head and then promptly called Los Alamos and Igor's extension.

"Knyazev," rasped the reply.

"Igor, it's Nic. I got an e-letter in Russian. Must be for you. What do you want me to do with it?"

"It cannot be for me," Igor said quickly.

"Well, I can't tell anything about it. Do you want to see it?"

"I do not! You understand my position here, yes?"

Nic chuckled. "You mean after that newspaper article?"

"No!" Igor replied hastily. "I mean, in any way. It would be disaster for me to engage in any correspondence with anyone outside this country. They know I have no family and therefore no reason to speak with anyone, do you hear?"

Nic picked up the rising note at the end of the sentence and finally realized that Igor was speaking for the benefit of listeners.

"Oh, OK. Well, it can't be for me either so I'll just erase it."

"Do what you think best. Are we not meeting today for dinner and the movies?"

"Oh, yes, so we are. How about Tune-Up, 6 o'clock. You know, Hickox Street?"

"I will find it. Nic, I see you later."

Turning back to his keyboard, Moncrieffe pulled up a search for online translations and found one that would do short sections of text for free, max 250 words. He blocked the first several lines and entered them into the translation space and waited. In a few seconds the words came up, stilted but intelligible.

Beloved,

It is happy I am hearing thus from you. Finding your soul, it is indeed time. I am so desirous of such opportunity. You know how all is here crime and danger, so little food, these two horrible rooms, Mama has been sick and Ilya missing school. It is shocking to have a son with his spasms and his difficulty in memory that with computer I search between the nets among symptoms and now sure that he has bloody clump in his brain from the fall. I will make encounter with specializing doctor in Kiev, soon. Paying is impossible. There is no idea what to do if surgical penetration is needful. Criminals operate hospitals. They are without hygiene comfort, not even medicine, blankets, food. You know all this.

Your friend seems good for you. I would love to meet him. Is he married? I never hear from Leonid again, which hurts but yet am I rejoicing, I just discover that Mama had plans for termination of him, can you believe it? I am pure desire for that day when beams can transport us like on TV, fly to you like sorceresses and will make fine dinners for you and have many crazy dancing friends, and laugh and sing and cry to stupid old sentiment songs from mother country. This is horrible time to be alive in most dirty town Zaporozhye, we can never open windows for the bad air. The new fall of snow turns black within two hours. You found this place for us during sea wind in summer, you did not consider. Just what we breathe I do not know.

The program reached its block limit, so he had to repeat the process to see the touching remainder.

So, dearest, if you are only safety-rope to be alive even one-tenth like Hollywood seen, please I beg you take care your life. We would grapple the end of it and you would pull us all the way over. I am so grateful to read you. For me, the most enviable quality is to fear nothing. Sometimes I can do it for 20 whole seconds, like holding breath. Forever Elena.

Nic sat and stared at the screen unmoving for several minutes, astonished at the poignancy of the message, aware of several blanks that needed filling. On his first visit to the house, Igor had somewhat shyly asked to send an e-mail from this computer. Nic had left him in privacy and never enquired about it. This had to be the reply yet Igor was openly denying it, therefore his connection with this Elena must be compromising, but to whom?

Shrugging it aside, he went back to editing a new manuscript, but as he worked, the tone of the letter kept returning, hauntingly. Most imposing was the thought of his own son aged 12, and in the pink of health. He thought of the newly-opened organic food store, now the fifth and largest in a city of a mere 80,000. Standing inside on opening day, he'd gaped in near horror at the cascading opulence, musing ruefully that the Third World would rise *en-massacre* at the mere sight of it. It seemed like sheer defiance.

This in turn raised the ticklish question of knowledge of conditions. Through the media, the West was fully aware that a third of the world was not only starving but also media-deprived, meaning that it did not necessarily have any awareness of anyone else's privilege or that starvation was anything but normal. The emotions raised by the letter kept intruding and hampered inspiration. He tried to conjure a picture of what Elena had described, a scene so pitiful and potentially abject, yet a bright spark of courage and forlorn hope seemed to glow through it. He felt a strong desire to respond although pure logic fought the idea alarmingly.

From his window he had a clear view of the Sangre de Cristo Mountains with the light capping of snow above the aspen line. He grimaced at the thought of this turning black within hours of settling. Clicked onto an Atlas program, after some searching he found a short description of the Ukrainian city of Zaporozhye, a half-million souls and some seventy manufacturing plants. He found no good reason to dwell on this and in a moment grinned to himself at the thought of some possible leverage over the Russian, with this connection he was presumably forced to hide. After the first meeting and a later visit to his house for coffee, Knyazev had left clutching bemusedly several books which he vowed to return intact. It was after a subsequent visit, seemingly as an afterthought he had come back from his car holding up a flash-drive and diffidently asked if he could send a message, saving a trip to the library. Moncrieffe never asked why he didn't just use his smart phone.

After a sporadic work-spell, a snatch of conversation from his current manuscript seemed to take over. Unaware that he was still in the alter-ego of the writer, he started to compose a reply:

Beloved! he wrote, *I just wanted that to be the first word I sent in reply to yours. For sure you must be someone's beloved! A message came to me in Cyrillic. On translation I found it not addressed to anyone. I have been asking myself, "Why has this been presented to me?" Perhaps there is no reason, but still I am intrigued by my own response to it. I am a writer and almost every time I focus on a story and get myself out of the way, characters take over, something mysterious or miraculous turns up to support it. I was touched by your note even though it was not intended for me. I have been considering my extreme privilege of where I live, and it seems to be imposing a responsibility on me.*

I also have to trust that this is based not on guilt but on a whole new understanding of reality, and that there may be something I can do for you. I realized that if my son (age 12) had a problem such as your Ilya's, I would find a way to take care of it. I do not have much spare money but a strong belief that ways get found, mysteriously. It seems that the Universe loves to surprise which is why expectations seldom materialize, at least in the way we expect!

I look out of my window and with great delight I see that it is RAINING! You might not be able to imagine the joy of this but in the high desert of New Mexico we have 300 days of cloudless skies and recurring drought, while rain creates daily gloom where I was born (300 days of gray) in England. My roof is leaking but it doesn't seem to matter.

A strange feeling comes over me as I write this, as though I am getting to know you just by directing thought towards you. I have no feedback (I don't know if that word will translate, it means more information in response) so I have no knowledge of your age, temperament, outlook or relationship to anyone here who can admit to having a correspondent in Russia. For all I know you could be a 200 kg mud-wrestler, a politician looking for votes or a Mata Hari sent sweetly to trap me!

He worked the text into blocks for translation and just before sending it off added, *I repeat, What can I do for you? Wishing you blessings from this strange encounter, Nicoll Moncrieffe.* He canceled the program's attempts to translate his name.

Glancing at his watch he realized that everyone East of Europe would be long asleep. He thought of a single mother on the other side of the globe, living in cramped quarters, the windows shut tight against polluted air, hopelessness, despair and bafflement, yet riven with flashes of optimism, of spirit, like a prisoner dreaming of freedom and some wild rampageous behavior.

The tiny finger-stroke required to press Send seemed all at once as a distant star compared to the possible enormity of its earthly consequence. The matter was suddenly out of his hands, the message on its way at the speed of light - already arrived and irretrievable. Without calculation or forethought, he'd been prompted to ask a question that could be a lifetime juncture, or a consequence so self-inflating that pride would promptly try to own it and contaminate the pure well from which it came.

Left to itself, he decided, whatever this Elena's wishful response, it could be granted effortlessly by a benevolent, responsive Universe as easily as a brook bubbles up from the earth. Or else some interfering self-appointed hero could try to force its issue, perhaps binding the poor heroine to a life of unrepayable debt.

After chewing on this from many angles, Nic concluded with warped relief that the only motive guaranteed for purity must be utter selfishness.

CHAPTER 2

The quest for enlightenment is but the inchworm of conceit, measuring a leafless cane.

Ludmilla Simonova

Tune-Up was crowded and steaming. They found seats across from each other at the community table, where Moncrieffe watched intently as Igor perused the menu.

Once their order was taken he asked, "Tell me something. Suppose one fine day someone of great power should say to you, 'Igor, old chap, what can I do for you?'"

"You mean, *'djinn v boutylke'*. - the genie in the bottle. *'Tri zhelania'*, three wishes?"

"If you like."

"Well, a few million dollars would solve all my problems. Uh, please!"

"Excellent. In reply, the genie does something unexpected. You know the expression about give a man a fish?"

"Instead fishing lessons, to feed for life, yes?"

"*Da.*" Moncrieffe grinned back. "The genie says, I will teach you how to make a million dollars, then you can do it whenever you like. How does that feel?"

Igor rolled his eyes. "Delicious. Full of power. Is this the big secret you were talking about on the bridge?"

"No. But listen, let's suppose it's all energy. You heard about the statistics of people who win big lotteries? Within 3 years they are virtually all, as close to 100 per cent as makes no difference, back where they started. Lack-belief, which is what prompted them to buy the ticket in the first place, has not been transformed by the gift from outside, it's still there and soon reasserts itself. But if instead someone says 'I lack for nothing. Every second, every encounter is an opportunity to declare this, to express my gratitude for living', what happens then?"

Igor said nothing at first, staring straight ahead as if testing the notion. Finally he nodded. "So, this is the most enviable quality?"

Nic grinned and toyed with the mischief, shaking his head. "But it does seem like a choice, right? A decision to make. It doesn't depend on externals, other people, circumstances; it's purely an attitude, whether you're a pygmy hunting a meal, or a Trump chasing a deal, a response to life?"

Igor's eyes narrowed suddenly. "Why are you asking me this?"

"Well, you know that message I got, the e-mail mystery, remember?"

The Russian nodded darkly. "No. What about it?"

"I replied to it."

Igor's gaze held perfectly level, like someone trying to look trustworthy. "Oh? What was it all about?"

"I'm having trouble believing this myself," Nic smiled wanly. "It didn't sound like she was having too much fun, so I went and asked what I could do for her."

"Just like that?"

"More or less."

"And what do you expect for reply?" The Russian's pupils may have widened enough to betray his duplicity but Nic, looking casual and ingenuous, simply shrugged.

Letting it go, Igor said, "You are not rich, I think? You said you were mortgaged up to the nostrils, no?"

Nic nodded. "Right. So let's call it New Think. It *seems* like a choice. Let's say something comes up, is presented, or prompts a thought. We have the response thought, the pure motive, and the Universe takes care of the details, the form of it. If my co-operation is required, it'll supply me with an idea, one which is practical and fun. Otherwise it will just send me a cheque. The form and details are none of my business. My concern is simply to respond without fear or consideration, from a notion of abundance. It seems the lady's son has a medical problem. If my own son needed an operation, say, I would certainly find the means even if I had to hock the whole shop to do it, right? Look at the power of her thinking, her desperate plea to the genie - it's a done deal, pfft, like that. Maybe she just doesn't know it yet."

Igor sat astonished. "But this response, it doesn't make sense. You don't know anything about her, she could be—"

"It doesn't matter. Something got conveyed and a response was evoked. If I don't know something, maybe I don't need to. It's actually a relief to come from a place of no ulterior motive, no pre-formed notions."

"I don't see how that's possible," Igor said. "You form a notion when you receive a message. You start to imagine circumstances, personalities, problems."

"True...It touched me. But I tried to keep mind out of it."

Igor continued to stare and finally shook his head in disbelief. Reaching casually for his wallet, he extracted a photograph, slid it across the table. "What does that tell you?" he asked.

Nic took it without expression and moved it under the lamp. He stared at it wordlessly for a full minute, setting it aside as their plates arrived.

"Isn't this a famous face?" he asked, but Igor shook his head firmly.

"Then I take it this is a snare?" Nic grinned finally, "You're a dastardly double agent using this person to entice and entrap me. OK, deep breath, my first response to this picture was, well frankly, alarm. I got jolts both here and here." He quickly indicated both chest and solar plexus.

"What does that mean?"

"I think it means she's exquisite enough to fall quickly in love with, but that in itself is scary. See, so-called 'Love' takes control. It interferes with choice and autonomy." He tapped the picture. "But look what her expression says: 'You are taking my picture so I do hope you like the look of me, even if I am a little shy, yes, I know I am tiny and pretty enough, but then again I cannot care what you think so take me as I am, my left leg is slightly advanced because it looks sexy and I feel sexy, I am very gentle and kind but tough as a tigress, I love beautiful clothes and generous people and wild parties, I love to give and receive in equal measure, I know that something wonderful is coming my way, I am a brilliant cook and a very skilled lover, I am just waiting for him and I will never nag or criticize him or find anything to make him think less of that first delirious impression and I will be very careful with his money and--'"

Igor finally erupted with laughter. "If you can get all that from a photograph I think our Security gives you a job on the spot!"

Nic chuckled. "Yeah, right. But you never know about chemistry, do you? And the language thing–I wonder if that could be an advantage? Do I assume she's Russian? We all chatter, criticize and analyze so much, try so hard to make people understand. Feeling gets bypassed, with all its fine subtlety. Igor, have you wondered what you're *really* doing here?"

"What do you mean?"

"Well, you responded to a lure, from the National Security Agency or some such. You spilled your guts in return for a post and a visa and now that you're pumped dry, they give you some crummy job in Los Alamos working for a total pork head. What did you have to tell them, anyway?"

Nic's question came with a mischievous twinkle since he expected no reply but Igor surprised him, looking quickly left and right and speaking just above a whisper. "You tell no-one, right? I bring FSB satellite pictures from the morning of 9/11. I know for certain that they were not shopped, but I heard nothing more. I was naïve enough to believe they would be useful, but of course there must be gag-order, incredibly far-reaching. Now I am completely in limbo and feeling it was all for nothing."

"Hm...But still, something draws you down the hill to Santa Fanta, Mecca of the New Age, Woo-Woo-land, it must be like another planet for you."

Igor nodded as if agreeing but still mystified. "It's mixed, though. There's a special atmosphere in this place, but I have not put my thumb on it."

Nic leaned forward intensely. "Igor, I believe there's something very big coming up, it's the sharp end of a great wedge which might be about to split and shatter the old world, the fiction, the world of fear and lack and separation. Consider, you may be here as a witness, like they came to see the first atomic bomb-blast. Here you are in the world at the most awesome and important time in the history of *homo sapiens*. This next decade is critical, even sooner. Some say that from the end of 2012 the known world has been moving into a new paradigm, a new way of thinking."

Igor looked skeptical. "Are you talking about a, how do you say, Coming Second? Who's behind all this?"

Nic chuckled without correcting. "But it's coming from within, see? Finally creating what we've always wanted, after eons of checking out what we *don't* want. The only way to be part of it is by becoming aware of what's really going on."

Igor said nothing but opened his hand as if inviting more information.

"Here's the conundrum. How do you talk across paradigms? Imagine talking to a late-nineteenth-century farmer about the aerodynamic problems associated with breaking the sound barrier. Total incomprehension. Then a few years later he actually sees an airplane fly, his curiosity might be fired to hell and he has to make a major shift in his thinking - prompted by a massive desire for this greater experience. Thus with the Age of Truth, let's call it. The talk doesn't cut it anymore. To some extent it will point the way, but what's the real carrot?"

Igor's head swayed doubtfully.

"It's coming across people who are serene, energetic, grateful, gracious, all-embracing, un-judging and 100% delighted with their existence - as opposed to the lives of, quote, 'quiet desperation', trudging through this, quote, 'Vale of Tears'. Simple question for you - what do you want?"

"Money."

"What for?"

"Freedom. And not just for me," Igor added quietly.

"Ah, but are you free to have money?"

"I don't understand."

"OK. Submit the question to Central Processing and forget about it. But be ready for a glimpse that is truly delicious. Next question: who is answering the question?"

"I am."

"All right. Want to try something? Close your eyes and take an internal step back, observe who is answering the question, can you do that?"

Igor fluttered his eyelids for a moment and finally nodded.

"Good. Now observe that observer from another step back, who is that?"

The Russian pondered even longer and finally shook his head. "There's no-one. It's just watching."

"Brilliant! Now, what does it want?"

"Um, nothing. Well, just to watch. It feels............"

"What?"

"Delicious. Very calm."

"Perfect! Now, who is it?"

Igor covered his face for a moment but a mighty crash of plates from the kitchen broke the spell. Opened, his eyes were full of alarm and wonder.

Nic nodded with a smile. "You can't hold onto it. Wanting to hold is old Ego stuff. Now that you've seen the observer as no-one and nothing, you have to see everything in a new light. It's pure consciousness. Well, I suppose you can forget it and relapse, in fact the Ego will try to make you forget, but it's a monster carrot."

Igor picked up his fork and waved it in the air. "It feels more like a dog chasing its tail, from back here, at this table. And hungry, because you won't let me eat."

"Yep. But suppose that is all you really are, all you really want to be, except of course that it doesn't want for anything."

Igor brightened. "That's what it felt like - just being, and nothing else, but with no limits."

"Hah!" Nic's eyes were bright with mischief. "Now then, what can we DO with it?"

Igor's quickness and intelligence were suddenly streaming from the added humor. "You mean, how can we sell it? I - I don't think you can, you can only *be* it. The question is, *how*?"

"The farmer's curiosity was piqued. He became an aviator. Nothing changed except his *perception* of himself and his surroundings. Now tell the aviator that he is really a cosmic super-voyager, as well as the ultimate instant creator of everything he perceives. He can't believe it till he sees it. When he sees it he wants to fly it, it's falling in love, this time with Reality, All-That-Is. Where does that wanting spring from?"

"What is Reality?"

Nic let out a long breath. "Now you can feed," he said with a grin.

Both men ate for a long time in silence, restraining crinkles of humor when their eyes met. Eventually Nic asked, "Can you ever go back?"

Igor shook his head vigorously.

"How about that amnesty thing in the newspaper, the chuckles?"

Igor shot a glance at the ceiling in complete dismissal, his mouth still busy.

"Couldn't your bosses fix you up with papers so you could go as someone else? And we could hypnotize you to get that haunted expression off your face - that's the big giveaway!"

Igor's chewing slowed to halt, his eyes widening. "Are you serious?" he asked, swallowing hastily.

Nic leaned forward. "I think you hate what you're doing, you probably regret a whole bunch of other stuff, and you think that money will solve it all. Into this frame of mind the spirit of abundance cannot come. It's repelled. And on some level you know this, so it haunts you and affects your expression."

"Shit!" Igor spluttered. Wiping his mouth forcefully he demanded "What can I do about it?"

"Huh, whaddo *I* know? But here's the problem: it seems the right answer cannot come to the asker of that question." He held up his hand to Igor's protest. "Hold on....The asker of that question is a do-er, see, and the answer doesn't lie in doing but in being. That means reconciling, coming to an understanding of who's there."

Igor made no attempt to hide a sneer. "So who am I really?"

"Ah-ha, the great New Age trick question. But same problem, there's a built-in catch. It's a personal, ego-centric question looking for an ego-free answer. It demands the quantum leap. Note also, the ego-mind gets terrifically repelled by this topic and wants to get drunk or stoned or have sex or go to the movies, any similar distraction, you notice?"

"Yes, please. Let's finish and go!" Igor drank some beer and attacked his food again. After a little while his jaw began to slow, his head turned and he watched Nic from cornered eyes.

"The observer of me eating does not feel hunger."

Nic nodded. "It's kind of amazed by it. But the observer of the observer, that one just accepts -- everything -- just as it is." Glancing up as the door opened, he added, "Is someone looking for you?"

Igor turned towards the entrance, grimaced and brought the heel of his hand to his forehead. The figure in the doorway simply nodded and vanished. Igor reached inside his jacket, made a movement with his hand, spoke something quietly from the corner of his mouth then returned to normal.

"Explain," said Nic, bemused.

"I have to check in, about every hour. Inside here is a GPS locator so they always know where I am, but of course I have to be there as well, not just park it and go somewhere. If I'm more than half an hour late the watchdogs are on me."

"Does it monitor your conversations as well?"

"It can if I wish, if I leave it switched on. They allow me that privacy."

"Hm. Decent of `em. Are you sure?"

Igor's head jerked forward on his neck. "I cannot believe I never thought of it. They just showed me the talk button, for my check in. I think you have a devious mind, no?"

Nic shrugged. "I just have a thing about exploring possibilities, so my sources are very -- Igor, what are you doing now?"

The Russian was muttering again inside his jacket. "Movies. I had to tell them I'll be off-air for a couple of hours."

Nic took out his wallet but continued to stare blandly. Although expressionless, his face had somehow an upward trend to it, the eyes fractionally widened, as on the brink of excitement.

Igor watched him for a while in silence, then asked, "And you, Nic, what do *you* want?"

"*Moi?* I think—I want to be always in love with my own responses, to whatever comes up."

Twenty five miles to the Northwest, computers checked a voice ID for Igor and inserted an electronic tag for another voice in the background. The next morning, the words would be filed or discarded depending on significance. '*My sources are very--*' earned a red tag and a new voice ID, as permanent as fingerprints.

Creeping early light seeks union with a vase of yellow fuchsia. Each golden flower is a reminder of the exquisite and the limitlessness of possibilities. With this image the eyes close and conscious mind subsides. Awareness settles itself gently into vacuum, like a broody eider arranging her nest. The yapping of a terrier next door registers no longer as an irritant but as a reminder to drop deeper within. In this place there is no hankering, no wistfulness, no malice or other disturbance, only Is-ness, pure awareness of awareness. Overall there is a feeling that something momentous is coming in.

Unbidden by conscious thought, fingers seek the pen, the pen the page. *Beloved*, scribes the pen, *Yesterday I asked what I could do for you. I think I got the answer from an unexpected source. Tell me your version and we will see if it's the same.*

I have a notion that almost everyone feels bound or trapped by circumstances but is really seeking something much deeper. Everyone is trying to find out what is REALLY going on here so they can get a handle on it, control it somehow, change it for the better. They cannot find a trustworthy source. And the other problem is that they are looking at it with the wrong decoder, like through binoculars set for the wrong distance, so even when they get the answer, they cannot interpret it.

I'm sure you must be asking yourself "Why is this complete stranger talking to me like this?" Answer: It is because I feel that the world is about to have some incredible new secret exploded on it. And no, I have not yet been given any details. I am waiting, quietly confident. It's as if I know something huge is coming.

Just as you have almost no ideas about me, and there is no influence from gestures, pheromones or expressions, you are holding what we call a clean slate. Yet if I write on that slate, you interpret according to your own ways, influences and conditioning. You may not even be curious about the secret shift, as some people certainly are not. But if you do have curiosity, how did it get into you and not into another? Luck, fate, grace? Or some might say, ill-luck?

The pen's motion ceased. Nic got out of bed, found a bathrobe and shuffled into his token office. He stood quietly inside the door, sensing some kind of anomaly. He frowned for at least two minutes before it came to him, the laptop was fully closed. He always left it fractionally open to avoid wrestling with the catches. His breath expelled in a silent whistle. He felt sure he would have heard any intrusion in the night so it must have happened while he was at the movies with Igor. Senses on alert he became aware of the merest trace of an alien scent. Putting the two together left him in no doubt about an intruder, but if not for theft, then for what?

Aware of a curious indifference, he recalled the first time he'd been burgled, losing a vintage Hagstrom 12-string guitar and a Sharp stereo. The dismay had been intense enough to cause the opposite reaction: I do not want to feel this upset, therefore I declare that I simply do not care. The dismay faded quickly, to be replaced at once by a feeling of new adventure. Two subsequent burglaries now found the same equable response, so on this occasion he was at first curious and then strangely delighted.

Possibilities swarmed among thoughts like puppies chasing tails, too many to track. Tuning them all out, he sat until there was nothing but clear vision, a blank screen. He felt the corners of his mouth lift with the realization that he had no idea where this would go, only that it was loaded with promise.

Switching on the machine he typed in what he had first written on waking, blocked it into translation and sent it off. Then he began again directly into the computer:

Beloved, information and its twisted forms has always had an irresistible appeal for me, in fact I think it's what started me scribbling in the first place. So consider Shakespeare: "All the world's a stage, and all the men and women merely players." Let's say you've been handed a costume and a scenario. The people around you are also auditioning, all variously equipped, are chattering about the play's content, its meaning, how they are going to handle their parts and so on. Some are pundits, determined to make sense of it all, others are naïve, or meek, curious, awe-struck, scared, even indifferent. The pundits imagine that if they can get enough players to believe their version of what's going on, that will overcome their own uncertainty. Is this is how religions get started...?

Now you might expect me, at this point of detachment and observation, to come up with MY version of what's going on, thus lurching into the same trap. However, there's one very odd factor in this particular play—the very last part isn't in the script. Not the Director, not even the players know the outcome! Mystifying and exciting for everyone! Imagine the atmosphere, especially where all those desperate for some form of control are longing just to lean in on the whisper.....

Nic smiled at his own flowery language, knowing that the translation program would butcher it beyond recognition.

The hackers had already been thorough. The e-mail, in Russian, appeared simultaneously on the night watchdogs' screens. Instructions were consulted on the text filed for coding in the morning. The Western world slept whilst Ukrainians, Elena among them, bundled up in winter clothes, breath steaming, and plodded dismally for the buses and subways.

In the bleak half-light of a Monday morning, she unlocked the engineering design office where her part-time job gave access to a computer. Every day she logged in and checked for messages which, though reduced to rarity, brought tiny distant glimmers to the darkness of her isolation. *"Vy poluchili soobshenie - You have messages"* always jolted her into animation, a feeling which delighted just for itself, especially after weeks of no contact.

This time her eyebrows arched to see two messages, one quite chatty from Igor referring to a new friend, the other a long, weirdly phrased and disturbing self-introduction to that person. Reading at first eagerly, she found herself getting strangely upset and pulled two ways. Part of her wanted to dismiss the words as incomprehensible, yet in another way she felt curiously calmed. Some of the agitation came from a growing awareness of her confines, the tensions with her mother and all the other strictures of her life. There was no space or energy left for the luxury of introspection or flight above the torment of her days, yet the assurance of the words seemed to contain a gleam of hope. There was also the sudden yearning triggered by the question, *'What can I do for you?'*

Feeling sure that Igor would not endanger either of them, since he had used some incognito address, she changed her screen name and then began to tap out a cautious reply in her native Russian. On translation in New Mexico it would come out as *'I am delighted to hear from you, mystery man. I will make print and try to uncover the meaning later. It frightens me because it feels filled with hopes and I seem to be a in a place without these. Perhaps I am mistaken already, but that is how it seems on first response. So you think something very serious is about to happen?... Just now the chief approaches so I must finish. Thank you and again thank you from Elena.'*

The outer door had opened signaling the arrival of Arkady Kozlodoyev, the icy partner responsible for staff hiring. Even though only part-time, this job was perilously precious to her, and as one who normally smiled whenever she spoke, she was always set back by his stone-faced response. Still, she felt stubborn about modifying her ways, even if it made him squirm under its apparent teasing.

Kozlodoyev nodded perfunctorily to her and made for his office, his eyes immediately lowered from her bright greeting. For a brief second she caught a clear glimpse into the pain of such repression, and became suddenly aware of the change in herself as fear switched to compassion. The moment seemed to pass swiftly as he came out again and barked an order for some files and drawings but to her surprise the mood had taken hold. The abject hypocrisy of her stance seemed to vanish into a sensation that she much preferred.

She got up and delivered the documents, feeling a gentle patience mixed with pity. No longer obsequious, she evoked a response from Kozlodoyev that astonished her as he nodded his thanks.

"Elena Knyazeva," he said with a small hesitation, "Your work is good. Do you wish for more time here?"

Startled, she considered a moment. "Thank you, sir. Yes. But I have a young son with medical problems, and I do not wish to be unreliable."

"You will not be. Lydia is leaving. Work as much as you wish. That is all." His hand movement made clear that the conversation was over. He neither acknowledged her response nor noticed her long deep breath of gratitude.

Returning to her computer, she quickly composed a note to Irina Popova, a longtime friend whose genius for languages had paved her way to the West. Irina now lived in a smart apartment in London's Hammersmith with an income unheard of by legitimate Russian standards.

"*Dearest Irina,*" she wrote. "*I received an e-mail from a man in Amerika, in New Mexico. He is English and is a writer. Like you he talks of matters I have trouble understanding. I think back over the things you have shocked me with, including your view of sexuality and relationship, so refreshing and yet so frightening, your complete rejection of this corrupt and hypocritical society, your mockery of the egotistical and the fearful. I had long wanted to know why I could not do the same and this morning I had a quick look at a new possibility. I had actually had a moment of pity for the pig Kozlodoyev and one instant later he turned almost human and offered me some more work time. Can this be true that my attitude actually affects his, and instantly? Well, I must go now and be a good little worker.*

P.S. I wonder, could you translate my message to the Englishman and pass it on? He made translation by machine and it comes through with little sense and no humanity. I relay it to you, see what you think. I also received a list of very important books, an attachment, it came from a different address, a library perhaps. He is sending me some money to buy them. Amazing! E.

Irina and the rest of London still slept while New Mexico prepared itself for night-time. Elena felt a sudden further awareness of her boundaries shifting, her mind expanding beyond these walls, the tiny concerns and the bleak morass of hardship, beyond this evilly polluted industrial town where no-one would dream of opening a window unless a full Southerly gale was scouring in from the Black Sea. Irina's tales of jet-set parties and bankers in limousines, trips to Paris and the U.S., had always seemed like fairyland, like shiversome novels of romantic fantasy.

The phone rang, her mother saying that Ilya had gone to school but seemed pale and listless. The notes of blame ran perennially in her mother's voice, blame for Ilya's deadbeat father, her own dead husband, the politicians, her disgraced and vanished rebel son, the weather, the teenagers, the Mafia and above all the manifest unfairness of God.

Elena thanked her gently for the information and then asked what she would do today. There was no reply beyond a plaintive moan and Elena decided not to pass on her news of more earnings.

Hungrily she went back to her keyboard to re-read the e-mails, both received and sent. As she scanned the lines it seemed that something moved within her small chest like nothing ever felt before, swelling, like early spring petals pressing urgently against the confines of their calyx.

CHAPTER 3

Them that asks no questions isn't told a lie......
Laces for a lady, letters for a spy,
Watch the wall, my darling, while the Gentlemen go by.

Goldsmith, Old smugglers' song

Several days passed before all the intercepts were put in place, by which time Security Specialist Frank Uren was once again feeling the hunter's quickening. He stared at the printout, his heavy brows furrowed. He jabbed a button in his intercom, waited for the gravelly response.

"Knyazev."

"Igor, get your Roosky rump in here, pronto."

When the knock came a few minutes later, he gestured brusquely towards the chair. "Igor, they're on to us. How did that happen?"

Igor shook his head. "I am sorry, I do not follow your thought."

"Dammit, man, they've put in a cutout. Think they're being smart, look." He turned the page and pushed it across the desk.

Igor read in silence, fear creeping up the back of his neck.

Dear Nic,

I felt certain that I was missing your real meaning; the translation is so obscure it cannot be what you are trying to say. I have a dear friend in London who is a master of both languages (that's me, Irina!) And she has agreed to check our dispatches. She has no allegiances (and is a complete cynic! - Ira) I know this will take longer but it will be much safer, don't you think? She has explained to me your symbols but of course they mean nothing until I receive the hardcopy. I will order the Course and the other books when I receive your draft from Western Union. I am grateful and astonished. I do not know what to say. This is such a great mystery.

I am also shaking whenever I think of your words. This suffering I would not have known was suffering, without the TV and the Internet and letters from abroad which now they can no longer stop, (or can they? Irina) *now this suffering is worth any price to end. Short of endangering or losing Ilya there is nothing I will not do to make it so. You can rely on me 100%. When will you know the secret? Will it change everything? And after this we all fly away to a warm and magical tropical Isle?* (And are you going to let ME in on it? I have ordered the same books already! Irina). *I absolutely have to get this information, or it will kill me to know that it is there and I do not have it. I am eager for our next rendezvous in writing. Elena'*

Igor looked up and slid the paper onto the desk, trying to disguise his difficulty in meeting Uren's glare. "Where do we go from here?" he asked meekly. "We couldn't get the attachment, about the books."

"Never mind, it's a piece-a-cake! One word from you to your old bosses in Moscow and this skank Elena gets debriefed, reamed out and cranked into bratwurst. Puts you back in favor and then we can use your double status. Moncrieffe conveniently commits suicide by arrangement. Score: 30/Love for Frank Uren." Uren's eager grin turned to disgust. "But No, Langley's having me play this out, crack the codes, find all the sources. This engineering office she works for, must be a front, right? Zaporozhye sounds like a serious shit-hole, six dozen smoky plants *inside* the city, crisakes, must be a chunk of `em on defense work, `cos that burg's on our Master Target list. Guess I shouldn't have told you that, Igor, heh-heh, mention it and you're toast, Christ, you stink of those frickin' coffin-nails, prob'ly kill ya first."

"Frank, if you are still treating me like an enemy alien, why would that ever change? How can I ever be trusted here?"

Uren nodded seriously as if sympathizing. "Yeah. To be honest, what've we really got to threaten you with? No lover, no relatives here, no-one in the old country we could use against you? You don't fit the pattern. A horrible death is about the only thing we can hold over you, heh-heh! It's all in your file, matter o' fact."

This thought brightened Uren's frown into a crooked smile, then he snapped back to business.

"Right. You know what to do. 'Codes' can get insiders at all the email encryption outfits, if our villains decide to use `em—hope they don't, it gets tricky and expensive. Everything else, in any language, send it in. Hey, make a list of all the books out in his study, including this Course thing."

Igor nodded, making notes on his hand in ballpoint.

"Good. They'll use abbreviations for the book titles and misleading numbers for the pages. Get me a single co-relate and we've got 'em, right? This Moncrieffe feller is looking at Terminal Island for about two hundred years. Over to you."

"But Frank, you don't --"

"Oh yes I do, betcher ass! Somehow they have to convey the key, the book and the page. Usually by another conduit, can go in a whisper, like *'Crime and Punishment, page 22'* If you don't know the key, the code's unbreakable. That's what you gotta find."

"I don't understand -- '

"Didn't they teach you anything in the Lubyanka? Look, say on page 22, first time the letter A appears, you substitute whatever is the next letter, or two after, whatever is agreed on beforehand. Next time it comes up, go three ahead so there's no discernible pattern. Next time the same book is used but it's page 25, whatever. Computers can't crack it, see? 'Kay, go find 'em and sick 'em."

"But if they're reading them in a different language, it won't correlate."

"Yeah, it will, computers'll just allow for it. Get outta here."

Outside, Igor leaned against the wall, his face set in rage and dismay. The worst part of his dilemma was knowing that he himself had a part in creating it and at the same time excluded and endangered the one person with whom he could have shared it. Less pressing but urgent enough was Moncrieffe's apparent innocence, at least as far as the correspondence with Elena was concerned. On the other hand the man's quiet but abnormal confidence was mystifying enough to be sinister.

Nic Moncrieffe had woken around 3 am without knowing the reason. He tested and found no thirst, no bathroom urge, just a clear alertness as though a mist had cleared.

He tried to remember what had prompted or arranged his first meeting with Igor. He recalled gaily talking up one of his old story lines with a cocktail acquaintance and at a certain point the other had switched off his humor and clammed up, leaving the party soon after. Two days later, after an umpteenth baffled visit to the mystic staircase in the Loreto Chapel, munching a sandwich and not even knowing why he was there, he met the Russian émigré, gaunt, grey and cadaverous as Rachmaninov, leaning over a very significant bridge on the pathetic, ruined trickle still called the Santa Fe river. Then the mysteries began to mount. The first message from Elena, disowned by Igor, the secret search of his office, all had potentially worrying implications. Then Igor had shown him a photograph ostensibly to enquire what it told, yet when asked who it was he'd simply put it away.

Without conscious decision he put on a bathrobe and padded out to his office. Signing on, he found an email from *Ursaminor*, Little Bear, alias Irina in London.

"Dear Moncrieffe,

Our friend Elena writes again. I think she must be hot-to-trot. I don't mind doing this at the moment, my workload is not so heavy and your stuff is starting to get me excited. The English have this wonderful and disgusting phrase 'vicarious pleasure', which is beginning for me as I write. Of course, you will not know if I am to be trusted not to embellish! No, I sort of promise to be faithful, because now I too want to know the secret to end all, so please don't leave me out of the loop at the crucial moment. Here is the latest:

Dear Nicoll (Are you Nic for short? The affectionate for Nikolai in Russian is Kolya. Can you be code-name Kolya?)

I am astonished by your question. I will be taking Ilya to see the Professor in Kiev in a few weeks and will have more to tell then. At the moment I cannot write about the crisis, to what extent it is.

To answer your question, I take up very little space. In your measure I am 5' 2" and weight 95 lbs, exactly the same as the divine skater Ekaterina Gordeeva whose husband died on the ice and left her as the darling of the people. Her heart-melting smile was responsible for much of the global warming and she used to be the most beautiful woman in the world until she emigrated to United States and is now therefore officially considered a sack of turnips. I am told that I look like her, but that would certainly be one of my three wishes because it cannot be so. Google her and lose your breath! However, I feel her spirit exactly, with this longing to share grace, beauty and compassion with the entire world. I am as if in a dream state when I speak like this, my circumstances here being very different.

So I must ask the same question, what can I do for you? I hope you will not answer 'Nothing', even if I cannot make any suggestion from this little corner of hell. No doubt when I have the big secret you will tell me what to do with it, maybe let me sell it for a mountain of rubles. Meanwhile I do understand, at least I say I do, that it cannot be conveyed all at once, that there is critical background information. Is it that our current mechanism cannot receive this? Do we need to upgrade our equipment? Be sure that I am otherwise prepared, even if I am not clear about its purpose. I await the keys, day by day. Miracles and secrets are so thrilling! Your friend Elena."

Moncrieffe stared at the screen for several minutes but with eyes glazed. At some point intuition found a chink in the process and his gaze snapped into focus on the fax and phone wall-plate. No more than ½ mm of white paint showed on one side of the plate. He reached out to test it and found it tight and unyielding. Fetching a small screwdriver he removed it and examined the recess. Four of the wires had small plastic nodes crimped onto them, innocent looking items like wire-nuts except that he had fitted the outlets himself when converting the office space and knew they didn't belong. After the initial surprise at the additions, he felt his face lifting again in involuntary amusement.

"Dear Irina", he typed in the reply space, *"Thank you for doing this. The web translation programs cannot carry flavor or nuance. I feel sure you are an expert at reading between the lines accurately! Please decode when you have time and send on:*

Dear Elena,

More background. My contacts with scientists from Los Alamos, which in case you do not know is where the atomic bomb was developed just up the road from here, point to a serious problem. They have to do their work as if physical matter existed, otherwise they would lose their jobs! This in spite of the fact that their own latest discoveries are now proving that Einstein was right, there is no such thing as matter, at least not as we know it. A while back they even succeeded in isolating the "top quark", the smallest theoretical particle, they actually cornered the little imp and found there was nothing there! It was simply energetic potential.

It has also been known for some time (Search 'Heisenberg') that a particle of matter alters itself between wave (or potential) and particle (or actual - according to our notion of actuality) depending on whether it is being observed!!! Thus the action of observation is critical to its appearance as so-called matter. This means that the observer and the observed are essential to each other, which should be obvious for any such activity, but the implications are limitless and are the first stage of the upgrade you mentioned. The foundation of historical thought is trembling and must collapse. Talking of which, it's 4 am and I'm going back to bed. More soon. N.M. in N.M.

P.S. Quote some guru: 'Nothing in the Universe means anything at all, except the meaning I bring to it.......' So, who is this "I" and what does IT mean? CM, W32, T613.. Thanks Irina, for you both I accept code-name Kolya!"

Moncrieffe drifted back to sleep brooding about meanings, how once when the earth was believed flat, a host of erroneous notions followed. And stars in a named constellation, given meaning by its shape yet each differing in hundreds of light years distance from earth, would show a totally different pattern when viewed from another position in the Universe.

As he did so, the wires between Los Alamos and Langley VA were already buzzing and intercepts between London and Ukraine were automatically activated. When Igor Knyazev checked in for work there was already an irritated message from Frank Uren.

"Igor, get your Commie carcass in gear. Find out what this means: ACIM, W32, T613. Go figure. Check the book list."

Hurrying over, Igor watched to see if Uren would look up at him and show a spark of humanity but was disappointed. The American, his face suffused to an unusual shade, was barking further orders into his speaker-phone. Igor found his own stress rising as Uren handed him a list without looking up. He took it carefully and left without a word.

With reluctant diligence he examined the list of accessible books found in Moncrieffe's office and bedroom. He made a further list of the titles in abbreviation and finally with simple initials. Shortening still further to what seemed like a convenient minimum and at last came up with one single possibility.

Not yet having any of the books available, a guess was no practical help so he left a brief memo for Uren and drove his old Chevy Blazer down to Santa Fe. In the Ark bookstore on Romero Street he was politely shown to a whole shelf devoted to A Course in Miracles, which came in either one or three volumes, accompanied by numerous commentaries and a huge reference book. He felt suddenly both ignorant and intrigued so he sat down on the sofa to examine the original text. He had hardly opened the onion-skin pages when a handsome, middle-aged woman dumped herself next to him, threw off a bright silk stole and settled herself with a rattle of bracelets and long turquoise earrings. Returning his curious glance she pointed at his tome and chuckled.

"Won't get through that by lunchtime, that's for sure," she said heartily.

"I don't know anything about it," he admitted sheepishly, "But it's a strange title."

"Indeed. Where are you from, Eastern Europe?"

"I am from Russia." Igor made his voice and accent sinister since it amused Westerners and sometimes their eyes grew large with alarm.

This woman answered bright and unabashed. "Cool, splendid. Well, a New York Jewish woman, atheist, psychologist, starts hearing voices, eventually hears an actual command. The Voice says to her, 'This is a Course in Miracles, please take notes.' What should I *do?* she asks her colleague. Well, *Duh*, quoth he, or its latter-day equivalent, Go channel, sister. Seven years and 1200 pages later, you hold it in your hands, Text, Workbook for Students, Manual for Teachers. The Voice implied that it was Jesus but she never admitted that, she just called it The Voice. Difficult writing, especially if it's not your native tongue, it's almost in verse, fine cadences."

Igor looked at her gratefully. "I do not suppose you could give me a brief synopsis?"

She gave him a rueful glance. "Certainly! It's a brilliant if rather thorough exposé of the total falsehood of the Ego-based world. If you like, it's the complete formula for freedom, how to exist in truth, gratitude and perfect relationship."

Igor stretched his mouth and hefted the book. "It must be more difficult than I thought," he said with mock resignation.

The woman chuckled and put a heavily-bangled hand on his arm. "There's several groups in town, they read from this together. Laugh a lot and tease each other, for the Ego-stuff, you know."

Igor looked uncomfortable and said quietly, "I don't, I mean I don't know, er, what it means."

She stared at him for a long moment, her eyebrows arching, then exhaled "Ah," as if she'd just heard a terminal diagnosis. "Damn, I meant to get some *chai*. Like a cup?"

Igor shook his head and cautiously opened the book as she heaved herself up and bustled off. The density of the printed pages made his eyes glaze, then for a moment they cleared on a single sentence.

"The ego is quite literally a fearful thought."

As he tried to examine the phrase his mind seem to run into blocks, like a rat lost in a maze. After a minute the woman returned and sat carefully this time, long leather boots creaking and a waxed cup of insipid liquid balanced in a napkin.

"There," she said. "My name is Rose. My family calls me Rose Madder. East Coast. Old Money. Not a soul between them. And you?"

"Igor Knyazev. I find it difficult to believe you need 1200 pages to understand what means the Ego. What happens for the uneducated, or the just too busy?"

Rose chuckled. "Ha, now *there's* an Ego-thought.......All right, listen up. Don't be alarmed."

She cleared her throat and then hummed up and down as if testing an instrument for pitch but the background of bland New Age music threw her off. She shook her head and said "Can't sing in here. Just the words." Unexpectedly in a quiet, clear voice she began to recite:

"There's a single note in a symphony,
Without which the music has no sound.
Yearning for harmony, that special tune,
But do you think it knows its way around?"

She hummed a little longer as if words wouldn't come, then resumed a new verse,

"I am a single drop in the ocean of desire
Without me the tides can't ebb and flow,
Can it be the wave and the rain and the river
And still believe it knows just where to go?"

"I am a single blade in the prairies of the All,
And yet what is it makes the meadow green?
If beauty's in the eye, the "I" could never die,-
– Without the seer, what is ever seen?"

She smiled at him as she finished and then said, "There's more, but I haven't written it yet. Now, where were we? Ah, Ego. Yes. Basically it's a false belief in who you are. Are not, rather. Know what I mean?"

Looking at his expression, she smiled gently. "Hm. Alright. Let's say you're an actor. You are given a part and if you're a really good actor you get right into it, *become* it. But then when the play is over, if you go on behaving as to the part, everyone will think you're schizo, right? Good. Just so here. Director says: Here is a play, it's called, ah, Time. You will play Yesterday, She will play Tomorrow, and he will play Today. Tell me, what is the flavor of Yesterday, what kind of character do you sense?"

Igor frowned and finally answered. "Regret. Guilt. A few happy memories, perhaps."

"Good. The memories, are you just delighted with them or wistful 'cos they're gone?"

"Wistful, I think I know what that means."

"OK, and the flavor of Tomorrow, how's that?"

Igor considered. "Anxiety. Wishing for more, wealth, peace, loving. Fun. You know."

"Uh-huh. And if you are to play *Now*, how does that feel? Totally, this moment, no future thought, in fact no thought at all, just feeling what it feels like to be in this moment. How about that?"

Igor closed his eyes and was silent for a half minute. Abruptly he opened them, looking haunted.

"I can't do it. I mean, I had a glimpse but then anxiety comes, what I am going to say, what am I supposed to be feeling, how do I play this part with no experience, and so on."

"Ah, yada-yada, I know. Future thoughts, plus some past thoughts, guilt for not doing it right. Now try again. Just be Now. What is happening within you?"

After a pause he answered, "Inside? I am very aware of your presence. My heart beats."

"Are you sure, can you feel it?"

Igor smiled. "No, I just presume. No, wait, yes, I do sense it."

"OK. Now put full awareness in your chest, see if you can pick up the rhythm, just from the pulse pressure in your body." To Igor's slow nod she added, "Is your skin tingling, hands, feet, scalp? Good. Anything else?"

"Yes. But if I told you, you might leave. Or slap me. A vital feeling."

Rose laughed gaily. "Wonderful! I guess my wicked body must have sent you a pheromone and you picked it up—maybe the only reason you agreed to play! But that's the best "Now" gift, to feel delight in your urges, instead of longing to have them sated. And all the time you've been aware of your insides, what's been happening?"

"Nothing...Well, it is feeling good."

"There you are. Now you can play Now."

Igor opened his eyes and gazed at her boldly. "Thank you."

"You're welcome. So, the Ego is everything else but this moment Now, and everything connected with it is pure fiction."

"I am sorry." Igor shook his head. "It is so difficult to make sense of this."

"Gotcha. That's because there's one little problem here, the mind receiving this information cannot understand it, because the mind is a temporal thing in a temporal body with an apparent history and an apparent future."

Igor protested. "The history is real. Once I was small, now I am grown. I know this."

"Um. And history gets written, I know. But it's still subject to the mind's interpretation in the moment. Matter, Time and Space are inextricably linked. Prove the fiction of just one of them, they all disappear. But Time we know is arbitrary, space is emptiness measured in Time, like light years, see, and matter has been shown to be just pure energy."

Igor shook his head bewildered. "But I bump my head, it hurts. Five minutes later it still hurts."

"True. Or at least your mind tells you it still hurts. If someone were to inform your mind that it doesn't really hurt, it will resist. Then you can be hypnotized to get out of your mind and go into Now and be told it doesn't hurt, and suddenly it doesn't. If I tell your mind that neither it nor the future exists, it will resist. Switch off your mind, for instance by dwelling in your heart or just being in gratitude for simple awareness of beauty and this resistance vanishes. The ego-mind is the wrong equipment to receive this information, that's all. Someone said it's like trying to do microscopic eye-surgery with a chainsaw, it's the wrong piece of kit! Now they've found that the heart has a brain of its own which is powerful enough to override the head-brain and accept beautiful information like this, because it only functions in the present. That's another book for you - the *Heart-Math Solution*. And two other books for you, quite new, *compulsory* reading -- "

"Please, I --"

"Alright, I'm sorry. All in good time. But it's a new life, a new world, I'll go further, it's a promise of the return of the Garden of Eden."

"Do you not mean *to* the Garden of Eden?"

"Hey, you're clever! Neither, really. It never went away. It's all attitude. But it does seem to take time because of the mind's resistance, since the mind is reading the book. But laughter is a huge help, it's a very Now thing, and of course there's hypnosis, as I said. Local ones I know, look up Edward Rice. Or Julia West, Harriette King. Or Nic

Moncrieffe."

Igor stared at her in surprise but she stood up abruptly.

"Gotta go. It's pamper day. I'm having a colonic, a girls' gossip lunch, a massage and tonight a tantric workshop. Can you believe this town? It's like the Mecca of the New Age! Call me if you're confused. Here's my card. Just think, you could take happiness back to Russia, all neatly packaged, make a fortune. Well, I'll see you perhaps. You know, you have such a noble face."

Igor looked up at her from the depths of loneliness, caught himself and smiled. "Can you tell me, if there's a reference in this Course to T613, what does it mean?"

"Oh.......maybe T is text, that's the first, the big part......." She peered over as he turned to the page. "Brrr, just a great wall of print. What springs out at you there?"

"Um, let's see..........There's a quotation, in italics: '*I do not know the thing I am, and therefore do not know what I am doing, where I am, or how to look upon the world or on myself.*' And then it says, '*There is no statement that the world is more afraid to hear than this. Yet in this learning is salvation born. And what you are will tell you of itself.*'"

"There you are, then. See ya." Rose chuckled gaily then bent down to touch cheeks. She smiled into his eyes and swept out, the creak and jangle of her passage clearing a way between the browsers.

As Igor watched her go he became aware of a figure near the counter, his raincoat foreign among the jeans and casual wear. Pale eyes glared from under a hat-brim and the man tapped at his chest, twice abruptly. Resignedly Igor reached inside his jacket, thumbed his GPS, spoke briefly and nodded. Raincoat pulled a finger across his throat, pointed menacingly at Igor and then left without acknowledgement.

As the tendrils of conditioned fear subsided into disgust, Igor finally remembered his mission. Consulting his notes he quickly made sense of the other indicator, WB32, as a reference to the workbook. It wasn't clear whether 32 was a page or a lesson number. One was headed "*I have invented the world I see*," while another read "*I am determined to see things differently*." Both would have to be tested against the text of the letters for any recognizable patterns. With a sigh Igor realized he would have to buy the costly book which meant an inevitable fight with Uren over expenses.

After paying he watched in astonishment as the young assistant, so gentle in her movements as to seem almost stoned, touched her lips reverently to the cover before placing it in a bag. As the receipt printed, he thumbed his phone to call Moncrieffe.

"Nic, it's Igor. Is lunchtime for you…? Yes, I know it. One o'clock then?"

The assistant waited till he finished, gave him the book and receipt, then placed her hands together and bowed over them with an angelic smile. He felt as though he'd been blessed by the wand of *Dobroya Feya*, the good fairy.

"What've I caught you with?" Moncrieffe said over Igor's shoulder, startling him.

Igor shut the book sheepishly and craned his head around. "A woman in the Ark recommended you. As a therapist. Her name was Rose."

"Rose Madder?" He looked agreeably surprised.

"Yes. She seemed to think it would solve all my problems. Why would she think I have problems?"

Moncrieffe grinned and sat opposite. "She's a real kick. Well, maybe it's your long face, your grey complexion and your furtive behavior. Or else you've been eating pork and she read it in your aura. Along with homesickness and romantic yearnings."

Igor looked pained. "Anything else?"

"Uh-huh. Paranoia and resentment of authority - and perhaps utter bafflement that a mature man of high intelligence has yet to find the key."

"If you could meet with 'authority' you would know why I resent him. Paranoia is simply that they cannot ever be sure whose side I am on, no matter what I tell. What else? Oh, the key. I am sure that it is in here." He patted the big blue book with its gold lettering, re-opening it to a marked place.

"'*Truth*'" he read, "'*Can only be experienced. It cannot be described and it cannot be explained.*' Yet is this not 1200 pages of explanation?"

"Catch-44," Moncrieffe chuckled. "How do you explain the inexplicable, to the mind that cannot comprehend it anyway, and cannot recognize truth?"

After a long, gravid pause Igor surrendered. "Well, tell me, if you're going to. It sounds like those Greek philosophers, Sophists."

"They tried their best. Let's go and order. It's all Middle Eastern."

As they waited in line, Moncrieffe asked casually, "What sort of education did you have?"

"Privileged. I got degree from Military school in Kiev, then to the Moscow Institute for International Relations, a course for future diplomats and, er, Intelligence. In military service I had four years of flying, fighter jets and later helicopters, Mil-24. Gunships, you call them."

"Four years and they let you go, after all that investment?"

"I was in court-martial."

"Oh, cool!" Moncrieffe said with some glee, "What did you do?"

"Um, I neglected a protocol."

"Do tell."

Igor sighed and rocked his head. "I did not report my gunner for missing a target he could not miss."

"What was it?"

"Running refugees. Afghanistan."

"Ah. So they stuck you in the KGB, or FSB rather?"

"You cannot be told anything more." Igor looked away quickly.

Moncrieffe gave a deep rumble of scorn. "Damn cryptomaniacs," he said, "Or that's what one of my heroines called them."

"Meaning that's what *you* called them?"

"Uh-uh. I've actually no idea what my characters are going to say next. I'm simply a word processor. The people just take over."

"Oh, so you are not the puppet master, like God?"

"'Course not. But really yes, just like God, as all creativity. See, if ideals ran the show, all the 'bad' guys would vanish and there'd be no duality action. So, if you like, God - actually I prefer to say Godness, like an essence - threw everything conceivable into the possibilities pot and let it ferment, according to all the laws of probability. So Godness does not interfere but instead witnesses outcomes through the eyes of

7 billion participants."

"Puppets."

They ordered Tabouli and Falafel amid friendly banter with the Egyptian owner, then returned to the table where Moncrieffe resumed with a chuckle. "Up to a point, puppets, yes. Because of our programming, characters, proclivities, genetics. But when we bring those things to awareness we discover we don't necessarily have to follow them blindly. It's the most important discovery."

"Why?"

"Because freedom means blossoming into the sheer delight of who you really are, instead of the programmed robot running entirely on fear and greed."

"Who you really are, there is no fear?"

"Check. Just like you found yourself watching the hungry man, yourself. *A Course in Miracles* explains all that, how there is *nothing* to fear, a concept unimaginable to the ego, which cannot hear it, and which mistakenly believes it is a separated individual and can be harmed, suffer and finally croak. This is true if you believe it, of course. Same with everything. But it's possible to wake up out of this limited belief into another realm of knowing. At that point the Ego-world becomes a giggle and love is allowed to run the show instead. Shit still happens, or seems to, but one's attitude to it is different. I take my hat off to you for your willingness to take on such a mighty opus. There are other more succinct titles. Marianne Williamson wraps it up in *A Return to Love.*"

Igor shrugged slyly. "Then why do you use it? I saw it in your office."

"Oh, I think it's because reprogramming does seem to take time, like you pound and pound away with what is unreal and fearful and then one day a huge laugh erupts and there's a great sigh of relief. It's like a software upgrade. I guess if the mind can be battered with the real truth for 1200 pages it might just give in and get off it. Laughter seems to be a crucial tool. Of course, the Ego will then attempt to own 'enlightenment', which it cannot, of its nature. There's plenty of laughter in watching it try. Ego-mind is like an old 286 trying to run Windows 10. The very notion of an unreadable program is a real threat to its own existence."

Igor shook his head. "This word *Ego* is too close to my own name. And it is made to sound like something bad."

"No, it isn't bad, it's just mistaken identity. We have this perfectly valid mechanism that helps us cross the road and take care of ourselves and our children. I can identify with it and writhe under its helplessness and mortality or I can happily and gratefully observe it doing its little job perfectly. Same with my personality, I can identify with it or be amused by it. The mistake is identification because --"

"But --"

"There's no freedom in it. It's bound by its narrow walls and its fear of being nothing and powerless. Actually, I think it's just an app!"

Igor shook his head in more bewilderment. "But you treat it as a joke. This business of freedom and happiness is the most serious subject of our lives. And you can't go round pretending you are not who you are."

"I know. I think I've got a foot in both camps. Like a frog trying to be on two lily-pads at once. Ah, trough-time, that's our number, I'll get `em."

Igor was still looking unhappy when Nic came back with their dishes, sat down again and said, "You know, you can't pretend to be eating when you're eating, like you can't pretend to be having an orgasm when you're having an orgasm! You have to really engage in it or you can't savor it. When I engage in it with delight and gratitude, it's transformative, but when I go into need or desperation or fixation, I am locked into this third dimension, yes/no, attractive/repulsive, alive/dead. The shift comes like the grateful actor saying to the writer/ director, 'Thanks for giving me this part to play. It's exquisite and full of limitless subtleties and nuances. I can really get into this!' Imagine how gratified the Director, with actors like that. Yet most of the world's players seem to play their parts in bewilderment, in opposition or reluctance, or even in fear of losing the part. They don't understand that they've been perfectly cast. And the world is consuming itself simply for lack of this information, and runs almost entirely on fear."

Igor ate in silence for a while. "This is the second intensive I have had to-day," he said eventually, "I feel like my landing gear is locked up, hydraulics are gone. I am declaring an emergency."

"Eject, eject, eject!" Moncrieffe hissed gleefully.

On trained instinct Igor made to tuck in his lower legs and elbows, then reached his fork above his head for an imaginary handle. "Fire canopy. Limbs in tight, pull face mask. Deep breath, scream: *KATAPOULTIRUYSYA!!*"

His hand jerked down and there was a long silence as his face cleared of tension, though he kept his eyes screwed shut.

"Did it work?"

Igor smiled. "It did. I am floating free. I am no longer the Mig-23. I am detached – till next time!"

"Good job."

"Were you in the military?" Igor asked opening his eyes, "All that flying in your stories."

"No."

Igor's look narrowed at this abrupt denial but Nic glossed over it. "People love telling you what they know."

"So do you," Igor replied pointedly.

"Ha, right! But cryptomaniacs, they're not allowed to, are they? That must be mighty restricting."

Igor went still as he considered this and finally nodded. "It's like yearning I have, to find a beach in the South Pacific and throw my past and my clothes away forever."

"Hm.....Are you alone?"

"Oh no, I am not! There are many delectable ladies with sweet dispositions, and a very friendly barman."

"And how is it without them?"

"I could predict you would ask something like that. Please, let me hang in the parachute a little longer."

Nic's broad smile agreed. "Bravo," he said quietly. "So the Mig 23 was an extension of your pilot identity. But suddenly it just wasn't doing it for you anymore and you punched out. For a very brief period you are in control of nothing, just the observer, floating in bliss. Then comes the bump, return to apparent reality. Hitch-hike back to base for a new Mig and a resumption of identity."

Igor was listening intently. "But you cannot stay in the parachute."

"True, but it gives you the glimpse you need, at least to see what you are not."

"And if you are over the sea you can drown with a new outlook," Igor growled, adding, "Russians dig morbid humor."

"You know there's one of your a Mig-17's here at the Santa Fe airport? An outfit called Jet Warbirds, they've a couple of your trainers as well, L-29 and L-39. It lets ordinary folk fly military jets, if they've got about $2000 for an hour, that is."

Igor's face assumed a momentary keenness. "I was instructor on those for almost a year," he said before shrugging, "So what? Old days, old world. But it is not like riding a bicycle, for sure. Bicycle on high wire, maybe."

"Where?" Moncrieffe asked slyly.

"I cannot tell you that," Igor grinned, "But it was just outside Novgorod."

"And you've no family over there? No kids, ex-wives, close friends?"

Igor's eyes narrowed but he gave a heavy shake of his head. "It's the only reason the CIA let me come here. Otherwise I am considered a risk, if FSB can use them against me. Was KGB, same thing almost. They just changed the name."

Nic nodded absently. "Does Los Alamos know you're talking to me?"

"They must, of course. I am watched constantly. It does not amuse me to check in every hour, especially since I believe in taking longer to have erotic encounter." Once again he reached inside his jacket and muttered a few words quietly. Looking up, he added, "I am encouraged to socialize."

"Meet the natives? But me, I'm a foreigner."

"Yes, they....probably know that. But they want to know what you were doing in years before you came here."

"Hm…Are you supposed to find out?"

Igor said nothing but inclined his head inquiringly.

"I don't talk about it much. They were dangerous years. I was in aircraft repossession. Can you keep it to yourself?"

"I can, I am less and less inclined to co-operate. Uren should deduce something from your stories but maybe is too stupid. For repo you have to know many types, yes?"

"Scores, hundreds. Hey, where are my books?"

"I forgot, I will bring them next time. You have devious ideas, where do they come from?"

Nic shrugged. "The mysterious Biggall mostly, my best source. And contacts, you know. Somebody always knows someone."

Igor tried to smother the jolt, a hint of success. "Who is Biggall?"

Nic chuckled. "A pseudonym, no doubt, one of many. For example….I was doing a story about this agent chap one time. He was wired so the bosses could keep tabs on him 24/7. It was a simple matter for the other side to slip him a mickey, scan his transmitter for the frequency and then they always knew what the first side knew. But the first side didn't know that they knew, of course."

Igor's hand started involuntarily towards his GPS but checked itself. Frowning he asked, "Why did the second side want to know?"

"Some people feel they have to know everything, just to feel safe, which of course they can't, ever."

"But if first side guess what is going on, they could use him to spread some misleading information."

"Yup. Devilish, eh? So, what shall we slip `em?"

Igor's face assumed a faraway look, tinged with both alarm and speculation. Moncrieffe watched him in cautious amusement.

"Igor, are you thinking what I am thinking?"

"No, I am not. Whatever it is, I am not. Uren wanted me to slip *you* some misinformation, as trap. I tell you this so do not make any mischief for me, do you hear?"

"My dear chap!" Nic exclaimed in snooty English, unsure whether this phony protest translated.

Igor's scowl confirmed that it did. "I have watched much television since I came here," he said slowly, "It is noticeable that America likes to use Englishmen to be bad guys. They show them as suave and untrustworthy, with educated accents and well-tailored suits, you have noticed?"

Nic nodded, exaggerating the Oxford accent. "Inferiority complex, old boy. If one can't have something, one's got to knock it. I mean, dammit, old boy, how can one suddenly acquire centuries of good breeding, um? Ah well, I'd best be orf."

Igor watched him stand and raise his face with a vacuous expression and imagined he understood. He mused, how could Hitler and the Nazis have been so deluded to imagine themselves the Master Race, in the face of such aloofness?

With a smug nod, a self-mocking wink and a sympathetic pat on the shoulder, Nic slipped out towards the side door, leaving him with even more conflicted feelings.

CHAPTER 4

Art can never exist without Naked beauty display'd.

William Blake

"Gotta run! Love ya! Click the lock, Annie." Meg the yoga teacher vanished, somehow leaving the trace of her bright smile by the door.

Alone in the studio, a bulkily dressed figure approached the great mirror, twisted this way and that for long moments and finally addressed herself.

"Anastasia Wojerkowski," she grimaced, tilting her head in cajolery. "You are trapped by your own personality. Your smile is ambiguous; your normal face is severe. You do not know what it is like to be popular or even liked. And when some angel like Meg shows unconditional affection, you get suspicious. How does she see past your mean streak - and is there anything past it? Thoughts of revenge fuel every waking hour and poison most of your dreams. Meanwhile, what hides inside those thick woolly socks, sweat pants, and three tattered T-shirts is completely wasted, hidden from the world, untouched by loving hands."

Keeping an easy balance, she unwound her right leg horizontally, stretched herself languidly over it and plucked off the sock with thumb and forefinger. She repeated with the other, then turning away from the mirror she bent slowly, put her hands on the floor and pushed up carefully into a handstand so she could see herself again but upside-down. Using just her toes, inchingly she lifted off her sweatpants and flung them away, revealing slim and tautly muscular, silk-hairy legs.

She lowered them in a split, stood abruptly, pirouetted and then peeled off all the T-shirts as one. Revealed was a neat upper torso split by a broad, shapeless sports-cinch from armpit to armpit, which seemed to strain against confined inner swelling. With a nervous glance towards the door she unhooked the cinch and felt the rush of relief as her breasts sprang free. As usual, but heightened now by the chance of intrusion, of being caught in nothing but the merest black thong, they filled her with gratitude for their ripe fullness. Astonishingly for her 40 years, they jutted proudly without any crease beneath, as long as she held her shoulders back. A long-ago lover, a college art student, had pronounced them useless, that he couldn't even park a toothpick under them, let alone a paintbrush when he needed one. The thought held both humor and sadness, since Carlo, the art student, a lover of true heart who saw past her bitter expression, had gone down on a minor dope charge and died mysteriously in jail.

She twisted her body lithely, inspecting it for ominous signs. Once a considerable teen athlete in her native Poland, a middle-distance runner, she still kept in rangy shape by swimming, jogging and climbing 14,000 foot Colorado peaks in summer, and cross-country skiing as soon as the first high winter snows settled in. With a mind also unusually gifted, she had graduated *magna cum laude* from Cornell and was fluent in seven languages.

She was constantly surprised that the cinch didn't collapse her breasts but seemed to stimulate them into added resilience. She wore it mostly to work, a fairly unsuccessful attempt to defy those who would speculate on its release - particularly her disgusting, lip-smacking, crotch-scratching pig of a boss, Frank Uren. The very intruding thought of him opening the door right now had her scrambling quickly back into her cinch and her everyday clothes, overlaid with concerns about her new assignment. The worst thing about Frank Uren was how he relished calling her Mz. Nasty, a knowingly dreadful slur on her patrician name.

As she dressed, Anastasia reflected how gently the teacher Meg called her Annie, and how something inside her tried to resist yet seemed to swell in grateful response. She moved closer to the mirror for a little experiment, closing her eyes for a long moment while she considered Meg's sweetness, then opening them suddenly as if to catch herself unawares. She was met with a gentle and delighted smile, quite unlike anything she saw in her bathroom routine. She was acutely aware that despite her intellectual gifts, her ascent of the intelligence ladder had been virtually halted by her sour expression, a wit as penetrating as a plasma-cutter and a cynical disrespect for authority like mole-poison in the tunnels of officialdom. She dearly wanted to know how Meg was able to bring unremitting sunshine to every interaction and wished there was some easy, digital way to download the teacher's benign and buoyant program.

As a teenager in Poland, the young and ripening Anastasia had witnessed her father's imprisonment as an over-active member of the Union *Solidarnic* and his never-explained disappearance. When Lech Walesa became the Union leader, he had learned through his own sources that Anastasia was herself death-listed because of her outspoken efforts to find her father, despite her youth. She had been hastily wafted out to the USA just before the jackboots kicked the door down at 4am, when her already heart-broken mother had died from a rifle-butt stoving in her skull.

On hearing the news months later, Anastasia had foreseen her next steps with rare clarity. She prepared herself meticulously for acceptance by the West's most insidious Intelligence outfit. Once ensconced and trusted, she would use her connections in any way necessary to track down the perpetrators and exact a slow and excruciating revenge. She reasoned that the eye-for-an-eye syndrome had been plainly ineffective long enough and it was time for a meaningful upgrade in reprisals. Ironically the bitterness which had carved itself into her face over years of grief and seething had become her chief obstacle to advancement in the Agency. She kept receiving horizontal promotions which had eventually landed her in furthest New Mexico, doing routine work and fighting daily battles for autonomy against a philistine with a two-digit IQ, backed by the sensitivity of a rhinoceros - a philistine moreover who would fix his bug eyes upon her flattening breast-band and cluck his yet uncaring disapproval.

She had been careless in some way, she knew, though it took most of a day to work itself through her subconscious. The laptop on Moncrieffe's desk should have been left slightly open but her helper-cum-hacker had been too zealous. After milking the contents of Moncrieffe's hard drive, including all the items from Recycle believed dumped forever, the nerd Ben Storey had lost interest and grown inefficient while Anastasia was photographing and finding herself somewhat intrigued by dozens of abstruse book titles. She actually wished she could spend a few more hours perusing such as "*The Power of Now*", "*I Am That*", "*From Onions to Pearls*" and other well-thumbed items. She had lately begun to enjoy pitting her skepticism against religious and other proselytizers and mentally shredding them.

Back at the lab, she discovered that Ben had also downloaded an entire unpublished manuscript together with about 60 pages of a work-in-progress. She speed-read them both before lunch whilst attempting to oversee Ben's destruction of poached passwords and Moncrieffe's private business. Anastasia found that there were aspects of the writing which intrigued her, where it ventured into the abstruse and spiritual, while the novel showed extensive knowledge of aeronautics. Clearly Moncrieffe had little tolerance for hokey and was also disinclined to be serious for more than five minutes at a time. She couldn't decide at first whether this was admirable or despicable. Part of the world's programming, she realized, was to take all matters metaphysical as deadly serious and here at last they were perceived as the biggest joke of all, the ultimate Ego-catch, the perverted midwives of sanctimony, religiosity and *ex-cathedra* pontifications.

In a flash of personal insight, Anastasia realized that her own feelings about the murderous history of religions were equally murderous and unbearably serious. She found herself wishing there was some way to question Moncrieffe about some possible cure for this affliction, or if there was some way to break the syndrome. Her next thought was that a Jihad warrior might need more time than his allotted span to make such a change, especially if curtailed by his/her own suicide bombing. For thousands of years, the great religions had claimed to be fighting evil, thus giving it validity and promoting it and themselves to unwarranted status. The suicide bomber had added an incomprehensible folly, turning his *raison d'être* into a reason *not* to be, the bloody approval-seal of belligerence. Anastasia had even voiced the opinion that suicide bombers should somehow be brought back to life so they could be properly and cruelly executed.....

"*To die for.*" Her private smile faded as the phrase crept into her thoughts. She realized that her own ferocity for life had a similar motive—revenge and destruction. It simply took a different form. Given the chance to destroy her parents' killers, would she then want to go on living? The prospect seemed listless and empty. Perhaps if somehow she could corner the guilty ones, give them enough suffering for six lifetimes, have them finally repent and spend the rest of their lives as her abject servants....Even this seemed hollow, giving her enough discomfort to look for distraction.

Her 19" screen zoomed repeatedly on the book titles photographed from Moncrieffe's study, the Lab's 20mp camera picking them out clearly. She was then able to cross-check instantly with those contained in the Lab's library, but correlations were very few since spiritual matters had little congruence with the Los Alamos agenda. She found her nose wrinkling with nervousness at some of the titles, which feeling she found strangely at odds with some kind of curious longing. She also wondered why there were three copies of *From Onions to Pearls* and four of *Conversations with God*, Book 1. There were also several copies of a purple manual entitled *How to Startle Yourself—Life after Self-Help Books*, which was also available as an ebook. She decided to have one of these borrowed since it was essential to seal all the rat holes. Multiple copies of anything could indicate their use as code bearers.

The dreaded Frank Uren stuck his face round the door with a snide attempt at a friendly grin, his eyes as usual unfocussed and speculating below her collar.

"Busy, Miz Nastyasia?"

"Yup."

"Moncrieffe? I smell the blood of an Englishman. Go for it."

"Fee fie foe fum, boss."

"Roger that."

"You'd roger anything that wriggles," Anastasia thought, though aloud she said evenly, "For you, boss, anything." Uren shot her a dubious glance and left abruptly. She pulled an evil face at the door just as it opened again and the porcine snout reappeared, seeming not to notice her abrupt change of expression.

"Hey, Nastya, that cut-out in London, this Irina. Find out who and where, then send someone in to list her books. First look for a new pile that hasn't been shelved yet, `kay? We gotta narrow this down or it'll take till doomsday."

"On it, boss." Anastasia spoke evenly, avoiding any emphasis or nuance. She'd learned that the slightest wrong stress could give offence, especially without a pretty smile to defuse it.

She waited a few moments before picking up the phone to call London Center. She gave detailed instructions, ending with a terse reminder. "This time, don't blow it. Send a non-smoker, clean armpits, no perfume. And no appetite. And no kink for women's underwear, for God's sake. Can you manage that?"

The only answer was a sly cackle. Anastasia sighed and turned to her own new list of requisitions. *The Eye of the I....Journey of Souls....The Awakening.* The overwhelm had her balking at the prospect of wading through turgid everglades of woo-woo.

To Anastasia it seemed obvious that if there was a cosmic answer, the key to humanity's unlocking the secrets of the Universe, it couldn't possibly lie in any of these desperate-sounding tomes or they would have ceased production. Instead and to the contrary, more and more scribblers believed they had the answer for everyone, thus proving the opposite. She remembered with utter delight seeing a painting of an early brigantine under full sail, rushing to catastrophe over the cascading edge of a flat earth, her bulwarks knuckle-clenched beneath the dumbstruck faces and bulging eyes of the ultimately convinced.

Maybe, she mused, our business is not about solving the cosmic riddle, since we mostly find satisfaction from seeking, not finding. On the other hand, some people seemed to exude the joy or smug satisfaction of some secret knowledge. It wouldn't be long, she reckoned, before this Moncrieffe was hauled in for some serious interrogation, and she might get to be on the team. Any chance of promotion would help her own deadly aims, but there was little prospect of that without patronage from Uren. She recoiled from the picture of what this might entail.

Grateful for the interruption, Nic threw down the heavy iron bar and picked up the cordless phone from a tree stump.

"Greetings, comrade," said the voice rough as pumice, "What are you now doing?"

"Digging a trench. Why?

"I am in town. You like I bring sandwich and beer?"

"I like. Beer I have."

"*Pronto.*"

Nic attacked the trench again, the cement-hard *caliche* soil resisting every thrust, jarring his joints and baiting him with the certainty that a backhoe would complete in twenty minutes what would certainly take him two days at least. He was cutting the foundation for a small conservatory, an addition to his latest addition. It was another typical New Mexico day; the early spring sun beat down with relentless power and only a few puffy and cartoon-like clouds dotted the sky. To the North, not yet hazing the sky, a hatch of jet-trails spread in ordered crisscrosses. Scowling at them, he worked steadily for another half hour before Igor's old Chevy ground into the turning circle and the Russian emerged grinning.

Nic thrust down his shovel but it failed to penetrate even the dry topsoil and simply fell over. "Impotence looms," he muttered, wiping hands and brow.

"Why do you do this?" Igor asked, mystified, looking down into the trench.

"'Cos I'm what Americans call 'ornery', we'd say 'contrary' in England. I got this ferocious Mr Fixit complex from my Dad, who got it from his Mom. She wouldn't let him do anything, she'd say, 'Oh John, *don't* do that, pay a *man* to do it!' He rebelled eventually. Like bumblebees being told they can't fly, y'know?"

Igor nodded, familiar with this scientific dictum. "Is there only yourself here? And I presume, from the sign, a silent dog?"

Nic looked around and put a finger to his lips. "And sometimes my son, Jamie. Anyway, a man needs room to pace! Plus, I usually throw a big thrash once a year. It got too crowded, so I doubled the dance floor and the next one was completely crammed as well. My fault, really. The invitation said 'Only Two Articles of Clothing Permitted', and I had a wicked little pole dancer as well. You know, she could twirl her tits in opposite directions."

"I would like to have seen. You know, that's gyroscopically sound, for balance. Like counter-rotating propellers on a twin."

"I hadn't thought of that," Nic grinned, "Let's get out of the sun. I'll get some plates and beer."

Inside the house, Nic popped two cans and returned from the kitchen, Igor ventured, "I never asked you about being married?"

"Hm. I had a wife, Miki, she's an airline pilot. We were together seven years. Her grandparents were Russian by the way, from St Petersburg. She fell in love with a flight attendant."

"Oh…Male or female?"

"Female. Ironic, huh, with the stereotype of male flight attendant as a gay. They were equally gorgeous, I could have loved them both, the idea of a *ménage-à-trois* had serious appeal but Miki turned me down flat, total conversion, born again. A therapist told me that the average Lesbian relationship is seldom sexual beyond three years..... What a waste, eh? So I still wonder if she might come back. I loved her company. She was, is, a marvelous pianist, loved to cook, didn't get seasick - or any kind of sick for that matter. But as a lover she was, say, elusive, distant. I guess she hadn't realized her real orientation. Our son Jamie alternates between us 'cos Miki lives in Seattle. She still comes to visit, stays in the spare room. It's always fun, no bitterness, fine meals, affection. Nostalgic even. Very puzzling for me. But at least she stopped saying sorry, thank God. Hardly her fault, is it?"

"The Papists would have something to say about that."

"Yeah. Amazing how long it takes to change perceptions, judgments, how some claim to be loving and condemn in the next breath. It's changing though. Slowly."

The two men ate and drank for a little while in silence until Nic drained his beer and said, "Bring yours outside, I want to dig some more."

"Good, I smoke and witness," Igor barked laughingly.

Nic set to digging again. Igor lit a cigarette and went to fetch a graying plastic chair.

"Is a long time since I was digging trenches," he said inhaling deeply, shifting the chair into a stable setting, "I was waiting for *voenniy sud* - court martial." After a protracted silence, Igor took off his jacket and placed it on the wall a few yards away. Returning, he put a finger to his lips, and Nic stopped in mid-plunge with the digging bar.

"Whassup?"

"Could you sell up and leave?" Igor asked quietly, "I mean - vanish."

Nic looked startled. "Why, what's going on?"

"The hounds have scent. You know that whole business a long while back, with Wen Ho Lee? They had him months and months in solitary, without trial, finally cleared yet he's still under suspicion. His life turned into a nightmare, just for downloading some classified files which he was cleared for."

"So?" The two men looked at each other for a good half-minute. Finally Nic broke the forced silence. "I'm just a fanciful scribbler, Igor. If they just want my sources, there's nothing they can --"

"Not true!"

"What isn't?"

"They can do anything they fucking want! They don't bother with warrants or judges— they never did, even before Patriot Act. People vanish, have car accidents, heart attacks. Fall off a high building. Anything they like."

"Santa Fe hasn't got any high buildings."

Igor flapped with annoyance. "Listen! People have jobs. They need jobs. If the job is really stupid or pointless, they'll invent something to give it purpose. Like a dog barking at nothing, at least he feels like he's being a real dog. Where is your dog, anyway?"

Nic shook his head dismissively, with a sly grin.

Looking puzzled, Igor continued, "In this case dogs have picked up scent of rabbit and are getting excited, you understand?"

"But --"

"I cannot say any more, I have my own stupid job and much depends on it."

Nic went very still and watched the Russian in silence, but found his gaze avoided after the first few seconds. "Someone's been in here," he said finally.

"I know. Do you understand now?"

"Hm....Supposing the hounds believed the rabbit could lead them to other rabbits, or some bigger prey even, do you think they'd let him run?"

"*Niet!* Dog is too stupid and too hungry. And needs to please the master."

"Do they know you're talking to me? I mean, like this?"

Igor shrugged and pointed to his jacket. "Perhaps, I don't know. It doesn't make a difference. Rabbit is scented. What's that they say - Tally-Ho!"

"So what is it they want from me?"

"Your sources, of course. And someone you called Biggall, right? As soon as they have those --" Igor drew his finger across his throat.

Nic nodded thoughtfully, a slow grin spreading. "Could be a problem there."

Igor looked agitated. "You should be very afraid, Nic."

"Nah. I'm trying to give it up. No future in it."

Igor looked first incredulous, then slumped in resignation. "Well, at least give up e-mail and consider leaving the country. You were a sailor. How about a yacht and a pseudonym, maybe. I mean, for writing you can be anywhere, right? Wen Ho Lee had good reason to be afraid - if you remember what they did to him."

Nic hefted the spade and leaned on it, his gaze towards the mountains. "I do want to go back to sea sometime, but not full time, just no longer marooned in the mountains at 7000 feet…Have you noticed how sometimes we're just plain reactive, to people, circumstances? Your boss, he makes your blood boil, right? But there's a choice. You could just watch, obedient of course but unruffled. Not insolent either. Or in everyday life, something unpleasant. How to react, there seems to be a choice. Imagine being able to go into the heart, see every characteristic as endearing, even with bad drivers."

Igor shook his head wonderingly. "Nic, you are talking to a Russian. It is the land of lines, and lack, and needless suffering. You have no idea how lucky you people are."

Igor took a final drag on his cigarette and began a bout of coughing. Nic watched him with wry concern. "If—not when—you do get to the tropical beach, my friend, all those buxom bikinis will run from your dreadful smell. But you're afraid to stop, right?"

"Afraid?" Igor ground his stub into the dirt and set his jaw to look fearless.

Nic shrugged and began digging again. Igor watched in silence and then went to his jacket, thumbed the GPS and mumbled a quick check-in. This time there was a pager-alert waiting for him.

Igor dialed the lab and asked for Wojerkowski. The operator primly corrected him by adding a Miz. When Anastasia came on the line, she simply said, "Igor, while you're there, there's a title we can't read from the photos. Bookcase in study, near center, middle row, just to the right of *"Collision with the Infinite."* Small book, red spine. OK?"

"Wojer. Out." He heard a brief chuckle as she hung up. Turning to Nic he asked, "What was that book you said stopped all your reading for two years?"

"From Onions to Pearls." I bought a whole box of 'em, I think there's a couple left."

"Can I take a look?"

"Sure. In the study. It's like being hit by a train, but I suppose if you had to ask, maybe you're ready for it."

"What's to lose?" Igor moved away with a shrug. Having made a note of Anastasia's request, he returned with a copy of Nadeen's little blockbuster and hunkered by the trench.

"You were right," he said, "It just occurred to me, if I asked you for hypnosis to stop smoking, it might actually work and the idea was terrifying!"

Nic gave a short sympathetic laugh, which set the Russian off immediately on a longer version. After a moment Igor stood from his crouch and moved back to the plastic chair, which the high-altitude sun had invisibly destroyed. He sat heavily and the chair reached the end of its short working life. Seeing it collapse in almost slow motion, Nic yelled out gleefully "KATAPOULTIRUYSYA!!"

Igor wrenched wildly in mid-air at an imaginary ejection handle and subsided into the dirt, his laughter reduced to a helpless wheeze.

"Law of Attraction," Nic muttered eventually, "Feel ridiculous and the Universe promptly supports the notion." He let the spade drop and heaved himself out of the trench. Igor held his hands behind his head as he lay in shards of plastic.

"You said that serious," he observed quietly.

"Well, a Law is a Law, y'know. Feel grateful and in no time at all you get more to be grateful for. Go to Victim and you get enough shit to drown in. Go to abundance and abundance pours in."

Igor's mouth fell open. "That's it? It's that simple?"

"Uh-huh. So, whatever the flavor, the *feeling* of your life, that's why it stays."

"But - can you change it?"

Nic nodded long and slowly, a grin spreading. "Yep. Takes work, not just habits to break but brain's subconscious responses are hard-wired and have to be ferreted out before you can re-program. You cultivate the feeling and then, like it says on your screen, *Now reboot your computer to install these changes.*"

"That's what I want."

"How bad? And what do you really want?"

"I want to stop being a grey-faced, miserable, wheezing smoker with a horrible --"

"Hold on!" Nic interrupted, "Let's keep it positive. Negatives don't work in hypnotherapy, they just get reinforced, so I assume it's the same with wishes or intentions."

"Oh.....Well, in that case..... I may need a little time to re-think this, OK?"

Beyond a brief nod, Nic's only answer was a wicked bass chuckle.

"Tell me, is it negative if I want to be unafraid?" Igor asked after a pause.

"Good question. I suspect it is. The test is how it feels when you say it. Then try something like, I welcome anything that comes my way, I will relish it all as part of a great adventure. Bring it on!"

"Is that like this expression, paradigm shift?" Igor looked suddenly surprised. "I just got something. When you say 'I want it so bad', there's the sound of suffering, of lack, yes? Supposing I say, 'I want this so much that the thought thrills me, is delightful'. That's different, yes?"

"Yeah. And do you notice there's no flavor of fear of not getting it? It's like a done deal."

"But, I want to ask, where is that happening, what is the mechanism of it?"

Nic shrugged. "Quantum mechanics is starting to explain it. What draws anything together? Why is there gold in a seam, diamonds in a pipe, iron ore deposits, birds of a feather - when the Universe we're told has exploded and re-imploded several times already? We are literally stardust! Either someone is organizing it or there's a built-in law to govern its behavior. If you believe there's an Organizer, you might pray to Him/Her, but if there's simply a Law, a built-in system, then you just work with it.....I guess." He chuckled happily.

"So is that what means Enlightenment?"

"No. Enlightenment is when you get that there's nothing to get."

"I don't get it!" Igor brayed softly and sat up.

Nic chuckled again, "But you do want to make some big changes, right?

"Does the Pope poop in the woods?"

"I'm very impressed by your subtle command of English, my friend. Look, when I get *really* focused on a story, all I can tell you is that the most amazing things seem to happen. First one I did, I picked a location for the action in Western Scotland, more or less with a pin except it had to be by the sea. It was on the Applecross peninsula. I was driving one day and quite involuntarily, no idea why, I switched radio channels and immediately heard the announcement that they were going to build an oil rig right there, on my exact spot. The rigs are so huge that they have to build them in a big hole inland, then they breach the dyke, float them out to sea and sink them on location. Six months later, I again inexplicably switched to that channel and within seconds they announced that an 18th Century prophecy had come to light, from the sayings of the Seer of Ardrisaig, it foretold the whole thing, that the rocks of Applecross would open up and spew forth a stone monster, which would stand upon the ocean floor, its head would rear up to the heavens, its breath would be like snow, its voice like thunder in the hills, and there would be black rain! And I never listened to that station before or since."

Igor slowly gathered himself and stood up. "You hear stuff like that and you can only believe that we are tapping into something completely beyond."

"Right. So how can one focused thought have so much power-- and how are we connected to such a source? Who sends the prompt to switch channels? And every one of my stories had miracles like that, consciously unbidden. Or unconsciously bidden, I'm not sure which."

"I can't see any wires sticking out of your head. It must be everywhere."

"Uh, huh. The guru of all gurus, Ramana Maharshi, said that's all there is."

"What is?"

"Consciousness."

"Oh." Igor scratched his chin, mystified. "But where *is* it?" Suddenly he barked a laugh at his own question. "At least I can tell you where it isn't - in the person of my horrible boss."

"Well, you never know. Old Saul was a bit Right Wing until Almighty smote him with a thunderbolt. Then he was all brotherly love."

"Is that in Bible? How can we order a personal thunderbolt? Can we just wish it and it's done, is that what you suggest?"

Nic nodded to himself for a while. "Maybe consciousness is exploring that possibility, through you."

"So it has a purpose? You know, too much of this stuff makes my head hurt. Let's keep the doses small."

"Change of subject. What shall we talk about it - aren't I supposed to be afraid of something?"

"Is why I came. See, there's no way to stop hounds, once they have the scent. They could wreck your whole life. Everything you do is being watched."

"Even now?"

Igor's voice dropped to the merest whisper. "Even now. I'm one of them, I'm supposed to be at the front of the pack, do you understand?"

"Hmm....sounds like material for another story, maybe."

Igor shook his head with dismay. "The problem for me, Nic, is that I am under orders and I would prefer to be your friend."

"How about doing both? And before you say that's impossible, think about it, OK?"

Igor looked doubtful, tapping another Gauloise on the packet. He lit it, inhaled deeply, coughed and finally said, "I'd better go." He retrieved his jacket from the wall, thumbed the GPS and spoke his brief check-in. Turning back, he spoke quietly.

"They're deadly, you know. Especially after this Homeland Security rubbish, they can justify any action, confiscation, torture, death. If they had any notion of collusion between us, we'd both simply vanish. 9/11 was the excuse to bring back Fascism, pure and simple. If they didn't engineer it, they certainly knew about it and allowed it."

"For sure they engineered it," Nic said flatly, "There's a CIA memo to prove that they did. 3000 lives was a tiny price to unify a country of 300 million, to justify a war, total control and the end of freedom. A slew of architects and explosive experts all back that up. You can't drop a building neatly in its own footprint without weeks of preparation."

Igor said sharply, "What memo?"

"It was suppressed and it vanished. And the guy who revealed it also vanished."

"So where's the memo?"

"In a safe place."

"So you know who was really behind it?"

"Of course. And I'll bet you do too."

Igor stared in silence. Nic returned the gaze without expression.

"I'm going," the Russian said again, "I'm starting to feel like a hound in rabbit's fur. Or the other way round, shit, it's getting hard to tell. Thanks for the beer."

"And you for lunch."

Igor simply nodded and drove slowly away, smoke trailing from the driver's window. Nic went back to his dig, wondering grimly whether lemmings simply blunder over cliffs or have some prior calculated commitment. He heard the car stop some fifty yards down the road and after several minutes backed up again. Igor was waving something, so he got out of the trench and went over. Igor put a finger to his lips, handed him a piece of paper and drove away.

He had to squint even in the bright sunlight to read a faint scrawl: *"If I hear the hounds are off leash, I'll send you one word: KATAPOULT. Burn this."*

CHAPTER 5

Bad planning is the mother of adventure.

Anon

Half the world away, Elena Knyazeva groaned out of bed for the fifth time, drawing back the faded grey curtain dividing her mother's narrow sleeping place from her own. The sobbing which had kept them both awake had reached an unbearable intensity. A 15 watt bulb only added to the gloom.

"Talk to me, Mama. Please tell me," Elena pleaded, "What has happened to bring this on?"

"You wouldn't understand, child. I just want to die."

Elena felt impatience rising, wrestling with overstretched compassion.

"How about some hot chocolate instead?" Her tone left no doubt about her acid feelings but had an unexpected result. From mid-sob a short laugh tumbled. Her mother turned from the wall and sat up suddenly, wiping tears on a sheet-corner.

"You mean I have a choice?" The old face cracked an attempt to smile, stretching taut and unaccustomed tissue.

Elena giggled suddenly and reached out to her. "It depends which you want first, Mama. One of them would save us some chocolate. There isn't much."

"Can you give me something with hope in it?"

Elena had been saving her good news and reluctantly revealed it. "Mama, I will have more money. They have given me more work time."

"They're exploiting you," he mother said flatly into the sheet. Elena said nothing, just stared at her aghast. After a long silence, her mother raised her head and narrowed her eyes in the dim light. "What? Why are you looking at me like that, Lena?"

"I'm thinking about the choice. I don't want to waste the chocolate. I think you are already dead and trying to take us with you. What do you imagine we will remember you for, Mama?" Her voice rose indignantly. "Will it be for the sunshine smile, the kindness, the optimism, the helpfulness, the creativity? Why did you have children, Mama, to raise in your misery, so they could watch you grinding away your life in sorrow and complaint?"

A spark of defiance flared in the old eyes. "I raised my son well, he went to Academy, he was an officer. He would have made General."

"I know all *about* it, Mother!" Elena's whispered shriek provoked a sleepy moan from the other room. "You would have had a limousine and a dacha, caviar and diamonds and respect." Elena's voice softened, "But the son you raised was too noble to machine-gun defenseless Afghan refugees. If that was all the good you did in the world, it would be enough."

"*Good?* It made me lose him, my darling boy. No word in years. I do not know where he is and I will never see him again, and because of his disgrace we are exiled to this hole in hell! And I am officially dead, as are you, so that he cannot be compromised."

"He did that for you, Mama. You cursed him for an idiot, because he refused to be a cold-blooded murderer so you could live like a Tsarina. He thought you would be proud of him, like I am."

"It's those idiots in Kremlin. They invade an impoverished country, murder hundreds of thousands, they get their noses bloodied, 8000 soldiers dead and then retreat after 8 years of pointless agony."

"We agree on that. But you're still saying that Igor should have obeyed their murdering orders?"

"Soldiers must obey."

"And now it's the turn of other soldiers. Perhaps when they stop obeying there will finally come peace....Mama, I need to sleep. You will be quiet now, please. And don't give up hope for Igor, I will find him for you, I promise. But you, you must change. Find a way to become --" Elena was interrupted by a final sob, "-- to become serene. And pleasant company. Then I'll bring you chocolate every night, you'll see."

As her mother sighed and turned to the wall, Elena added softly "And you will sing to us again, and we will all go to the beach and eat ice cream, go to parties, ride in limousines....." She went on listing wistfully the imagined joys of the West as her mother sank back into despairing slumber.

"Imagine a real hot shower that doesn't spit boiling steam or cold black shit. Air to breathe that doesn't clog your nose every hour. Men who aren't misogynists and drunk and groping from breakfast onwards. A different dress for every day of the week—no, of the year! Daily beauty treatments, huge TV's instead of windows, I know that's silly. But freedom to come and go, quit your job and get another, shopping all day and night, walking in safety...."

Elena moved quietly into the other room. Ilya, 10 years old, had pulled his bedclothes into a solid mound, just his tousled head showing. She bent until her nose was just a centimeter from his hair, inhaling him deeply, absorbing the peace of dreamlessness. She wanted to touch and reassure him but willed herself not to recall his spirit from its silent excursion. She hunkered by the cot, filled with a strange wonder at the nature of being, who we are, where we go and how to elevate this state out of the cesspit of misery, uncertainty of anything beyond a short, intense flowering, maybe a few minutes of ecstatic forgetfulness, followed by years of disappointment, disillusion, decrepitude and death.

A spark flared within her, burgeoned and felt like it was spreading its tendrils like roots taking hold, in pure defiance. Not knowing where to direct its intent, she settled for the comfort of the feeling itself, a brief moment of pure certainty. In that quieting she knew how to answer Nic's extraordinary question, "What can I do for you?"

She went back to bed and fell immediately asleep, unaware of the smile which suffused her whole face, puzzled a few hours later that she felt so lightened in the morning. She went to work early and sent off a long e-mail, routed through London.

Dear Kolya, Irina here.

Because of an email from Lena this morning, during breakfast I made a list of all the privileged amenities in just this modest apartment. No doubt your own would differ slightly but in terms of what we regard as essentials, (which would be beyond even the imagination of countless millions) I had got to 17 before I finished my coffee. (Coffee itself – that's 18....) Anyway, a message from Elena, I translate without comment or exaggeration....

"Dear Kolya, The good fairy came in the night and it seems I am hearing her voice. Maybe she knows all the secrets but she only gave me one. It is the means of our release from this prison. It can happen any day, any time. I snap my fingers in command and the deal is done. The power this will give us so the greedy fiends who terrorize, oppress and make needless war from their comfortable offices, they will run in shame and terror and beg our forgiveness. We won't tell them yet that we will grant it effortlessly, amazed at ourselves.

I can see that adjusting circumstances will not work for everyone. For example, I could see my mother in a fine apartment overlooking the Bois de Boulogne or Central Park or the Caribbean sea, still she would find something to complain about, someone to condemn. The janitor has no class, too much fresh air makes her dizzy, young people shouldn't be allowed to have sex, a vindictive mosquito, the bikinis are too teeny....

Dear Kolya, it is so cold here and dirty and dangerous, food is so scarce, comforts so few and yet today I notice a spark dancing in me somewhere, growing into a little flame that is unaffected by these horrible conditions. Is it because it knows they are temporary and will soon be forgotten? Is it because I know you have something to convey, something of such great value that it could change millions of lives as well as my own? I am feeling so calm and confident, as if there was a team behind me.

You ask what you can do for me, well, you must have already done it, with just the thought, the optimism of another possibility, another way of being, with the books that hold the key. Something strange is happening to me. My grandmother told me that anything you give, freely and without condition, must come back 100 times. (Mind you, expecting the 100 times is like making a condition, so you have to expect nothing!) Anyway, as soon as I find out who is in charge of this process, I will demand an audit to be sure that it is being run properly and fairly. My mother will be chief auditor!

Greetings from a little spark in the frozen Ukraine, Elena xx

Nic, Irina here. She never answered your question.....If you sent her a hundred bucks, that would be two months' salary, imagine....By the way, what do you look like? – not that it matters, of course. Hrrmmph. Send me a photo anyway, please.

Nic shook his head and smiled to himself, wondering where all this was leading. There were, increasingly, times when he didn't understand his own responses, yet he also knew that somehow Igor had set him up for this intrigue, perhaps accidentally. Given an enlightenment dictum that "all minds are in communication all the time", it seemed that random sets of minds were constantly making plots, dismaying and amazing their own tenants. Every day brought new scenarios, complications and sometimes uncomfortable opportunities. Assuming that Igor would have to report it, he wondered what Los Alamos would do about his mention of the memo, the "proof" of complicity in the 9/11 Twin Towers fiasco. With his own inherent paranoia, Igor might even suspect Moncrieffe of being a plant himself, a test of the Russian's trustworthiness.

As these thoughts wove their intricate braids, Nic began to wonder if the e-mail he'd first received from Elena had been a set-up by Igor as a test, which he had innocently passed, or an intrigue designed to put him in enough danger that he could be manipulated. Deciding it was all too complicated and suffocating, he put it out of mind. In the evening he went to see a riveting wildlife movie about penguins, called his son Jamie in Seattle to tell him about it and went to sleep in a contented glow.

Dawn. As the spirit returns from its mystical flight, often there's a brief floating moment of pure existence, delicate, fragile yet somehow all-knowing. This is a moment of alarm for the struggling Ego-mind. Aware that it cannot dwell in this magical realm, it suffocates it with an overthrow of thoughts, remnants of dreams, anxieties, dreads and guilts. The Sensible Ones rise from bed in that moment, knowing that otherwise they can lie helpless prisoners of confusing concerns and speculations until optimism for the whole day is largely dissipated. If indulged, the sum of fears easily condenses into symptoms of neurosis.

On this particular morning, Nic made a decision to stay put and just observe the mind-play which, given its head, suddenly seemed like a hyper-active Collie shepherding crazed and bewildered brayings. All his recent online searches came rushing together like a stampede...

Like many a New Mexico morning, the day had started cloudless, but in the next twenty minutes Nic observed once again a dozen contrails forming crisscross patterns in the small patch of sky framed by his uncurtained window. He knew that the lefties and the environmentally sensitive believed the government to be dumping chemicals to make them either sick or compliant, or simply to experiment with weather control. Some even declared that mercenary, non-English-speaking Russian pilots fly jet tankers out of secret U.S. desert bases and seed the skies with poison. There was said to be proof, though it hadn't been revealed. Logic insisted that keeping such a massive operation under wraps was just not feasible, while official debunkers simply labelled the environmentally-sensitive as neurotic conspiracy theorists—despite confirmation from the founder of Microsoft himself, and the protests of two different women who had actually spoken out at the U.N. against the chemical spraying.

Googling *conspiracy theory* had turned up a plethora of unprovables, like the murder of JFK, the downing of Flight 800, faked moon-landing photos, Oklahoma City, the 9/11 Tower collapses, many of them supported by government refusal to release critical reports. The mysteries deepened and grew ever more complex, while conclusions remained the province of cranks. The provable stuff, like distortion of intelligence to justify an unjustifiable war, was simply brushed aside or obscured with red herrings. Despite subpoenas, the FBI records in the case of flight 800 had been simply "lost" (for the greater good, of course, because any question or proof of a missile strike, friend or foe, was politically unmanageable). Whatever the truth, all the obfuscations fully justified the public distrust of officialdom.

Some kind of dark mist suddenly cleared. Nic exploded with a bass guffaw, leaped naked out of bed and headed for the kitchen, gleefully boxing demons in mid-air. The patterns in the sky had given him just what he needed, with perfect timing, and the Universe must surely be complicit. As the ideas danced and sought and reformed in his head, he found himself trembling with gratitude for the mysterious Field whence the marvels flowed.

"Wotcher got, Wojer?" Uren looked up eagerly as Anastasia knocked and entered. He eyed her up and down appraisingly, smirking at his own wit. She was neatly dressed in a knee-length grey skirt, solid black shoes, her proud chest undefined beneath a loose green sweatshirt. Only her lower legs betrayed fine muscle tone. Uren tried to ignore her habitual scowl, having watched her with others and finally convinced himself it wasn't personal.

"It's about Enigma, boss. The book list he referred to, we never picked that up. Maybe sent from somewhere else."

"Can't you get it from the London end, this Irina piece?"

"They weren't onto her in time. I've ordered them to go back in, to get all her computer mail from a week previous."

"Yeah. Could be crucial. Meanwhile, we're getting everything of his?"

"Yes. I've set up a terminal which duplicates all his stuff."

"Including searches?"

"Everything."

"OK. Keep me posted."

"Will do." She flipped open a folder. "You want to hear the latest?"

"How long is it?"

Anastasia ignored the question. "*`Dear Irina`* he says, "*`I'll introduce it gradually, because the mind is averse to the Shift. Essentially, there probably isn't even one percent of the population which doesn't think there must be a better way. History is just a list of systems that don't work, Monarchy, Tyranny, Oligarchy, Communism, Capitalism, Socialism, Imperialism including religious Imperialism, even Democracy. Nazi-ism disguised as Patriotism. Now we are back to Fascism disguised as Homeland Security. The powers behind all the movements were each trying to find a better way. What's the common factor among them all? PEOPLE! And the common factor among the people? Notions of limitation because they don't understand who they really are. And why don't they? Because they're using the Ego-mind to do it with but the Ego-mind evolved specifically to explore and experience who-we-are-NOT!*

"*It seems we are coming to the point when Ego-mind is getting fed up with all that, and those who understand the problem have decided to accelerate things, for everyone's sake. They're calling it the Great Shift, and with reason, because something truly enormous is about to happen, is already happening. It's the exact reverse of what came to be known as The Fall. Do pass this on to Elena, if you have time. And watch this space! Love, Kolya.'*

Anastasia closed the file and looked up. Uren was flexing his fists, his glare enraged, his mouth a vindictive sphincter.

"Gonna nail this guy, Wojer. He's just dicking with me."

"Take it easy, boss. And don't take it personally. He doesn't know you're on to him."

"Yeah, well make sure it stays that way…Listen, I've an idea. I want you to meet him, pally up. I don't trust Igor, he may be getting too friendly."

Anastasia's scowl deepened. "So what do you want me to do?"

"Shit, I dunnno. Show some cleavage. Distract him. Make rumpy-pumpy. And gimme details!" Uren leered lasciviously. "Ask the watchers where he hangs out. Get familiar, get laid. Maybe you'll get promoted."

"Away from here?"

Uren ignored the taunt and waved her out, watching the lean-muscled legs and a defiant swirl of honey-ochre hair. Simply eyeing her beauty made his throat dry.

Anastasia felt secretly elated to have a job in the field, anything that would allow her more freedom. Over the next days, her assigned watchers reported little movement from Moncrieffe who seemed to spend the mornings in his study and the rest of the day in some kind of construction. On Saturday mornings he hung out with friends in a bakery-cum-coffee-shop, on Sundays he attended a kind of New Age non-denominational outfit called The Celebration, which described itself as an independent spiritual community embracing all paths, bring your own God. Checking its website, Anastasia found herself with warring feelings. Profoundly atheistic from childhood experiences, she yet felt a gnawing hunger for some deeper connection, mostly buried beneath her bitterness and brittle cynicism.

Her assignment, she decided, required a more adventurous spirit, and maybe some extravert new clothes. At yoga the next morning, Meg the teacher remarked that she seemed different, somehow lighter and more animated.

Saturday morning found her seated in the Santa Fe Baking Co with a wireless laptop and a single earphone. Beneath a napkin lay a directional microphone which she aimed at several tables, shifting her position unobtrusively. There was no sign of Moncrieffe whom she would recognize from photos taken by the watchers.

A rowdy group at a corner table seemed particularly animated. Tuning in, she caught something which startled her, a woman's voice.

"…..Forty million dollars a month, Nic said. They were talking flying and the man opened up. So when it was made illegal, he shifted production to Central America and sold it in Europe. Had his own jet, took the cash to Singapore, then back to Costa Rica for more. He truly believed it would change the world."

"Did you ever try it?" asked a male voice.

"Ecstasy? Not me, I'm chicken. But Nic said it was an eye-opener— or heart-opener rather. Ego set aside, complete presence and appreciation of everything. And a total conviction, understanding that the Ego-world has everything bass-ackwards, that the whole of humanity is insane not to be feeling like that all the time."

"But you can't live on that stuff, it'll kill you. That's after you go nuts!"

"Sure. But a glimpse is all you need…Oh, here's da man himself."

Anastasia watched the newcomer eagerly as they shuffled chairs. Nic Moncrieffe looked around before sitting, his eye passing over her as she quickly looked down at her screen. Peripherally she was aware that his glance returned, perhaps took in her summery blouse, slightly unbuttoned, swelling, lean arms, no excess bodyweight, exquisite hands, hair up but carefully untidy, a studious face with wide-set eyes and a somewhat sour, intimidating downturn to the mouth.

Moncrieffe stood around 5'10", lean muscled, wearing jeans and a tattered bush-shirt. His face was crinkled and smiling, topped with thick and unruly brown hair. She wondered idly if he liked to seem indifferent to his appearance or was genuinely so. He put down his coffee and sat half-facing her as the conversation switched. He glanced again in her direction which was flattering; she couldn't know that he'd seen or felt some anomaly.

"I heard from Leo this morning," said a new voice, "Says he's feeling much better in California. You know he fled New Mexico because of the chemtrails."

"Oh, that's all such total bullshit."

"Not according to Leo," Nic said, "I suggested it must be attitude because they didn't affect me, nor millions of others, so he said it could be a matter of personal sensitivity. He lent me a book called *Death in the Air*, fantastically well researched, by Leonard Horowitz. I could only take so much of it because the sheer scope of government and big business skullduggery is enough to give you terminal paranoia. There's no doubt whatever that they've been experimenting with weather control using aluminum oxide and with radio communications using Barium salts. Google that for 5 minutes and you'll be convinced. They've even admitted it at the UN. A guy I met from Los Alamos says at least that's all true. The stuff about population control is a little harder to prove, let alone digest."

"Wow," said another male voice, a thin-faced athletic character given to silent percussion with his fingers. "They could use stuff to snuff out our libido, in all but the most resistant. Call it Government-induced survival of the horniest!"

"Is that why you're keeping so fit, sugar?" said the tall woman next to him, squeezing his arm affectionately.

Anastasia caught herself smiling at the notion and quickly adjusted her expression when she saw Moncrieffe glance her way again, unaware that his inspiration from the other morning had suddenly kicked in with astounding synchronicity.

During a lull he ventured, "Anybody heard of Prist," but was met with silent headshakes. "It's something they routinely add to jet-fuel in case there's any water present, it prevents ice-particles forming and blocking pumps and fuel lines. It's for the high flying jets in extreme low temperatures."

"How do you know all this and why are you telling us—oh I get. How do we know what's in it?" The percussionist's fingers stopped and he looked up archly.

"Good question." Nic lowered his voice causing the others to lean in closer. "Y'know, nothing much happened for 10,000 years until electricity was discovered, now suddenly there's world-wide communication gone exponential, talk of new dimensions, new awareness. It'll peak shortly, and that's the end of the establishment, once enough people make the shift. They tried it in the Sixties, the Hippies and so on, but it got stamped out. Now it's all different. It's gone world-wide, it's the establishment doing it and they don't even know it!"

"What are you *talking* about?"

Nic looked steadily at the questioner without expression. "I shouldn't say any more. Walls have ears."

This remark claimed everyone's focus, especially Anastasia's. She made a conscious effort not to look inquisitive as an onslaught of questions ran round the other table. Nic smiled and shook his head repeatedly but finally relented to one.

"Well, just a hint, then. Latest polls show that 1 in 3 Americans have developed an interest in matters metaphysical. That's gone from 1 in 4 only ten years ago, which is exponential of a very high order. Why is that? Here we have the luxury of being able to afford a basic brunch and the leisure to discuss other levels of being, when most of the world is on the pure survival level. You can't thrust high-flown ideas on virtual cave-dwellers, especially if they're hungry, angry, jealous and threatening. It's as stupid as going to war to enforce democracy."

"You didn't answer the question," complained the percussionist.

Nic nodded. "Sorry. You know how the psychotropics change perception? Some can give freaky bad trips, but some of them seem to shift the mind to a world-view that is simply benign and appreciative. From there one naturally goes on to compassion for others, for the earth, for the well-being of all, and seeing that it's intrinsic to our real nature. So, if fear for self is the prime motivator of the Ego-world, when fear is set aside, there's only gratitude. Anyway, some chemistry wizard made a discovery that there's a DMT derivative or equivalent that's being surreptitiously distributed all over the world. It's very slow acting, but cumulative, so I'm told."

"The establishment wouldn't be doing that, it's suicide. People aren't controllable when they're not afraid."

"That's the whole point, they don't know they're doing it. Yet."

"Oh wow…Is it in the water supply?"

Nic shook his head. "Too many points of distribution. There's a single source and it's affecting everyone."

"Aha!" the percussionist announced gleefully, "It's in that stuff you mentioned, the jet anti-freeze. Who makes it?"

"Prist? No idea. But it should be easy to find out. I think they're in Texas."

The tall woman leaned in closer. "D'you mean we're all being affected, right now, like it or not?"

Nic put a hand on her arm, gently. "I would say you like it a lot. You spend your life being kind to people and you never gossip, which is quite annoying but a lesson to us all. Maybe you got more exposure to the stuff!"

She looked thoughtful. "Well, I do spend a lot of time outdoors." Seeing Nic's sly grin, she pushed at him. "It is in the air then, or the chemtrails?"

"It's much subtler than that. But I'm gestating, there's a saying "never discuss work-in-progress.""

"But, but how come *you* know?"

Nic shrugged. "Sources. You know." He downed his coffee and stood up. "Can't stay, I'm on a scribbling jag, the Muse is harassing me. See you later, folks."

His leaving was followed by laughter and groans, and as he turned his glance fell on Anastasia. Meeting her eyes, he gave a slight smile which she returned curtly and looked quickly back at her screen. She listened with only half her mind to the bedlam of speculation which followed. Intently and rapidly, she outlined everything she'd heard and filed it before getting up to leave. She felt real elation at a fruitful morning, delighted that she had something to both excite and mystify her horrible boss. He must be one of the denser ones, she decided, doubting that even the strongest chemical would get through.

On the way to her car, she passed the Radio Shack store and glanced in the window. To her surprise, Moncrieffe was inside just completing a purchase. Although no excuse came to mind, impulsively she pushed at the door, almost turned away but the salesman had looked up to the sound of the chime. Should Moncrieffe also notice her, a sudden turnabout would be suspicious, so she quickly decided to brazen it out. Searching in vain for a pretext, she went and stood next to Moncrieffe at the counter where the salesman was trying to explain something. Moncrieffe glanced her way and looked agreeably surprised.

She nodded her own startled recognition and enquired, "Transfer cable—what's that for?"

"Oh. New laptop. You can move all your old files across. I saw you in the bakery just now, very intent."

"Just catching up. That's a very lively crowd you were with."

He chuckled. "They're the best. All musicians. Did you hear them? You have a slight accent, where's it from?"

"Poland. So do you, I detect."

"England. So what brings you here?"

"Los Alamos," she answered, "I work at the lab."

Nic kept his face neutral. "Ah, physics and bombs?"

"This and that," she said evasively, "And you?"

He laughed, "I'm a this-and-that too. At the moment I'm writing half the day, messing around the rest, construction and stuff."

"So what brought you here?"

"I married an American."

"And before that?"

"Europe. I was a yacht broker and did some deliveries."

"Are you published?" she asked ingenuously.

"Some. A few novels a while ago. Working on a new one. No title yet."

"Cool. What's it about?"

"A brand new genre. To do with the Shift"

"Oh…Can I ask, what is the Shift?"

"Let's see…you could call it 'moving into conscious consciousness'. They say there's going to be a big Re-set. Well, actually it's already underway, since end of the Mayan calendar and all that buzz. Did they let you in on that?"

Anastasia looked at him evenly, as if innocent of eavesdropping. "Well, if they did I'd probably be skeptical. This country's full of brute Neanderthals, in my experience."

"Maybe you're moving in the wrong circles. Me, I'm fiercely optimistic. It might need helping on a bit but it's getting exponential, maybe inevitable. Surveys show that many more Americans are becoming seriously aware that there's a better way and it's not just with some new "-Ism." It's a complete outlook shift and we're seeing it everywhere."

Anastasia looked doubtful and gave a slight smile. "My boss says New Age rhymes with sewage. Are you still married?"

The salesman interrupted, handing Nic his receipt and looking to the next customer. They moved aside and Nic looked at her for long moments without a word. She met his gaze with a measure of defiance.

"Divorced," he said eventually. "And you, what brings *you* here?"

"I got a day off."

"I mean, from Poland?"

Her mouth twisted even further than its habitual downturn. "I left in my teens, but it's a tortured story. I don't like to talk about it."

"OK. I hope things are better now. Do you have the whole day, I mean, can I take you to lunch?"

"Why?" Anastasia recoiled at her own truculence. "I'm sorry, that was rude of me. You seem like a nice guy and your friends seemed to enjoy you. Can I still accept, but not today?"

"Sure. Shall I call you? I guess I'll need your name. Mine's Nicoll, Nic for short."

She delved in her purse and handed him a card, which described her as an archivist at LANL.

"Anastasia Wojerkowski," he read aloud, smiling. "That's quite a handle. You must be a countess at the very least."

She chuckled and inclined her head agreeably. "*Naturellement*. But they're ten-a-penny in Poland, didn't you know?"

"And of course they have to be beautiful. And tragic. Dispossessed. A difficult fit anywhere, right?"

"Damn right." She wrinkled her nose at the sly compliment. "Well, you look as though you have to go. You may call me sometime," she added with pretended hauteur and then a shy smile.

Nic exaggerated a courtly bow, pocketed the card and left. On the way home, he mused about this encounter, recalling Igor's warning about surveillance. Thinking back on the conversation in the bakery, he wondered how much had been overheard, considered the topic and felt a huge grin spreading. His idea on waking had already begun to materialize, effortlessly.

Musing about Horowitz's *Death in the Air,* and its numerous proven references to designed and targeted population control by the shielded potentates, the PBTT, the Powers Behind The Thrones, of Big Business, many named therein like the Bushes, Rockefellers, Morgan, Rothschilds, Kissinger and numerous others cited therein, Nic had begun fully to appreciate the helplessness of the abject, ignorant and controlled U.S. voter. Long a skeptic himself of conspiracy theories, the book had completely changed his mind about the real intentions of the PBTT puppet-masters, their openly declared philosophy of "eugenics", their clear intention to forcibly control or eradicate entire populations considered "useless" or non-productive. The USA was by far the world's largest producer and experimenter of chemical and biological weapons, and was also the main supplier of such to a former ally, the ill-fated Saddam Hussein of Iraq, who had to be eliminated when he wouldn't kowtow to marauding U.S oil policy. As one who had spent months researching the whole topic, Nic was able to appreciate more than most just how pernicious were these policies. He had also come to deplore his own former skepticism and the helplessness of the too-rare objectors. With a media tightly controlled by the same puppet-masters, the inevitable result was Fascism, already well underway under the speciously-named Patriot Act, and thus a *de facto* relapse of the U.S. into a Nazi State and its inevitable destruction—after sixty million deaths.

But for their purposes the puppet masters would need to remove twenty times that number...

CHAPTER 6

Art is a message, from the beyond, to the fearful, That Love is all there is.

Frank Schwake, Ibiza.

"Whathafuck is Prist?" Uren demanded, scowling.

"I looked it up, boss," Anastasia replied eagerly, "It's a fuel anti-freeze, for high-altitude jets. If someone's putting stuff in it that we don't know about, it's being spread all over the world. As we speak," she added with a twitch of mischief.

"What sort of stuff? What's in it? What would it do?"

"I think it's DMT, short for Dymethyltryptamine. It occurs naturally in the body in very small amounts. What I gather, it could change your thought patterns, like a psychedelic. Wouldn't work for everyone," she added pointedly.

Uren didn't miss the nuance. "You mean, if it worked for me, what would it do?"

"I'd rather not say, boss."

"Don't pussyfoot me, Wojer."

She gulped and gathered her courage. "Perhaps it would reveal and set free the sweet and gentle nature that is the real you."

Uren stared at her, his eyes like gimlets. Without looking down he punched a button on his intercom.

"Knyazev," came the disembodied voice.

"Igor, you flew jets, right? Get your Bolshevik butt in here, prontissimo."

Anastasia faced his brutishness again. "Never mind the chemical name of Prist itself, health-wise it says only that it's an eye- and mucus-membrane irritant, along with causing fetal and fertility abnormalities. But that's not to say they couldn't put anything else in it."

"Holy hot shit! And dump it on us every day?"

There was a knock and Igor put his head round the door.

"Ig!" Uren barked, "Whaddya know about Prist? Where can we get some?"

"I have no idea, but Santa Fe airport probably. Why?"

"You know about it? Go. Get some here to be analyzed."

"Why bother, boss? All the info will be on the MSDS – Material Data Safety Sheet."

"Igor, that shit's all they want you to know. What else might be in it that we don't know about, get me?"

Igor stepped in and closed the door. "What are you after?"

"We think something's going on. Someone may be putting happy-juice in the jet-fuel and changing people's thinking. Makes 'em non-compliant. We gotta find it and stop it."

"Whom is it affecting?" Igor asked mildly, causing Anastasia to giggle.

Uren glared at her. "What's with the smirk, Nasty?"

She smiled. "Like he said, boss. Some people are more sensitive than others, so it takes a little longer."

Uren exploded. "Whathafuck's with you guys? Here we have something to get our teeth into and you're getting jollies out of it. Igor, get me some of that stuff and put the damn chem-lab on it. Get a gumment requisition form, Big D's secretary"

"Whatever you say, boss. But Prist goes in such small quantities, an additive would be minuscule, I don't see how it could affect anyone. And wouldn't it burn up in the engines?"

"Don't ask me, tell me! Find out, get on it."

Igor nodded solemnly and went out. Anastasia remained seated, waiting.

Uren rapped at her. "So, you had a chat, he asked you to lunch and you said No—why?"

"Feminine strategy, boss. You don't want to seem eager."

"Shit, what if he doesn't call you?"

"He'll call," she answered confidently. "We know he doesn't have a girlfriend and he seemed interested, sort of."

"Too damn subtle for me. You got a coupla days, then we bring him in for a going-over. Any more emails?"

"Not yet, I'll let you know." When Uren looked down dismissively, Anastasia got up and left without a word. She decided the man was like a frothing Rottweiler, or a time-bomb looking for a target.

Dear Elena-via-Irina,

I mentioned the Shift as if it's future although really it's been happening forever, but now there's a massive acceleration, exponential, quantum jump. What does everyone want and what is everyone desperately striving for, in their so-different ways? Ponder…I'd love to hear your answers. Your very thinking about this is part of the Great Shift and there's nothing you can do to stop it! It must be something in the air…. More anon xx Kolya TS106-1

PS for Elena. Little genius, you hit on something vital with your moment of kindness for your boss. The power of this is extraordinary to the ordinary mind, while to the heart-mind it's as natural as breathing. I guess we can never predict the result but transmissions of love seem to take no time--and bring instant peace to the sender…Sending you some! Kolya xx

Anastasia read the message three times, her breath shallow, goose-bumps slowly subsiding. She could feel her mind trying to understand the ideas and resist them at the same time, also wondering how Frank Uren would react. Almost certainly he would bypass any philosophical notions, latch on to "something in the air" and rant about the code letters. Knowing she'd better have an answer for the practical stuff, she turned to the book list from Moncrieffe's office. Abbreviating titles, she finally got to "The Shift" by Owen Waters, 106-1 stated simply, mysteriously: *"Infinite Being is All That Is. Nothing exists outside of it. The Universe exists within the consciousness of Infinite Being. The physical world exists within the consciousness of Infinite Being. We exist within the consciousness of Infinite Being. We ARE Infinite Being."* Her mind overstretched in an effort to grasp the true meaning.

Dutifully, she blocked the text and sent it on to Codes and Ciphers with a request for computer analysis. Despite her own serious doubts about any cryptic content, she knew that Uren would be looking for something sinister and she herself would be reamed out for ignoring protocol.

Igor Knyazev drove down to Santa Fe in a speculative mood. En route, he had the whim to call Rose Madder and he felt a curious stirring within when he heard her voice.

"I remember you," she answered joyfully, "The sinister Russian from the Ark bookstore. When are you going to stop smoking?"

Igor gulped at the painful prod. "I—I don't know. Did I smell bad to you?"

"Awful, frankly. But I used to do it too. And I found I could only stop if I made it into something joyful, like freedom. Or becoming kissable by a handsome smoke-hater! And I put five bucks a day in a box to give myself a gift. How's it going with The Course?"

Igor felt another twinge of guilt. "Well, I'm waiting for your short synopsis. Can I take you to lunch somewhere? I'm on my way down the hill."

Rose answered gaily. "Delighted. I'll be out of yoga by noon. How about Saveur at 12.30?"

Igor noted directions and asked, "Did you finish your song?"

"I did. Tell you later."

Igor ran his eyes over the sleek lines of the L39 Russian jet trainer, fresh painted blue and white instead sinister camouflage, and a wave of wistfulness swept up from his solar plexus. In that moment he realized that the nostalgia stemmed from the sheer intensity and concentration required for high-speed flying, a perfectly effective distraction from introspection and other self-defeating mind activities. In his experience, even that was blighted by the cold and authoritative flavor of both the schools and the battle background of Afghanistan. The combat duties themselves were tainted by thoughts of the pointless and inhuman nature of the entire mission, while with instructing you never knew if the student was really some government infiltrator sent to test your loyalties. Too few were the opportunities for pure flight.

He sensed an approach, heard a confident voice, "Can I help you? Looks like you're hankering after my honey."

Startled, Igor turned. "This is yours? I used to instruct on these, back home. I am Russian."

"Really? My name's Larry. Are you still current?"

"My license? At home, yes, but I haven't made conversion. Who would pay for that, do you think?"

"I might. My other guy just failed his medical, heart murmur. Don't know if he'll be back. How many hours you got?"

Igor frowned into his memory, bewildered, held out his hand. "It is good to meet you. I am Igor Knyazev. I think I have about 4000, maybe 1200 on this one."

"What else?"

"Um, L29. Mig 17, Mig 23. Many others. Helicopter also, Mil-24." He looked at the American with curiosity. He saw a lean figure in an olive flight suit, with a craggy, pugilist face who must have won all his fights judging by a perfect set of teeth in a broad smile.

"Good. So what brings you here?"

"Ah, political reasons."

Larry chuckled. "Come in and have a coffee. Let's talk."

"Thank you. Actually, I was sent to get something, a sample of Prist. I work at the Lab. They want to check it out for content." Igor's scorn was undisguised.

"Why do they want to know?" Larry asked, "Something new for the no-snort list?"

Igor had no answer beyond a shrug and a palms-up gesture. They walked into the hangar and Larry spoke quickly to a young apprentice who wiped his hands quickly and ran off to the refueling bay.

Igor looked around appreciatively. "Isn't that a French Fouga, with the V-tail?"

"It is. You ever flown it?"

"No. But I shot one down once."

"You *did?* Where?"

"Egypt." Igor's abruptness seemed to close the topic. Larry led him into a small office, its wall covered with photographs. The man's passion was as obvious as the intensity of his gaze. He poured two coffees from an urn and said quietly,

"Sometimes I wonder who's listening. Only this morning I realized I was stuck without my guy, then you show up. How much spare time do you have?"

Igor stared back, his mind reeling. "At the moment, not much. I--"

"OK. If that changes, let me know. There'll be rolls of paperwork anyway. I've got a maintenance delivery coming up. You interested?"

"Certainly. Which one?"

"L39 to Phoenix, Arizona. Ride back in a Lear. Bring your log-book and license."

The mechanic hurried in with an aerosol can. "Here we are, sir. I put it on your bill."

Larry said, "Shit. How much?"

"I will get it," said Igor, reaching for his wallet, adding with a gravelly chuckle, "It's on the Government."

"You think they'll notice?" Larry grimaced, "You know how much our new fighter costs, the F-35? Over four hundred million apiece. They want 85 of them. That's enough to conquer the entire world in a matter of days. Look, if you've got to go, call me in the morning. Ferry flight on Wednesday, probably. Glad to meet you."

A phone rang somewhere which Igor took as dismissal, already anticipating his lunch with the eccentric Rose.

Rose Madder filled her plate from the buffet with unrestrained gusto. Her creaking leather outfit had been replaced with a sleek black velvet dress over short ankle boots, outlining a figure that that was full but tautly healthy. As soon as Igor had paid and found a table, she startled him with a question.

"Did you see any of the crop circle pictures from last summer?"

Igor shook his head, "Were they not discredited?"

"Good heavens, no! It's one of the sweetest mysteries that ever came to earth. Google them, you won't believe your eyes, they've become so complex and exquisite. Anyway, I was wondering if they contain messages, why aren't we able to decode them?—and finally it occurred to me that it's communication on another level. I'm writing a song about them…Remember when I first met you, we were talking about how the Ego-mind isn't able to understand stuff that the unconscious can—well, I think I get it. All we're meant to do is look at them with an open and grateful mind and the message they contain gets imprinted on our deepest selves. Our DNA, or even our souls, if you like."

Igor stared back at her, shaking his head. "All this esoteric—I just don't feel I have the equipment. So what is the message?"

"I've no idea!" she answered gaily, "Ah, this salad is delicious…I suppose if I had to say something about them it would be just the feeling I get when I look at them. There is awe, there's gratitude, and above all a sense that this is benign and well-meaning, a sense that on the soul level, all is well. Any time spent brooding about the evils in the world, the criminals in power, the greed, the needless suffering and warring, it's all wasted time. Ego dwells in the fearful and all the yada-yada, none of which is reality. Staring at a crop formation is just like meditating on a Tibetan mandala. It brings peace and reassurance. The first verse goes:

> *'Teasing are the secrets in the golden summer grain,*
> *No manual to tell us what they mean,*
> *Hasty follows harvest, only pixels now remain*
> *Of mandalas in meadowlands serene…'*

"Well, it goes on a lot. But the chorus is:

> *'Mystic circle-makers, we thank you for the call,*
> *Your messages from godly far domains,*
> *That till everything's let go, love cannot conquer all,*
> *But when everything's let go, Love remains."*

Igor said nervously, "I'm still trying to catch up here. So you're saying they're definitely not man-made?"

Rose tossed her head back. "No and No and No! There were some hoax attempts, one of them certainly by the British Government, to try to discredit the whole notion. It backfired actually, if you read the reports. One that really got me was from an article in the New Scientist; it went something like 'The crop formations become more complex every summer. How long before we see a complete Mandelbrot Set diagram?' A year to the day after the article, the so-called Mandelbrot

Set appeared in the fields just a couple of miles from Cambridge where Mandelbrot once taught. It's an immensely complex mathematical graphic. Others appeared while people were watching, and hundreds have seen balls of light at the same time."

"And flying saucers?" Igor twisted his lower lip, but Rose just smiled.

"Who knows? I certainly don't. But the patterns are much too complex and perfect to be man-made, at least by any means we're aware of. The media have dropped it all, probably on orders, Category UFO, and anyway, no-one's got an explanation so far, so it's not usable except by, as I say, just allowing it in and accepting that the esoteric denies interpretation by the mind. But one thing is certain, if these are visitors from other realms, they know how to circumvent Time, because other worlds are too far away to travel in a lifetime, even at the speed of light."

"But speed of light, surely, is the ultimate limitation?"

"Only for mortals, or only if you think so. But let's say this whole life is an illusion, just like dreams, but with the illusion of limitation also. Notice dreams don't have the same limits. Mind is not active, you can travel anywhere in dreams, instantly." She smiled dreamily, eyes shining before she continued.

"Meanwhile, it seems our subconscious is tapped into some mysterious matrix which links every one and every thing, what some call the Zero Point Field, where even every thought is lodged and bounced back into existence. And you sat in a bookstore wondering about A Course in Miracles and who should promptly sit next to you to tell you about it? And in another department, perhaps you were also just getting ready to meet an eccentric, impulsive, lusty and intelligent woman!"

Chin on hand, Igor smiled back and pointed his fork at her speculatively. "Perhaps you are right, such is the power of pure thought, a desire, is that what you're saying?"

Rose simply smiled and nodded. They ate for minutes in charged silence until she said, "But it has to be uncontaminated by expectation or by any negative emotion. In Ego-think, a desire is often expressed as a lack of something. The Field, shall we call it, immediately reflects back expressions of lack, so it continues. An uncontaminated thought becomes a feeling, often subconscious, but you can express it consciously, without the contamination, by going straight to the feeling."

"And how do you do that?" Igor sounded plaintive.

"Easy, by not being wistful, remember? You say to yourself something like, 'I love and relish the very idea of having a lively, interesting and succulent playmate'—the feeling being as if it were already so—and Bingo, here I am!"

Igor's mouth dropped open and he quickly covered it because he was still chewing. He stared at her in bald astonishment. Rose's laughter rang out, inviting grins and stares from other tables. Finally Igor said with pretended exasperation, "I don't think I've ever had normal conversation in this town."

Rose inclined her head. "What's normal? Gossip, bitchin' and blamin'. Disasters, nookie and sports?"

Igor laughed quietly. "But the esoteric stuff, where is it leading? You mentioned a name the other day, Moncrieffe—I'd already met him, you know? Now there's a guy who seems to give the impression he knows something."

"Well, I think he does."

"And—?" Igor's fingers beckoned as if to pull more from her.

"I don't know what it is," she sighed, "He doesn't tell, just shrugs and smugs. There's so much talk about the Shift, before and since the Solstice 2012, from the end of the world to the drowning of the lowlands, the disappearance of the entire West Coast, tornados, tsunamis, extinction by meteorite, decimation of the population, shifting of the poles, what else? All the way down to a simple change of attitude and perception, heralding or demanding world peace and the end of hunger. Bottom line, where do you want to be when it happens? Both geographically and mentally?"

Igor's laugh was like gravel in a bucket. "I was going to say 'on the beach', but that might not be such a good idea. Better here at 7000 feet. But Moncrieffe needs to find a yacht."

"Not for me, I get seasick. It's all speculation anyway, so I don't dwell on it. I think our only job is to get conscious, about what's happening right now, and who we are, in the great scheme of things…

May I speak frankly?"

Igor spread his hands, welcoming.

Rose hesitated only a moment before taking the plunge. "I think I'd like to take you to bed, one of these days."

Igor gulped and looked directly at her, finding truth in her left eye, a challenge in her right. Rose had flushed slightly and a slow smile came with it, softening her features into sultry.

"Is that Ok? What do you think?"

"It is indeed very Ok. I'm just not used to being, er, invited."

"But there's a condition. You have to have not smoked for 6 days. Is it a big enough carrot?"

Igor counted on his fingers. "It works well. Next Tuesday, right?"

"Good enough. I'll make you a fine dinner, and I'll sing you the One Note song. You've heard of the Seven-Date-Rule?"

"I can guess. So we'd have to date every day for the next six days? It sounds delightful, dear Rose, but I cannot say I am big on rules. How does the single-note end?"

Rose laughed, "Neither am I, don't worry. The song, the ending? It goes nicely, I think. It's meant to raise a smile:

> *"I am a single gleam from the crystal of Aware,*
> *With All-That-Is reflected here within,*
> *With everything in sight dependent on the Light,*
> *I'm wondering, just how did "I" get in?*
>
> > *Mysteries are not for knowing,*
> > *Who knows where the gleams are glowing?*
> > *Who knows why the grass is growing?*
> > *Only Knowing knows…*

And the final hook:

> *I am a single note in the Symphony of Time,*
> *Without me the music cannot play,*
> *If there's only harmony when I am in tune,*
> *Maybe I should practice every day….Every day."*

knew you cared."

"Yeah, well…If things are looking up I could turn warm and fuzzy. Where the hell is that Commie chum of yours?"

"Chewing his nails, Boss. He just quit smoking. Oh, and he asked me to ask you if it's OK to go flying again, they've got some jets he used to drive down in Santa Fe."

Uren tapped his ballpoint for long seconds. "Motive?"

"More pay, for one thing. He'd be instructing, he says."

"Oh, Shi-ite. It was me who sent him there…I dunno, let me think about it."

"Couldn't hurt, Boss."

"No? What if there's an incident? Moscow finds out where he is, they'll send someone to smack him."

"You could give him a pseudonym."

"Yeah, right, an alias for his alien ass, you kiddin' me? Just a photo would do it. Well, with a bit of luck he'll kill himself, so tell him OK. Let's see how he does with reaming Moncrieffe. Back to which, if there's anything in that Prist that's not on the Data Sheet, the Brit gets a going-over. This could be real hot shit. Ok, beat it. And good work, Wojer."

Raw skepticism filled her parting glance. Back in her office, she checked her emails in case of an early result. Instead there was a new message with a scam warning. Bypassing it, she found a surprise invitation.

"Nice meeting you the other day. Since you walk like a dancer, I wonder if you'd like to see the Aspen Santa Fe Ballet, at the Lensic, Saturday. I got great seats. N.M."

Duplicity beginning to haunt her, she gave a wry smile before posting her acceptance. Her social life could do nothing but improve but for a long moment she considered whether to get clearance. Her rebellious side finally won out and she tapped her reply: "Deal. Dinner on me. Before or after? A.W."

Dear Kolya, Irina from London. Your stuff is getting obscure. This is quite difficult to translate, though I have some help from the books and I

confess I enjoy the challenge. Knowing our little Lena, so angelic, but it may be over her head. We'll see. It feels like giving someone hope when they're stuck down a deep well and no-one's got a rope. But if it's really true, as you say, that we're all interconnected, it explains everything, does it not? All we have to do is see it, believe it, but that's the hard part, like an invisible rope! Or could she just go to Trust, so the well will fill up and float her to the top, out into the sunshine, yes? I'm enjoying this, my thoughts are expanding daily and I keep smiling. If nothing else, that's good, right? Asta la tarde. Irina.

P.S. Your excitement, if any, does not convey, but isn't this stuff momentous? Earth-changing—I mean stupendous, I mean absolutely shattering of all old beliefs and notions? Well, I think so!

The Italian restaurant *Andiamo!* was packed as usual on a Saturday evening. As Nic and Anastasia stood waiting at reception, she turned and looked at him directly. Her down-turned mouth seemed disapproving, but the instant he dismissed the thought, it broke into a sunshine smile.

She said brightly, "I haven't been on a date in so long, I can't remember how to behave!"

"Well, at least you didn't ask me why I invited you. That's a good start."

"But I'd like to. What's your answer? Were we lovers in a past life and was it incomplete?" She gave him an impish look and Nic chuckled softly.

"In the café, how much of our conversation did you overhear?"

Evasively she answered, "It was very noisy. Is that why you invited me?"

Before he could answer they were summoned to a small table. As they sat, he ventured casually, "I have the merest suspicion you weren't there by accident."

Anastasia tried to conceal the jolt, spreading her napkin with no expression. "Isn't it said there are no accidents? Is that just a matter of belief? And we create our own reality? And simple wishes, if they are pure thought with a delighted feeling, are always granted?"

"So `tis said. What on earth have you been reading?" He grinned, relaxing and picking up his menu.

"Me? All sorts of good stuff. Abraham for a start. What was your wish?" she asked innocently.

"Hmm...I guess it must have been for a provocative dinner companion." He looked up and their eyes met for a long moment.

"So what am I provoking in you?" she asked, "Apart from suspicion, that is. I hope you're not one of those wannabe knights who are drawn to people who look unhappy?"

"Ouch...I wonder about that. It's more that you're very interesting. You've a spring in your step, a beautiful smile but you must know that your normal expression is somewhat puzzling. Attraction is a curious thing, often the externals *seem* to be the reason but really it's on another level. That's why people keep attracting the same partners, the vibrational level is the same even though the form that shows up can be quite different."

"So it's the flavor of the pudding rather than its shape?" Seeing him nod and smile, she went on. "So you're saying you quite like the look of it but you're not sure about the flavor? Thus, according to the so-called Law of Attraction thing, I really am a plant? Or maybe *you* are—an unwitting tool in either my downfall or my evolution? A vibrational match?"

"Why downfall?"

"A distraction from my mission in life."

"Which is—?

"I'd rather not go into it. Something happened in Poland a long time ago and it needs a correction. But tell me about you, what are you up to?"

"Bit of home improvement and a new novel."

"Oh. Can I ask what it's about?"

"Not really. It's pure self-indulgence to talk about it and then it loses impetus. Let's just say it's about what's really going on."

Anastasia gave a wry smile. "Are you saying you actually know?"

"Sure. Don't you?"

"No, I don't, I'm completely mystified."

Nic chuckled, "Well, that's the best place to start, I guess. So, your walk is taut and springy, you're a dancer?"

"No, not at all. I run and ski and do yoga sometimes. I was actually thinking of dance lessons but with my future being uncertain... Everything I've done has been with a view to going back."

"Back where, to Poland?"

"Yes. And everything I've done has just moved me further away. I actually like it here, it's just this thing I have to do. I called it a correction. It's risky—hey, do you think a person can change their facial expression, I mean the one in repose?"

The waitress came and hovered with unusual respect. Nic said, "How about we share? The starters are great, a bunch of those and we spilt a main course? And some wine?"

She nodded eagerly. After the order, Nic found his way back to the topic. "Sometimes you see people with extraordinarily sweet expressions and I can only assume it's from years of thinking kind thoughts and being grateful."

Anastasia looked crestfallen. "I have a picture of me at twelve, it's serious but charming, light, kindly. Something happened and I've been having murderous thoughts daily for twenty-six years. That would cause this face of mine, don't you think?"

"Maybe. Or we could think of it as a flower, new growth, waiting to open. This correction you speak of, would that do it?"

Anastasia went silent and thoughtful, finally venturing, "I hadn't thought beyond it. But I have to say, it does feel bleak."

"Can you tell me? You're being a bit mysterious."

"Keep it to yourself?"

"Of course." Nic ran a zipper across his grin.

"Ok. What would you do if someone murdered your parents?"

He gulped visibly. "Do you know who did it?"

Anastasia gave a long slow shake of her head. "But I mean to find out."

Silence hung for a while, other conversations intruding from nearby tables, banter, arguments and laughter.

Nic drummed his fingers, stopped and looked at her intently. "My perceptions have changed. Twenty years ago I might have done something drastic, but now I get there's no peace in that course. When you get intensely focused on an idea, it tends to block out other possibilities, other ways of looking at things."

She flattened the air with her hand. "Look, I don't care to hear any pacifist crap. For me this is something that has to be done."

Nic stared at her evenly, his mind scrambling with conjecture. "Do you have to do it yourself?" he asked finally.

She scoffed, "Well, who else is going to?"

"I mean, if someone else was to take care of it for you, would that deprive you of the satisfaction, personal involvement?"

Anastasia went suddenly rigid, growing taller in her seat, her eyes huge, her mouth a straight line, her lips quivering. Nic said nothing, watching her unblinking and when the waitress came with the wine he held up his hand. She started to speak and caught the gesture, turned away without leaving the glasses. This was witnessed by couples at the tables on each side, curious and aware of seething tension.

Anastasia blinked suddenly and two tears squeezed out. Her hands began to shake and she quickly moved them to her lap, ignoring the teardrops. Nic extended a hand across the table, palm up and waiting, but she made no move towards it. The adjacent couples continued to stare. With his other hand, Nic slowly reached across with his napkin towards her face but Anastasia angrily whipped her head. The tears flashed and fell to the tablecloth.

Abruptly she stood up and without excusing herself, picked up her napkin and slipped past the table. Nic made no move, just watched her empty place with no glance to either side. The waitress returned and set the two glasses down. Nic nodded silently, then again in sudden amazement as the girl put a gentle hand on his shoulder and left again. Minutes passed as the conversations on each side slowly resumed and after a while he reached out to take a sip. A hand fell lightly on his wrist.

"Wait for me," Anastasia said quietly, then eased back into her seat. She picked up her glass and held it out. "Thank you," she said as they clinked and sipped. "I'm not sure what happened. I'm sorry."

Nic shook his head. "No problem."

"Oh, there's a problem all right. I just haven't worked out what it is yet. Total confusion. You just tossed a big rock in my pond." She reached out a hand which felt dry and cool and very strong as he took it gently and covered it with his other. Her grip responded gratefully.

"This pond was a trifle murky, methinks," he said with a smile which was slowly returned. The contrast from her normal downturn was like clouds parting for a sunbeam. "Twenty-six years, you said. Poland under the gun. Solidarity getting under way, against massive resistance. Was it 'authority'?"

Seeing her nod, he asked, "Was it soldiers?"

"As far as I know."

"So they'll be at least in their 50's, retired or dead. Russians?"

"I assume so, but not necessarily."

"And do you want the soldiers or their commander?"

"I—I don't know. Certainly the commander."

"Who's going to be in his 70's, right? In a defeated regime. Dead or retired and hitting the bottle."

"Probably."

"Hm…So let's imagine we go and find this guy, tie him to a chair and wave a shiv in his face and confront him with his crime which will be one of many, so he won't remember specifics. He's sad, defeated, dejected, let's say. But you, you're determined, so you shoot him in the groin and take your time explaining your feelings while he's writhing and moaning and praying for death—"

"Stop it, please!"

"Ok." Nic paused, took a sip and then their starters arrived, the waitress smiling and relieved. They shuffled and split the portions, then Nic continued.

"I heard this guru-ette, she's what they call a channel, a voice from the other side. Abraham. She said nobody comes into the physical without a clear acceptance of their life conditions, their willingness to act out a part, if you like. This would include both the soldiers and your parents. So, if we all come from some mysterious source into this Time/ Space duality which is simply a limitless morass of possibilities—let's say, and I'm just speculating, it's all by prior arrangement and things are going to happen both good and bad, depending on your personal perception. The soldiers probably thought they were doing the right thing or at least their unavoidable duty. Mostly we have no control over what happens or what other people do, in fact the only control we have is over our own choice of attitude."

"This is beginning to sound like a sermon, Nic."

"Not intended. I'm doing a 'what-if' scenario. Have you heard of regression therapy?"

"Vaguely. Did you do it?"

"Some. It was very interesting. It seems that on the level of detached observation or perception, there is no suffering, there is just what is. To quote from a famous monster tome, "All suffering is of the Ego."

"What tome?"

"I think you know. A Course of sorts."

Anastasia stayed silent, not wanting to divulge her acquaintance with the title, and the circumstances.

"Well, anyway," Nic continued, "In one of these sessions, which seemed perfectly real by the way, under hypnosis I was a medieval monk who got hung for heresy. When the session ended and I told the therapist about the hanging, he just laughed and said 'Yeah, I've been hung a coupla times, no big deal!'—which in retrospect it isn't, just a quick *squunch* and on to the next thing. It's only in prospect that it's a bit alarming. Another thing from the tome, 'Always remember that you never suffered anything from anything anyone ever did to you'. We're transcending ego-level here, you understand?"

"But—but you're talking to someone's ego-level, so on that level how could she begin to understand?"

"That, ma'am, is a very smart observation."

"Oh. Thank you. So is it possible for the ego-mind to forgive and forget, is that where you're going?"

"No, I don't think it is, if you stay stuck there. But what if that Ego-mind evaporates when you croak? Doesn't that mean it's all an illusion, a strictly temporary construction? It must mean it's not who you really are, don't you think?"

After a long silence and several mouthfuls, Anastasia ventured, "Are you suggesting, first, that my parents actually and willingly, if unconsciously, accepted their lives and their demise, and second, that on some mysterious level they never suffered? On that level it was simply another adventure?"

"That's what seems to be coming down, yes. Since ego-mind cannot accept it, one would have to shift levels to see it that way."

"But you can't get rid of Ego-mind, it's where we live."

"Check. But if it's not who you really are…? You can by-pass it, set it aside so it's not dominant."

"How?"

"By sheer trickery!" Nic grinned broadly. Anastasia gave him a quizzical smile and shook her head.

"I'm not taking the bait. But from what you were saying about illusion, you think none of this is really happening?"

"It seems that if you put your attention on it, that's like deciding it is happening. Otherwise it's not. You and I have a consensus that we're sitting at this table. Then your mind goes far away to Poland, creates a scenario, doesn't like it and wants to correct it. It can't, so it's frustrated and looks for some outlet. Someone should pay. Suppose they already did?"

"How would you know?"

"Well they'd surely have experienced a miserable existence, disconnected from their joy, fulfillment, amazement and wonder at this incredible experience of being an aspect of Source or consciousness, exploring the physical realm. Tuning into the marvel of it inspires the ego by-pass trick."

Anastasia lowered her head, conceding. "I give in. Tell me the trick."

"Oh, there's dozens. Art, music, sport, adventure, stories, gardening, studies, inventing, love-making, hearing children laugh, smiling at people, sharing a meal, above all and essentially, instead of using these things as a distraction, enjoying them consciously in pure appreciation and gratitude. Let's coin a new word for it—appreciatude! Whatever the circumstances that apparently brought you to this very point now, where are you really? You are beautiful at least in someone's eyes if not your own, you're healthy, vibrant, very clever, you have a job and somewhere to live well, you have education and mobility and an appetite and no doubt all kinds of desires. Let's say a charming prince has his eye on you, loves to watch you eat, imagines holding your hand at the ballet and sharing being transported by beauty in movement, afterwards a walk along the river in the moonlight, maybe that beautiful sad mouth would change shape with an oh-so-gentle kiss goodnight, y'know, stuff like that. What d'you think? Wouldn't your Mommy and Daddy, wherever they are, want that for you instead of dark and miserable thoughts of vengeance?"

Anastasia put down her fork and covered her face with her napkin. Nic took the opportunity to eat, his eyes away from the shudders that wracked her body. He tried to ignore the other diners sensing a drama and when Anastasia's crisis subsided, he saw her lower the napkin to reveal just her eyes, huge and glistening, but minutely expressing amusement.

From behind the cloth she muttered, "I think you're just a wicked seducer."

"Really? Did it work?"

Still partly hidden, she nodded vigorously. "Oh, yes. And then, guess what, my mind immediately started looking for snags and called you a seducer."

"But I suspect everyone's a seducer of sorts, including you. We all love to elicit response from others, but that's just another thing to be grateful for when it works! Look, I just had an idea. Write down your parent's names, where they lived, dates and stuff, and I'll see what I can do."

In astonishment Anastasia exclaimed, "You? How could you possibly do anything?"

"Well, you never know. It's who you know, y'know." He grinned cryptically.

"Who do you know?" At that moment she realized she been disarmed, recalling that she was supposed to be working for Uren, that a meeting was supposed to be a probe, an ulterior strategy. She found the thought seriously dismayed her, especially since it was clearly failing.

Nic simply put a finger to his lips and shook his head. "Just leave it with me, Ok? And we should eat up or they'll start without us."

CHAPTER 7

Love is in the air....And I don't know if you're an illusion.

John Paul Young

"Ok, Comrade, whatcha got for me?" Uren's bulldog face looked up from his computer screen, his right fist clenching a yellow marker.

Igor stood before him with a sheaf of papers and a blank expression. "Nothing. The Prist analysis is pretty well identical to the Manufacturer's Data sheet."

"Holy hotshit damn! What in hell is going on here? There's only one manufacturer, right?"

"Well, no. There is one other called Dice but it's the very same thing, same analysis. Do you want it to get checked as well?"

"Time wasted. Moncrieffe was specific about Prist anyway, right? It's gotta be the stuff itself that's doing something. Shit, I'm going to have to go higher on this. The cloud-seeding, what the pinkos call the chem-trails, that's strictly local and mostly experimental."

Igor's eyes opened wide. "So you admit the truth of it?"

"No. What I'm getting here, bottom line, is that there's something in the jet fuel itself being spread all over the goddam globe and it might be fucking with our heads."

"Don't we already know about that?"

"Get up to speed here, Boris, we already know about our own stuff. What we gotta find out is what someone else might be doing."

"Please then tell me what we are doing, Frank. If I don't know that, how can I tell what else is in the air? And my name is Igor."

"Yeah, yeah, I was being generic. Look, we're doing whatever the fuck we like—Igor. But we sure as hell ain't using happy juice, get me? Ok, split for now. I'll call you. By the way, that woman you're seeing, she's got a record, didja know that?"

Igor stiffened in surprise. "Who do you mean, Boss?"

"This Rose puss you're trying to tomcat. Two arrests, one for possession, one for a protest chain-up to the White House railing. Seems she wasn't too fond o' Georgie-Dubya. Better watch your step, Comrade, associating with felons…"

"Frank, I am allowed private life. There's nothing sinister. I simply met her in a bookstore. Anyway, how did you even know about her?"

"Listen, sonny boy, you've had an implant since Day One. We always know where you are."

"Where?"

"Where what?"

"Where's the implant?"

"None o' your friggin' business. Go on, get outta here."

As the door closed, Uren made a call to a number in Virginia, one he was loath to use because it always diminished his authority. The call was picked up instantly.

"Ross Boyd. What is it now, Frank?"

"Morning', Ross. I've got something, might be huge. We've been checking on a guy who seems to have sources, kinda global, seems he's onto some hidden additive in commercial jet fuel which is dicking with people's minds. Makin'`em aware of what's really going on."

"And what might that be, Frank?" The voice sounded slightly bored, also hollow and disembodied.

"Aw, c'mon, Ross. The thing that's never spoken of, like who's really in charge of things, y'know?"

"No, I don't know. Do you?"

"I've a damn good idea. It ain't the President, that's for sure. I bet you know them all. Begins with B, they meet every year, right?"

"Is that B for Bankers or B for Bilderbergers?"

"It's the same goddam thing. I heard another word for them—Zionazis. Or the Corporate Goliath. So, if they're losing control of people's minds, what d'you think's gonna happen?"

"There'll always be some mavericks, Frank. But we'll soon be taking care of that."

"No, listen, if this guy's right, it'll be everyone. Including you and me!"

"Umm....I see what you mean, Frank. Hold the line."

As he waited several minutes, Uren pondered his own observation. Loss of control would mean the end of his job, there'd be no need for it. No need for the nuke program he protected, no need for ICBM's, F.22's, B.2's, F.35's, HAARP, Predators, Tomahawk missiles, drones and assassinations. A population out of control, Military/Industrial Conspiracy defunct, World peace, America defenseless and over-run by diaper-heads…*"Not on my frickin' watch!—."* The thoughts cascaded as the call held for long stressful minutes.

"Frank," the voice finally came back, "Had the Joint Chiefs on conference. We gotta nip this in the bud, whatever it is, rumor or real. Take your time, but nail it good. If you can't handle it, strap this guy's ass to a Bizjet and send him up here."

"I can handle it, Ross."

"Good. You better. Keep me updated."

The line went dead. Uren stood up and stared at the wall, his body rigid, fear coursing through his entrails. If this was a red herring, it was egg all over his face which spelt doom. If it was real and unstoppable, he was equally doomed. If it was real and he failed to get to the root of it—rage suddenly boiled like a rocket moving up his spine. All he wanted right then was to bugle up the cavalry but there came a sharp pain in his chest and left shoulder. He sat down in bewilderment, feeling his arms wanting to reach out and smash things. It took him several minutes to get his breathing back to normal.

There came a knock on his door. Anastasia came in beaming, a fresh glow on her face.

"Better be good, Wojer. Need some action about right now. What're you looking so pleased about?"

"New email, Boss. You're going to love it. Shall I read it to you?"

"Go."

Anastasia sat down and took a deep breath. *"Dear Irina/Elena. The truth of what's happening is not believable to the regular mind, because we've only a limited view of what's really going on. It's been discovered in fact that we only see about .5 per cent of the visible universe because we don't have the equipment for more, it's like we have a very small frequency range. There's a tale about Captain Cook arriving somewhere primitive, the crews went ashore and the boggled natives asked them where they came from—they couldn't see the ships at anchor because they'd never seen one before so they had no reference! Some of them went on board and changed their perceptions. Now we're being asked to do the same but in a totally different context.*

Most of humanity sees only what they are programmed to see, strictly 3-dimensional, and they're conditioned to worry, struggle, age, sicken and die, and to believe that life is about mostly bad news, suffering, fighting and a preposterous struggle to stay alive until you croak! Now suppose someone comes along, hypnotizes you into believing that you are a cosmic voyager on a brief stop on a little vacation planet called Eden/Gaia and says, Hey let's explore this place and create some amazing and wonderful things like water, flowers, music, trees and bizarre animals, and move around in a special feeling vehicle called a body with weird controls that take a lot of learning and with a highly sensitive perception and feedback mechanism which is, by the way, up- and down-linked permanently to the mother-ship so it can't get lost and can convey all its actions and feelings immediately both to the ship and all the other explorers who, by the way, love to interact with each other in all kinds of different and deliriously delicious ways!"

Uren thumped his desk fretfully. "How much more of this crap?"

"Patience, boss. You might learn something. Just listen, Ok?"

He gave her a disgusted look but gestured to continue.

"In order to do this effectively, it has to forget all it knows about the rest of the Universe—except for one thing: this is strictly temporary, so there's absolutely nothing to fear. Now for quite a while, this worked so well that they forgot they were forgetting something vital, and so they got fearful, and some became so fearful that they had to do something to control the situation and somehow make themselves safe. The feeling became so powerful that it got transmitted through the mother-ship's matrix and spread all over the place. A few who were the most desperate to control, let's call them the Superfears, found a way to commandeer all the money and isolate themselves and essentially employ everyone else to protect them, and once they had enough agreement about this, the whole program changed and permeated all the other receivers.

"Not everyone was totally thrilled about this." Anastasia paused and gave Uren a saucy look before continuing. *"In a few isolated places, they*

found that some of their discoveries or creations in the vegetation realm were able to disrupt the program by opening their minds to let them see once more the greater view, and the way of fearlessness. They started to spread the good news but as soon as the Superfears got wind of this, they determined to shut it down for their own protection. Now Eden/Gaia, the planet they were visiting, was also vibrationally connected to this matrix and realized what was happening; she had never fallen for the fearful program. She also knew that some of the plant residue from eons of growth and decay were trapped within her many layers so she waited quietly for the travelers and their progeny to extract them. This they inevitably did, using these residues to provide the means of speeding travel around the planet. Over the next 100 years or so, more and more of this residue was extracted and carried worldwide along the jet-streams, very slowly opening the minds again, the least fearful at first, then the others more gradually. At last it began to accelerate exponentially, not without a little push from some clever chemistry whiz who realized that a small dose of help was required to speed things up before the Superfears got wind of it and had to ground all the aircraft, demanding the invention of a 'safer' system of propulsion. The Supers also had a back-up plan which was to inject everyone with an implant so that they could be monitored, controlled and restricted in all their movements. It became a race against time, though of course only the Supers were racing.

Those who re-discovered fearlessness weren't bothered about this, they understood the reality, i.e. the illusory nature of their existence, and they also knew that the Supers, poor bastards, were missing out on the best bits of exploring, like love and sex-in-love, making baby vehicles for other visiting souls, discovery/invention, mind-bursting beauty and joyful interaction. They also knew, with utter conviction, that all was well because the little planet Eden/Gaia understood their position and was even using them to release her secret recipes so they would change their thinking and take care of her properly. The time of wars, inequality, starvation, disease and terror was coming to an end and Eden/Gaia would once again be the vacation spot of choice for the Cosmic traveler. Now then, darlings, go outside and breathe deeply! T60.111.1 By the way, if you're unconvinced, I heard a recording of a recent secret meeting of the Superfears. It's very revealing. They seem to know that if they cannot keep us in fear they will have nothing…! Love Kolya." (Memo, Send précis to Jamie)

Anastasia left out the last four words as a precaution and looked up, beaming into the scowling face of Uren. She said breathlessly, "So, what d'you think of that, Boss?"

"Did Bilderberg meet recently?"

"I've no idea, Boss."

"Well, find out quick and get back to me. That's all. Good job. Oh, has he called you back yet?"

"Er, yes, we went out to dinner and the ballet, couple of nights ago."

"You did? Why didn't you tell me?"

"It was the weekend, Boss."

"I mean right now. Are you holding out on me? Didja hump him?"

Anastasia gave him a disgusted look which he ignored. "He was very respectful. He also assaulted my notions about going back home."

"And?"

"And nothing. He walked me to my car and kissed me goodnight."

"And that's it?"

"Actually no, Boss. Last night was different."

"Tell me. Everything!"

"He made me dinner at his place."

"And that's it?"

"The rest is private, Boss."

"No, it ain't! C'mon, spill it." Uren made a vigorous come-hither with his pudgy hand.

Anastasia hesitated long moments and with a reluctant sigh went on, "Afterwards he took me to his room and had me lie face down and pretend to be asleep. I think it was kind of a trance thing."

Uren leaned forward in his chair. "Go on."

"Eeuw, Boss, you're not asking for details?"

"Damn right I am. You're on assignment here, remember? Don't leave anything out, might be relevant."

Anastasia twitched her mouth in reluctance, looking away with pretended shyness but actually disgusted by Uren's lascivious gleam. "Boss, come on, you can't—"

"All of it!"

"We just lay down and fondled."

"Who fondled who?"

"Well, mostly he fondled me, I think he put me in a kind of hypnotic state. To be honest, I was up for anything but he didn't go for it. He asked permission for everything he did. Then he stopped and lay down beside me. He had all his clothes on, by the way."

"You gotta be kidding! What about you?"

"I kept my underwear on. He just said it was enough for now. Then he just held me gently for what seemed like seconds but was more like an hour."

"No shit. How were you with all this?"

"I was blissed out. He asked me if I was warm enough. He wrapped me in a duvet and asked if I wanted to sleep. I roused myself after a while and told him I should go home. He brought me a cup of hot chocolate while I was dressing, then he walked me out to my car. That was it."

"Goddam, I never heard you. So, you didn't hump him, but did you pump him, I mean for information?"

"There wasn't any opening really. I did ask him what his new book was about, although I did read some of it before, remember? Lot of conspiracy stuff, but he only said it was his little contribution to the Great Shift."

"What the hell is that?" Uren asked with suspicion.

"He only said it was the new consciousness, and who we really are and what's really going on. He wouldn't elucidate. I thanked him for being so respectful and he said it was easy because I commanded that respect. I must say, Boss, I do feel quite different today."

"Hell, woman, weren't you horny by the time he, ah—?"

"No kidding, Boss." She lowered her voice shyly. "Actually, I was at screaming point. But then he told me about just reveling in the *feeling* of desire, instead of the need to move on it. The room seemed to blaze with, well, love. All around, in the very air—Oh, my God, d'you think he might have sprayed some of that stuff around?"

"What stuff?" Uren asked sharply.

"You know, whatever's in the Prist?"

"Damn, I never thought of him actually having some. Right! We'll have to go through his place. Make it a burglary, there's no chance of doing a whole snoop without him sussing it. When are you seeing him next?"

"I've arranged the day off, day after tomorrow. We're going sailing."

"Where?"

"Heron lake, it's about eighty miles north, we'll be gone all day."

"I'm gonna have to pull you off this, moochacha, I think you're getting attached."

Anastasia paled visibly. "But, Boss—"

"No buts, honey. After Heron, you aren't seeing him again. He'll be gone anyways."

"Gone where?" she asked in alarm.

"You don't need to know. Somewhere out of earshot, that's for sure. Gimme that email, lemme know the moment there's more. Ok, that's it for now. Good job."

Igor Knyazev lay back in the goose feathers, breathing deeply. By his side, Rose faced him, her head on clasped hands as if in prayer, her eyes shining. "Don't even think about a cigarette," she cautioned, "Get by this moment and you're done forever."

"I am done forever," he answered hoarsely. "Perhaps I mean undone. I only wish I was 18 again so I could—"

"Uh-uh" she countered. "Men can't do that at 18, they're too driven. Thank you for your patience and restraint, you're a brilliant pupil. How do you feel?"

"I—I feel like I have nothing more to ask of the Universe. I can go now, anytime. Nothing matters any more. How is that possible? I think maybe it's because I felt the absolute most that this body can feel."

"You ain't seen nothin' yet, sunshine." Rose moved up and kissed him lovingly. "By the way, you do smell gorgeous? Was it a terrible struggle, giving up?"

"Hm, I'm not sure which was worse, the missing smoke or the waiting. If I had known there was such mighty carrot befront my nose, it would have been a piece of fruit-cake."

"Just cake, *Lyubimiy*. That's Russian for 'darling', right? I looked it up, just in case."

"*Da*. You are *korrek*t, *Lyubimaya*. Your song was quite lovely, will you sing me another? And there's no need to dress."

"*Au contraire*, I think there is. One breast hanging over a guitar would look rather foolish, don't you think?" She giggled, leapt up, squeezed on a T-shirt and ran out of the room. Igor watched her retreating backside in quiet wonder at her taut condition, as well as her confidence in it. He had never felt such an afterglow, the experience of restraint and pure appreciation being something quite new, although slightly dismaying that he'd never known it before. And Rose's expertise in Tantra had him speculating about how much practice she must have had. Dark thoughts vanished as she returned with two glasses of champagne in one hand, a guitar in the other. He held the drinks while she sat on the bed and began a delicate picking rhythm.

If I could see you as we're all seen, as through Creation's eyes,
And all the spaces in between, as Graces in disguise,
I'd see you as perfection, as you were meant to be
No need for re-invention—perhaps a little therapee!

She stopped to chuckle for a moment, then continued with the chorus:

Does a candle on the altar of the All,
Does a flower in the Eden of the Sun,
Does a drop in the wave of the mighty ocean,
Dream of going it alone?

If I could soothe you as I would me, in heart instead of mind,
Where love reigns fearlessly, what treasures would we find?
No questioning intentions, no fear of being deceived,
What appetites for loving, we hadn't dared relieve?

We are candles on the altar of the All,
We are flowers in the Eden of the Sun,
We are drops in the wave of the mighty ocean,
And at last we know that we are One.

She put the guitar down and reached for her glass, then caught the look on his face. He shook his head, not hiding his amazement. "You should be famous," he said quietly, "That was so beautiful. But how can you say that we are One?"

"Didn't you feel it, when we were making love? And now, still, no separation? Fact is, only the Ego-mind sees itself as separate, when in fact we are all simply aspects of the same consciousness. It creates individuality so it can see itself from every possible aspect, that's all. Once this is seen for what it is, everything changes. Peace descends and permeates everything you think and do. It seems we came here to forget who we really are, so we could have the thrill of re-discovering it. After eons of unhappiness, minds are finally demanding a better way and it's gaining momentum at a tremendous rate, exponentially."

Remembering his brief, Igor asked innocently, "Can you tell me what's propelling it? I mean, does this new awareness have cause of some sort?"

"I've no idea, except that everything that's ever been tried hasn't worked and people are getting truly fed up. I think that things needed to get bad enough that a reaction would happen—I thought this might begin with the two Dubya stolen elections, if that lawless, feckless, brainless and amoral man got in he would screw up badly enough that it would cause a reaction, for good. But he was just a patsy, a tool for the real powers behind the thrones, and so too was the utterly reprehensible Supreme Court who enabled him. I dunno, maybe it has to get even worse, because we're up against entrenched powers who like things the way they are, so they can control the world, decimate those they regard as useless and make fortunes from getting them to fight each other. They clearly have no concern whatever for the suffering, maiming and death they cause, but don't get me started on that. I'm sure you know that 9/11 was a fabrication, they invent enemies deliberately, Iraq and Afghanistan were spun into mass-belief—it's quite simply about controlling the oil and the pipelines, in fact the whole of the Middle East. They justify it to themselves and to all the saps and patsies by declaring it protection of our vital sources, meaning of course that if we didn't have any oil, we couldn't run our battleships, tanks and bombers. I told you not to get me started—this is hardly bedroom sweet-talk, is it? Are you hungry?"

"Yes. And about 9/11, I brought satellite pictures from Moscow proving the fabrication. They just vanished. But I have to say that the people I have to work for are essentially paid to be defenders of the system, so their job is to eradicate all opposition, and in this they are unspeakable ruthless. I am concerned that my friend Nic Moncrieffe, you know him, yes? He may be targeted, and you do not want to come up against these people. They are completely above any law you care to name because Homeland Security comes first and justifies any action. I know they break the law in any way they choose and have been doing it for years. It is just the same as in Russia but they disguise it better here. You have so-called free elections and do nothing but put mass-murderers in power, who of course all think they're on the side of right, with God to back them up!"

"Igor, we must stop this now," Rose said, patting his knee, "The attention gives them energy. You're breathing heavily and getting upset, which is not appropriate for a man who is naked as well as hungry. I will give you the answer when we've eaten. Follow me to the trough, kind sir. By the way, what are you doing tomorrow?"

"I am to fly Russian jet fighter, but on peaceful mission."

"I'd never have guessed. *Qué hombré!* Is there room for another?"

"There is, but I regret that I am the other. Maybe someday soon, though."

"Hm…" She looked doubtful. "What's the miles-per-gallon, Igor?"

"Um, I think it's a little bit less than two."

Fuel tanks topped and external checks complete, Larry and Igor stood to the left of the sleek jet trainer, a Czech-built L.39 Albatros. It gleamed blue and white in the early sunlight, hunkered as if eager for flight.

"No ejection, no `chutes?" Igor asked mildly.

Larry shook his head. "Nope. Not many do for non-military. Did you see James Bond stole one of these, in *Tomorrow Never Dies?*"

"I saw it! He made it look easy, did he not?"

"Well, I guess it is. You want to take the front?"

"Thank you. Where we are going, Phoenix, Arizona?"

"Yup. Tell me if anything's unfamiliar. I put all the needed frequencies on your pad."

Igor clambered up the stirrups eagerly, stepped down on to the seat and strapped himself into the full harness. On Larry's word he hauled over the heavy canopy and latched it. Head-phones jacked in, he said, "I remember where everything is, but I'll need to translate in my head, give me a minute."

"Sure, take your time. APU when you're ready."

"I assume Auxiliary Power Unit?"

"Yep. Contact."

As Igor scanned the cockpit, something of the old headiness returned, the clear need for total focus which heightens the feeling of aliveness. Evidently Larry was watching carefully as his hand went to adjust his altimeter.

"Airfield height 6350'. Altimeter 30.52."

"Affirm. This harness is much simpler. We used to have leg straps, weight settings. And of course, ejection seat. APU is at idle."

"OK. Switches check, then start main engine. I'll talk to the tower, if you like."

"I like."

"Santa Fe Tower, this is Albatros 24189. Taxi for departure, Phoenix."

"Roger, Albatros, clear taxi to runway 33. Hold short, contact Tower on 119.5." There followed some background muttering, then, "Correction, hold your position! Someone wants to talk to you. One coming over."

A hand slapped on the outside of Igor's canopy. Unlatching, he opened it a few inches and looked out, expression inscrutable inside his helmet, the noise from the spooling up engine overpowering. He removed his helmet, straining to hear.

One of his watchers stood there scowling. "Where the hell are you going, Knyazev?"

"Ferry flight. I have clearance. Check with Uren. I return by lunch."

The rain-coated man shouted back, holding up a warning finger. "Hold while I check." He thumbed his cell phone, waited and then had to move away from the noise to hear, running to the side of the hangar.

Igor cranked his head round to see Larry's hands go up in a what-the-hell gesture. Unable to communicate without his helmet, Igor simply gave him a thumbs-up and a 2 minute wait signal. Larry was clearly annoyed, not unreasonably with an engine already running at $2000 an hour. Igor replaced his helmet and heard Larry speaking to the tower, then on the intercom, "We've got clearance as far as I'm concerned. Let's roll."

Igor closed his canopy, released the brakes and eased the throttle forward. "Paranoid idiots. Where do they think I'm going, with no passport and a bug in my butt?"

The controller's voice came on. "Albatros 24189, this is Santa Fe Tower, dunno who're these sonsabitches, they have no authority here. Clear taxi, runway 33, no conflicting, hold at your discretion, clear takeoff, left turnout, climb on course to One-Seven thousand."

As they swung in a great circle, they saw a figure running from behind the hangar. Igor simply looked the other way, keeping the taxiing speed high as he ran his checks over the panel. Larry watched admiringly at Igor's consummate skill at steering with the brakes, a big hurdle for students. They passed the holding point, Igor swung hard onto the runway, braked sharply, ran the engine up to full power, checked engine instruments and released the brakes. The speed built rapidly, the tail-pipe roar receding and ten seconds later, at 110 knots indicated, they were airborne in almost complete silence, the loudest sound being the hiss of the air-conditioning. Igor raised the landing gear just as the Tower cut in urgently

"Albatros, Santa Fe Tower, these goons are demanding your immediate return. Runway—"

Larry cut-off the transmission with his own. "189 airborne, climbing to One Seven thousand, heading 245, switching to 128 decimal 9. Good day."

His professionalism completely recovered, Igor asked, "I don't have that frequency on my pad, what is it?"

"No idea," Larry said shortly, "Enough crap for one morning. Sit back and relax."

Eighteen minutes into the flight, level at 17,000', the L.39 cruised comfortably at 350 knots, the sky fiercely blue, with some scattered cloud off to the west, Albuquerque to the left and behind them. Larry changed frequencies and reported their positions to ABQ approach.

An answer came immediately. "24189, ABQ, it seems you have company."

At the same moment, Larry barked into the intercom, "What the hell? Look left!"

A National Guard F.16 nosed alongside a mere fifty feet away. On instinct, Igor craned his neck both ways. "We got two," he said quietly as another long snout appeared to starboard. They both saw pilots gesticulating.

"Well, what have we here?" Larry said calmly, adding, "We don't know what they want, do we? Let's pretend to be shocked. I have control."

"You have it."

He rocked their wings and hauled back on the stick, cutting the throttle to idle. The Albatros pitched up to the vertical. The two F.16's followed at once but forged above them as the Albatros' speed fell off abruptly. Unable to risk a tail slide, the F.16's lit their afterburners, veered apart and rolled level, hauling into opposing turns.

With the last of their momentum, Larry eased on left rudder and the Albatros winged slowly over into a steep dive. Seconds later, one F.16 streaked by, half a wing's length from their canopy, still in afterburner.

"Well, well," Larry said quietly after the awful roar diminished. "What do you think, Igor?"

Igor chuckled. "They must know who you are, Mr Aerobat. I think you should give them a show."

"Gallup's not far off, we could go in there." Larry pulled steadily out of the dive.

"That would not get us to Phoenix, plus your friend waiting in the Lear. It is certain they do not have orders to shoot. They would not do it over a town anyway. I think we pretend we are just having play-time, yes?"

"Well, aren't we?" Larry chuckled, "I like it."

"That cloud bank to the west, it looks good and long. We could use that."

"Not much use. They've got radar that'll pick up a needle."

"Yes, but they won't know what we do in there. What's the cloud base, would you say?"

"Four thousand, give or take. Bit scattered, with layers."

"Is good. Tops at 11."

"What're you thinking, Igor?"

"Flat spin. They can't do that, we can."

"All right, I guess. Till the juice runs out. It's all yours, you have it."

"I have it." Losing more height, Igor headed for the cloud-bank. The F. 16's closed again alongside, both pilots hand-signaling fiercely. From the Albatros the two waved back gaily, just before they slipped into cloud. Igor throttled back to idle, popped the airbrakes, extended flaps once enough speed had been dumped, pulled hard on the stick and waited for the rumble of the stall. At 90 knots, the aircraft shuddered briefly, dropped its left wing and fell out of the sky, gyrating madly like a sycamore seed, losing over four thousand feet a minute, flashes of whirling horizon in the cloud layers, the violence of the spin making speech difficult. Larry's voice cut in sharply, strained from the spinning.

"Better allow a good 12 seconds for engine spool-up."

"*Da.* Ugh, I do it in fifteen more for full, but starting now. You see anything?"

"No…Wait, oh Moses! D'you see that?"

"*Ohuyet! Pizdets, blyad!* Idiot! Spinning. He got too slow!"

A final layer of cloud enveloped them for a few seconds as Igor applied full power, watching the engine RPM carefully before opposing the rotation, dropping his right wing with rudder and aileron, dipping the nose to get flying speed and snapping out of the spin, nose pointing straight at the ground.

"One-fifty, one-sixty, one-eighty, pulling out now—there he is!"

Below them the flat-spinning F.16 was in a death-throe struggle, dropping like a stone slab, afterburner blazing to no effect. Igor heaved the Albatros level at 2000', then banked steeply so they could witness the action below. They saw the F. 16's canopy fly off, followed instantly by a rocketing ejection seat. Two seconds later there was a massive eruption of flame and dust from the desert as the jet-fighter impacted, no more than a couple of miles from the town of Gallup. A parachute flared, swung and collapsed in seconds. The pilot had clearly stayed with the aircraft till the last possible moment.

Climbing hard on their original heading, the two were quietly pensive for long minutes. Larry broke the silence.

"Uneventful sort of day, don't you think? I didn't see anything, did you?"

"Nothing. Where did the other one go?"

With a calico-ripping roar, the second F.16 answered for itself, passing mere feet above their canopies. For a second they were staring into the flame of afterburner before wake turbulence slammed them against their harnesses and flung the Albatros into a steep rolling turn.

"I got it," Larry said, surprisingly continuing the movement instead of fighting to correct it. The rolling turn was so violent and uncomfortable, a sickening see-saw between positive and negative G, that neither could speak until he rolled out of it.

Igor feigned a vomiting noise. "Why did you do that, Larry?"

"Make him think we're crippled."

"Ugh. It was maybe crazy enough."

"OK, let's see what we can do really badly. God, look at that guy, gotta be on his maximum Nine-G, he's coming round again!"

Larry pushed forward into an inverted half-loop, rolled into a full barrel, finishing inverted, and from there did three vicious snap rolls, a split-S, and finally an Immelmann turn off the top which took them back on course.

Igor was vastly impressed with this precision flying which could seem wildly erratic to all but the expert eye. The F.16 pilot couldn't seem to think of anything to do but circle them ferociously, pulling hard enough to black-out if not for a combat G-Suit.

"Your turn, Igor."

"No, I think that's enough. I don't compete with your aerobatics. I think he's leaving, look."

The F.16 had eased out of its turn and broke off to the east and Kirtland Air Force Base, its afterburner stifled.

"OK, take us back to One-Seven, we need to watch our fuel. It could be close after all that messing around."

"I have it. Using so much burner, I think he runs out of gravy."

"That's for sure, I wonder even if he'll make it back? Igor, you know you just cost the US tax-payer a cool forty million dollars?"

"Bummer, isn't that what you say? They can take it from my paycheck. Anyway, I did not do anything. Tell them I got scared and over-responded."

"Oh, I will, don't worry." Larry cackled, "I'll say you reacted like any normal chicken-shit Russian at the sight of two American F.16's playing Gotcha... Y' know, we burned a lot of extra gas ourselves, at eight bucks a gallon."

"You send bill to National Guard?"

"No comment."

CHAPTER 8

"Everybody loves an accent. It you've been unlucky in love, consider pulling up stakes and moving to another country. Then you'll be the one with a neat foreign accent."

Marilyn vos Savant

Ten square miles of sparkling blue water, a single sail far distant, a solitary fisherman casting from a tiny rowboat. The only sound was the breeze teasing the piñon and juniper near the water's edge and impatiently flapping sails. The sky was a pigeon's egg blue dotted with frivolous marshmallows. Nic helped Anastasia onto the trampoline and pushed off the Hobie from the muddy shallows.

Two swift tugs on the main sheet quieted the mainsail and the little catamaran surged forward, bright water chuckling along the hulls. He reached across and handed her the jib sheet.

"Haul it in a tad. It locks itself. You can hold it lightly. You just flick the line up to unlock it."

"When?"

"I'll tell you, don't worry."

The Hobie scurried to a sudden gust as they rounded the western point. Nic eased the main before the windward hull could lift and cause alarm, but Anastasia squealed with delight.

"Wow, it's so fast, it's amazing."

Nic grinned at her and then said, "Can we talk now?" At her nod he asked "Why did you want me to bring my laptop?"

"Oh, it was just an idea, doesn't matter now."

"Well, how did you know I even had a laptop? You didn't go in my study the other night, did you?"

"Nic, it's my job to know stuff like that. Anyway, you were buying a transfer cable. Which one did you bring?"

"The new one. I tossed the old one."

"Oh...But I have a more pressing question: why didn't you want to make love with me, did you think I was unwilling?"

"Hm. Well, actually I did want to, and I did make love to you, in case you didn't notice." Nic chuckled gently and went on, "But it was all in the heart-space. Once that's made sure of, there are no other limits. I haven't earned your trust yet."

Anastasia was silent for a full minute, feeling a rush of expansion deep in her chest. Finally she said quietly, "I think you have. It was the sweetest thing that ever came my way, I can tell you that now."

Their eyes met and held for long moments as the little catamaran sped across the lake, eager as a colt. Quietly he said, "Thank you for that, a huge thank you."

She kissed her fingers and reached out to touch his face with them. "You are most welcome."

"But tell me, why did you shush me in the car?"

"Because I don't want anyone to know whose side I'm on."

"You mean my car is bugged as well?"

She shrugged. "I don't know for sure, but it's more than likely. They don't miss much. They also don't tell everything to each member of the team, a kind of built-in check. If I sit nearer will it upset things?"

"No. Come." She slid towards and he put his arm around her.

"They said they're going to stop me seeing you after today, Nic."

"Hm. I wondered why you'd gone down-mouth on me. So they even mess with your private life, how can they do that?"

"By removing you."

"So you mean it could happen tomorrow?"

She put her hand up and turned his chin towards her. "I cannot say for sure, I don't know exactly, but you seem to have poked the hornet's hive."

He kissed her squarely on the mouth, lingering until a gust caught his attention. Easing the mainsheet, he said casually, "You haven't asked me why this is happening. I think this means you know more than you're letting on."

"Not just more, you dear man. I know just about all of it. You're tapped out. They know you're sending coded material to Ukraine and London. Eek!" She squealed quietly as the cat surged forward and cold spray came over the windward hull. "And about an additive in the jet-fuel. They can't find it, at least not in that Prist stuff, or Dice, was it? Is it really in there?"

"Certainly. I have it on the best authority."

"Then how do you have such incredible sources? They haven't found anything incoming, at least not lately."

Nic shrugged, grinning. "I get around. The Internet's a minefield, there's not much you can hide anymore."

"But CIA and NSA, neither of them had any inkling of this."

"Ha. They also said they had no inkling of 9/11, when in fact they were in it up to their necks, they were behind it on the President's orders. The real question is, who ordered the President?"

"You can't be serious, Nic!"

"Deadly, honey. I know it for a fact. So would anyone who ever bothered to research even superficially. The cover-ups were a masterpiece of bull-dozing—and the media just lay down in front of it. Quite a few journalists resigned or got fired, refusing to be prostitutes for their jobs."

"But how do you know it for a fact?"

"A CIA memo got out. Of course, no-one will publish it. That would mean certain accidental death."

"Where is it?"

"How badly do you want to keep your job?" he grinned, "Or your life?"

"Wouldn't it bring down the whole house of cards?"

"It should but it won't. What's Joe Public supposed to do? Millions of people all around the world now know it was a fix. Afghanistan and Iraq were pre-set targets long before 9/11. Dubya got caught in a lie. He said he saw the hit on the first tower on TV. It wasn't on TV! He ignored the questions about it. And the day after 9/11 Dick Cheney was heard to say, 'It's time to attack Iraq.' Saddam Hussein had no more to do with it than Walt Disney. They needed a war, plain and simple. They'd also been preparing for war in Afghanistan for two years already."

"But why do such a thing, especially when everyone hates war?"

"Because war makes fortunes, reduces populations, expands control. First principle of politics: Get in and start a war, scare the folks and get `em focused. Dubya even said it bluntly: 'War is the best way to boost the economy.' And he also said, 'The war in Iraq will pay for itself.' They think they have to control the whole of the Middle East, it's been on the Master Plan for years. Why? Bottom line: Protection for Israel, plus the gas pipeline from the Caspian and the oil in Iraq. They also needed to control Kuwait—that was clever, they got Saddam to invade so they could come to the rescue and get their oar in there properly and have a just war. The fact that all of this has taken millions of lives and caused untold misery is quite irrelevant to the Powers."

"And you know who they are?"

"It's common knowledge, sweetie. They've planned all the wars since the 1800's. And nobody gets to be President anywhere without their sanction—Whoops!"

Another flurry, almost a squall, lifted the windward hull clear of the water. Turning slightly downwind, Nic held them balanced for a while then eased the sheet and brought them level again.

"That was fun!" Anastasia exclaimed.

"Teetering. But we don't want to capsize, the water's still mighty cold."

"I felt it. How high are we here?"

"Over 7000'. So, you were saying, about them removing me?"

"Yes. I'm really scared for you, Nic. I think they will, unless you give up all your sources. And there's still the issue of the coded messages. They've all been intercepted."

Nic laughed out loud and then caught himself. "And decoded?"

"What's funny, Nic?"

"It's just that I'm torn. I'm hugely attracted to you, I want to tell you everything, but, well, there are constraints, tricky circumstances. Could spoil everything. I presume they know you're with me today and you're supposed to go back with something meaty?"

"It could save you. If I go back empty-handed, there's more than a good chance they'll come straight to you. I'm not sure if you know what that means."

"I think I do. First the polygraph, then solitary, some very harsh treatment and possibly rendition. Water-boarding. It won't do them any good, you can tell them that much."

"Why not?"

"Because I only have the truth. That CIA memo is locked up. It gets released if I croak."

"So why not reveal it?"

"Because then they'd *have* to kill me!"

"Oh, God… But you'd be locked away already, for passing secrets. They don't need any proof, you know. Are you at least able to tell me how you got the memo?"

"Um…Ok, friend of mine, CIA, known him for years. He came by one day and showed me something terrible. He was enraged about what the CIA was up to, all the falsification of evidence. He spoke out and next thing you know he wakes up in a hotel room with a hangover and a sachet needled to his chest. They told him he'd been injected with a toxin and the sachet contained the antidote. The antidote lasts 72 hours, after that you sicken and die, but the sickening is absolutely intolerable. He tried it, told me he had to cave in, couldn't take the pain and sickness. He had to beg for more antidote. He'd done that only once when he came to me. We sorted it out."

"Heaven's above, that's horrible. What did you do?"

"Do you have to report everything I tell you? I mean, could you leave this answer out?"

Anastasia nodded silently, though still looking shocked, then crossed her arms in a promise.

"Ok. So much of our conditioning is a matter of belief. There was a guy who drank a whole glass of cholera-infested water with no ill-effects. There's a sect that drinks strychnine believing that God will protect them, and it works, apparently. You can fire-walk without injury if you're sure it can be done. If you're not sure and you do it anyway, you actually get your feet burned. My friend agreed to hypnosis, threw away the sachet, faked his death, robbed a bank, got a new passport from a buddy of mine in the INS and lit out. I got a wish-you-were-here postcard from Papua New Guinea a few months later."

Anastasia's mouth hung open for long seconds. "Boy, you've given me something awful hard to keep to myself. So, what *can* I tell them?"

"You can say that the DMT is a natural result of the combustion of Prist in the jet fuel. DMT is also produced in our brains, from the pineal, so it's just a natural occurrence being given a boost. And fearlessness also boosts it."

"How on earth did you find out? I suppose I'm asking for your sources and you won't tell?"

"I could whisper," he grinned saltily.

"No, don't! Then I'd have to tell."

"Hell, it'd be easy to find out. Many people in Santa Fe know about Biggall."

"Really? Where's he hang out?"

"All over. Tell `em to just ask around."

"Don't you think they'll just ban the use of the Prist stuff?"

"It's too late." Nic made no attempt to hide the glee in his voice. "It's everywhere by now, affecting everyone by differing degrees, depending on their openness. Rigid belief systems really get in the way, as with fundamentalists. Pilots would refuse to fly without Prist anyway."

"Then they'd force the Prist-makers to change the formula, or make it just pure kerosene maybe?"

"They could try. But like I said, it's too late. World consciousness is already changing, and they wouldn't want to risk a bunch of crashes, so many that people would stop flying, especially long very high flights where freezing is more likely."

"So you really believe it's actually happening, that consciousness is really evolving?"

"Definitely. You know, I think they may have already got wind of it, that's why the war-mongering is getting more dangerous all the time. It has a purpose behind it. It's to make us all feel unsafe so we'll ultimately agree to One World government."

"Wouldn't that be a way to end all the fighting?"

"Sure it would. But that's not why they're doing it. The Powers-Behind-the-Thrones are not philanthropists, though they might pretend to be, or even believe they are. They simply want total control, which really means complete enslavement. They would then be in a position to reduce populations, with massive genocides of those considered unproductive. They believe that 3 billion is the maximum that the world can tolerate, preferably even fewer, which would in turn solve the climate crisis."

Anastasia blew her cheeks in disbelief. "How the hell do you know all this?"

"Honeychile, it's there for all to see, if they only care to look. Check the minutes of the last Bilderberg meeting, for instance."

"I was already told to do that, but I couldn't find anything after June."

"There was a more recent one, but only for the real insiders. The press had no warning. What's most clear overall is that they value ordinary people no more than nuisance cockroaches."

She opened her hands in despair, then looked back past the quickly vanishing wake. "The speed is amazing. Look how far we've come."

"Yeah, let's try the marina, see if we can scrounge up some lunch."

"Super! Hey, did you hear what happened to Igor?"

"That he'd found some champion nookie? He sounded breathless on the phone."

"Heh, no, not that. He was flying a Russian jet, pulled some stunts, next thing you know, Uren tells him he owes the taxpayer forty-two million bucks. Apparently he caused an F.16 to crash in the desert. Pilot ejected safely, but barely."

Nic looked at her, wide-eyed, grinning broadly, so she joined in with a chuckle. "I just had a thought," she said, "Igor has no passport, he's kind of shackled here. He's also got an implant."

"Where?"

"He doesn't know, so he can't get rid of it."

"He must know, there'd be a mark."

"No," she answered, "They put 'em in with a hypodermic, they're only the size of a grain of rice. He had a series of jabs when he came over."

"Hm…We'll have to get him an MRI to find it. I know a radiologist who works at the Imaging Center."

"Female?" Anastasia queried, grinning.

"Er, yes, now you mention it."

"And you're still friends?"

"*Touché.* Ok, we were lovers once, but she's polyamorous."

"Oh…And you're not?"

"Nope."

Anastasia went silent, leaned across and squeezed his hand. He transferred the sheet to his tiller hand and continued to hold hers for the rest of the ride. When they arrived at the marina, he swung them deftly into wind alongside a tarp-covered sloop.

"You get to drive on the way back," he said with a smile, standing up to drop the flapping mainsail and bundling it loosely.

"Are you sure?" she asked nervously.

"What can go wrong? C'mon, let's go hunt up some lunch."

From the unmarked van in front of Moncrieffe's house, Ben Storey and his two helpers emerged wearing work-clothes and carrying tool-boxes. The road in front was deserted. After seeing the sign in two languages, "*Cuidado con el Perro, No Ladra* – Beware of the Barkless Dog", they got pepper-spray from the van, went round the back, switched off the electrical panel and shorted the phone line. After a quick check to see if any window was open, they hit the front door-lock with a sledgehammer. No dog appeared and no alarm sounded. Storey directed one man to the study, to go through every file but without leaving traces of a search. With the other man, he tossed some stuff around, knocking over some chairs and lamps and rifling drawers, then examined every item of household cleaner, taking samples where unmarked and simply sniff-testing the rest. The workshop contained dozens of different paints and chemicals but they were able to spot anything recently touched by marks in the sawdust. Finally they checked the fridge and freezer, then took the TV and stereo, guitar and keyboard from its mahogany case out to the van. The other man emerged from the study, shaking his head.

"No laptop?"

"No. Not where it was last time. Nowhere else either. No dog, not even a feed bowl. Files are all innocent. I got his passport, Uren said to bring it."

"Ok, let's go. Wedge the door to make it look closed. There's the cavalry, you hear that?"

Distantly a police siren sounded. They scrambled into the van and took off, rounding the corner before anything came in sight. Gathering their breath they looked around at the haul.

"Man, that's a stupid old TV, not worth 10 bucks. We're gonna look like real dumb robbers. No computer. No guns. No drugs. Who is this guy, anyway?

"Dunno. Must be a fucking cleric, or a green-wank. No condoms, no stains, no skin `zines. How old is he? Must be decrepit. Or a poof."

"He's forty-eight," Storey answered, "Divorced. Has a kid. Supposed to have some inside dope. I think we're going to have to bring him in."

"Sounds like a pushover. Won't be any fun, right?"

"Nah, none at all."

CHAPTER 9

*The nose of the bulldog has been slanted backwards so that he can breathe without **letting go***

Winston Churchill

Anastasia gripped the tiller-bar and mainsheet nervously as the Hobie-cat sat head to wind, sails agitating.

"In a moment she'll swing off and fill. Here we go." Nic held the small jib out to starboard, easing them off the wind. The mainsail filled and quieted, urging movement. "Ok, now she'll want to come back so resist with the rudder, bring the helm towards you. Yes, like that. If it gets alarming, let off the mainsheet, the rope in your hand."

Her anxiety eased as the little cat streamed away southeast. After a few minutes she even began to experiment with the pressures in her hands, though still puzzled about the dynamics.

"I wish I understood what's happening," she ventured.

"It's like squeezing an orange pip. The sails pull one way, the water pushes back, the boat squeezes forward. Sails are like wings but vertical, their lift is just ahead of center, so the squeeze takes us forward, not back."

"Hm...It's such a beautiful day, I don't want to think."

"Just feel it, then." Nic locked the jib sheet, fished in his pack for a camera and scooched forward to the mast. "Step one," he said, "Smile. Show me your beautiful teeth. Pretend you're in the Caribbean."

She raised an arm in front of her face, protesting, but then with an effort she lowered it, felt the sun on her face and offered a delighted grin. Nic took several shots and thumbed the replay.

"You have no idea, do you?" he smiled.

"About what?"

"What a gorgeous woman you are."

She looked at him in astonishment, a blush spreading. "Eye of the beholder," she said flatly.

"Uh-uh. Look for yourself." He turned the camera for her. Clearly surprised, she looked at the sequence and then at his face.

"That's not my normal expression, is it?"

"Frankly, no, but it could be. It's your get-out-of-jail card. You know that smiling instantly changes body chemistry? And regular smilers live 23% longer?"

"How do you know? Oh, you and your sources! Well, I should be croaked already, I don't smile from one week to the next, or I didn't till you came along. Do you have to have a reason? I mean, if it's just mechanical, it's not going to work, is it? Oops, what's happening?"

The wind gusted and spray hit their faces as Nic quickly bagged and stowed the camera. He looked back to see Anastasia gripping both tiller and sheet with a grim expression. Before he could say anything the windward hull lifted sharply.

"Ease off," he said calmly, but with nothing else to hold onto, she tightened her grips and cried out in alarm.

"Let go!" he called urgently, "Just let go!" but it came too late. Her pull on the helm took them further off the wind, increasing the sails' angle of attack. The windward hull reared up, hung for a second then arced agonizingly over the vertical. The masthead seemed to search for the surface, touched and dug in, pitching him into the mainsail as Anastasia fell backwards into the frigid water. Grinning, he shouted for her to hang onto something, sloshed off the sail and dived under it, seeking to buoy the mast before it went vertically down. After a long struggle, he surfaced with it, relieved to see her through the trampoline, clinging to the upper hull. He swam quickly to join her, hampered by his clothing, both of them gasping from the exertion and the cold.

Her teeth were vibrating as she tried to apologize, but Nic just grinned at her. "All part of the fun," he gasped back, "If we hang on here, she'll come up. Hold the edge of the net. Put your feet on the hull under water. Lean back, far as you can."

Reaching up to the base of the stay, he unfastened the trapeze line to the masthead, hauling himself up until he could scramble onto the upper hull and lean out almost horizontal. Gradually the mast and mainsail came unstuck from the water, the wind sneaked under the sail and suddenly flicked the craft upright. Anastasia disappeared and the cat started to accelerate downwind, rounded up and almost capsized again, Nic holding grimly to the trapeze bar.

When he finally got back to the helm and regained control she was nowhere to be seen. He scanned all round in rising alarm until he heard a shivery laugh from under the trampoline, then she emerged astern and hauled herself over the aft cross-beam.

"I'm so s-s-sorry," she chattered, "H-how are we going to get warm, it's miles back to the car."

"Air's warm. Squeeze out your clothes."

"What? Take them off?"

He shrugged. "You'll be warmer." He busied himself sorting out lines and quickly got them under way again, the breeze settling back pleasantly. He was aware of her wringing out her clothes and made an effort not to look until she spoke.

"What about you, aren't you freezing?"

Still shivering, he nodded and dragged off his sodden sweater and T-shirt. Only then did he look up to see her standing on the windward hull, both hands on the stay, facing forward, shaking water from her hair, covered only in goose bumps. Her lithe body drew his eyes in admiration.

"That's a pretty nice earth-suit they fixed you up with, *Querida*. Just my opinion."

She turned her head to smile at him. "I think the heater's packed up. But thank you. Mind, the way you phrased it, is that a hint not to take it personally?"

"I guess," he nodded, grinning.

"But you like it?"

"Understatement."

"I should have just let go, shouldn't I, like you said?"

"Right. There's a parallel, if you think about it."

"How d'you mean?"

"Poland. Do you see the darkening on the water ahead? Another gust coming, you can hold onto that bar and lean out."

Her canted weight kept the hull down as they accelerated to about 14 knots, forcing a jubilant squeal as she leaned her body over the water. The gust subsided and she instinctively moved back in.

"You're a natural," he called out happily, "In spite of what you might think."

"Natural *au naturel*," she grinned, turning and revealing all of her remarkable physique. "How come you're still wearing pants?"

"Not enough hands."

She answered with a mocking smile, delighting him with her changed demeanor. He made no secret of his admiration, shaking his head in wonder.

"Oh, I am feeling so liberated, thank you, thank you!" She balanced precariously, holding her arms out, piping "Queen of the World! Remember the movie? They wouldn't have lasted 30 seconds in that ice-water, even inside the ship."

Nic nodded. "And when they yelled 'Hard-a-starboard', the helmsman turned the ship to port."

"Really?" she chuckled, "You can't rely on anyone, can you?"

"You're relying on me, right now."

"So I am. Is this OK, me flaunting myself before you?"

"Much better than OK. But thanks for asking." She faced forward again, relishing the warm breeze on her skin. Nic thought of a William Blake quote he'd used before and called out, "'The nakedness of woman is the work of God'."

Anastasia paddled her buttocks in rhythmic appreciation, causing more laughter, but after a moment she turned her head towards him. "Nic, seriously, what are you going to do when we get back?"

"Me? I'll wait to be invited."

She shook her head delightedly. "I meant about Uren and the bloodhounds."

"Like I said, I'll wait to be invited."

"That's crazy. Don't you have a plan?"

"Uh-uh. I think it's all going to plan."

"How can I help?"

"Oh, just stay naked. It stops me thinking and worrying. Let's just be now, for now."

"Ok. Oh, Nic, this is gorgeous, my goose bumps have gone. Should we have been wearing life-jackets?"

"Probably. We never had them as kids, in England. I'd be five miles offshore in an open dinghy, nobody gave it a thought."

She sat down next to him, hands over her breasts but not big enough to cover them. "My nipples are still like corks…Do you like big breasts?"

Nic laughed happily. "I couldn't care less. Oh, I note that Americans say, 'I *could* care less,' which doesn't make sense…If I like the woman, they don't matter. It matters that you like them, that's all."

"I love them! They distract people from my gloomy face. D'you want me to cover up, are you sure?"

"Certainly not. I'd stare at you for hours if I thought I wouldn't get caught. Gust coming, up you go again."

She leapt to the trapeze, leaning out against the breeze with a little cry of exhilaration. They sped across the lake, sun and wind warming their bodies. Anastasia became aware of an ache in her cheeks from long minutes of unaccustomed smiling. When the breeze softened again she swung down and hunkered next to him.

"Interesting, isn't it, how the mind roams and focuses. One minute I'm sitting self-conscious, the next I'm busy with a little job, then I'm sitting self-conscious again."

"Yeah. So how long can you hold a thought, such as 'I love being naked and I love being next to a man loving my nakedness'?"

She was silent for a long moment, her smile bemused. "Not long, I guess. The thought arose, settled to my satisfaction and immediately the mind went off exploring for something else to worry about. Why on earth is it so prone to not be in the moment, all these gorgeous moments—hey, there's another car next to yours, d'you see? Now I'll have to put wet clothes on, I suppose."

"Not yet, let's go off again. We'll be even warmer downwind." He swung the helm and let the mainsheet run. With the breeze behind them and sudden quiet from the hulls, the atmosphere changed once again.

"Can you kiss and steer at the same time?" she asked mischievously.

"See? The mind is always on to something else, even when everything's perfect. Well, try me."

Nic locked his toes around the almost slack sheet, wedged his rump against the tiller-bar and waited for her. Anastasia shuffled across the trampoline on her knees and reached up for his face. He put his hands on her bare shoulders and they locked eyes, the moments turning to minutes. He saw the years of pent-up rage and sorrow, while in his gleam of quiet satisfaction she saw clearly the quality for which she'd yearned. She became aware of her own fear for him and what might soon come between, the thought jolting enough to remind her of the lesson. He seemed not to share any of her fears. Resorting to the present, she brought her mouth to his, softly exploring, feeling the kiss permeate her whole being. His hands ran over her shoulders, beneath her arms and merest fingertips caressed her breasts. She shivered in overwhelm and the kiss intensified into a quiet moan, then erupted into laughter as he harmonized with her note, first a minor then a major third.

"My God," she squealed, "I never knew."

"What?"

"That laughter doesn't spoil it, it sort-of glorifies it."

Nic nodded, delighted with her response. He abandoned the helm and drew her down to the canvas, playful and undemanding. Left to itself, the Hobie rounded up to the wind and drifted, sails flapping idly.

The watchers on the shore sat disappointedly. One of them kept raising binoculars while the other chewed on a cold burrito, cell-phone to his ear.

"What the hell are they doing?"

His accomplice lowered the glasses. "Can't see now. Lying down. Sunbathing maybe."

"Humping, more like. You seen the rack on that chick?"

"Not till today. She dresses like a box in the lab. D'ya think they saw us?"

"Who cares? Main thing is, they weren't meeting anyone and they went where they said.

Ben and the others have finished at the house. Didn't find shit, he said. We can scram now."

"Are they going to do him over?"

"Moncrieffe? They'll have to, won't they? They're certain he knows something he shouldn't. Uren's gone all hyper about it. Classified, he says. What d'you think'll happen to the Russian, Igor whatsisname?"

"Dumpster, I guess. That F.16's a hell of an embarrassment, if it gets out."

"He hasn't talked. Neither has that jet guy, Larry."

"No, but they could. C'mon, let's split."

"Come in, Comrade. What's up? Never mind what's down, like F.16's and so on." Uren's growl seemed without bite, and Igor sensed he might actually be amused.

"You know, Frank, it comes back to you. You did not tell the watchers that you'd cleared me. Anyway, I told you I did not do anything. Those cowboys did ambush us, and one of them made a mistake. We were in a forty-year-old clunker with no guns, how could we do anything to them?"

"Yeah, but they tried to stop you taking off in the first place. There's going to be a hell of an enquiry."

"They had not the authority, not for Captain of my aircraft. Anyway, I'm not here for that. I fill in for Anastasia today and there's a new email from Zaporozhye, via London."

"Read it."

"Yes, sir. It says, '*Dear Kolya, Lena says she looked up the reference but couldn't make sense of it. She sends back ACIM T464.9.4*' I looked that up, boss, and passed it to the Crypts. What it says in the book is: '*If you choose to see a world without an enemy, in which you are not helpless, the means to see it will be given you.*' Anyway, going on, she says, "*So it's entirely a matter of I-Spy, but where shall I put my little eye? Perception is everything, right?* Back to Elena's email:

I have been recruiting for several days and my recruits are amazing me. It seems like everywhere I go they come up and ask questions, did I get plastic surgery, some I've known for a while don't even recognize me. They have asked me to speak at a meeting. We are calling it a secret meeting in order to flush out spies sent by SAV (That's Ukrainian KGB). If the ideas work on them we will know we have a Movement! I have also been promoted yet again, in just 2 days, and have been promised trips to Berlin, Warsaw and Paris for trade show work. There was no way I could get an exit visa without this, and anyway I did not have the money. All this AND you sent me 200 dollars! My mother is very suspicious; she thinks I am selling my body. I told her if it was by weight it would not be worth much so now she wants to fatten me up! Alas, sometimes I feel that any sex is better than no sex, but then I remember what it is like after and desire vanishes, pouf!

Kolya, tell me please, how much is your influence, did you get me the promotion somehow? Or does it all stem from my moment of compassion? Mon dieu, if it's just that, think of the miracles to come…Do you ever come to Europe? (Berlin, Warsaw, Paris, um?) Well, back to the books. Blessings from Your Elena xx"

Igor folded the note feeling a lump in his throat, and wondering if Uren could possibly have any inkling of his connection.

"What bothers me, Igor, is how Moncrieffe got hold of this skank and then actually got her promoted so she could travel?"

"No idea, boss."

"Hm. Question is, do we bring him in now or let him go and meet her, grab them both red-handed? Trouble is, that's out of my bailiwick so no credit comes here. Or we could get on to Moscow, tell them everything. After all, any stuff in the Prist, it's gonna be affecting them too."

Igor tried to stifle his nervousness. "I would not bother with telling Moscow, Frank. They would only see it as tricky."

"Maybe. Or we could send you, Igor, with a beard and an alias. Codes is getting nowhere with those book references, can't crack 'em for shit. You get this Elena in a small room in, say, Warsaw and pull bits off her till she blurts. You up for that, comrade?"

Igor actually felt his face go ashen. "Frank, you know that is not my business. I was never in *mokrie dela*, the wet squads, you know this."

"Yeah, well, just an idea. The burglary yielded nothing, complete waste of time. This Moncrieffe is mighty fly. Let's wait till Nasty gets back, see if she pried anything out of him. If not, we'll haul him in tomorrow, Ok?"

Igor nodded and went out silently, feeling close to the edge. Even though he hadn't directly caused the F.16 crash, it had certainly jangled his nerves and with the threat to both Elena and Moncrieffe, he felt doubly powerless.

From his office he placed a call to JetWarbirds, wondering if there'd been repercussions. Larry answered with a chuckle.

"Yeah, they came and grilled me, coupla suits. I told them I saw nothing, we were in cloud after all. They said that if I changed my mind about it and said anything to anyone, the consequences would be, let's say, prejudicial to my health, my business and my license, not to mention my five children and my dog. It's obviously a huge black eye. Rookie pilot, I guess."

"Do you have guard for the planes?"

"Only the airport security. Should be alright, if I keep my mouth shut."

The breeze had dropped to a whisper as they drifted slowly downwind. The only other sound was the outboard motor on a faraway fisherman's skiff. Their smiles both faded into kisses as desire flared but then their gazes met in a truce of truth. Nic had kept his shorts on and was gently tracing lines on her belly and torso when there came a bump against one of the hulls. They both sat up startled and looked over the side to see half a dozen huge Kokanee salmon, a gravid female surrounded by suitors, milt in the water and a wild, determined excitement.

"Look, look, look, they're spawning, right now, look!"

The quiet water suddenly erupted as they were surrounded by dozens more, huge silvery pink bodies swirling and swarming, oblivious to all but Nature's command. Tails thrashed the water as competition flared. Anastasia leaned over and tried to touch them, making several contacts and squealing with delight. They looked at each other with wonder and amazement, then back to staring down at a mystic private theater, pointing and exclaiming. The melee lasted a full five minutes, finally moving away and erupting again at a distance.

Anastasia closed her eyes as if in prayer, her joy untrammeled. "Do you think they picked up our vibes?" she asked gleefully.

"Speak for yourself," Nic answered gruffly but with a happy grin. "They're spawning very early. That's weird. A smuggler plane crashed here, remember? Loaded with cocaine. Wonder if that had anything to do with it."

"Nic, there's a difference in what you do, how you are with this— like the other night, you just lay with me, just being there. You're not, ah, lacking in any department, are you? Would you like me to check?"

He chuckled. "No need, sweets. It's just I have no goal beyond just being here with you, being gentle. Just like the salmon, the bodies seem to know exactly what to do if other notions don't interfere. Goals take us away from now. Delight gets wasted."

"These are new notions for me, takes some getting used to. I'm imagining your sexual encounters are rare, if this is how you are. How long has it been, for you? And would you call me Annie, please?

"Sure. About three years. You?"

"Longer than that, but still, I'm having to adjust here. New notions. I came across a new word the other day, it's not in Websters: Appreciatude."

Nic grinned broadly, remembering his emails "Now I wonder where you came across that one?"

"I think my skin is burning, I mean from the sun."

"Yeah. We should head back."

"To reality? I want to swim again first."

She rose in one fluid movement and dived over the side. Surprised and amused, he waited till she surfaced and hauled her back on board.

"God," she gasped, "I forgot, it's wicked cold in there!"

He handed her damp clothes. Struggling to put them on, she said "End of idyll?"

He laughed. "Projecting again. This damn Now thing needn't ever stop, had you thought of that?"

"I hadn't. But I think I'll buy it. I did read *The Power of Now*— why didn't it change me? I mean, suppose there really wasn't anything except Now, how would everyone behave? It's unimaginable, that's the trouble. But you'll help me, right?"

Nic nodded eagerly, handed the main and set the cat moving again. Fingers twined in rare contentment, they were silent all the way back to the launch site.

On the road south, after taking the mast down and leaving the Hobie in a farmer's yard, Anastasia broke another long silence.

"I have to let it go, don't I, about my parents?"

"Not necessarily. But if you were to find out that all involved were dead, how would that feel?"

"I'm not sure…Guilty for not having acted sooner? Deflated from all that wasted angst? Or suppose the one who gave the order was now in some institution with Alzheimer's?"

"Ok. Then how about you hear a definitive statement—but you have to believe it?"

She stared at him in silence as he drove, eyes fixed on the road until he slowly pulled over. He parked and said quietly, "I'm going to put my hand behind your head and then draw it into my shoulder, firmly. Ok? When I do that, I want you to just drop in, drop down, like the other night. Just let go and go with me. Can you do that?"

"Sure I can, gladly."

As he pulled her head towards him he said abruptly "Sleep!", then waited long moments until it was clear she had relaxed. He lifted her hand and let it drop limply. He spoke close to her ear, with quiet authority, "Two of them, soldiers, were killed in the Solidarity riots. The officer was sent to Siberia, for life, hard labor. No reprieve. He died there. It's over. Do you understand?"

Anastasia simply nodded into his neck, without answering. He held her for several minutes and finally said, "I'll count to five, and when I get to five you can come back. You will remember this and we'll get going again."

After the count she opened her eyes, stared forward unfocused and then started glancing at him quizzically, brightly. "It seems I have a new belief. But you were making it up, right?"

"We make everything up, honey. Everything. Quote: `Nothing in the Universe means anything at all—'"

"--`Except the meaning I bring to it'."

"Now where did you hear that?" Nic opened his door and beckoned her out with a toss of his head. They walked a few yards from the car.

She said with a shy smile, "It must have been in some email."

"Ah…So you've seen them all?"

"Should have, if I've done my job. That's why they want to know what you know."

"So aren't you at risk just telling me?"

"Maybe. But I suspect you already knew or at least you guessed. Nic, your house was to be burgled today, that's why I said to bring your laptop."

He turned to her with slow grin. "Thank you. How thoughtful."

She gave him a satisfied smile. "Welcome… I have a question. How did you know about the secret Bilderberg meeting and what was discussed? I couldn't find anything about it. I even ran movements of all the big boys, Kissinger, Rockefeller, Bush, Cheney, Rumsfeld, Wolfowitz, Rove, Castries, Blair, dozens, there's no time in the last four months when they could have coincided."

Nic raised his eyebrows and answered quickly, "It was a midnight tele-conference here, breakfast in Europe. Friend of mine hacked in."

"Anything earth-shaking?"

"Well, usually they just cover their bases. Mostly they know what's going to happen and they're set to take advantage of it. They talk about the wars matter-o'-factly, like backgammon or a chess game. The wars are wickedly profitable because the defense budget keeps going up. Now they're worried about the Internet, too many people know too much because of it. Some of them want to be able to shut it down in the event of a crisis, and a crisis can be invented with ease."

"Do they know about the stuff in the air?"

"I'm not sure. Is your boss keeping quiet?"

"Uren? No way. He's getting all knotted up, he's furious that it may be going beyond his pay grade; he wants all the kudos, for promotion. He knows he'll get demoted if he doesn't handle it right."

"So, he's going to want to have a chat with me, is that it?"

"I can't say anything about that. Can you make yourself unavailable?" Anastasia tried to keep regret out of her voice but a little crack gave her away.

"Should I tell you? What's the first thing they'll do, anyway?"

"Well, first a very nasty interview, then the polygraph. If that's inconclusive, they start the softening up, shackled to the ceiling, naked in a cold room and frequently doused with ice water. That's been known to go as much as forty hours, then they might let you sleep a little and wake you up every ten minutes."

"What if they're in a hurry?"

"Straight to the water-board. No-one lasts. Average is about 9 seconds, tops."

"Don't they have to rendition you for that?"

"No, not if they've decided to rub you out when they've finished, so there's no complaints."

"And you've actually witnessed this whole process?"

"'Course not. But we all know about it. Enhanced interrogation, their sugar-coated phrase, you know it messes people up for life, assuming you live?"

"Yeah, I know."

Anastasia gripped his arm fiercely. "I want to scream, Nic. How can you be so matter-of-fact about it?"

"Listen, sweetheart, I don't know how much to tell you. You've got a foot in both camps and I don't want them messing you up as well."

"So give me something useful which doesn't endanger you. Like, who was at Bilderberg, what was said, stuff like that. And don't forget, they'll want the name of whoever hacked in."

Nic grinned and nodded. "Mainly it was about controlling the Middle East for big business interests, since the Big Business Goliath completely controls the U.S. Administration. And the Bilderbergers and Banksters completely control Big Business."

"Got it. So who controls the Bilderbergers and the bankers?"

"Well, that's the tricky part. When you have massive power, wealth and influence, all it needs is a word in the right ear and you will be obeyed, all the way down. There's not the slightest doubt that there is an anonymous ruling cabal with neither racial nor religious allegiance. I don't believe there's a single emperor type at the top whom you could pin-point and classify, but the moment you try, you're entering a minefield. If you look at the list of who attended the last Bilderberg meeting, they come from all points of the compass, and they can't be accused of anything except informal but very high level talks. They're mostly white, of course, but belong to no exclusive racial or political faction. They call it a friendly get-together to discuss world affairs but single out any of the very richest and get ready to face the consequences. They're aligned in their intent, that's all, not their allegiance to any creed beyond One World Order. It's all about to change, you know that, right?" "How?" she asked, her expression changing from dismay to eagerness.

"Well, because the entire mind-set of humanity is about to shift, is already shifting."

"From fear to love, just like that?" Anastasia didn't hide her skepticism.

Nic simply shrugged and smiled. "Lez git on home, honeychile. Don' y'all worry about a thang. It's all bin' tooken care of."

As they walked back to the car, she looked at him with a puzzled smile, "Like, it's in the air? Is it really possible to turn away from centuries of horror and oppression, wars and starvation, desperate inequality, cruelty, genocide and so on, you really see that possibility?"

"No, inevitability. Done deal."

"They're going to want to know how you know this."

"And why will they want to know?" he smiled quizzically.

"Because they want to stop it, of course."

"And when they find out they can't?"

"Hm…I suppose they'll adjust to a new reality and see how to take advantage of it."

"And if the new mind-set doesn't go that way?"

"Utopia…Heaven on earth. I'm trying to imagine what that'd be like but I can't get my head around it."

"Well, at least you're trying, that's all it needs, so relax. Maybe it's like leaning naked over the side of a boat watching salmon spawn with a maybe-wannabe-lover's hand on your incredibly exquisite butt."

She laughed delightedly, "I thought you Brits said 'arse'? But surely, not everyone can have a mansion and a jet and a yacht and a limitless clothing budget?"

"Which makes them oh so happy? Who are the happiest people on earth? Do you know the word *boddicitta*?"

"I've seen it somewhere. I don't know what it means."

"'Mind of enlightenment' or 'Mind of love'. It's like a request, or delight perhaps, which comes from within, to realize who we really are and then, automatically, think and work for the well-being of all. There's no happiness in power, because of the inherent fear of loss of it and the need to protect it."

Anastasia turned to him and locked her fingers into both his hands. She shook her head sadly, flinching as a big yellow bus roared by, loaded with river rafts and trailing laughter. As it faded into the distance, Nic smiled down at her.

"What do happy people do? Think of one."

She mused for a moment and Meg promptly came to mind. "My yoga teacher. She's a jewel...I guess they do whatever they are drawn to do, but they behave lovingly to everyone. I'm not one of them, for sure, my job is—"

"Stop! No guilt, no recrim. The changing mindset takes care of everything. You're doing it right now, just with your inquiry. There's a longing in your tone, for something better, more fulfilling, right?"

"I guess," she murmured doubtfully.

"What happens when people trip, do 'journeys', like mushrooms, DMT, MDMA, acid, peyote, ayahuasca, even pot sometimes?"

She freed her fingers and reached up to caress his face. The road stretched empty across the cooling desert of Tierra Amarilla. She drew their heads together and kissed him gently.

"Do they feel like this?"

He returned the kiss as restrainedly as he could, lightening the moment by rubbing noses. "It depends on the kind of kiss, is it a giving one or a getting one? Are you seeking reassurance or giving it? Anyway, what mostly happens is an attitude adjustment because of how the chemicals affect the brain. Generally, the ego gets set aside and as soon as that happens, it gets replaced by wonder and gratitude. With MDMA, Ecstasy, the heart-space seems to open like a cone expanding to feel overwhelming love for everything, sheer amazement, often the thought that the whole world is absolutely crackers not to be feeling like this *all* the time. It seems you can do only good from this space and also that there's nothing to worry about, nothing to fear."

"So you have to do drugs to have this attitude?"

"'Course not. But they can give you a glimpse, so you do know there's a better way. Millions manage without, like the one you thought of perhaps. How do they do it?"

She nodded slowly and put her head against his shoulder. "All I can think of is how to do it myself, since I am largely not. But it's what everyone wants, isn't it? They—I mean we—simply don't know how."

"Do you know what a meme is?"

"I think so. Sort of memory packet?"

"Kind of. Thoughts have weight, energy, or significance, and they convey. If they have validity they get taken up in other minds and spread, like a virus. But the mind has to be ready to receive them. If you'd talked to someone in the Middle Ages about cell phones or radio waves, they wouldn't get it. But once it's accepted, everybody gets it. So a new meme comes along, such as 'There is nothing to fear', we test its validity, reject it completely because of our ego-world experience, hear it again, meet someone who's actually fearless, gradually the idea percolates and becomes an acceptable possibility. A welcome possibility."

"And now you've found a way to accelerate it?"

"Not me! C'mon, let's get going. I suppose I'll have to report the burglary."

"That's the idea. Then they'll catch someone who doesn't exist and you'll get your stuff back."

"Neat. I may not want it...So what were they really looking for?"

"Sources, of course. Your laptop. Where you got your information."

Nic smiled to himself as they approached the car. Noticing, Anastasia spoke earnestly.

"If you told me, perhaps it would avoid all the trouble that's coming."

As he opened the door for her, Nic said, "The old laptop's in the landfill by now, after I ran it over with the truck. Anyway, if I told you, they might give you a promotion, when really we want to get you fired."

She looked up at him in shock, but he closed her door softly by pressing with his knee, as if he hadn't seen her expression. There was another long silence as they set off again until Nic asked casually, "Were you afraid, back then?"

"About my job? Yes. Terrified suddenly. Then I started to relax. I told myself there's nothing to fear, but I'm afraid myself did not really believe it! We're working on it, right now. How can I convince this skeptic, myself?"

"What are you grateful for, right now?"

She looked across at him, chuckled, fondled his upper arm. "You, for a start."

He smiled. "What else? Make a list."

"Wow.... Let's see...My brain. My health. My body, which loves you touching it. So do I! Feeling my mind expand with new notions... Just being here. A new awareness...Tell me, sir, are you playing with my emotions?"

"Isn't that a fear-based question?"

"You're answering questions with questions, Nic. That's called avoidance—even if you've got a point. So, are you afraid to answer?"

Nic shook his head and smiled at her. "Makes me think of that Carole King song, *'Will you still love me tomorrow?'* Everyone wants a guarantee. But think of the fearless explorer, whom everyone enviously calls insane, setting off into the unknown, the jungle. No rescue possible, no guarantees. What on earth could be his motive? He could stay home safe and get a job in a bank or something."

"He wants to feel alive...Do I make you feel alive?"

At first crestfallen when he shook his head and didn't answer, she took time to reconsider. "I think I get it. Correction: It's just allowing fearless feelings that makes me feel alive, I mean, *let's* me feel alive. How's that?"

For answer he simply held out his hand, palm up. She placed hers in it contentedly, but continued her questioning. "So, tell me, overall, what is it you want to come of all this, Nic? Where do you think it's going?"

"Can't tell. I mean I can't, not I won't. It could go all the way to the top, then we might find out who's top. The Asians might take `em out first, it's said they're ready. Does your boss know about that?"

"He hasn't said anything, but I know he wants all the kudos. Hey, that's something I could tell him. Where's the info?"

"Internet. Just Google Green and Red Society. It's all there. But I should wait on that, let's see where this goes, OK?"

CHAPTER 10

I assess the power of a will by how much resistance, pain, torture it endures. And knows how to turn it to its advantage.

Friedrich Nietzsche

Uren's phone roused him at 3.30 am. "Who and what?" he barked furiously.

"Knyazev. He didn't come home, boss. Moncrieffe."

"Well, shit. He can't have run....Did you check Wojerkowski?"

"No, boss. You think he might be there?"

"Likely. They were together all day yesterday. Check the bugs on her place."

"I didn't know that. I'm down in Santa Fe. She's in Los Alamos. Anyway, there's no-one monitoring at this hour, just recording."

Uren thought quickly. "Ok. He doesn't have a cell phone, at least that we know of. I'll call her. Call you back."

He thumbed Anastasia's number but there was no reply. Groaning, he got up and dressed, stumbled out to his car and drove to her condo. A silver-grey SUV was parked outside. Uren waited in dilemma for a few minutes, saw no sense in immediate action and drove home back to bed. Part of standard softening up was to drag the suspect from deepest sleep, bewildered and scared, but he didn't want to upset or embarrass his assistant. At least they knew Moncrieffe's presumed whereabouts.

At 7 am he woke to his alarm and called her again. This time she answered. "Yes, boss?"

"Moncrieffe with you?"

"No, boss."

"The fuck he ain't! Where did he go?"

"He went out to get us breakfast."

"Huh. Well, did you get nasty with him, Miss Nasty?"

"No, boss. It was nice. Very, very nice. If you must know."

Uren felt a rush of jealousy. "Screw that. It's D-day. Did you get anything from him?"

"Nothing useful, boss. But—" she paused.

"But what?"

"Well, he's just a good guy, boss. Nothing sinister, I'm sure of it."

"Bullshit. And why doesn't he have a cell-phone, goddammit?"

"Says he doesn't need one."

"That's ridiculous, this day `n' age. Call me when you've finished breakfast. And better hope he hasn't put you in the club, you'll be a single mom. Out."

The phone rang again while she was in the shower so she ignored it. Picking up the message a few minutes later she heard only one word but Igor's gravel accent was unmistakable.

"*KATAPOULT!!*"

When Nic returned with two breakfast toasters, she put her finger to her lips, picked up the phone and replayed the message for him. Nic, his mouth full of sandwich, simply nodded, pondered a moment, peeled his car key and remote off the ring, handed it to her and picked up her keys from the kitchen table, his look questioning. She nodded without a word, spun hers off and handed it to him, then shoved him towards the door. As he backed out, she put her hands together in a prayerful gesture. He answered with a deep and solemn nod and was gone.

An hour later Uren called again. "Why'nt ya call? Gimme Moncrieffe."

Anastasia put some pain in her voice. "Can't do it, boss. He hasn't come back!"

"Shit, woman, you warned him, didn't ya?"

"No, sir. I'm still waiting for my breakfast."

After a spate of muttering, Uren said quietly, "Ok, get in to work. We can find him, there's a tracker on his car." He paused, his voice heard muttering to someone else, before he exploded. "What the hell, Nasty, his car is still outside your place!"

She looked out of the window. "What? Let me see....So it is. But mine has gone! The keys...Oh, his are here, looks like he took mine, boss."

"Goddammit, woman, did he leave anything else? Gimme your license number, an' get your ass in here."

"I don't remember it. I'll have to look it up."

Anastasia hung up and calmly finished her breakfast, flushing the wrapper as a precaution. The phone rang a few minutes later, this time from Igor.

"Anushka, where is Moncrieffe?"

"He was here, but he left. After barely one word."

"Ah…Uren says there's no GPS on your car, he took it, yes?"

"Yes. Are you going in to work?"

"No, I'm in Santa Fe. I take over watch in an hour, in case he shows up home. Looks like it's over. Uren is boiling up, he's out for blood, and he's going to grill you. Drive slowly."

"*Da*. Later. Oh, I've got another call. Bye."

She pressed her Flash button and Nic's voice both soothed and alarmed her. She asked, "Where did you go?"

"Doesn't matter. Could be for a while. You Ok with my wheels?"

"Of course, but Nic—"

"I need to get going, sweets, I just wanted to tell you, about yesterday and last night, in case you were wondering, desire is divine, so is sex, but, well, that shouldn't be all that binds us. Trust is the most important thing, and discovering if we're on the same wavelength. If so, then lovemaking is truly that. I'm enchanted with what I've found so far, you're so clever and deep and open to new ideas. And dumping the vengeance, that'll be a whole new world for you, limitless. Can you feel that?"

"Yes, I can. But now I'm afraid for you. Do you know when…?"

"No. I need to let this thing run its course. It could turn out to be huge."

"Nic, are you talking about us, or about the jet fuel thing?"

"Both. They both need exploring completely, if you're willing."

"You know I am—but I can't wait!"

"Don't wait then. Do it already. Trust, and just imagine I'm thinking of you constantly, with delight."

She sighed heavily. "Alright, I'll try…Keep safe, wherever you are."

"Where's safety if there's nothing to fear, right? And note the difference in feeling between expectation and expectancy."

"Ah, *merde*, you and your stuff. How can I believe this?"

"I wrote it down somewhere, for Elena." There was a rustle of paper, then he said, "Here it is: T.34. 2.7. And 8."

"What? Let me write that down."

Nic repeated it and said, "Gotta go, sweets, be in touch. *Bezos*. Love ya."

Without her car's badge to match her own she had a long delay for admission to the lab, finally getting clearance from Uren with a demand to see him immediately. In defiance, she went first to Igor's office, rummaged his desk for *A Course in Miracles*. Sifting quickly, she found the quoted text, which immediately made her think of the Hundredth Monkey syndrome: *"If a sufficient number become truly miracle-minded, this shortening process can be virtually immeasurable. It is essential, however, that you free yourself from fear quickly, because you must emerge from the conflict if you are to bring peace to other minds."*

Reading before and after the quote, she deduced that the shortening referred to the time required for healing of the minds from centuries of belief in separation. Taking the book with her, she went to Uren's office where she was met with infuriated incomprehension.

"This guy is just dicking with us, Nasty. I've got an All-Points out for him, Washington's breathing down my neck and all hell's about to break. Any clue where he's gone, which direction? He's got about two hours' start, could be out of the state any minute. Colorado's nearest, I got traffic cops all the way north. Nothing yet. We know he didn't go home. I told Igor to report the burglary to the local cops. Gimme the keys to his wheels, we need to go over it, and get our bugs back. Tell me about yesterday."

"Well, let's see, boss...He talked about the last Bilderberg meeting, the one I couldn't find anything on, remember? Seems it's completely a given that Kuwait, Iraq and Afghanistan were all a put-up job, strategic if you like, to control the Middle East and the oil and gas. Also the Israelis needed a bigger US presence for their own safety and the implication was that they control most of what happens here. Also he talked of some leaked CIA memo implicating White House and

CIA or NSA collusion in 9/11, absolute proof that Mossad knew in advance about the Trade Towers. He says he's seen it, but it's now in secret hands. That's about all I got except that the entire mind-set of humanity is about to change, actually is already changing."

"You mean, because of the goddam Prist?" Uren's face was suffused with both rage and bafflement, and he seemed on the edge of control. He slumped in his chair, drew his hands over his face and silently waved her away.

Outside his door, Anastasia found herself tense and shaking but as she walked away down the corridor, a soothing change came over her, remembering Nic's parting words. She began to smile and felt her steps lightening. A colleague coming the other way didn't hide his astonishment at her expression, usually so dour and disapproving.

"Why, good *morning*, Anastasia," he said in passing, his irony unconcealed.

"It *is*, isn't it?" she replied, hearing his footsteps stop and turn. Turning herself, she saw him point at her and mutter, "Must've been good. Or bad, as they say."

Her response, just a nod and a smile, seemed to re-infuse her whole body. Testing it, she was surprised to find no trace of apprehension. While mystified at Nic's intentions, his confidence somehow allayed her anxiety, and she felt that her own role, though ambiguous, shouldn't jeopardize him further.

Rose turned from the stove, her robe swinging open. She smiled to see Igor's focus, over a satisfied grin.

"You like?" she asked with rare confidence.

"Is Ok," he answered flatly, trying to sound indifferent and munching his toast.

"And that's it?"

"Yes." He swallowed lengthily. "I am not aware of any design flaws. The landing gear is sturdy and sleek, moving smoothly. Did you get an alignment?"

"What?"

"The fuselage is Teflon-smooth and aerodynamic, the power unit purrs like Cadillac, but the control systems are very advanced, how do they say, above my expertise level. I think I would require many more hours with instructor to avoid serious mis-happening, before it was mine to command. Unless you know of simulator, perhaps?"

Rose's expression lifted from concern to pleasure. "Comrade, how come you know just what a girl wants to hear, compliments deeper than skin, the superficial? I take it you quite like me? Oh…And oops. Why did that make you frown?"

"Like is not correct word. I will try to think of one more appropriate. Right now, though, I am worried about Moncrieffe."

"Why, what's up with him?"

"There's a big *huynya*, like nonsense, Homeland Security. They want to bring him in for questioning but he seems to have vanished."

"Oh God, what has he done?"

"They think he's passing secrets."

"You're kidding! Is that why he disappeared? And how did he know to disappear?"

"Hmmm…Let's say he has friends." Igor glanced into the living room to reassure himself that his check-in transceiver was safely under a cushion. He still didn't know if it was voice- activated. He continued quietly, "One of these friends is supposed to be getting a passport for me. Another is going to find my implant."

Rose closed her robe and stared at him for long moments, her eyebrows arched in questioning surprise. "Surely they're bound to find him?"

Igor shrugged. "I'm not sure. He seems confident."

"And you, the passport? Where were you thinking of going?"

Igor waved his hands non-committally. "It would be nice to have a choice. At the moment I am completely restricted."

"And the implant, what's up with that? Do they, for instance, know just where you are?"

"Probably…I mean Yes. Certainly they do."

"And?" She glared at him intensely. "Does that put *me* on a list?"

Igor was silent for long seconds, his eyes down. "I'm sorry," he said eventually, "I really hadn't thought of it. I suppose it's possible, but they'd have nothing on you, nothing at all."

Rose clattered dishes in the sink, her face set. "Nowadays they don't *need* anything, they do whatever they like, you know that."

Igor wisely stayed quiet, finishing his breakfast. Rose dried her hands and then of a sudden spoke earnestly.

"There's something in the air, not quite right. I think you haven't told me the whole truth. Did you have anything to do with his disappearance, hm?" She stood over him and squeezed her thumb and middle finger together in front of his face.

"Of course not. What are you doing?"

"Muscle testing—kinesiology… Igor, it tells me you're lying. And you didn't sound surprised about him leaving, like you expected it."

"Alright. I was ordered to bring him in. I did not want to be the one to do it. We had a signal."

"He has a house here in Santa Fe. How can he just leave? I mean, wouldn't it have to be forever? And besides, there's nowhere they couldn't find him, surely?"

"I do not know. He has strange ways, strange ideas."

"Dammit, Igor, if he's guilty, that's treason and he's got it coming to him. If he's not, then why did he run?"

Getting no answer, she sat down and began eating a bowl of fruit and cereal, talking between mouthfuls. "Igor, let's be clear. You must never lie to me…I understand your motives but even so…This has given me a feeling of dread…it's funny, being here in a peaceful, civilized, New Age city and half an hour away they make atomic bombs and must guard it like grizzlies…Is there anything we can do for him?…I guess not, if we don't know where he is…What are you going to do now?"

"What I am told," he answered with a shrug. "I am to wait and see if he comes back home. I am sorry for the untruth."

In forgiveness, she forked a piece of melon into his mouth, playfully, while their eyes went deep into each other's, as if searching wistfully for truth. Just then the phone rang.

"Yes?"

"Is that Rose?"

"Yes. Who's this?"

"Is Igor there?"

Rose scowled. "I asked, who are you?"

"Give him two numbers. Got a pen?"

Stiffening, she quickly reached to the counter. "Go ahead." She wrote down the numbers, one in Santa Fe, one in Albuquerque. "Got it," she said quietly and the line clicked dead. She pushed the paper towards Igor.

"For you," she said, "I won't ask, I don't want to know, if that's who I think it was."

Igor looked at the numbers, frowned and then brightened, folding the paper and bringing himself back to the present.

"You make my heart feel like Jellyo", he said quietly.

"Likewise, Comrade. Let's hope we have plenty of time to explore it. Do you think they trust you?"

"Of course not. They trust no-one. Is first principle. I have to go now, to keep watch. I'll be relieved at 5 pm. Can we meet later?"

She nodded with a shy smile. "Are we getting hooked, Igor? I'll make dinner and give you a surprise."

"I may have one for you."

Anastasia's day was long and inconsequential, interrupted by Uren's mounting frustration. Unable to consider anything else to do, she spent the next evening buried in A Course in Miracles, trying to cull aphorisms from a tome that seemed to be nothing else. One in particular stuck in her mind because it was delivered several times in different ways and she noted how difficult it was for her mind the grasp the full import, let alone the implications. Half wisely and half from exasperation she decided to let it percolate, mixed herself a generous margarita and went up on the roof of her condo to watch the sunset. She'd photographed many of them, so startling in their miraculous variety and improbability, but her thoughts constantly veered towards Nic's inexplicable behavior. She felt a deep trust, mainly because of his restraint in face of her obvious availability, and the respect seemed to fill her veins with added desire. A curious pull, something more than sunsets, seemed to come from the West and she wondered if that was the direction he had taken. She heard the phone ring below but it stopped before she could clamber down. The caller ID showed the local area code 505, name unavailable, but there was no message. It rang again, this time from the monitors at the lab.

"Miss, there's an email intercept from London, shall I forward it to you?"

"Sure, go ahead."

In seconds she saw the message on her screen and read breathlessly: *"Kolya, Irina here. What is happening? Elena is being sent to Warsaw next week, can you believe it?! She is so gutsy, she wants you to come and meet her. I translate:*

Beloved Kolya, there is a conference in Warsaw on the 28th, I will be at Le Meridien hotel, it's got five stars and costs $141 per night, that's more than two month's pay for me, they are sending me there!!! I'm sure it is too much to ask for you to come and meet me but I so earnestly wish....I did wonder, because of you being in Cuba, I assume you are on your way somewhere else? I fall over my feet with excitement, I would give one of them to learn English overnight...I am completely overwhelmed, and I just know it's all a result of my change in attitude, from being a sufferer to being simply grateful. When I told my mother, she screamed and said she knew it, I was leaving her and would never return. I told her I could not do that because then her martyrdom would be complete. She was silent for more than an hour, finally she smiled and made a big fuss of me! Oh, so many wishings but mostly thanking thoughts, as the whole world seems to be opening to a little soul that thought it was forever in prison....Love Elena."

Anastasia was dialing Uren's number even before she finished reading.

"Boss, Moncrieffe's in Cuba."

"*What!* But you can't go there from here, there's still an embargo."

"Well, he can, Boss, he's not American."

"Shit! What else? Is he overnight or staying?"

"There's no more information. The woman in Ukraine must have received a message from there, we couldn't track it."

"More shit. I'll see if the local CI in Havana can find him. Going to Code Red here, how the hell did he get out of New Mexico, I wanna know? He just hung my ass out in the wind."

Uren hung up just as the phone clicked. Anastasia picked up immediately before the caller ID registered.

"Annie? How's it going?"

"Nic! What the hell are you doing in Cuba?"

There was a pause for absorption. "Oh, well, I was just wandering around. I've decided to go in retreat, lie low for a few days, get myself sorted out."

"What do you mean, about us?"

"No, sweets, no doubts there. It's about what's coming. But you, you move me to my core, it's like a whole-being response, believe me. But I don't know how you feel."

"Me? I have lost cool, no subtlety, I cannot play coquette. I feel like an open invitation."

"Love it—but rain-check. I'm guessing there's a big showdown due and I need to get really clear."

"And that's it? When will I see you?"

"Give me a few days."

After a gulp and a long pause, she asked, "Can I really believe you, I mean about my parents and the killers? How could you get such information, so quickly, I mean—?"

"Just believe, honey. All is well."

"Are you still in Havana? The CIA—"

"Stop."

"What?"

"Just stop. No more questions. Bye for now. Big kiss." Click.

Anastasia's hand rattled the phone into its slot and a muffled shriek emerged from deep inside. She held her hands to her heart and rocked herself quietly into submission until she was steady enough to pour the remains of her margarita. With an inspiration to face her fears, she went out and rented the movie *Rendition* but had to switch off at the first signs of torture. She wanted no more dreams of sadism and powerlessness, but they woke her anyway, drenched and screaming soundlessly. Comfort came with memories of the day on the lake, touching the frantic and gleaming Kokanee salmon, response to the mating urge and being gently held without demand.

The monastery appeared at the end of twelve miles of dirt road more suited to his SUV than Anastasia's little Corolla, no longer green but deliberately daubed with adobe mud. The vast expanse of sky was blistering clear, the air crystal with peace. Rounding a bend he was startled by a family of purple-black wild turkeys scuttling into cover. Multi-colored cattle roamed freely, watching him with unconcern. Finally the track followed the Rio Chama down to a wide expanse where beige buildings nestled into the landscape amid ancient cottonwoods. Nic had to park and walk the last quarter mile to the main building, almost embarrassed by the utter silence. He couldn't imagine a better place for contemplative retreat. At the main building the guest-master greeted him with a gentle smile.

"Welcome to Christ in the Desert, my son, have you come to stay with us, did you call ahead?"

"I did not, I'm sorry. Do you have any space?"

"I believe we do. You passed the guest rooms so you just have to go back. I am Brother Gerard. We are entirely silent here. You'll find details in your room. We rise at 3.30 am, for Vigils at 4. Are you perhaps in crisis?"

"Nice of you to ask, Father. Not exactly, no, but I need to prepare myself for one. I'm not a believer in your sense, though of course I respect it completely."

"It's Brother. I understand. Mysticism and spirituality need no conformity. It is simply a choice of ours, a faith if you like. So you will not be receiving sacraments?"

Nic smiled and shook his head. "Many paths, brother. I hope that's all right?"

"Indeed. How would you like to be addressed? You sound English, is that right? I thought so. Well, we do not need names, it's up to you. Our discretion is absolute. The rooms do not lock. I put you in number 4. Perhaps we'll see you for the evening meal, at 4.30."

"Thank you. Tell me, living here, does that mean you have no fears?"

Surprised, the monk eyed him speculatively. "On the earth-plane, I suppose not. There is perhaps some apprehension regarding the afterlife, if we fail to fulfill our purpose."

"Hm," Nic chuckled before adding, "And how do you know what that is?"

"You ask, in humility, and the answer comes."

"From inspiration or an actual voice?"

"Either way."

"It strikes me that there's an arrogance to even imagining we have a purpose."

"All life has a purpose."

"Even for the mass of men leading lives `of quiet desperation'? Does it make you special if you're not quietly desperate?"

"Perhaps in quiet introspection you will find the answer. Do you feel that you have a purpose?"

"Frankly, I can't tell. I certainly had an inspiration. Now I need to decide if it was merely a vanity. The consequences of acting on it could be dire. A Course in Miracles has a whole section called "*I Need Do Nothing.*"

"I see. That sounds interesting. My curiosity is aroused but I will curb it. If your conscious mind is in pursuit of something, perhaps it would help to switch it off and see what the unconscious mind comes up with. I wish you grace and blessings," he added with what looked like a pained smile.

Walking back to the guest house, Nic found a neat little room with single bed, a desk and a chair. He sat and opened a notebook. The first thing that came to mind was a question: "How can even the most cloistered saint escape the vanity that his smug and chosen way of life is pleasing to his Deity and not just to himself?"

Bringing his thoughts back to the present, he began a letter to his son:

Dearest Jamie,

Hard to believe, but I'm holed up in a monastery! I may have started something with heavy consequences so I may be out of touch for a while. I can't really go into it because those consequences are so far unknown, but I'm quite sure the facts will tickle you when you finally get them. I'm not going on a sea-voyage, I wouldn't want to without you, the coolest First Mate I ever had.

If the outcome should appear unfortunate, remember that appearances often deceive and ultimately "All is well, no matter how it seems." It could be a damp squib or an amazing grace, there's no way to tell yet. Remember when that squall hit us in Puget sound, we were both calm and confident, trusting ourselves and each other completely? Since I'm certain that will always be how we are, please trust again even if I'm out of contact. I'll fill you in as soon as I can. Sorry to be mysterious. A hint: Remember my last story, about the Ministry of Misinformation? It's something along those lines....

Love forever, Dad. xxx

He considered a PS but instead wrote a note to himself:

How can you love the desert? Some people do! Would they love the sea, as Jamie and I do, or fear it? As a doer, my response to the desert is frustration about what to do with it, but some are able simply to gaze in awe at this vast extension of beauty. And what has driven these saintly people to carve a quiet oasis in the middle of an arid nowhere, build it into a thriving community of contemplatives who are mostly silent in their efforts to block out the madness of the world in order to communicate with God, personally? Well, I'm not here to solve that mystery—I'm here to set the stage within myself, to stand on that stage without a script or prompt, to get ready for anything and just see what happens...

CHAPTER 11

*Feel it now: there is a power in me to grasp and give shape
to my world. I know that nothing has ever been real without
my beholding it.... My looking ripens things and they come
toward me, to meet and be met.*

Rainer Maria Rilke
(Tr Barrows/Macy)

Summoned again the next morning to Uren's office, Anastasia
faced rage personified.

"They turned up nothing in Havana. Someone must have
tipped him off. Most likely it was you. You or Igor. Whaddya say to
that, Polack?"

"Wasn't me, boss. But he must've known something was up. He
knew his house had been searched last week, he suspected about the
intercepts and—"

"Yeah, but not necessarily about us being onto the coded emails to
Ukraine and the cut-off in London. Did he, huh?"

"It wasn't mentioned. Anyway, all he knows about me is that I'm
here as an archivist."

Uren growled in fury, "And a naked one, at that! Carnal knowledge,
right? Equals pillow talk, how the fuck can I trust a woman in love or
lust or whatever...They're waiting for you across the way. Polygraph.
Go."

"Me? You're wasting your time, boss, I'm on the level."

"You lent him your car!"

"Did not! He just took it."

"Gonna file charges, are you? Get outta here."

Short, bald and bespectacled, Dr Henderson seemed quietly
detached until he consulted his clipboard and Anastasia suspected a
gleam of prurience. The plastic of the chair felt sticky and her arms

were held with nylon ties at her elbows. He had to ask her permission to remove her cinch for the rubber tubes to cross her chest, sensors for respiratory rate.

"You can keep your sweater on, however," he added, with a hint of disappointment. Galvanic sensors for sweat were taped to her palms and a blood pressure monitor clipped to her index finger. After a few test questions, Henderson, reading from a clipboard she guessed was provided by Uren, jolted her with the first formality.

"Are you and Moncrieffe lovers?"

After a pause, Anastasia answered quietly, "Please define the term."

He looked up, frowning. "Is there a sexual connection between you?"

"Please define sexual connection."

"Have you been having sexual intercourse with Mr Moncieffe?"

"No."

"But you have slept with him?"

"Yes."

"But there was no intercourse? That is a question."

"Correct."

"Why not? Is he impotent?"

"That's two questions. To the second the answer is no."

"How do you know?"

"Listen, Doctor, I am not here to answer prurient questions. They are not a matter of National Security."

"They could show motive. You best answer."

"Uren put you up to this, right?"

"I ask the questions here. So, you're saying that you have shared a bed but not consummated?"

"Correct."

"Thank you. Did you warn him that he would be arrested and brought in for questioning under the Patriot Act?"

"No."

"Even though you knew he was under suspicion?"

"He knew that himself."

"Did he discuss it with you?"

"No."

"Then how did you know that he knew?"

"I made reference to one of the books, and he realized that the only way I could know of the reference was from reading his emails, which we have been monitoring."

"Were you aware that those references were coded information intended for foreign or hostile receivers?"

"No—that is, there was such an assumption but Codes has been working on them without success, as far as I know."

"Now about this, what is it, Prist?"

"What about it?"

"Does the use of Prist in jet-fuel constitute a threat?"

"To whom?"

Curbing annoyance, he asked. "To anyone?"

"Not that I know of."

Henderson made a note on his clipboard and glared ominously. "It would seem you told an untruth."

"Not so. I myself am not aware of any threat. Others may not see it that way, the paranoia goes much higher. Nothing has been found in the Prist analysis that might constitute any threat. As far as I know." She grinned at him smugly.

"Why did Moncrieffe run?"

"I imagine he saw himself under suspicion."

"For what?"

"For having some knowledge that was classified. That's what brought him to our department's attention."

"Did he reveal any sources?"

When Anastasia hesitated, Henderson pressed her tersely. "Answer the question."

"Yes, but it was quite vague. Only one."

"And what was that source?"

"Somebody called Biggall."

"No other name or description?"

"No."

Henderson's face set in a kind of triumph as he watched oscillations on the print-out.

"Let's try that again."

"That's all I know. No, wait, the emphasis was on the -All, so it wasn't like Biggle."

"Ah, that's better. Thank you. Do you know the whereabouts of this Biggall?"

"No."

"Or any other description?"

"No."

"Do you know where Moncrieffe is now?"

"We have deduced that he is, or was, in Cuba."

"Has he called you since he left your apartment?"

"Yes. He said he needed to sort himself out, in retreat or something."

"He didn't say where?"

"No."

"Did it sound like he was enamored of you?"

"Yes."

"Did he say he would return?"

"Yes."

"Did the Russian Igor Knyazev warn him about possible arrest?"

"How would I know?"

"Answer the question!"

"Oh, sorry. I don't know."

Henderson frowned, shrugged and switched off the recordings, plucked off the sensors, handed her back the cinch and spoke abruptly, "You can go now, thank you."

She put it on awkwardly, stood up and smiled. "Well, did I pass?"

"I'm sorry, I am not permitted..."

"So whisper," she smiled impishly.

Melting slightly, Henderson allowed himself the merest of nods and a fractional lift to the corners of a severe mouth. He was rewarded with a gentle hand on his shoulder as she passed him, her steps lively. Turning in the doorway, she saw him shake his head, bemused.

When she returned to Uren's office, Igor was standing in front of the desk, while Uren's face on the other side was pale and drawn, gnashed with frustration. Igor was in the middle of saying something when the email alert beeped and Uren held up his hand, turning his screen to read the message, which seemed to give him some satisfaction.

"Ok, Nasty, seems you are on the level. How do we find this Big-fucking-All guy?"

"No idea, boss, but I gather lots of people know of him, in Santa Fe."

"Ok, get down there and do some asking around. Langley's screaming at me, where's your man? How could we lose him, how did he get to Cuba, fucksakes? Get onto all the General Aviation terminals hereabouts, flight plans, number on board, names, of all private jets going east, specially Miami or South to Mexico. CIA in Havana hasn't turned up shit and he may have moved on already. Nothing from the airlines. What about the credit card monitoring?"

"Nothing except a withdrawal, here in Los Alamos, took out $500 in cash."

"Huh, well that won't get him far…we're lookin' like rednecks here, idiots. Couldn't you keep him in bed, Nasty, another half hour and we'd have had him? What the hell's with you, woman? You look like the cat that ate the cream. He called you, right?"

"Yes, boss. I asked him what he was doing in Cuba but he didn't answer. Said he was going in retreat for a few days, that's all."

"Where, dammit?"

"Didn't say."

"Listen, it's my bet he's headed to Warsaw, seems this Elena chick is hot-to-trot. He's two-timin' ya, Nasty."

Anastasia's eyes narrowed. "But he's never met her, boss, we know that."

"Huh. I thought of tipping off Moscow FSB about her, but then we'd lose our carrot. Then I got a better idea, someone who speaks Polish—and Russian—and who even wants to go there." He tried to grin at Anastasia but it came across like a cruel sneer. "Open ticket'll be waiting for you at admin. You stay at the Bristol Meridien, same as the Ukrainian bitch. I'll get you some local back-up in case she's a tigress. Go when I tell you, Santa Fe direct to Dallas, London, Warsaw. Don't enjoy. And call me when you find this Biggall feller. Get him and maybe we won't need Moncrieffe, we'll just—well, never mind."

Anastasia stared at him without expression, her normal downturn twitching up at the corners, reaction shocked but still unformulated.

From somewhere a bubble of humor erupted.

"Thanks boss. Would that be First or Business Class?"

"*What?* Get outta here."

Uren dismissed her with a flip of his pudgy fingers and turned to Igor with a snarl. "Get that grin off your Fascist face. It had to be you, Comrade. Somebody tipped him off and if it wasn't Nasty, it was you. Whaddya say, huh?"

Igor shook his head as if baffled. "How could I have done this? No cell-phone, and he didn't go to his house where I was waiting. But he must have known something that he was being investigated."

"Arrgh, listen up, you blundering Boris. This thing with the Prist could be the biggest fucking turd to hit the turbine in 50 years. I'm willing to bet you gave him the alert, but in any case we've lost him, and how in holy hell did he get to Cuba? Either way, what the fuck am I going to do with you? You're no more use to us. You owe the National Guard about forty million bucks and you've nothing more to tell us… I can't see how I could double you…I'd send you back to Moscow anyway except that you know about Prist….But then if Moncrieffe's gone East with it, they'll know soon enough. Far as I can see, you've got a choice between Guantanamo and the Lubyanka-slash-firing squad. Unless you do everyone a favor and take a 600 foot swallow dive off the Taos bridge… I dunno, look, just in case he comes back, get back down to Sannafay, do not speak or let him see you, just call it in. I doubt it but it could just save your ass. Ok? Get the hell out."

"Is there to be enquiry, about the F.16?"

"Nah. Ya don't go out in public when ya've pooped ya pants. Go."

In the refectory, a dinner largely of fresh and surely organic vegetables was accompanied by a surprise reading from Eckart Tolle's "*A New Earth.*" Though there were occasional glances, mostly the silent monks ate expressionless and inscrutable. Nic found himself bemused at the way characters still exhibit themselves, some with fatuously bushy beards, others shaven and ascetic-looking. All except one seemed serious and self-conscious before half a dozen visitors, the exception being a round-faced and cherubic character who seemed to be in Buddha-like bliss, aglow with such happiness he seemed almost deranged.

Dinner was over by 5.15 followed by Vespers and lastly Compline in the Church. As Nic walked over to the guest-house still in a meditative trance, the utter silence of the valley seemed to support every mystery, the sky an absolute black, the stars winking insistently but with one anomaly, a satellite right overhead moving at tremendous speed, presumably the orbiting requirement of 17,000 mph. In his room the rechargeable lamp cast a dismal glow as, unable to consider sleep at such an early hour, he reached for his notebook and began a tentative discourse with himself.

More notes from the Cloister:

"Tyrannies are falling all over, with the help of Social Networks and leaked cables. Prist Paranoia reverses the fear factor onto the Banking Gangsters—the Banksters! are up against something they can do nothing about.

Fact: this generation is beginning to think in terms of the New Freedom, thinking outside the Ego/fear box, becoming aware of its power. The Overlords/Corporate Goliath are protected by the media and Big Business which they own and which in turn owns the politicians....?:Will they try to suppress the information (and therefore me) hoping it's ineffective or at least won't take full effect in their lifetimes, or will they try to discover the full extent of it?

Fact 2: The Shift is provably happening and will intensify according to every soothsayer, channel and even plain logic. When enough people envision a fairer world, 100th Monkey and Law of Attraction must make it so. As the Overlords recognize what's happening they'll begin to make their compromises. So, do I stay out of sight indefinitely to add conviction or roll up like a good boy with solid information? Gut says the latter. Poke the nest and expect to get stung, but—the fearless bee-keeper doesn't get stung, he's not sending out fear pheromones. How can anyone ever be happy until they recognize it's the Ego-world that is making them miserable? And that's just the first step!

Only the fearless find happiness. If you get killed, so what? Get killed for the 'right' reasons, you die happy. Hmmm...I once thought that confrontation is impossible but now we hear there are legions of Asian ninjas ready to take these guys out. Anyway, confrontation is more of the same= creation of enemies= strife. What you resist persists, etc...

As the little lamp dimmed, sleep came effortlessly, but only lasted a couple of hours. Nic got up and padded down the walkway for another lamp, in awe at the utter silence under the blackest of skies, but the desert night was typically too cold to linger. Back at his desk he resumed his scribbling, wide awake and filled with a strange calm.

The B's, the Overlords, have limitless resources and yet seem ever intent on gaining more power. Need for control is fear of loss of control. Some have even described them as possessed, whether by 'Dark Forces', simple avarice, or terror of powerlessness. The general public is not really aware of their machinations, how even they supported, and were paid by, both sides in the two World Wars. How they have admitted plans for population control and funded research and dissemination of both viruses and vaccines, provably lab-created in the US, such as several carcinogens, HIV/Aids, Ebola, West Nile, H1N1, Zika and more, including female sterilization concealed in vaccines. Talk to any one of them, they'll likely come across as urbane, highly educated, cosmopolitan, reasonable and even philanthropic. They'll tell that the only way to avoid more wars (all of which in the last 200 yrs could only have happened with their say-so) is to have One World Government, and to avoid revolt or opposing factions, everybody would have to be 'chipped'. To be acceptable, the chip would be introduced as a safety device, benign and protective and eventually cash money would be abolished, all exchanges made through the chip. Thus are you protected by Big Brother—and by the way, step out of line and we simply switch you off, so you cannot move, transact or buy food and fuel. Bye bye. How's that for a deterrent?

I've seen only a tiny fraction of the beauty in this world, and the love that emanates from unselfish people. Equally I have seen only a fraction of the beauty in other worlds when Ego-mind, 3rd Dimensional mind, is by-passed. I'm gifted with an (apparent!) physical body and with the knowledge that it is only a vehicle in the (apparent) physical world and my body is not who I am. The moment this is fully understood, fear evaporates and the possibilities of the 4th and 5th Dims open up—and they are only the beginning!

Consciousness is simply Godness showing up in myriad forms. Osho said something like: "Life has to be fun, a rejoicing, a dance, a song, a love affair. Taking life seriously is wasting an opportunity to have everything in playfulness. Rejoicing is my religion." I watch and listen as Ego-mind says, Yeah, right, that's all very well, BUT....!

It's as if the last thought induced instant drowsiness...Left the window slightly open, and later a great wind sprang up with a multitude of different tones and voices, some querulous, some soothing, some argumentative, all clamoring to be heard. It made for coziness, reminding me of being snugged in a bay with a full gale from offshore tearing at the palm trees and howling in the rigging, two anchors out and a quiet certainty that all is well—unless the wind backs 180°! My boy sleeping below but always ready in an instant...Slept for an hour, woke with the thought that the only thing I <u>know</u> is that all is well right now. I have no idea what will happen when I turn myself in.

The mingled voices died with the wind about 2 am, the debate seemingly resolved. Slept through the 3.30 wake-up bell and first light revealed a fine dust from the desert covering everything. Is this a metaphor? My thoughts are similarly settled. I know nothing of what's going to happen, my only choices are 1) put myself in the way of opportunities, miracles and hazards or 2) disappear for a long time and see what happens without me i.e., would my disappearance intensify the alarm? Will I even know?!

Truth is, I can't run. They can trace any credit card transactions and I have limited cash, maybe enough to get to Canada, then what? Closed bank account for sure. So....Steal a 50' ketch in Vancouver? Then what?

Anastasia: I am filled with delight at your liveliness and cleverness, a wonderful mind, a chrysalis emerging from years of hate and determined misery, now determined on another course. Cannot avoid thoughts of your physical beauty, but since I'm not under its sway, I can simply rejoice in it and see it as my delightful creation. I will not fantasize, but take you as you are in any given moment. And avoid the big No-No of falling in love with someone's potential—there is no more you need to be. We can explore wherever it takes us... Unless—oops: fearful thought, Dismiss!

Sleeping through both Vigils at 4.30am as well as Lauds, Nic showed up at 6.30 breakfast, dismissing guilt. With no glances of reproof, he recalled with a grin the ACIM dictum that guilt is self-induced and is simply fear of retribution. Something in this clarity conveyed, he was sure, because the guest-master asked no questions, took his $50 for the night, promised to mail his letter and wished him many blessings on his journey.

The day was warm with a light breeze so he turned North on the highway and spent the day sailing on Heron lake, borrowing an old Jeep from the farmer to tow the Hobie to the water. He spent the following night at Ghost Ranch and took a long hike just after dawn up to the box canyon. A great calm seemed to have settled itself and after a two hour drive South and an early brunch, he presented himself at the entrance to Los Alamos and asked to see the head of Security. There was a long wait at the gate while the guard phoned for clearance, then two burly uniforms came stealthily from behind, slammed his head onto the roof of the car, twisted his arms, cuffed him with gritty triumph and frogged him inside. Despite the pain from too-tight manacles, Nic offered no resistance as they started to drag him, deliberately hurting as well as upsetting his balance. He grinned at each in turn and felt the pressure ease gradually, though eye-contact was fleeting. Brutality and humanity are mutually exclusive.

CHAPTER 12

Necessity is the plea (excuse) for every infringement of human freedom. It is the argument of tyrants, it is the creed of slaves.

William Pitt 1783

In Santa Fe, Igor dutifully hung around Nic's house shortly after dawn, called in that he was going to breakfast, and went instead to a secret appointment at the Imaging Center on Hospital Drive, leaving his transceiver in the car. There was no-one at reception, but when he tapped the bell, a small-boned and very pretty woman emerged from the passage with a dazzling smile. She had raven hair and sparkling eyes, at least half-Hispanic.

"You are Igor, Nic's friend? I am Jasmine. Come with me." She led him into a spotless room dominated by the huge O-ring and trolley of the CT scanner. "We must be quick, we've only a short time before the quacks get in. Where's the promised burrito?"

Igor pulled a wax-paper wrap from his pocket. "Vegetarian, yes?"

"Yes, thank you. Clothes off, and your watch, any chains and so on, you can keep your underwear on. Lie down on here. Do you have any idea where it is?"

"No, I do not. Not in my head, I should think. Hand or arm most likely. I thought you were going to use MRI?"

"No. It has a huge magnet underneath. If there's any metal in the chip it could explode the thing right out of you. You only want to know where it is, right?" She peeled her burrito and took a bite, talking through the mouthful. "I'll be in the box over there. I'll stop the scan if I see something."

He stripped to his shorts and lay down on the table while Jasmine punched numbers into the control panel. The machine began to whirr, the table lifted and Igor's head went through the huge ring. It stopped and the X-ray annulus began to spin, the table moved and stopped again after 20 seconds. The table then backed out and lowered as Jasmine reappeared from the box, still munching, a sprout dangling comically from the corner of her mouth.

"Got it," she mumbled, "Right arm, inside, about five inches below the armpit."

"Is it deep?" Igor asked, sitting up.

"An inch or so. Look." She showed him the printout on which she'd circled a tiny outline about the size of a single long-grain rice. "Did you want it removed?"

"Yes. But not yet. The timing is critical."

"Take this with you then." She tore the heading off the paper and handed it to him, then went and punched some buttons on the control panel. "Ok, it's re-set. You were never here. You have never seen me, is that clear?"

"Yes, of course."

"I wouldn't do this for anyone but Nic. I hope he knows that."

"I'll make sure he does." Igor finished dressing and added, "You are very beautiful. How was it between you?"

Jasmine blushed and then shrugged. "Merely perfect, except he wanted an exclusive. I regret it every day. Now I'm told I have a personality disorder—I'm paranoid about being controlled."

Igor nodded and then chuckled in his gravelly way, pointing to his right arm. "That is two of us. Tell me, would the magnet of an MRI disable the chip?"

"For sure. It's so powerful it would fry it."

"How about high voltage?"

"Probably. If it killed you then it wouldn't matter, would it?"

"Hm. Then one more favor, when I'm ready to switch off?"

Jasmine sighed theatrically. "I get you. Weekdays, same time. Call me first." She brightened impishly. "I do eat fish. Pickled herring from Denmark, salmon paté, caviar, Moët et Chandon."

Igor held out his hand. "You have a deal, though I may not have time. You know, he's not a controlling type?"

"Yes, I do. That's why it's called paranoia. Give him my love, won't you?"

"If I can. He seems to have vanished."

"Bloody man. He wouldn't get a cell-phone."

"Hm. Maybe I'll give him mine when I leave."

"Damn. Then I'll have his number, won't I?"

"On that subject, can I use yours, from here?"

"Help yourself. Better be quick, though. The quacks'll be here in a few."

Igor followed her gesture into the booth and called the number in Albuquerque Nic had given him. After introducing himself, he said quietly, "Can I pay you extra to come up here, to Santa Fe? I don't think I can come to you...You got the photos by FedEx?...You can, in an hour? Yes, Harry's Roadhouse, 10 o'clock?"

He turned to Jasmine. "One more, OK?" Seeing her nod, he dialed a local number. "Larry? It's Igor Knyazev. I was wondering when the L39 would be ready in Phoenix?"

He gulped at the answer. "What? Really? But I'm not legal yet. You did? Well, OK, yes, I'm fine with that. No. No bogeys this time. See you, then."

Jasmine hung in the doorway, her shiny black eyebrows raised. Igor touched the back of his hand to her cheek, his nervousness soothed by her beauty. He nodded his thanks quickly and left her smiling. Back in his car there were two messages on his cell-phone, the first demanding his call-in, the second a single word, a woman's voice with a distinctly Slavic inflexion: "KATAPOULTIRUYSYA!"

A bare windowless room, a table, three steel chairs and half one wall a huge mirror. The two guards frisked him intimately and shoved him roughly into a chair. One double-knocked the door and was let out, the other stood to attention, staring ahead.

"Can you loosen the cuffs, old chap?" Nic asked mildly, but there was no response. He felt his hands begin to tingle urgently, numbness setting in. He put his thoughts elsewhere, a fine warm breeze, a schooner leaning her shoulder into sapphire sea, Anastasia standing naked with a hand on the shrouds. A feeling like a smile spread through his body and expanded for the next twenty minutes, the reverie shattered with the door crashing open. A furious bull head appeared, collar and tie askew.

"Moncrieffe?"

"Yes. How do you do?"

"What? How the fuck did you get here from Cuba?"

"I drove, why?"

"Don't shit me. You emailed from Cuba, right?"

"Yes. Would you mind loosening these clamps, I'm going to lose my hands."

Nic's mild tone had the desired effect. Uren stared at him incredulously and finally nodded to the guard who produced the key, released him viciously and pocketed the cuffs. The relief that flowed into Nic's hands was delicious agony. Watching him rub his wrists, Uren barked, "Private jet, right? Why'd you come back?"

"Well, I couldn't think of anywhere else to go. Are we talking about the same Cuba?"

"Whaddya mean?"

"I stopped on my way to Farmington. Cuba, New Mexico. It's about forty miles from here, northwest."

Uren stood dumbfounded, actually blushing, acutely aware of faces behind the one-way mirror. He sputtered, "So you never left the goddam State? Where'd you go?"

Not wanting agents bothering the monastery, Nic answered simply, "I went camping. Needed a break."

"Break from what?"

"All the fuss. Burglars often come back. I'd rather lose stuff than have to kill one."

"You haven't got a gun."

Nic made no reply, simply met Uren's furious face with a slight smile.

"Do you?" Uren barked.

"Well, I have a nail-gun. Does that count?"

"How did you know there'd been a burglary, you spent that day with Wojerkowski?"

"Hm…How did *you* know about it?"

"Listen, we got no time for this shit. It's beside the goddam point."

"Look, Mister er—"

"Uren. Frank Uren. We're after your sources. You got one chance before it gets heavy. How did you know about Prist?"

"Oh, that…Well, you'd have to ask Biggall."

"Who the fuck's Biggall? C'mon, answer!"

Nic's only reply was an exaggerated shrug, then he said quietly, "I think you're about to have a heart attack."

"Fuck you!"

"No, seriously. I know the signs."

"Shut up! This isn't about me, it's about you."

"I think you know everything I know."

Uren bunched his knuckles fiercely then took a deep breath. "Just tell me how to find this guy and you're off the hook. Maybe."

"Take another long breath and let your body relax. I can help you if—"

"Answer the fucking question!"

"I don't actually know. I've been trying to find out for a long time. There's whispers and rumors, but everyone's got different ideas. I guess he's kind of mysterious, keeps to himself, you might say. Sorry I can't help you."

"Well, you better help yourself or things are going to get very nasty. You've no idea what we've got lined up for you…You saying there's, like, a chain, you heard it from someone who heard it from who?"

"Whom."

"*What?* Jesus!" He looked at the impassive guard warily and said, "This guy is about to get some chunks ripped off him and he corrects my fucking English. Jesus!" Turning angrily, he strove for control and finally said, "Moncrieffe, start me on the chain. Who'd you hear it from?"

"No idea. I can't remember."

"Bullshit!" Uren took another long breath. "I'm trying to be reasonable before I hand you over to the cattle-prod and pliers team. Where does this guy hang out?"

Nic gave a huge shrug, suppressed a grin that was trying to form and added "I suppose you could ask around. Should be plenty of folks in Santa Fe who might know."

"We've tried that. I got people down there asking. Does he work for the Prist company?"

"That I doubt but I really couldn't tell you. He could be a chimera for all I know."

"Ok, who did you last talk to about him?"

"You must know that. It was Igor the Russian."

Uren struggled for composure again. "That was *you* telling *him*! From who, oh fuck, from whom, did ya get the information about Prist?"

"I'm trying to remember…It was ages ago, I can't—"

Uren banged his fist on the table. "Gimme names, Goddammit! Who it might have been?"

"I can't think of anyone. Cocktail party gossip, maybe."

"Ok, like the stuff about the Pershings not having nuke warheads, where'd you get it?"

"Same source, I guess." Nic opened his hands helplessly. He saw Uren was about to erupt again but there came a sharp knock, the door opened and the other guard's head appeared.

"Mr Uren, call for you. Says it's Urgent."

"Tell 'em to call back."

"Sir, it's the Secretary of Defense, in D.C."

Uren's eyes narrowed, his lips forming a snarl. "Holy fuck! Ok. Come in and watch this guy." He stormed out leaving the door ajar and before the guard closed it, Nic heard a barked question. "Wojerkowski, she leave yet? If not, stall her. Send her down here, have her wait—"

The door closed off any other words, leaving Nic with the impassive guards. He sat still and silent for several minutes until the little asp of mischief emerged unbidden.

"Are you chaps married, got kids?" he ventured. Getting no response, he added, "I know a great wife joke, you want to hear it?"

Both men ignored him, simply gazed unfocused and impassive.

"Reason I asked, I wouldn't want to upset them, I mean, would anyone miss you if death was to come to you, rather than the other way round? You know, if I was to kill you both, right now?"

Still neither man looked at him but both stiffened visibly. Nic pretended disappointment. "Oh well, I suppose it's not much of a conversation starter. Just wondered…Ok, who wants to be first?"

The guard nearest the door, about 6'2" and 250 pounds with an aggressive close Marine cut, simply smirked but also flexed his hands with anticipation. The other drew his sidearm and clicked off the safety with menace.

Nic grinned at him. "C'mon, soldier, you know you're not allowed to kill me. Besides, I'm talking bare hands. How many ways did they teach you? I bet I know one you never heard of. Can I show you?"

He started to get to his feet and both men moved at once. The nearest swung and shoved his semi-automatic in Nic's face, then pushed him forcefully back into the chair. Nic raised his hands submissively and then waved them in front of the man's eyes, blurring his vision, pointed over his shoulder, locked his fingers on the wrist pressure point and took the gun from an impotent hand. The guard immediately swung his other fist, missed, leapt back in astonishment and lurched into his colleague who was trying to draw his own side-arm. Both men reeled and recovered at once, crouching tense, rigid with adrenaline.

Nic flicked off the safety and said to the other, "Take it out, two fingers. Put it on the table."

The big man complied warily, obviously looking for a chance but his face was filled with fury and embarrassment.

"Face the wall, both of you. Hands above your heads."

"Don't be an idiot," the smaller one said, "The door's locked from the outside. You can't get out of here."

"Yes, I gathered that. But this is more interesting than what we were doing before, don't you think? It's a different dynamic. Just be quiet and think nice thoughts. I'll quiz you in a minute or two, Ok?"

Both men turned to stare incredulously as Nic placed both weapons on the table in front of him, clicking the safety off the second.

In a strained voice one said, "Where d'you think this'll get you? You can't get OUT!"

Nic sighed. "I know. But it's something to do while we wait for the ogre. You really shouldn't have messed up my wrists, that was unnecessary, right? Hey, we could play a game. I'll face the wall as well, then we go 1,2,3,GO and see who can get to the guns first. What d'you think? Wait, suppose I empty them both but leave one round in one of them so only one of us gets shot? Remember that three-way shoot up in *The Good, the Bad and the Ugly*? Mm, no, that's not fair because you're not allowed to shoot me, are you? Let's see now, M9 Beretta... Did you know a priest's hat is the same, but spelled differently, Biretta with an 'I'. Isn't that weird?"

Nic chuckled to himself and worked the slide on one of the M9's, shells clinking on the table until the clip was empty. "Ha. Ten rounds and none in the chamber. See, you weren't even ready to shoot me."

He started to empty the clip on the other gun, watching with a grin as he saw them counting. "One up the spout here. Five, six, seven. Three left. Don't move, chaps. I'm quite nifty with these. Boy, you'll be so in the doghouse when the ape gets back. You have to promise me you'll be gentle next time you—In fact, let's try it now. You," he said to the smaller of the two, "Keep one hand on the wall, take out your handcuffs and put them on your pal. Behind his back."

When neither of them moved, he pointed at the nearest thigh. "I have three left. A nine-mil does horrible things to bones, could lose you a leg. Do it now, slowly, and not too tight or he may resent you. Hands behind your back, big guy."

Slowly the first guard complied and shackled his colleague. Both kept giving him furious but anguished glances. "Ok. Now lift your left leg and put it down between his hands."

"You're kidding, right?"

"No. Do it now, I'm getting itchy here."

With baffled reluctance the guard complied, lifting his leg and inserting it carefully through the shackled arms. Both were shaking heads with agonized expressions.

"Now take his cuffs and clip one on your left wrist. Quickly... Now put your left arm between his as well... Good. Now bring your right arm round in front of him, through his legs and cuff yourself together."

The man stared at him incredulously. "I can't do that, I'll be—"

"Do it! Three seconds before I pop you one in the butt. I've nothing to lose here. One, two—"

After a brief and horrified wrestle, the man finally shackled himself. Both were grimacing in disbelief at their positions, their hands forced into each other's crotches, humiliation and defeat making them wide-eyed and desperate.

The smaller one gasped out, "Listen, man, we'll lose our jobs over this. We wouldn't have hurt you, you know that!"

"Really? I thought you just did. Anyway—"

The big one ventured, "Hey, asshole, have you thought about what we'll do to you when they open the door?"

"Not really, I hadn't got that far, sorry. Well, at least it was a different sort of day for you chaps. What's the worst that could happen, anyone? I suggest it's being on the receiving end of sadism. Have you heard reports from Iraq, for instance? Sufferers cannot understand where this cruelty comes from. I mean, imagine right now, if I cut the clothes off you, drench you in ice-water, knock all your teeth out, kick your nuts to pulp, ram a truncheon up your ass, tie you to the ceiling from your cuffed hands, you shit where you hang and live with it, no water or food for a week, no one to appeal to, no kindness…Prisoners lives completely shattered, tens of thousands of them, zombies, unable to function, even worse if they haven't done anything wrong."

"Hey," hissed the smaller guard, "We were both in Iraq, we didn't do those things."

Nic stood up and read from their name tags. "Snelling…and Price. Nice to hear. What if you'd been ordered to, would you have obeyed? And I bet you'd like to do it to me, right now. You gave me a taste already. Tell me honestly, what does it *feel* like, being needlessly cruel to someone helpless? Feel powerful? Or an outlet for fury? What's it like? Suppose they'd actually left you in here to beat me to a pulp, would you have done it? And enjoyed it?"

Both men stayed silent, heads bowed, aghast and squirming at their intimate tangle. They looked up sharply when he spoke again.

"You know, we could change things around. Where are the cuff keys?"

Price, the smaller of the two, spoke quickly, hopefully. "Front of my belt, the little one."

"Got it. Ok, here's the deal. I unhook you. You stand in your proper positions and I'll keep your hardware behind me on the chair."

Their expressions of relief were quickly dashed when Price said, "But they're watching us, behind the mirror."

"Oh," said Nic resignedly, "Are you sure? Don't you think they'd have come rushing in? Well, Ok, then stay as you are."

"NO!" both men hissed at once, their whispers loud and urgent.

"All right." Nic took the key from Price's belt, staying carefully out of head-butt range. He unlocked one shackle, put the key on the floor and stepped back as the two frantically freed themselves, put the cuffs away and resumed their sentry positions. Both were trying to slow their breathing, their relief palpable. Nic gathered up the ejected shells and put them on his chair with the two M9's. He sat awkwardly but silent, letting the two process their predicament, but then the door clicked open cautiously.

Anastasia's head appeared, her face transformed with a bemused smile.

"Who's outside?" Snelling asked her, his tone grating.

"Only me. There's a huge flap upstairs. Boss is going nuts."

"I mean, did you see, through the mirror?"

"Nothing, relax. I saw nothing." Her lie was betrayed by a giggle. "Prisoner giving you any trouble, soldier?"

"No, ma'am," Price said quickly, "None at all."

"Model prisoner," Nic added with a grin, his eyes widening as she stepped inside. She wore a knee-length turquoise skirt, her legs shaved, a regular bra just visible under a flowery blouse seductively unbuttoned. "Going somewhere?" he asked mildly.

Leaving the door open, backing into shadow, she pointed to herself and made mirror letters with her hands: W-A-R-S-A-W.

He made no attempt to hide his astonishment, considering all the implications, his mind overloaded. "Any trouble for you?" he asked.

"Not yet, far as I know. Nic, can't you give them this Biggall fellow, whatever?"

"Nope."

"It's the only way, otherwise—"

"I know, sweets. Can't be helped."

A distant door slammed and commotion followed outside. Anastasia was pulled back from the doorway and Uren's flustered face appeared, glaring at the nearest guard. "Why the fuck did you let her in?"

"We didn't, sir. We can't. She just opened the door."

"What did she say to him?"

"Er, not much, sir. She asked him to give up Al or someone, and he said No."

"Damn! That better be all…Ok." Turning his back to the room he spoke to Anastasia outside. "Igor's on his way, he'll take you to the airport."

They heard her protest, "But, boss, I was—"

"No! We have to go over your car. Call me when you get to—destination. Check your email and phone whenever you can. Go."

"Can I give him a KGB?"

"*What?!*"

"A kiss goodbye, boss."

"Fuck No! Scram!"

Her face reappeared for a second, fingers touched to lips, returning his smile with a wan attempt of her own before she was pushed roughly away. Uren turned and spoke to the room in general, not meeting Nic's eyes, his voice cold. "Take him over to the airfield. There's a Grumman jet on its way. 15 minutes."

"Where am I going?" Nic asked mildly.

"None o' your business. They took you out of my hands. Can't say you didn't ask for it. God help you, that's all. You are completely screwed, feller, and you *will* talk." He read from a clipboard, tearing off the sheet. "Ok. The Registration is NG2587. Get his jacket and toothbrush 'n' stuff from the front desk. Here's his passport. Put him on board, see the door close and watch the take-off. That's it. Any trouble in here?"

Both men shook their heads woodenly.

"Don't you want someone to go in the plane with him?" Price asked hopefully.

"Not necessary. I would have gone but they need me here. Anyway, he can't go anywhere else at 40,000 feet. He'll be met at the other end."

Uren turned abruptly and left. Nic stood as the guards nodded to each other and moved quickly, one beckoning him toward the door, the other hastily scooping their hardware from the chair. In turn they peered outside, grimly holstered their weapons, pocketed the shells and formed casual escorts down the corridor, making no attempt to touch him. After collecting his few belongings, they went out to a black van and drove south through the complex. Waved through the airfield gates, they waited below the control tower and a few minutes later a long, sleek twin-jet came in over the threshold, touched down and distantly back-tracked towards them, its engines a low scream. The two guards walked him to the aircraft as the steps came down. Price handed him his small bundle in a plastic bag with his passport on top, shouting over the jet noise. "Thanks, pal. Point taken."

"Yeah, thanks," Snelling yelled, "Have a good journey."

Nic went up two steps, put down the bag, turned, put his hands together and called out, "*Namaste*, gentlemen."

Price looked puzzled, waving at the air, stepping closer. "What? What's that mean?"

Nic cupped his hands to shout an answer, "Look it up. See ya, boys."

CHAPTER 13

Nothing is more terrifying than fearlessness.

Cornelia Funke

With polite hisses, the steps folded in and the door shut. Nic sat alone in a tight but luxurious 18-seat cabin, engulfed in a fine champagne leather armchair. Keeping his thoughts strictly in the moment, even though his mind kept trying to speculate on the future, he found a wry amusement from the interaction with the guards and Anastasia's sassiness with Uren, overlaid with the warm memory of being with her.

The cockpit door opened briefly and shut again while the engine noise increased ominously. Nic glanced out of the port side window to see the two guards getting into the van but before the aircraft could move another car appeared, moving fast to block their way. The engines subsided, the cockpit door opened and a white-shirted officer emerged to re-open the access door and unfold the ramp. A bullet head appeared at the top of the steps and spoke briefly to the pilot, who nodded and vanished again.

Frank Uren waded into the narrow cabin while the engines murmured down into silence. As if trying to pierce darkness, his eyes bored into Nic's as he moved his bulk sideways and lowered himself into the opposite seat.

Nic watched him impassively. "Heart holding up?" he enquired, seeming genuinely concerned.

Uren had to check a hand's instinctive movement towards his chest. "None o' your business. Listen, change of plan, we've got a few minutes to talk. Could save your ass."

"And yours, presumably? Why all these seats anyway, who's coming?"

"Only one we could get at short notice. $4000 bucks an hour. As it happens, there's been a change of destination so we need its greater range, unless--" He clenched in frustration. "I was going to come with you but they stood me down."

"Oh, what a shame! You were saying, unless…?"

"Yeah…Look, you gimme this Biggall guy or tell me how he knows about the Prist, you get to go home and no more hassle. First they wanted you in DC for questioning but now they want you in -- somewhere else."

"What for?"

"Questioning. Different kind. Guaranteed results. So, spill the beans and save yourself the—I was going to say trouble, but I won't bother. Just save yourself. They don't come back from Egypt, especially if they go on to Djibouti or Diego Garcia. End of the line, get me?"

Nic nodded. "Got it," he said equably.

"So spill it, why don't you? Gimme this source and you're off the hook, free and clear."

"I can't, sorry."

"Why the hell not? You can't be more afraid of him than what'll happen in Egypt."

"Well, I don't know him. Did you look in the phone book?"

"Ah, fuck off!"

"Well, I don't know what he looks like, where to find him, nothing. Didn't you ask around?"

"Shit, yes, but we found no-one else with anything to tell us. There's only you, far as we know."

"Hm. In that case terminating me isn't going to do you much good."

"Listen, asshole, termination's the least of your worries. You know what they'll do to you first? I've seen it. It's a freakin' nightmare, still haunts me. You think there's really any rules in this business, huh? Not even the President can save you once you're out of US airspace—why the hell are you holding out?"

Nic sighed theatrically. "I'm not. I don't have anything else to tell you, except that conscious perception is changing all over the globe, in case you haven't noticed. People are beginning to understand that our elected leaders are not the ones in charge, they're only there with the sanction of a bunch of anonymous power-mongers whose days are numbered by this new consciousness."

"Caused by some fucking chemical reaction spread all over by jet engines, right?"

Nic nodded with heavy emphasis, a grave finality.

"And it can't be stopped? 'Less we ground all the flights?"

"I suppose. But it's too late for that. Everyone's had a good whiff by now. How are you feeling?" Nic managed a salty grin knowing he was risking a wild backhander.

Uren stared back in silence, his brow ferocious, knuckles clenching on the arm-rests. Another car was heard approaching the stairway, squealing. Doors slammed, there were light steps and a bag slid in, followed by an anxious face. Anastasia.

Uren cranked his bull neck to face her, stood up in the narrow cabin and backed squeezingly into the crew-relief cubicle. "Ok, Nasta, so ya didn't get First Class, ya got one better, all the way to Europe. Guess I saved the gumment a fare. Better polish your Polish, heh. You got about twelve hours to get this fucker to talk. If you can't, they'll rinse it out of him, get me? Come here a minute." Uren took her roughly by the arm towards the back of the long cabin, out of Nic's hearing. One of the pilots peered round the cockpit door, his expression questioning, followed by a nod and retreat. The engines began to spool up again as Uren strode forward.

Barely pausing by Nic's seat, he said "I was going to say good luck, but it looks like you're fresh out of it. Adios, sucker." He paused in the doorway, turned and shook his head. "I wanna know something: Why the hell aren't you scared shitless?"

Nic shrugged and smiled back. "What's the point? It's alright so far."

"Yeah, well, enjoy the Pyramids." Uren shot him a disgusted look, turned, ducked in the doorway, staggered, tripped and tumbled down the steps. Nic and Anastasia both moved to go to him but the co-pilot emerged at that moment and motioned them to their seats as he turned to close the hatch. They leaned across and stared out of the port window to see Uren sitting on the tarmac, disheveled and clutching his chest. The drivers of both vehicles ran to help him but by the time they'd wrestled him into a rear seat, his body had gone inert.

Nic put his arm around her shoulders. "Looks like Adios to me. Hey, does anyone else know where you are?"

She looked back in strained amazement and shook her head. "Only Igor, as far as I know. But Uren says he's toast, he's sending him back to Moscow. He would've been with us on this flight but they couldn't get hold of him in time. Phone didn't answer, which was the last straw. I left him a message. One word. Heaven's, what if the boss actually croaks?" She chuckled nervously. "The implications, my God, I—"

She was interrupted as the Gulfstream began to move and a disembodied voice spoke suavely. "Good afternoon, folks. This is Captain Pistoff speaking. Real name's Piston but I'm supposed to be in Barbados for the week so thanks a lot. We could do it in one but we'd be over our legal hours' duty time and they couldn't find a relief pilot. We couldn't even get the usual lovely and succulent flight attendant, so you're on your own back there, have to help yourselves to the goodies. Man, I told them we couldn't get outta here with this much fuel unless they let us take off to the West, which they don't *ever* do regardless of wind conditions, so you must be mighty important. Lucky too we gotta westerly wind at 20 knots, so we should make it out, huh, guess you'll know if we don't! Anyway, we'll put down for our break in the Azores. There's a full bar in the galley, snacks if you need 'em, dinner whenever you want it, push the call button if you need anything else. We got hundreds of movies and a million tracks and after climb-out there should be no turbulence since we should be over any thunder at 51,000 feet. If you wanna sleep there's benches aft, pillows and blankets in the lockers. Buckle up and enjoy the flight, folks."

Nic shook his head, grinned and sat down. Catching Anastasia's hand, he spun her so she collapsed on his lap. She tried to fasten the seat belt around them both but couldn't make it reach. He pulled her head into his neck and murmured, "Let it go. What was the word you said to Igor?"

"Same one he sent to you, in Russian."

"Hm… Hope he doesn't die of thirst in the desert."

Rose opened her door to the bell and stood back startled. "Igor, *Lyubimy*, have you seen a ghost, Holy or otherwise?"

"*Niet*, but I heard it. Do you have any vodka?"

"Of course. This early? Come in, sit down, unload. Tell Rosie what's the matter." She went quickly to the sideboard and poured him a stiff one. "Ice?"

"No matter. Look." He produced his new passport, opened and flicked the pages. "I am now a Mexican National, but there's no visa, so I am not legal here. So I cannot leave."

"So stay, why don't you? Let me see it."

Igor shook his head distantly and put the passport away. Haltingly he explained his predicament, how the likelihood of being sent back to Moscow guaranteed end of life in Siberia, with no hope of helping his three most beloveds. The sympathy in her eyes encouraged him to tell the whole story, how he had faked the deaths of his mother, sister and her child and escaped to the West, almost frozen solid in a crate designed for a Kamchatka bear.

Wide-eyed, Rose listened and finally giggled. "Did you end up in a zoo, then?"

"Al*most*! Fortunately I could still talk. But now they are going to send me back, so I must leave immediately."

Rose paled visibly. "Where to? And how?"

"It cannot be regular, they would pick me up for sure. Besides, I have limited money."

"Relax, my dear. I have scads of it. I'll smuggle you into Mexico, I have a place there, did I tell you?"

Igor shook his head forcefully. "No, sweet lady, I cannot permit it. If you were caught—"

Rose thumped the table and yelled in his face. "*Mon cul, c'est du poulet?!*"

Igor sat back, startled by her ferocity. "What did you say? Is French?"

"Yes! It's very, very insulting. It says, 'Do you think my ass is that of a chicken?'"

"No. I don't get this."

"The implication is oh-so French and subtle, that you are a chicken-fucker and I resent that, Ok?"

He shook his head, trying to understand. "Dear Rose, I am so sorry, but they told me you have a record and an offense like this would—never mind, listen, I have another way to go, but I must not speak of it. I just hope that we can meet again in another country....Did you say you have a place in Mexico?"

"Right on the beach, baby, in Cosumel. I have another in Buenos Aires, another in Byron Bay, that's in Australia, one in Bali. There may be others, I forget. Here—" She scribbled quickly on a pad. "Memorize this for Yucatan. How soon can you get there?"

Igor gulped. "Two days. But—"

"I know. Money." She turned to pull a book from the dresser, opened it to reveal a stuffed hollow and scooped out a wad of notes. "Should be about ten grand, give or take. Open an account when you get there so I can reload it and get you a credit card. Is that all now? When must you go?"

Reeling, Igor tried to gather his wits. "Right away, I have a very long drive. But *Querida*, I cannot take your money."

"I insist. Please remember that you are doing this for me, for my delight, Ok? And I will never use it to control you, and you will never owe me. Is that clear, please?"

Igor sat with his hand to his forehead. "I am in disbelief....I have no words at the moment. I already thought you could not be real, but this....I will find a way to—" He stood up decisively. "But first, identity. Where is your fuse-box?"

"There, by the fridge. Why?"

"And some wire. I need it to become without whereabouts. But I don't want you to watch."

Rose shook her head, her stance stubborn. "There's wire in the garage, I'll get it."

Opening the breaker box he added, "And a screwdriver, please. Slot, not Phillips."

When she returned, Igor had his jacket and shirt off, causing her brows to arch in puzzled amusement.

"And scissors, please." Igor cut two feet off the coil of wire and stripped the ends. Opening the fuse box and unscrewing the faceplate, he carefully screwed one pair of ends into the two positives in the fuse-box. With the other ends, he held one against the back of his arm and the other by its insulation in his teeth, which accented his grimace as he thrust the stripped end into the opposite side of his biceps. There was a loud flash and his body convulsed, almost dropping him to the floor. Rose screamed and clutched at him as he recovered and unscrewed the wires from the box, to a whiff of burnt flesh. He sat down heavily and reached for his shirt, while Rose simply stared at him open-mouthed.

"What the HELL was that about? Were you trying to kill yourself? I thought you never miss!"

"In a sense I did, I mean I kill myself," he said hoarsely. "You could say re-invention, using 220 volts like in Europe. I wanted to make sure, since my implant might have been designed to withstand 110. My name is now Narciso Valenzuela. *Como estas?*"

Rose tried to steady herself and sat down instead. "And how-do-you-do to you too."

"*Bueno, gracias.* Do you think Narcissism is worse than Egotism?"

She giggled, "Probably—but I think I love it! So you already speak Spanish?"

"*Si. Desde muchos meses.*"

"You really are the man with a plan. *Excellente.* Are you hungry, *mi* Narciso?"

"I am now—but more hungry for you and I may not have much time. They will quickly know that Igor has ceased transmission."

"*Dejeuner en boudoir*, then. I'll bring it up. Go shower. I'm feeling deliciously promiscuous. Two different lovers in one day. Hasn't happened since Woodstock. Do you need some burn ointment?"

"Not yet. Maybe later."

"Very funny."

"Aren't you too young to have been at Woodstock?"

"I was nearly fourteen. You got a problem with that?"

CHAPTER 14

"The man who believes that the secrets of the world are forever hidden lives in mystery and fear....But that man who sets himself the task of singling out the thread of order from the tapestry will by the decision alone have taken charge of the world and it is only by such taking charge that he will effect a way to dictate the terms of his own fate."

Cormac McCarthy

Elena Knyazeva sat bemused in a window-seat of the Tupolev 334, neatly dressed in jeans and a flowery blouse, her light brown hair swept back to a ballerina twist. Not only had she only flown once before but her new executive status was confusing. Apart from her own scant luggage, she'd been given charge of several packing cases of literature and display items for the upcoming trade show, and the confidence they had placed in her was still toying with her head. Kozlodoyev, her boss, had fortunately not changed his sour demeanor so she wasn't too concerned that he might have romantic or lustful motives. He'd remained brisk and business-like as he handed her an office credit card and several hundred euros for expenses. Looking around the cabin, she felt her own excitement must be palpable to other passengers especially when a well-fed *muzhik* in civilian clothes sat next to her with a too-friendly greeting. She made an effort to pull in her energy when assailed with stale cigarette and alcohol fumes and, sharply aware of her questionable status, she fished in her purse for her wedding ring and slipped it on. The gesture didn't go unnoticed, though Russian language doesn't distinguish between Miss and Mrs.

"Greetings, *dyevushka*, I am Sergei. So many married women are disappointed, and so they become targets," he said easily. "Is that so in your case?"

Elena looked back at him, wide-eyed with surprise, anger rising, her mouth open but wordless. She took a little while to gather herself for a reply.

"Targets?" she questioned flatly.

The man grinned at her shamelessly but was met with puzzling silence. Elena kept her face expressionless, her gaze fixed on his eyes, unwavering even when his grin broadened to cover his disquiet.

"Beautiful women are targets of desire. It's just nature. You would prefer to be ugly and undesirable?"

She was suddenly mindful of the lessons of the last few days and decided to quell the urge to humiliate. "If you were to respect me and not simply see me as a target, you might learn a great secret. If not, then I would ask you to sit somewhere else, so I do not have to move."

"The seating is assigned. Your accent is from Moscow, *nye tak li?*"

"My wish is to be quiet and enjoy my own company." Her voice softened slightly. "Your compliment was sly but real, so thank you. And you are very handsome, but I detect the aromas of a long, hard night. So, let us be strangers again, please."

Attempting finality, she turned to the window as the aircraft lurched in the push-back from the ramp. As excitement spread through her she glanced around to see people still standing and settling hand-luggage. She saw many faces jaded with air-travel and no longer interested. Her neighbor pulled papers from a briefcase and appeared to be studying them, but his next move gave her a jolt of pure terror, since she was certain it was deliberate. She had no way to tell whether it was to induce submission to fear or simply a gambit to re-open conversation.

One of the papers was clearly a printout of emails. In the middle of the page Cyrillic letters gave way to English, of which she knew enough to recognize a message beginning "Dear Kolya."

The mix of emotions seemed to tear at her very core, the blush spreading over her neck and head, the fury at not being able to stop it and the wave of fear rocketing up from her midriff. She clasped her hands tightly on her lap and forced her gaze out of the window. A rain-squall obscured her view as the aircraft was turned into it, ending her attempt at nonchalance in the face of certainty that this Sergei was some kind of sinister agent. She closed her eyes and began a frantic prayer, mostly focused on the small boy left tearfully behind for the first time in his life, and her promise to be home in four days. Her last mental picture was of a despondent Ilya holding the arm of his grandmother whose drawn features spoke as always of impending doom and perdition.

Ignoring the seat-belt warning, Anastasia remained standing and watched the take-off through the window above the galley. Recognizing that her thoughts were in ferment, she was trying to step outside them by doing something unpredictable. Facing forward in his seat, Nic watched in treasured amusement, not only at her posture but the entire circumstance. The Gulfstream 5, very light on passenger and payload, used only half the Los Alamos runway and forged out steeply, illicitly, to the West followed by a steep 180° turn. After a short while and some deliberate shaking, she brought her attention back inside and groped to her seat down the steep angle of climb. Though expressionless for several minutes, their eyes met and held quizzically, an indefinable twinkle. All that was needed to break the impasse was Nic's merest grin, causing her to erupt with nervous laughter.

"Did you look in the fridge?" he asked when she quieted, impishly.

"No, why?"

He heaved up and groped to the galley, hunted briefly and returned with two flutes and a 2003 Vintage Roederer. He made an elaborate ceremony of release in quiet reverence, easing the cork with exaggerated restraint, just as the P.A. crackled. The Captain spoke drily, as if sardonic. "Lady and gentleman, we are now in cruise-climb and you are free to move about the cabin."

Nic picked up on the tone immediately. "They must have a camera on us," he said quietly, "Better guard your moves."

Anastasia giggled. "If they're relaying to Uren, we should give him what he wants. Might aid his recovery."

"Could be the best party I've been to all day." He leaned forward and asked, "Do you have your cell-phone with you?"

"Yes. And my tablet."

"Well done. Would you come here a moment?" He patted his lap and she swung across lightly, linking their arms holding glasses. They clinked and kissed with exaggerated ceremony, then Nic spoke quietly in her ear.

"The cockpit door has a keypad. You see how shiny the walls are, must be twenty coats of epoxy? I was thinking we might get a reflection."

"What for?"

"I don't know yet. Well, cheers, old girl. I must say you are looking most fetching."

"*Merci*. How far to the Azores?"

"About 4000 miles, seven, eight hours."

"How in earth shall we pass the time?"

"Eat, drink and be merry, for tomorrow we—"

Instead of a finger, Anastasia pressed her glass against his lips, commanding silence. "Today, *Cariño*, there is only today." She took her first sip, then another, her eyes widening. "Oh my God, *zbawienie!* I know comparisons are invidious, but honestly, I don't think anything finer ever passed my lips….I am completely in awe…Just hold me so I can at least pretend to be real. That today is real. That you are real. And that…" She paused and sipped again.

"Yes, and?"

"And that there really is nothing to fear?"

Nic sipped for himself and nodded slowly. "It remains a choice, as I see it. Fear doesn't arise in Now-ness, only in projection."

His face softened in admiring surprise when she answered carefully, "Hm…And love does the exact opposite?"

Marienbad, Czech Republic

Shadowy figures in a dim, baroque and heavily draped drawing-room. A butler serves from a silver tray, puts a log on the fire and withdraws. One of two bodyguards leans in and closes the huge carved door. The mood is somber as they drink their coffee. Finally a rasping, hesitant, accented voice rumbles from a deep armchair.

"It seems that Langley is panicking... It seems that some of you are doing the same."

A measured, patrician American voice answers. "Let's just say we have reason for concern, Henry. We could be looking at a worst case scenario, forgive the phrase. I was going to say 'by all accounts' but it appears there is only one, and that is unconfirmed because we do not have the source. If the facts hold up, what we are facing is a complete reprogramming of the minds caused by a chemical known as DMT. I'm sure you recall the great surge in the 60's, the hippies, the drugs, the disobedience. It is the nature of surges to wane and we were able to suppress that one. Despite the protests and the ending of the war, Vietnam was an effective diversion. 9/11 was also a great success and shaped the next ten years. Now our nominee for US President is showing signs of going his own way and if it's more than we agreed, well, need I say more? Meanwhile, back to the point."

"How are we to unearth the source of the rumor, which is all it is at the moment?" The voice is English, its upper-class timbre almost exaggerated.

"That is not known, Philip. The link we do have, he refused to clarify beyond a single name which we have not yet located. That link is being flown to Europe as we speak and he will certainly be made to divulge. We had to get him out of the U.S. in case his health suddenly failed and it became public. There's a pernicious document to be released should that happen, very prejudicial, concerning the truth of 9/11. Of course, finding the information source does us no good if the facts hold up. The stuff is supposed to be already in the air and the stats are clear that the perceptions of the general populace are changing. Also, the percentage of opinions that 9/11 was a put-up job is now over 75% and growing, largely because of the Internet. How could you ever have let that toad Silverstein be interviewed, with his ludicrous explanation about Building 7? Our control of the media only goes so far, and censoring the Internet—well, we've gone over that. China can still do it but not for long, in my view. And the people are becoming utterly sick of war. If this new so-called threat has any validity, we will have to come up with a more palatable diversion. A war with Iran or North Korea, well, it's really too soon for that."

The gravelly voice interrupts. "Ach, they'll never get sick of war as long as threats remain viable. Kosovo went away and now with Iraq and Afghanistan winding down, a short breather and they'll be ready for another. As are we, of course. Then we bolster up the Patriot Act and start locking up dissidents, that way the Internet will perform its own censorship, based on fear of reprisal. Anonymity has to be stopped, that's the first thing. I'm told it will be quite easy. Next comes the chip, the ultimate solution."

"Henry, the chip will take years to implement. We're talking about an immediate threat here. Our president does have the power to shut down the Internet if National Security is threatened. What we have to consider is the consequence of ah, persuading him to do just that. Anyone?"

"If he did, David, he'd also have to declare Martial Law, to control the protests. But realistically, we're halfway there, we can lock up anyone indefinitely for subversion. FEMA will have plenty of new prison space. For the rest, any outside threat has 'em begging government to keep 'em safe. But this problem is completely different. It doesn't threaten the sheep, it threatens us, it threatens the Grand Plan, for population reduction, for a controllable world. So, the only question is, how can we stop it?"

One man standing behind the armchair clears his throat pointedly, then speaks with a noticeable Dutch inflexion. "Why has no-one asked this question: if it is in the air and everywhere, why are we not being affected ourselves? And are we not forgetting that Amstel's original concept was to bring order to the world, no matter the cost—was this not a benign philosophy and is there not a benign means to bring it about?'

An extensive murmuring follows the question until a gaunt figure stands, goes to the fireplace and regards the room solemnly. His voice is a drawl. "Sounds to me like you bin inhaling the stuff more'n we have, Willem. I don't ever recall the word benign being used among us. For the greater good, yes, but never benign. Let's just lay it out here. The Internet doesn't matter. There's any amount of stuff out there, against us in one group or another, be it CFR, Trilat Commission,

Bilderberg, the Illuminati. It's all there, writ large, millions of words, much of it true and the list of our uh, diversions is very long. Going back only as far as JFK, then Bobby, then Martin Luther, Cuba, Gulf of Tonkin, to Vietnam, Kosovo, 9/11, Desert Storm and so on.

"The Internet, take a look, it's riddled with conspiracy stories. Latterly it turns out that JFK Junior had been handed a revealing file on his dad's murder. That file went down with his plane and vanished, and no copies, right? Well, that's why his plane went down."

There was a murmuring in the room and two heads nodded knowingly.

"All these thousands of reports, including the ridiculous Warren Commission, that *prove* the public has been lied to, hey, think of Flight 800—they make no difference because Joe Public cannot DO anything, regardless of proof. Literally millions know about the chemical spraying, so what can they do about it? Those with good immune systems will survive, and those who don't, won't. And the next virus will make sure. Literally millions believe that Dubya, Cheney, Rumsfeld, Wolfowitz, Powell, and you, Henry, should be doing life for war crimes, and what can they do about it? And don't forget that anyone searching the conspiracy sites or tweeting them or sharing, goes automatically on our lists for, ah, compromise if necessary. You mentioned that our current link, who's on his way here, right? So he has a CIA memo about the truth of 9/11 which would be revealed in the event of his demise—does that worry y'all? Through the media we can easily discredit it. So let's remember that certain happenings are intended for the general good. Compared to that, a bunch o' lives here and there, they don't just mean nothing, they mean that they paved the way for the Grand Plan, for which many millions are expendable. More the merrier, in fact. And keeping the public afraid enables this Grand Plan, it enabled the Patriot Act so now we control America and will effectively control the world. Look, I'm sorry to preach to the choir, it's just a reminder of principle. So, to return to the reason for this meeting. You're implying that a mental virus is now endemic in the world, borne aloft by millions of jet flights and the minds of men will not be able to be kept fearful—well, I say, You Wanna Bet?"

"George, first we don't need the reminder but this prospect is indeed sinister because it's a worldwide chemtrails type of deal, not strategically localized, which we did not initiate and therefore do not control. Now, how can this possibly have come about without our knowing about it? Anybody?"

"More to the point, gentlemen, how do we get it stopped?"

After a long silence, a mild voice ventures, "It would appear the damage is already done. Perhaps we need to find a way to work with it. We come through on the side of public opinion, or appear to. Stop the GMO's for one thing. You gave them free rein and look what happened."

"What are you saying, Sir Ian? It was a basic business venture which was meant to benefit the whole world, seeds that are impervious to blights and twice as productive!"

"Then why are GMO's banned in Europe and Japan?"

"We're still working on that. They'll come round."

"Oh, rubbish! Don't you keep an eye on the nay-sayers? Your aluminum spraying in Hawaii is killing the crops and the palm trees and rendered the soil too acid to grow crops conventionally. That's irreversible. So you sell them seeds which can thrive in the acid soil and now they've no choice but to buy them from you. The damage, though you doubtless wouldn't call it that, is already done, as a permanence. Now we have an alarming reverse: the minds have apparently all been affected and continue to be, TWENTY-FOUR-SEVEN! You wouldn't listen. The research into selective viruses was so promising, well, it still is, and we all agreed that the world can only thrive with a population of no more than three billion, yet you persist in finding ways to grow enough food for TEN billion. Where the balance point where the earth thrives, the climate is controlled and the population contained to our satisfaction? I always said this was dangerous folly and I never understood your motives. You personally have enough resources to feed the entire world all by yourself!"

The gravelly voice intervenes. "This is no time for acrimony, gentlemen. We are all now perhaps facing a very different threat, an uncontrollable populace, and about which we are still in the dark. I suggest we adjourn until the informant is delivered here."

"Here—no. After one stop in Poland he's being renditioned to Egypt."

"Get it changed. I suggest we at least have a word with him first, agreed?"

With no dissent, all stand to leave the room with one voice adding, "We should get a polygraph in here. And a hypnotist. And a doctor with a truth serum. And his contact from the Ukraine. And a Russian translator. Anything else? When does he arrive?"

"He's due in Warsaw around midday tomorrow. You know, I suggest we go there rather than try to get them all here."

"Good thinking. I suggest you all leave your aircraft here and come with me, so we don't draw any more attention, and perhaps divert it. I have a 737, plenty of seats…Agreed? Very well… So, cars at 8, take-off at 9. Let us set aside our differences, enjoy all the amenities and later a fine dinner. Not vegetarian. Mostly organic. And non-GMO!"

Glazed and still breathing heavily, Igor quickly dressed and wrenched himself away. He was running out to his car when Rose called from the upstairs window.

"Narciso, wait!"

Confused, he ran back to the door just as she ran down and opened it, wrapped in a crumpled bed-sheet.

She asked, "One question, *cariño*: How far to go in that heap?"

"Five hundred kloms. Why?"

"Can't they find it easily? And what if it doesn't make it?"

"What choice do I have?"

"Take it to the covered car-park by the Round House. Walk to the Kaune's food market across the Paseo. I'll meet you there."

"But—"

"Go, quick!"

Igor shrugged and ran, watching his rear-view mirror all the way into town. Outside the legislature car-park, he spotted a young Hispanic man in a woolen skull-cap slouching towards the Plaza, clearly dispirited. He lowered his window and called out.

"Hey, you want to make some *dinero*? You have driver license?"

The man looked up eagerly. "Sure."

"Three hundred bucks. Drive this car to Taos, leave it by the bridge. Leave it open and the keys under the visor. Do not tell anyone. Can you swear to that?"

"Damn right. You go to fakin' a suicide, *señor*? Dodgin' cops? Alimony?"

"You got it. No prints, so wear these gloves, the whole time. And you say nothing, *nothing*, not to anyone, Ok? Show me your license."

The man slid it out of a battered wallet and Igor pretended to note his name. "So, we good? You go right now?"

"Whatever you say, boss. How do I get back?" The man snatched at the proffered notes.

"You take fucking bus. But you tell anyone, I will come suddenly back to life and yours will not be worth a *peso*, got it? Keep quiet and you need not worry."

The man spread his arms, signaling dereliction, laughing. "Me, worry?"

Half an hour later, Rose swung into the lot driving a shiny new Nissan, startling him with a short horn-blip.

"What's this?" he asked, getting in quickly. "Is not your car."

"It's a rental. One way, right? Ok, *camarado*, which way?"

He stared at her, bemused. "South to Albuquerque, then West, I-40."

"*Bueno, vamonos.* Not going South?"

"*Cariño*, I wasn't to tell you, remember? If you don't know, they can't incriminate."

"*Ay, cojones!* I'm coming with you. But surely South, it's only 300 miles to Mexico."

"It is, but that is border crossing, I cannot go that way, they will be looking for me. Anyway, it is my turn to make surprise."

Rose bounced her seat as they headed up Old Pecos Trail towards the freeway. "I just *love* surprises, Narciso. In you I think I have found a treasure."

He put his hand gently on her knee. "Hm….Findings keepings, isn't that what you say?"

"Close enough, *mi* Narciso."

"And you have a word for reciprocation, I think...Yes, it is 'Backatcha'!"

She chuckled, "It's a deal. It sounds kinda Russian. So, where are we headed?"

"West, I said. Many hours. No luggage. I call you Rosita, *es mas romantico, no? Tienes pasaporte?*"

"*Si, siempre. Qué aventura, mi caballero misterioso!*"

Trying to quell panic, Elena couldn't decide whether to confront her neighbor or pretend not to have seen his blatant display. She wasn't entirely certain that she was meant to see the photocopy with the name 'Kolya', but quickly realized that it didn't matter, that the man had somehow been assigned to shadow her. She stared out of her window with a feeling of mounting outrage, distracted from the excitement of only her second flight, and her first in many years. The implications were at first quite baffling, but gradually she calmed herself and in her innocence felt her spirit returning. She even suppressed a chuckle, watching the rain streaks angle back as the aircraft accelerated and the runway began to blur beneath. As with all new fliers, she felt disbelief and astonishment as the trundling stopped and the earth fell away. Within moments they were enveloped in cloud and with nothing more to see, she turned to her left and spoke quietly.

"When I booked my seat, yours was already taken. How did you—?"

He flicked his fingers for interruption, looked at her and smiled confidently. "That person cancelled at the last minute."

"And are you staying in Warsaw?"

"Of course. My room is next to yours."

All doubts removed, she asked boldly, "So what is your brief?"

"Ah, it is to make sure you are safe and comfortable and all your desires are met, *Skolko dousha ugodno.*"

"All the desires of my soul, indeed? And you were also ordered to give yourself away like that, with the paper?"

He looked at her slyly. "Of course not. But a clever young lady like you would surely have guessed, so I thought it better to be clear from the start. I would not like to look in the eyes of a beautiful woman with a lie in my heart—and she would understand that, for her, much depends on the favor of my report. So we should get along very well. The *organy* do not care how I do my work, only that I do it. I am very good at my job." His confident grin left no doubt about his line of thought.

Her voice deliberately gentle, Elena said, "Surely a man of such great honesty would not enjoy the fruits of coercion?" While speaking, she put a hand on his arm and looked directly at him. "There could be no joy in it, only cruelty."

His gaze faltered, flicked away and then slowly came back. It alternated between her eyes and the small hand on his arm and in those moments Elena was reminded once more of her discovery. He was about to put his hand on hers when she deftly removed it.

"I have a great secret," she said softly, "But I will only tell it to a perfect gentleman."

She could see that Sergei was rummaging for an answer or perhaps trying to deduce how he'd been outmaneuvered. The cabin suddenly filled with sunlight as they emerged above the cumulus, timed perfectly with her own clarity and conviction.

CHAPTER 15

"Pain or love or danger makes you real again."

Jack Kerouac.

When the G550 reached cruising height, the co-pilot emerged from the cockpit for refreshments He was handsome, jovial and seeming oblivious to any sinister mission. He poured two cups of coffee and told them to help themselves from the well-stocked galley. Anastasia thanked him distractedly, making a show of storing a text but actually filming the oblique reflection on the shiny passage wall when he re-opened the cockpit door by keypad. She couldn't tell yet if it was readable in reverse.

Watching each other in subdued amazement, along with the champagne, Nic and Anastasia savored vichyssoise, caviar, duck paté, fresh salad, smoked salmon, pumpernickel, gorgonzola, raspberries, French vanilla ice cream, Kona coffee and even a 1978 Armagnac. Groaning after this joyous feast, Anastasia felt so relaxed she was ready for a nap. For Nic it had the opposite effect, enlivening; he asked for pen and paper but instead she handed him her tablet, clicked on the Word processor and retreated tipsily to one of the aft banquettes.

In brightest sunlight, far above stray puffs of cloud, they sped across the Southern plains at 51,000 feet, at least 10,000 higher than all the commercial jet routes and far above any threat of turbulent weather. Nic felt an urgent need to clarify his thoughts and get them down before distraction, typing rapidly.

"Amid the swirling of ideas and possibilities, a picture is trying to fix itself, right now, like a screen-saver. We're being flown half across the globe in the most luxurious form of transport imaginable, on my way to face the basest and most painful experience yet invented by man and back there dozing on a banquette lies the most exquisite creature was ever put breath

into, and the whole process of being simply Now, Here, Where I am has given rise to a range of mischief that I never could have imagined in the regular day-today paradigm of 'What now?' If Uren was here, this mischief would sky-rocket. But I have no mischief for Anastasia...

"If only we could see everyday happenings as being an amazing adventure, how then would we be? What could we not achieve? How could we even contain our delight without blowing a gasket?!

"Man's inventiveness and energy for exploration is limitless, relentless, incessant. Imagine being released into a modern apartment or a nice suburban house, with a loving partner, new cars, money, favored possessions, comfort, books, music, TV, movies, tropical vacations, concerts, fitness, dance, yoga, kindness, openness—suddenly, after spending 20 years in a soul-less, freezing, forced labor camp...But then, after a while, this bourgeois luxury gradually becomes the norm and the exploratory nature reasserts itself. The gratitude, elation and amazement start to fall away and little dissatisfactions intrude...We didn't really want comfort, we wanted adventure...

"I look back and across the aisle and notice that Anastasia's mouth, habitually down-turned when awake, has softened in sleep to a straighter line and there is even a suspicion of upturn in one corner. She is remarkable in her cleverness, her strength of mind, her passion for life, and now her ability to play two opposing parts at once. No-one can explain the mystery of what touches us deeply, viscerally—it just happens. We respond if we are ready, and sometimes that response is quite unwelcome...I wonder what Igor is doing now? And little Elena from Ukraine, wasn't she being sent off to Poland? I'm assuming that's why Annie is on this flight... I just thank The All (All-ah!) that Uren isn't with us, talk about a blessing, I wonder if he survived the heart attack....

Seething some nine miles below is more beauty and misery than any one million lifetimes could hope to experience, the world of duality that we came here to explore. And I have a strong feeling, perhaps projected or fueled by desire, that the essence of womankind, if uncontaminated by ambition, rage or envy, encapsulates divinity in its very nature, and so few women are aware of it. And the ones that grasp it, who shine like lonely beacons, must live in a torment of frustration that they cannot make their men, and other women too, see the limitless in loving possibility. Or maybe good champagne *tends my thinking to idealism. I'll ask Annie when she wakes…*

Has she wondered about my hesitation to consummate (Eeuuw, that word!), instead of being the eager, typical, single-minded, lusty male penetrator? It's so easy to interpret desire as love only to find it was nothing close. Is then love without desire a different kind of love, a purity without self-interest, like my love for my son? Does this then mean that raw desire emanates purely from self-interest, which is why it produces only guilt or regret? I have come to feel that the act is something so precious and sacred that, if not approached as such, it actually separates the participants. Total intimacy cannot happen without total trust, which requires much interaction over time, otherwise the act actually separates the pair—the sheer intensity as climax approaches, compels each within self and so there follows a feeling of loss—why else would they call it Le Petit Mort? In my experience, this 'Little Death' is just that, if it follows an un-loving, un-sacred act, the kind that makes you wish that one of you just wasn't there anymore, when the backs are turned to each other, seeking oblivion or denial. That's too sad for me— I want laughter, tenderness and gratitude, and renewal of faith in exquisite ideals…Life's too short for cheap bubbly, Ho Vintage or nothing….!

"She hasn't really asked me yet for my rationale for holding out against Uren and all the sinister powers on up the ladder behind him. Well, it arrived like one of those gifts that come to a scribbler, the kind that floats in like a blessing when the focus on the story is intense enough to side-line the pen-servant. Thus if I am just pure energy and thoughts too are energy, the power of their intensity takes over and seems to render the thinker irrelevant. This is, mercifully, how we can happily disappear during the act of putting thoughts to paper. Sometimes an idea wakes you at some ungodly hour (as if any hour was ever ungodly!) and you drag yourself from cocooned warmth like a servant, to sit and scrawl in acute discomfort without complaint, to emerge hours later, spent and mystified but somehow deeply satisfied to have been removed and self-forgotten—then to realize this self-forgetting is bliss and there is even dismay at returning to self again…

"So…I do not know where this current gift is taking me but I feel I have to be its servant to discover its purpose. Look what it's done so far: It has found me an exceptional and lovely woman whose life is changing minute by minute as she emerges from years of angst and venom, while the

PBTT seem to be in a royal tizzy with something they can't control and therefore must consider a serious threat—which might disappear for a while if I let the gift go and settle for safety and comfort. Then there was a very fine lunch and free trip to Europe and unknown possibilities for mischief.... Now I'm sleepy too..."

Leaving the tablet on the pull-out table, Nic stood up, banged his head, stooped and edged himself aft, then gathered blanket and pillow and settled himself on the opposite banquette. His last glimpse found Anastasia flickering a smile still in her dreams, her face only inches away across the narrow aisle. The sheer improbability of their situation scrambled his thoughts and he made a ferocious effort to repel speculation. Sleep descended like a featherdown the moment he found amusement and then gratitude.

An hour later, Anastasia awoke needing the bathroom and when she emerged and went forward, she saw the tablet lying on the table. Still sleepy, the blanket round her shoulders, she clicked it back to life, sat and read with reluctant wakefulness as a powerful feeling of connection swept over her. She looked up and outside from time to time as if attempting to grasp the reality amidst the unreality. As she finished reading, her own hand seemed to reach for the keys with none of her own volition.

"I have deep suspicion that yr restraint is just cunning device to accelerate my trust in you. Interesting that when woman insists on delay, she's seen to play coquette or hard-to-get. And now I am snagged up in your bland and ridiculous confidence while I know that it's insane. They are taking you somewhere to be brutalized and tortured for your knowledge and you refused the offered escape route—and from what you have written, you don't even know why you are doing it—only that you are compelled, like the cat dead from curiosity. I could cynically and cruelly watch from the sidelines as they mangle and dismember you were it not for my totally selfish desire to have you with all your members intact! You seem not afraid for you but I am terrified, and yet I am swept into levity by your absurd and frankly unproven conviction that all is well. In similar vein, maybe I should just kiss you while I can and wonder what's for dinner...

"As for my response to you, it has simply been spontaneous, artless, without strategy, I think because I saw no prurience in your eyes and you

didn't lock onto my tits like everyone else, and now I'm feeling strangely, delightedly, consummated by corresponding with you. It's intriguing, is it not, to be corresponding with another who is sleeping just a few feet away, while his spirit wanders in realms unknown? I just hope it can get back into this preposterous tube (what do these things cost, anyway?) doing more than 500 miles per hour—oh, I get it, the earth is turning the same way also at 500 mph so, cosmically speaking, we are doing 1000 miles per hour! And going the other way, Westward Ho, we'd be zero and the sun would never set. With continuous mid-air refueling, we might never age! Einstein would have something to say about that. What say you, Sir Moncrieffe?

"And my longing and intention is to use, no, to BE the sacred ritual, to get lost in you, not in myself and separated. Have you noticed that when you get lost in delight, you are literally lost and cannot even observe being delighted, only in retrospect. I suspect happy memories best implant themselves from times when we are lost in Now…I am so grateful to be here and now, and willing myself to be not afraid…xxx…

PS. I have been sent to Poland to ah, 'interview' little Miss Elena. I am to beat the codes out of her and/or to find out the secret you are supposed to be imparting to her. If I find out you have told her before telling me, you are nostril-deep in doodoo. I'm going back to bed because I have no-one to harass…Oh, but wait…"

Delighted suddenly with a cheeky notion, Anastasia pushed the call button on the side panel. A man's voice answered immediately.

"Cockpit here, can I help?"

"Can we go online up here?"

"Yes, ma'am. Good afternoon, the name's Dirk. I'll bring you the router code."

The door opened and the co-pilot emerged, clawing awkwardly over the center console with the Wi-Fi code in a plastic folder. "No need to use up battery, you can plug in on the panel."

"Thank you," she said, plugging in the tablet, "We had a very fine lunch. Can I fix you guys anything?"

He inclined his head while making an obvious effort to unglue his eyes from her cleavage. "Damn, that's very gracious. We're not supposed to touch the passengers' food—unless it's offered. We do have our sandwiches. Are you and the gentleman—?"

"Pre-packed and tasteless, I bet. I'll fix you a couple of nice plates. No booze, I assume?"

"No ma'am. Are you and the gentleman—?"

"He's having an erotic dream so we won't wake him. Aren't there any private rooms on this thing?"

Dirk grinned saltily, his teeth an impossibly white, inviting phalanx. "Can't help you there, sorry. There is one in our fleet, a 727 with a huge circular bed. But they don't do nine mile high like this baby."

"That must be so-o disappointing," she smiled with raw sarcasm. "*Altitudo reservatus.*"

In the face of perceived erudition, he retreated to his all-male enclave. Anastasia busied herself putting in the Wi-Fi code and then making up exquisite platters and didn't notice when Nic rose from the aft section, used the washroom and returned to the forward seat. When she saw him he was already reading her written contribution. She eyed him jauntily and asked him to push the call button. Quizzically he did so and watched her take the two plates forward as the cockpit door opened. She edged herself inside as it swung shut again.

Seeing the tablet alight, he hesitated and then logged in to his email server. There amidst the junk was a message from Irina in London.

"*Kolya, our Lena is in trouble. A Russian man next to her on the plane to Warsaw, first he has been sent to sleuth on her and second, he is trying to leverage this position to make intrusion into her undergarments. His room is even next to hers at the Meridien. That's the gist—I needn't translate. I'm in Gatwick airport waiting for my flight. Irina to the rescue! Where the hell are you, shining knight? Later. Ciao. Irina.*"

The captain had clearly been dozing when Anastasia chirped a good afternoon and held a plate between him and the yoke. He came to in some confusion, looking very stern.

"Ma'am, you're not supposed to be up here, we have strict orders. Dirk, did you let—?"

"Oh, shush," she said with her brightest smile, again conscious of its feeling, a new habit. "No-one will know. I just hate to think of you missing Barbados. In fact, why don't you just stick it on George, come back and eat in comfort. Then you could watch a movie with us. After all, you've got nothing to do up here."

With a show of reluctance, he took the plate and a napkin, his expression an odd mixture of gratitude and resentment. Anastasia surveyed the outside scene in awe, exclaiming, "Oh my God, what a view you have! Is that the coast up ahead, it must be, where, South Carolina?"

"North. Cape Hatteras," Captain Piston muttered over a mouthful of paté and black bread. "We're not allowed to leave the cockpit unattended."

"Oh pooh, who's to know? And there's no other traffic this high, isn't that right, Dirk?"

"S'right, ma'am, but still, you know, rules."

"Are for fools, burp, burp…But what've you got here, just TV screens, oh look, is that us there on a moving map? Fantastic. I can't believe you get bored. I mean, what a privilege, sitting up here all in charge, Lords of the Universe, safe in your little space-ship, no traffic, no jams, no cops, no speed traps, no smog."

She smiled cheekily at each of them as they ate the gourmet dishes with guilty gusto. "But I guess there is another viewpoint—this is really tightrope-dangerous, completely dependent on the wings staying on, the juice not running out, the engines keepin' churnin', then you have to know where you are and how to get down, all that knowledge and training and expertise, such mystique for everyone else, like you're supermen, which is presumably why you wanted to be pilots in the first place, and the irony—you're bored shitless and wishing you were sitting on a beach drinking rum punches in the tropics—"

Between mouthfuls, Piston muttered sourly, "Dirk, we got something to learn from this here female person of the opposite sex."

"Oh yeah, what's that?"

"How to speak for five minutes without drawing a single breath."

"Careful, Benny, she could be royalty. Or CIA. Or even FAA, sent to test us." He turned back to Anastasia, "Tell us, ma'am, what's going on here? Must be hellish important, frantic scramble, eighteen seats to take two all the way to Europe, bill to the Government about $100,000 I reckon."

She looked at each of them in turn, her finger to her lips. "Hush, hush, gents, it's safer for you not to know...By the way, do you ever see chemtrails—and I don't mean contrails?"

"'Deed we do, ma'am, all over, but unpredictable. Some days nothing, some days right across the sky—ya really see 'em up here, there's a whole slot of flight levels cleared for 'em, on vectors no-one else flies, neither passenger nor freight. Ask questions, forget it. Controllers have nothing to say, just look kinda blank at ya."

"Where do they fly from?"

"We ain't sure. Somewhere in Arizona, I've heard. And maybe Wright-Patterson AFB"

"But is it *true?*"

"Oh, shit yeah, beg pardon, no doubt whatever. But who ya gonna bitch to? I seen a video, some feller took the evidence to Congress and he couldn't find one single Representative with the slightest notion of what he was even talkin' about. And the media won't touch it. I mean, like, whaddya do?"

"So why do you think they're doing it?"

"God knows. Mebbe like ol' bad Billy Boy said, bee-cause they can."

There came a sharp knock on the door. Before anyone could say anything, Anastasia stood from her crouch and opened it.

"Come on in, Nic. It's party time, on Captain Piston's pissed-off airlines."

"Hey, lady—"

"It's Ok, captain, he's harmless, I promise."

"I don't care. He's not supposed to be here. He's in custody, right?" "I'll take your goodies back." She said this with such a bantering tone that Piston barked a laugh and moved his plate out of reach.

With no more space, Nic had to crouch by the open door, leaning in like an eager new-comer. "Wow, nice little office. Do you guys actually have to do anything?"

"Here we go again...Not much," Dirk answered deprecatingly. "We all jes' fire the ol' gal up and tell her where to go. She tells *us* if we're doing anything wrong. She plain refuses to fly into a mountain, won't land with her wheels up, if she gets too slow she yells at us and shakes the stick and even pushes it forward. This here cursor travels over the screens and we just click on whatever we want to see. Tells us we got just over four hours to the Ay-zores, then we get to refuel and take a break."

"Can we go exploring while you do that?" Anastasia enquired eagerly.

"Nope. We got orders on that. `Sides, it'll be night-time. You gotta stay aboard or get cuffed and locked in a cell. It's a Military base. You'll get a local hot meal sent in to you. S'all I can tell ya, sorry."

"Who gave the orders?"

"Gumment, I guess. That guy who came aboard, took a purler down the steps."

"What if he's dead?" Nic asked.

"Nah, he ain't. He's in the hospital gettin' a quad bypass. He was on the horn, checkin' up on ya. Oh yeah, he said to tell ya, point o' no return in two hours' time. Give the word and we can all go home."

"Oh…So we can't even take a shower?"

"Nope. You a Limey?"

"How did you know?"

"Thought so. Well, at least we got Rolls-Royce blowers. Ain't that a comfort, huh?"

"Not sure. They make `em in Germany now."

Marienbad, Czech Republic

Along manicured gardens, box hedges trimmed with ferocious precision, gravel paths delicately raked and even the ponds sparkling orderly ripples, two men walk, their pace set by the elder, a European. He is costly-suited, almost boyish, with a full head of dark brown hair and an expensive tan.

The other is American, mid-thirties, dressed casually with open collar and a blue felt jacket. He is pale and subdued, speaking very quietly with almost puzzled respect. The older man speaks well but with a slight Gallic accent.

"I want to thank you for coming, Jack. I was hoping this would be of interest to you."

"Well, thanks Henri. Sorry I was late and missed the first meeting."

"No matter, young fellow. The point is that you have created a social medium of enormous influence and frankly, for us, influence is the heart of the matter. We have been described as a bunch of, quote, 'Stuffy old men', and a younger perspective is perhaps in order. We have also acquired the image of super-rich, behind-the-scenes manipulators. Doubtless you are aware of that?"

"Well, yeah, I did a lot of research on the way over. There are conflicting views so I guess I'd like to know the truth."

"That you will have to decide for yourself. I would like your opinion about changing of awareness, a shift in perspective if you like. The average Joe, as you'd say, has a viewpoint derived from his circumstances and, naturally, our circumstances are quite different. We all have considerable wealth and therefore can command an overview not available to the majority. We do not make policy but I admit that we do influence it."

The Frenchman stopped and turned, his voice confidential. "You see, between us we own most of the banks and of course, your Federal Reserve. These banks own the corporations, which in turn own the politicians. They own the newspapers, Hollywood, most radio stations and so on, so they essentially dictate not only the news but also how the world sees itself. They do not yet own your social medium, but they do control the State Department, the Pentagon, the NSA, the CIA, the DHS as well as the Supreme Court and numerous other organs. This is irrefutable fact, right?"

"Sure. So in other words you're saying that business and politics, in the States at least, are mutually dependent?" The younger man speaks with a particularly soft voice.

"You might say that, yes."

"But they're all technically dependent on the will of the people?"

The older man snorts, "The people, the masses, have no more vision beyond their current limitations of survival, safety and comfort. Our influence has served to keep it that way, to prevent unrest and preserve the status quo."

"The vision is changing, Henri."

"Well, I believe it is trying. That's why you're here. We have received some disturbing news and we hope to get to the bottom of it, to see where it is leading. Perhaps as soon as tomorrow."

"Would you care to give me the gist?"

"There appears to be a worldwide influence, apparently unstoppable, which may be expanding the popular vision. It may be outside *our* sphere of influence which is frankly troubling. The world is a tricky place, always a tightrope, if you like, and we don't wish to see it tumble out of control."

"Huh…Henri, when I arrived, you were all dispersing. It's not exactly a slew of happy faces, in fact it was a bit of an off-put. It made me wonder about the general state of the average super-rich. It's hard to see how they'd be elated, or even just content, with mansions, supercars, jets, yachts, access to every conceivable pleasure. These things mostly require hordes of managers and minions, and thus no freedom."

"Some of us believe we have a grander purpose than accumulation and recreation. How is it for you, Jack, now that you yourself command billions?"

"Well, with wealth and influence you are constantly bombarded and ambushed, like by sycophants, sensation-mongers, interviewers, on-the-make chicks and so on, so you have to set barriers. Doing so inevitably creates more curiosity, and us-and-them scenarios. It's not comfortable. You can use the wealth to separate yourself but still you know it's always there, the gap, lurking. Me, I'm happy when I'm busy creating, with minimal or no company. I'm not sure yet about the trappings, it's all a bit new…But looking at you guys scares me."

"So tell me, do you have ambitions to be a man of influence?"

"For a better world? Yeah, of course."

"That is what we want to hear, thank you. Well, I think it's time for a nap. I hope you'll be joining us for dinner?"

"You bet…I must say, you seem to be worried, Henri."

"I tend not to worry, son. We once thought that Television spelled doom, if we didn't control it."

"So? I thought you bought it?"

"Indeed we did, and along with it all the folks who were paid by it. This is more sinister. The hordes of unemployed, who all seem to have computers, now have time and sufficient resentment to wage war by subversion, howling conspiracy accusations. They've even given us a sinister name: Banksters."

"Hm…Can't win `em all, eh?"

"Don't you believe it. If you're on both sides in a war, you can't lose, *n'est-ce pas?*"

The young man looked up aghast. "And that's where I come in, is that it?"

"That's what we're going to find out."

CHAPTER 16

How do we know if it's the real thing? Go within to see it well. No-one reveals how real love feels, real lovers never tell!

From a song: Lust is a Liar.

"Seat-belts please, gentlefolk. We have begun our descent into Lajes airfield, landing in about 15 minutes."

Nic and Anastasia remained seated side-by-side in one of the conference slots, touching hands frequently, engrossed in the end of a movie. She would type on the pad as her thoughts kept straying, though most she erased. Finally she had something she thought cogent, so she paused the movie and invited him to read. It delighted her that he looked interested and not irritated by the interruption.

"P.S. to my last. Of course it's idealism, whether fueled by champagne or no. But my disbelief is willing to be suspended, as it is for watching a boy sharing a lifeboat with a tiger. We do not expect men to suggest that womankind encapsulates divinity—it would have to follow that the recognizer also encapsulates—No? So perhaps you mean the feminine quality in all of us, and there's a mutual honoring of it. I had a thought to ask beforehand, rather than during, if our bodies could remain still for long, very long moments so that we could fully appreciate this sacrosanctity. What say you, Tiger? And what is the mischief to which you refer?"

She slid the tablet over and Nic took it with a grin, tapping quickly. *"Works for me. But before any such maneuver, or cessation of it!, I'd ask your patience while I outline and caress or tenderize every inch of your personal wrapping with my fingertips, not to drive you crazy but to emphasize this devotion and perhaps to help you focus love upon yourself…Writing is so different from speaking, 'cos interpretation of tone is entirely up to the reader—but at least with us it's instant. Imagine such love letters in days of yore, when the mail could take weeks—ah, the patience, the poignancy, the hankering, and finally the over-pent and hasty deed, over in seconds like primates...*

Mischief—I don't know yet, I'm still open. It will surely surprise us both. You know, this written dialogue is a ferocious form of foreplay, I'm just glad you're right there and not taunting with a pseudonym from somewhere hidden on the Web! Back to movie, pls."

Anastasia looked up from reading, her face alight. She took his hand and held it in both of hers, then retrieved the tablet, quickly tapping before restarting the video.

"Ok, d'accord. But when do I get to reciprocate the fingertip routine?"

For answer, Nic only shrugged as if indifferent, even though he felt on the brink of spontaneous combustion.

It was dusk when they landed, the vast airbase indistinct and with very few aircraft evident. Ground-crew directed their parking, placed the chocks and summoned the re-fueling bowser. As the engines wound down, the two pilots emerged, lowered the stairway and conferred with the ground-crew. Some of the conversation was audible as a tray with covered stainless dishes was passed inside and Dirk placed it in front of them.

"Seems we only just made it. This base is being run down so it often closes long before midnight. I'm told the Chinese want to buy it. Anyhow, we're going off to get some shut-eye. We'll be back about 3 am local. We already filed our flight plan and got our clearance. You guys can stay asleep back there. The lights'll stay on, we're on shore power. I'll just get our stuff and leave you to it. We'll close the ramp and lock you in. Those are the orders. Sorry 'bout that. Catchya later, folks."

He retrieved two bags from the rear compartment, hauled them through, nodded to each and left. The stairs hissed upwards and the door shut with finality. The cabin lights brightened as the base power-line was connected.

The dish was local mackerel, mashed potatoes and asparagus, obviously traveled some distance. The mackerel was tasty but the rest they discarded and raided the fridge for delicacies. They ate in charged silence while the noise from the bowser overwhelmed and finally ceased.

"What we gonna do now, Top Cat," Anastasia asked playfully, "I really want to change my clothes and at least make out with a wash-cloth. Can I get to my bag?"

Nic nodded and went aft. Since he had nothing but his small bundle, the only remaining items in the baggage compartment were Anastasia's case and two large golf bags, Barbados plans thwarted.

While Anastasia spread her clothes on another seat, Nic spent several minutes with the tablet, ignoring her questions, holding up his hand. She tried to get his attention, laughingly holding up different items, but he shook his head at every one.

"Well, that's all I got," she said, finishing, "There's only one conclusion. I have nothing to wear, *Nada*. I'm going to wash up. Oh, my, it's really dark out there."

His only response was a nod, non-committal, but as soon as she closed the washroom door, he seized her cell-phone and ran the video she had taken earlier, watching several times until warily satisfied. Reversing the keypad in his mind, it was a very obvious 1-4-7-unlock. With an intense feeling of critical juncture, his expression set, he went forward and touched the keys in order. The cockpit door clicked open and in that moment he knew the die was cast.

Jamming the base of the door with a magazine, he considered the main stairs and rejected the idea because of its likely glaring light. Instead he strode to the back and opened the baggage door, although from there it was a drop of six feet to the tarmac. He reached for the two golf-bags, hefted them to the edge, jumped down and carried them over to the nearest building. It had one lighted room but with no sign of an occupant. Distantly he could see the control tower, lit from outside but dark within. Running back to the aircraft, he unplugged the power cord and dragged the chocks away from the front double-wheels. He noted there was little or no wind.

Back at the baggage hatch he had to heave himself up with legs flailing, flopped inside and stood up, hunting for breath. He shut the hatch with a quiet squish. Anastasia was still in the washroom, humming happily. With deliberate, measured steps, he went forward into the cockpit, shut the door, hoisted over into the left-hand seat and sat for a long moment unmoving, until something like urgency broke the spell and his hands began to move.

Battery Master—On. The screens lit up and asked for information. He satisfied it arbitrarily, airfield height, pressure setting, surface wind, all required to bring the navigation systems online.

Overhead he set the APU to run and heard it winding up far in the rear. Outside the cockpit he saw distant lights which angled away, perhaps a roving security vehicle. He was forced to wait some 40 seconds for the Auxiliary Power to settle before selecting Engine #2—Run. Bleed air from the APU set initial spinning, registering on the engine controls. Knowing the engine was warm and shouldn't be restarted until the shaft cooled, he let the bleed continue for half a minute before the final act of commitment—No2, Fuel On. The engine monitor segment on the middle screen twitched and came to life, winding up slowly but with a nerve-cringing, tell-tale thrumming. Hastening and before it was complete, he repeated the sequence for No 1. The moving map showed their position by the terminal and the taxiways to Runway 15, so before No1 was properly up to Idle, he released the park brake, grasped the ground-steering tiller in his left hand and pushed the throttles forward with his right. The Gulfstream lurched and began to move and then there was a dilemma between haste and too much noise. To be less conspicuous, he reached up and doused the cabin lights, leaving also the landing lights and beacons off. Navigating by EVS, the Gulfstream's new infra-red system which he'd learned from the tablet, he followed the taxiway until its greenish glow revealed the holding point for Runway 15. By this time he'd completed his cockpit checks, engine RPM, temps and pressures, all good. Selecting 20 degrees of flap he checked to his right for any inbound traffic. Pressure off the brakes and the G5 moved eagerly onto the runway and turned to the centerline. He unlocked the tiller, flexed his feet on the pedals, seized the yoke and with dry mouth nudged the throttles forward. As if sensing intent, they advanced automatically to full power.

At that moment there came an urgent knocking on the cockpit door and some incoherent high-pitched yelling from beyond it. Grimly determined, Nic had to ignore it all, watching the IR screen for his heading and the ASI for speed. Lightly loaded, the G5 needed just 15 seconds to reach Vr, rotation at 122 knots as displayed on the screen. He hauled back on the yoke as final commitment and the rumbling of the wheels gave way to soothing, streaming air.

The knocking came again, louder and more frantic, then suddenly ceased. Nic reached for the landing-gear knob, moved it up and waited for three yellows. He eased up the flaps, trimmed to nose-high 25° and when the ASI showed 250 knots, he engaged the autopilot and set course and altitude with the screen cursors: 075° and 51,000 feet. When all the automation seemed happy with his input, he started to extricate himself but before he could get to the door, the lock buzzed and the door opened.

Cell-phone in hand, Anastasia stood there with her face a mixture of triumph, terror and amazement. She was scarcely wrapped in a too-small towel, gazing into the darkened cockpit, trying to make sense of the scene. With the cabin dark behind her, the light from the panel showed Nic's face grinning palely. Looking back at her, he put finger and thumb approvingly together, then waved her into the right hand seat. Clutching the towel and shaking her head in continued disbelief, she finally complied, her bare right leg probing awkwardly across the center console. She reacted to the cold leather with an exaggerated flinch.

Wide-eyed she gazed around, baffled by the compressed array of screens, dials, knobs and switches, an overwhelm she had to burst through. "Doesn't this thing have seat-warmers, Top Cat?"

Nic grinned back and shrugged. "It might, I dunno. Look around."

"You mean, push buttons until something happens?"

"Oh, just sit on the damn towel."

"Yes, sir." With a grin she pulled it off, folded it in half and slid it under her thighs. Her torso gleamed in soft reflected light. Silent, with arms across her breasts, she hugged herself in stretched disbelief, her mind a ferment of excitement, fear and finally a kind of desperate acceptance.

"When were you going to tell me?" she asked eventually.

"Tell you what?"

"That you've done this before."

"I haven't."

"You WHAT?!"

"Not this one. But it's just an airplane."

"It's just—but you're *stealing* it! What's it cost anyway?"

"About $55 million. But not stealing. More like borrowing. And it's 'We'. You made me do it."

"Did not!"

"Oh, come on. I thought you wanted to be alone."

"Yeah? Like alone in prison? Won't they come after us?"

"I don't think so. The tower was closed and they already had clearance. I left them their golf-bags, they'll be quite happy. They won't know for six hours anyway."

"Terrific…Would you mind telling me where we're going?"

"No idea. Where'd you like to go? You can be in charge, since I believe you work for the Government. Did they give you a gun?"

"Yes, actually…I don't think it'd be much use under the circumstances." She took a moment to look up and through the windshield, drawing in her breath and gasping. "Oh, my God, look at the stars… Hey, some of them are actually *below* us How high are we?"

"On our way to nine and a half miles or so. High in the lonely sky."

" Nic, I, er, something's happening, I'm on complete overload, I don't want to but I think I'm about to scream."

"Well, please do it somewhere else." He reached a hand across and she took it "Ok, listen. I had to do something unpredictable. I figured that if it had gone to plan, I'd be shackled and helpless as soon as we arrived in Warsaw. Now we can go somewhere else. Buy me some time, where there's no reception committee. Let me know when you decide. We're fueled for about 4000 miles."

"Oh, *merde!* I need to put some clothes on."

"I'd rather you didn't."

"But I'm chilly."

"Well, go and get into bed. I'll join you as soon as we get to cruise height."

"You can't be serious? Oh God, I think I'm going to scream again… How long?"

"Ten, fifteen minutes. I never thought of you as a screamer."

Her despair abruptly turned to mischief. She heaved herself up from the seat, retrieved the towel, leaned over and spoke breathily in his ear.

"What if I'm asleep?"

Nic's answer was a prolonged chuckle and a brief wave as she crabbed over the console and bent to jam the door open with her towel. He turned to see her sidling gracefully down the now lighted cabin, hands out to the seat-backs, an exquisite shape, her movements sassy as if she knew he was watching. Women always seemed to know, he thought. Only then did he become aware that his own emotions were at fever pitch and needed time to order. Very deliberately he ran his eyes over all the panels, engines all in the green, passing 38,000', Mach .75, altitude preset 51,000', radar showing no conflicting blips, rate of climb 2700 FPM. Satisfied, he opened both hands as if surrendering to fate, eased himself upright and left the G5 to its own myriad devices.

A green velvet curtain was drawn across the aft section where they'd been sleeping earlier. He drew it cautiously aside and found his way blocked by the two banquettes now joined together.

"None shall pass," came a throaty voice from within. "I found a switch and Presto."

"'They also serve who only stand and wait'" Nic grated in response, grinning in the dim light.

"That sounds ineffective. Do come in to my boudoir."

He knelt on the fine leather and closed the curtain. Hearing a purring sound from the depth of total darkness he began at the other end, finding her feet under the blanket, soles uppermost, and took hold of them gently. The subdued roar from the rear of the plane precluded whispering.

"We need to talk," he said sternly

"Uh, oh," Anastasia answered with a nervous chuckle. "What about?"

"Well, everything. Anything that comes to mind. You can direct my hands if you have preferences, like specific places. And you can tell me what you're feeling. Personally I feel like a piano wire that's been overstretched. In my solo sailing days there'd be long watches in a seaway and with self-steering you could only nap for twenty minutes at a time—that's how long before collision with anything just over the horizon. Pretty nerve-wracking. At least we should have no conflicting traffic up here, but still…you can't help wondering if all is well. I remember reading W.E.Johns as a boy: 'When you are flying, everything is either alright or it is not alright. If it is alright you have no need to worry. If it is not alright'—well, you get the idea. There's so much strength just in your feet. They feel beautiful. Maybe I'll just stay here."

"Teaser. My feet'll start getting bored."

"Oh well…moving right along."

"Ah…Nic, I can't stop *thinking*. And I'm not used to the talking, either. This is all completely bizarre. I can't pretend we aren't where we are. It's a wild and crazy stunt and you must be some kind of maniac. Oh, yes…but a very kind maniac. And before you ask, no, I have never been subjected to pure devotion, I've been too angry too long. Now I feel like I've left that all behind, but this could end up being the fire after the frying-pan. Yet I'm wildly, pathetically grateful."

"Your muscle tone is terrific…What I want for now is for both of us, *both of us*, to focus entirely on your delight, and that'll be my delight also. And it isn't leading anywhere, there is no goal. We'll let your body dictate all the moves and they can stop anytime if you're feeling overloaded."

"But what if I lose control of it? You're only at mid-calf and it's already starting to teeter. I just thought of that Sinatra song, 'And then I go and spoil it all by saying something stupid like—" She giggled into her pillow.

"You can say it if you like."

"Any more of this and I'll yell it. Was ever a humble Polack so exalted? I'll never be able to tell you to stop."

"That's good, 'cos I don't want to. Just put your attention on my hands, in each moment."

She took a long, slow breath. "I'm trying, believe me! But my disbelief is tearing at me and my thoughts are wild, like how will it be when he gets to my thighs, my butt, my waist, Oh, hands on the waist, aargh! Oh, hysteria: Back at the lab we were shrieking with laughter, there was a court case in the paper, this guy had grabbed a woman round her waist, but they'd miss-spelled it, w-a-s-t-e!"

Shared laughter tends to supercharge intimacy and Nic struggled to re-center himself.

"Future thoughts mean you're not present with where I am."

"But a woman can think of more than one thing at once."

"Ok, but anticipation isn't Now-think. Come back, lovely Annie. This is going to take a long time, better get used to it."

"Still thoughts intrude, like how long have we got, will you always do this, take so much trouble?"

"Trouble? It's pure delight. I feel I could explore you forever. Written guarantee…Kundera called love something like ceaseless interrogation."

"Yeah, right, till the gas runs out. I take it we're somewhere over the North Atlantic with no destination. Did you do a proper pre-flight check?"

"I'm doing it, in case you hadn't noticed. You're not ready yet."

"Hey! That word `yet', that's not a Now-thought... God, it's awful hard to keep talking… Anyway, I think from now on I'll be ever-ready, gassed up and ticking over. Come to think of it, I've always been ready, I just never got my clearance…Hey, you used the L-word…Oh, God, stop and don't stop—is there anything more gorgeous than a thigh, inside or out? Why does Nature lead us on so, always looking to the next thing and missing the last—No, please, don't go back down."

"If you don't shut up I'll have to start over."

"But you told me to talk. I'm beginning to love the talking."

"Ok, but no future talk. Tell me how you're feeling."

"Right now? Overwhelmed, absolutely blissed out, like I could never ask for anything more in my whole life. I'm churning like a washing-machine loaded with gratitude…My heart feels like jelly. I want to turn and sit up and hug the last breath out of you, it's wrenching to hold it back, the urge to reciprocate. Receiving is much harder, don't you think? We can never feel deserving enough. Oh…please don't go near the middle bit, or my inner thighs, I just know I couldn't stand it."

"That's Ok, I wasn't going to. It would change the focus. Are you Ok with buttocks?"

"Try me…Oh no, no, don't! Stay away, it's too gorgeous. Move on up or I won't be responsible…" She reached out to touch him. "Hey, you've still got all your clothes on."

"I'm busy. I don't want any distractions. But I think I should do a cockpit check, I'll be right back."

"Ah Jeez, you'd better. Tell me `afore you go, what's it like driving a $55 million plane?"

"It's quite fun. But it's not even a tenth as much fun as making love in the back of it."

"Oh…Is that what we were doing? I didn't realize. Will I have to turn over?"

Nic chuckled all the way to the cockpit, his nerves seeming to glisten with pent-up desire. The break gave him time to tame it slightly, to remember that desire itself can be delight and not anguish, not compulsion. With no radar watch over the mid-Atlantic, there were still a couple of hours before he'd have to report his position and call up EuroControl, and he wondered if any sleep was possible.

The panel showed no anomalies. Distance run 380 nm. Heading 075°. Altitude 51,000', Cabin Altitude 6000'. One blinking entry demanded Next Waypoint, enter Flight Plan—?

Ignoring it, he got up and made his way slowly aft, unbuttoning his shirt, loosening his belt and leaving items strewn down the cabin like an old burlesque. Burrowing past the curtain, he groped around the joined banquettes in the dark but there was no-one there.

He pulled the curtain aside to admit some light from the cabin, then moved aft to try the washroom door. Empty. Then past the half bulkhead into the baggage compartment, also empty. Desire and tumescence vanished abruptly. He knelt on the mattress in sudden alarm, his gaze fierce on the length of the empty cabin, the open door and the darkened cockpit beyond. There was only one possible answer, the crew-rest compartment just behind the main exit. Relieved and grinning, he padded confidently forward through his discarded clothes, stopped by the cubicle and with a triumphant "Gotcha", slid the pocket door aside. Empty…

A cold wave of terror seemed to hang up at breaking-point as logic suspended it. He looked aft again, assessing any possible hiding places, his head oscillating in bafflement. His very nakedness seemed to add to his confusion, so he retrieved his crumpled jeans and pulled them back on as if to establish some normalcy. He stalked all the way to the rear of the aircraft, eyeing every possible cranny, his mind in ferment of disbelief, yet still with a half-smile at the impossibility.

Returning forward, at the cockpit door he saw the pale gleam of an elbow in the left hand, Captain's seat. He stood behind the console taking deep breaths of relief, sensing his whole being had processed too many emotions in too few minutes.

"Nice one, Annie. Gotta give you that. Fifteen love."

"Thank you," came the chuckled answer from the dark. "Could you pass the towel? I think I've, er, your seat, well, you know. It's all your fault. Hey, remember, Confucius he say, 'Woman who fly airplane upside down sure to have crack up.'"

She giggled, stood up and crabbed out, took the towel, wiped the seat and handed it back to him. Her face was alight with triumph, her teeth gleamed and her aura somehow streamed around him and filled the whole opulent interior. She reached her arms around his neck, pressed her breasts to his chest, a thigh between his thighs and her lips to his in the softest, deepest, longing-est union either had ever imagined. Finally disengaging, she slid past him, took his hand and tugged him towards the rear. She turned and backing up said, "Don't we have some unfinished business? And did you miss me just a little bit?"

Pointing to his discarded shirt and socks, her brows arched questioningly. "If you'd waited I could have followed the clues. You know, Nic, I've never seen you naked. Are we indulging imagination too much? Like, where are we, who are we, what the hell are we doing, why are we doing it, where are we even going—oh, I'm sorry, I forgot the Now-rule. There was a clip from the Course: `*I do not know this thing I am*', was it? Yes, I remember now: `*and therefore do not know what I am doing, where I am, or how to look upon the world or on myself.*' Was ever the hell that true! Am I talking too much?"

"Just go lie down and take what's coming to you. Or were you getting bored?"

She let go of his hand and dived headlong past the curtain in a slither of leather. From inside came her muffled voice entreating, "Carry on, Captain….my Captain…."

He followed, spread the blanket over her, slid his hands underneath. "Let's see, where was I?"

"You were just past the danger zone, you'd got to around L3…By the way, Los Alamos doesn't know you have a pilot's license."

"Probably because I don't."

"Silly me, of course not. What else don't you have?"

"Um…A goal…Annie, dear Annie, you're thinking again."

"Or even a destination. That could be worth thinking about, don't you think?"

"Later. Just join in the focus. Feel how beautiful your shoulders…"

"You play an instrument, don't you?"

"A little. But this is a new one, it's very fine, a 5'6" Polivarius. It may be above my Grade."

"Oh, no. You're playing it very nicely. *Largo… Lento… Adagio…* The test will come with *Allegro…Vivace…Prestissimo…Scatenato* Oops, sorry. Thinking ahead again… *Decelerando… Soave…Lusingando.*"

"I don't know that last one. What does it mean?"

"Coaxingly. Shall I turn over now? Are we half-way yet? Point of no return?"

Nic sighed theatrically. "If you must. I'm supposed to put in a waypoint."

"I'll let you know, don't worry."

"Me, worry?"

CHAPTER 17

"Some of the biggest men in the United States in the field of commerce and manufacture are afraid of somebody, are afraid of something. They know that there is a power somewhere so organized, so subtle, so watchful, so interlocked, so complete, so pervasive, that they had better not speak above their breath when they speak in condemnation of it."

Woodrow Wilson, 28th President USA

Midnight in Marienbad.

The tall aging Texan sat in his room in slippers and bathrobe, deep in a leather armchair. He was sipping spring water and frowning. Fully dressed, the younger Frenchman stayed on his feet, leaning on the mantle shelf. The fire was down to glowing embers as he voiced his thoughts.

"I'm not sure about the young man, George, or at least he hasn't yet had the chance to consider the responsibilities of wealth and influence. He may still be harboring youthful idealism."

"Now don't you be troubling yourself, Henri, he'll get the picture soon enough. We all did, remember?"

"Of course, but if there really is a new breeze blowing, we may be too old to find a way to compromise it. Compromising new ideas has been our modus for a very long time." He laughed sourly. "Maybe we shouldn't have nixed that anti-aging formula way back, remember? Biolongate, wasn't it? Stay youthful to 120. We decided that prolonging life would simply add to the population problem, but now we could use some of it ourselves."

"What happened to it?"

"What do you think? Like so many other so-called improvements, we bought and suppressed it."

"Do we still have the formula?"

"Of course. But the placebo was almost as effective. You know what really aids longevity? It's attitude. Biolongate improves, that is, optimizes attitude. You know what's in it? D.M.T., and that's exactly what we're being threatened with right now. From the air. But apparently we're causing it ourselves."

"It's been a long day, my friend. I bid you good sleep. Perhaps we'll know more tomorrow."

Los Alamos Medical Center, New Mexico.

"Mr Uren—may I call you Frank?"

Without waiting for an answer, the cardiologist sat on the edge of Uren's bed and swung the platen of his stethoscope warningly.

"It seems you have a lot on your mind, Frank, which is doing you no good. You've had a string of visitors who do not bring grapes and flowers but messages and questions. Your cell-phone is also incessant and I am empowered to, er, sequester it and bar your visitors, in the interest of your survival. Do I make myself persuasive? Your surgery is scheduled for tomorrow morning early. In the meantime you need to find relaxation because you are on a cliff-edge right now. I do not like to lose patients, it's bad for my image. Will you do it voluntarily or do I have to load you up with Diazepam which could compromise your body's tolerance for the surgery?"

"Ok, Ok, Doc, I got the message. My team's on the way for a five minute conference, then I'll comply, Ok? I'm not the only emergency here, it's government business, get me? See, if I don't, my life won't be worth living anyway."

"Hm...Well, in that case, perhaps it isn't. Anyway, I mean."

Uren snorted. "Gee, thanks Doc, you're such a comfort. Go sharpen your knives, Ok?"

Minutes later, Ben Storey and two henchmen crowded his bedside. None looked particularly sympathetic.

"How's it pumpin', boss? Thought you should know, Igor Knyazev's gone off-air. We sent an all-points. Can't find his Blazer and the woman's not home. But her car's still there."

"Right, keep up the pressure. Nothing from the Wojer but I don't expect it. They'll be locked up all the way to Warsaw and our boys'll pick up there, right? So…The Ukrainian puss is on her way there too, and Nasty's gonna have words with her. Make sure Nasty has a ticket home. Moncrieffe goes to safe-house and then on to Cairo, right? Put three guys on him, I swear he's tricky. If we lose him before he squeals—well, I needn't spell it out."

"There's something else boss. The Ukrainian, Elena whatsit, she must be a piece because her shadow has gotten carnal ideas and blown his cover. But that may not matter if Nasty does her part."

Uren was silent for a moment, musing. "You know, it might be best to hold Moncrieffe there for a few days. I'll suggest it to Langley. We could maybe wrap this whole deal right there. Once he's in Egypt he's out of our scope and no kudos."

"Good thinking, boss. We don't want to look like hicks and bumblers."

"Ya mean, even though we are, is that what you're saying? Fuck you. Find Igor and tell Moscow FSB we're sending him home. Meanwhile he has a car accident, the road up here, where there's no barrier. Just to piss them off. You know the drill."

"What if he split already, boss? He must know you'd written him off."

"Nah, he's hog-tied, he can't get out. He's chipped and he's got no papers."

"He can still hide somewhere, out of chip-range. If he squeals to Moscow about the Prist panic, they could probably fetch him out."

"Mustn't happen. He knows too much about us. Just find him and fix him up, Ok?"

"It's a deal. Good luck tomorrow, boss. Hey, I was lookin' up the failure stats for bypass surgery. It's only about 2 per cent. Mind you, someone's got to be the 2 per cent. Would it be tactless to ask if you got any unused Viagra?"

Uren's face began his usual snarl but his very helplessness poured in on him suddenly and produced a weirdly human grin. He looked at the three in turn with what could almost have been affection.

"There's only one left. You'll have to split it three ways. But there'll be a whole ten-pack to whoever can find me this Biggall feller, which case I guarantee to be in the 98 per cent. Wake me up, even if I'm still gapin' open."

"You got it boss. Take it easy."

Sky Harbor Airport, Phoenix, Arizona.

"Narciso, you appear to be calm but you are not speaking much. I tried to interest you in a little side-trip to Sedona but you had to press on. And the wonderful Pipe-Dreams exhibit at the rental place, no interest. Now we are being driven by this kind gentleman to another part of the airport. Please don't tell me we are going to be nailed into crates and shipped out as aid packages to Central America?"

Rose chattered on as the agent drove them around the airport perimeter. Evening was closing in. Igor sat looking straight ahead, calm but expressionless, his right hand holding hers, his left cradling a slim folder. Apart from her hand-bag they had no other luggage between them.

In front of Pentastar Aviation ranged a pair of Learjets, a Falcon 50, a Citation and two King-Airs. They stopped in front of the offices, stepped out and the driver left without comment.

"Rosita, you will wait outside, please. I won't be a moment." His confidence left her dumb-founded but amused, standing in the still-hot sunshine, wearing jeans and a yellow light leather jacket, carrying only her purse. After a few minutes Igor emerged followed by a fierce-looking, overweight man who chattered mysteriously, reading from a clipboard. His spiel finished, he nodded, shook Igor's hand and pointed to the far side of the hangar. Igor thanked him and walked over to Rose, took her arm and smiled.

"You come with me now, please. Time for surprise."

Rose felt her grin expanding at his easy confidence. "Narciso, I am indulging you and your great mystery, but a little air-conditioning might help my condition."

"Then I will see to it, Madam, in just a few minutes."

He walked past the line of plutocrats' playthings as the heat from the tarmac rose to stifle them. Without hesitation, Igor led them straight to the blue and white Albatros, which gleamed wetly over a puddle of drying wash-water. The canopies were open, the stirrups extracted. Igor gestured invitation, now grinning broadly.

"Mi Rosita, you get to be back-seat driver. First time in your life, perhaps?"

Rose clasped her purse to avoid betrayal of shaking hands. She looked at him directly, trying not to smile, letting him relish every moment of surprise. He led her up to the aircraft, took her purse, showed her where to place feet and hands and half-hoisted her into the rear cockpit. Neither said anything as he leaned in and helped with her straps, handed her a helmet, plugged in the intercom and closed her canopy, signaling how to slide the latch. He quickly seated himself in front, then his voice rasped remotely through the headphones, speaking not to her but to the tower for clearance. A humming started up somewhere behind and in a moment the relief of air-conditioning wafted over her. She stayed quiet, savoring every second.

The main engine began its gathering growl as unintelligible information came from the tower. Igor acknowledged, released brakes and dipped the nose briefly to test them, then began trundling to the taxiway.

"Igor?" Rose strained tentatively, surprised to hear her own voice through the headphones.

"I am now Narciso, *señora*."

"Yeah, well, it is *señorita*. Now listen to me, Narciso, I cannot be seen dead in something that only does two miles to the gallon."

"I will put it on economy. Just for you. Are you comfortable, *señorita?*"

"No. I have to go to the bathroom."

"You are kidding, right? Can you wait 25 minutes?"

"Well, if I must....Yeah, I was kidding. I—"

Her words were interrupted by the radio instructions and then the L39 stopped at the holding for Runway 25L. She watched over his shoulder as Igor ran up the engine and his fingers walked the dials to his muttered checklist, in Russian.

"Albatross 2418Niner, you are clear to line up and take-off, left turn out, climb to 6000', route clear to Albuquerque."

"One-eight-niner rolling."

Restrained by bemusement, Rose sat tense and transfixed. The thought of return to Albuquerque held her mystified all through the take-off, but soon after she heard Igor requesting a change of flight plan, to low-level flight test to the South.

"24189, will you be returning to Phoenix Sky Harbor?"

"Negative Phoenix. Will inform shortly."

"Roger 189, you are clear to the South, stay below 5000'. Switch to approach 127.57. G'day."

After further muttering and static, Igor chuckled and spoke mildly. "Ay, Rosita, *Que piensas?* What do you think of it so far?"

"Is hokay, Narciso. Is this a jet fighter?"

"Is just like one. A trainer. It is Russian, a very fine aircraft."

"Not very dramatic, I must say."

Without a word, Igor rolled them inverted and held it for long seconds before completing. Hanging in the straps, with a mighty effort Rose held in her scream and resolved to stay maddeningly cool. She was in a turmoil of delight, terror and admiration. After several minutes of level flight she ventured cheekily, "Is that it?"

"Is not my aircraft, *querida*. I do not wish to be cleaning vomit. We will be in May-hee-co in twenty minutes."

"Come on, *hombre*. Show me what you got."

"Well, we can go plus+8 and minus-4 G. Depends on which end you want stuff to come out."

"Oh, stop it. Just be nice, and no *machismo.*"

He knew from long experience how to gauge when a squeal of delight bordered on distress, and he had also come to understand that this precious Rose invited or permitted only gentleness. He was pleased to note that no hint of sadism was evoked in response to her taunting. After a whole series of deft but smooth maneuvers, he brought the aircraft level and asked quietly, "Are you well back there, *cariño*?"

"More than well, I am enchanted. That was fun and the view from this bubble is incredible. And just so you know, Narciso, I could sense your kindness. But I want to be able to say I flew it, can I do that?"

"Yes, indeed you can. Just pull back on your stick, very hard. I will be with you and say when to ease off. Do it now, please."

Heart in mouth, Rose grasped the handle between her legs and hauled it towards her. The Albatros responded at once and aimed directly skywards, the great blue dome arching over.

"Ease off for a moment, then pull hard again."

She did so and in a trice the blue turned to arid terrain right beneath the nose. She could sense the speed building as the desert expanded alarmingly.

Igor's voice: "Pull really hard now, out of the loop."

The G-force seemed to flatten her buttocks into the seat and her cheeks sagged like old age. Instinctively she eased off the pressure as they came level again.

"*Excellente, señorita.* That was perfection."

"Well, it was fun. Now, do I take it you have a plan? What happens now?"

"We head due South at 5000 feet, doing 350 knots, about 400 mph. We are going to an airfield called Nogales, just over the border, which actually closed about half an hour ago. We will leave the aircraft there and find another way to Cosumel. I will call the owner and tell him Sorry and leave some *dinero* under the seat. I hope he will understand."

"Why don't we just buy it for you. Hey, that way you could have a job and stay out of my hair."

"Rosita, get serious!"

"Well, what do they cost?"

"Originally $10 million. Now only about 200K. Excuse, please, I need to pay attention."

"That's affordable. Why don't we fly straight to Cosumel?"

"We don't have the range. And I want to make it easy for the owner to collect. Please, I have only about 6 minutes to the border. Mostly they look for illegals going other way. I throttle down and dive for quiet. No talk, please, for a few minutes."

He spoke briefly on the radio. "Phoenix Approach, this is Albatros 24189. Non-emergency, I make precautionary landing in Nogales, Over."

"Roger 24189. Good luck. Let us know if you need anything. Out."

Engine idling and diving to maintain airspeed, they swept over the conspicuous barrier at less than 1000 ft. The Arizona side was empty desert, the Mexico side a crowded shamble of shanties, derelicts and trash piles. Just a few miles further, Igor spotted the airfield, its windsock hanging limply and no sign of other traffic. His practiced judgment brought them to the runway threshold without additional power, just as the speed diminished to 130 knots for touchdown. He had to spool up the engine to taxi to the shade side of a hangar, but quickly shut down and opened his canopy. From his folder he took an envelope and slid it under his seat, turned and beckoned to Rose to unstrap herself and unlatch her canopy. She removed her helmet to show her broad face once more expressionless, her real state betrayed by wide astonished eyes and the forced restraint of a smile.

"Don't you have to lock it?"

"Military aircraft do not have keys. You just get in and go. How do you think James Bond got to steal one?

"Maybe I call you *Jaime Vinculo*? Won't they be looking for us here?"

"I think not. I did not say which Nogales airfield. There is also one in Arizona, just a few miles north-east."

"Narciso, I think maybe you are one smart *galleta*. What is the next surprise?"

A confident traveler, on the last flight of the day, Irina Popova took a taxi direct to the Meridien and called up to Elena's room. The answering voice was both strained and relieved, urging her to come up quickly. They hugged lengthily and Elena looked up into a broad and generous face, well-fed and healthy, in a cascade of blonde curls. A joyful reunion after some five years gave way to anxiety as Elena spoke of continued harassment by her Russian shadow.

"I don't understand how this has happened. They must be intercepting our emails but there was nothing suspicious in them."

Irina shrugged, her fair curls shaking. "Well, maybe because of mystery references and talk of secrets. I know, it's absurd."

"I speak gently to him and he tries to behave, but underneath is just typical Russian misogynistic horny beast. To avoid dinner with him I had it sent to my room. Are you hungry, Irochka?" Elena's eyes were bright, in spite of her distress. "I am so glad to see you and that you are here. Next time he knocks, if you answer it?"

Irina giggled. "It sounds like he would go crazy and want us both, Lenochka. You are more beautiful than I remember. I think something has happened, yes?"

"I think so, but I don't know what it is. I feel like I am in love but not with anyone in particular. And I'm not sure what to do with it. It is certainly not to do with this dog Sergei."

"We could just get you another room. This one is adjoining, I see."

"Yes. He opened his side, but mine is still locked. He knocks about every half hour. It's scary if he's FSB, and he must be, don't you think? I mean, what might he do if I refuse him? I have to think of Ilya and Mama."

"I think you must be unafraid. Remember Kolya's messages about this being just a recreational planet? Even people like Sergei only want to have fun and joy, but they have forgotten how. Together perhaps we can remind him."

With the constant muted roar from the rear of the Gulfstream drowning amorous whispers, the need to speak loudly amused them both. Enough light filtered past the curtain for them to see each other's' faces, smiling, questioning, eyes closing for long internal moments, kisses restrained against passion's demand for gorging.

"I wish," Nic said, his hand lightly on her bare stomach, "I wish I could actually see the energies between, like those LSD paintings by Alex Grey. I know we sense them, but with only dim reception. But at least we can easily tell where we're coming from—I mean, like, with intention—are my hands exploring you for my own gratification, to savor all this beauty, or are they intent on giving you pleasure? It's a different energetic, d'you think so?"

Anastasia's mouth had settled into a squeezed upturn of delight and disbelief. "I do, I really feel it. You put your hand on my belly, it's like such a comfort but then you move it and I wonder where it's going next. What happens if I take hold of it and move it up like this, oh, I feel my heart swelling inside me, makes me shudder, and yes, I feel the difference—you cradle a breast because you want to feel it, rejoice in it, then it changes when you want to please it. And I want them both, both feelings. Can I move it back down here?"

She moved his hand down her body until letting it rest over her mons pubis. Against all instinct she kept her legs tight together. Nic nodded with a faint smile as she said, quite loudly, "Oh God, what happens there? How do hands know to send different energies? Is it all from thought? And then I notice that with stomach and heart I could still smile, but with breast and pussy the smile turns almost to pain, anticipation of the agony of pleasure, like how can we moan and groan and pretend enjoyment?"

"What happens when I do this?" Up on one elbow, his right hand lightly on her groin, he placed his other between her breasts and induced deliberately the thought, the streaming of energy between heart and vulva. At first her body arched rigid, then gradually relaxed, though still quivering. From a tiny pressure of his right fingertips her legs inchingly separated until her yoni was cupped in his hand and he could feel her seeping through his fingers.

"It's like an energy stream," she gasped, "It's like green and overflowing, it's so beautiful I don't know if I can stand it. And I can't tell which is sweeter, what you're doing or the fact that you're doing it. One distracts me from the other. And I keep remembering where we are, miles and miles above the Atlantic Ocean, or so you tell me, how do I know? Our lives like hanging on little threads of whimsical instruments which could fail at any moment, God, this is the craziest, the absolutely wildest—Nic, please can you take off your pants, so there's nothing left between us?"

"Annie, beloved, that's kind of a Rubicon. Let's try to stay in the hearts as long as we can."

"But I can't bear it any more. I long, I am all invitation, it's so joyful, but—"

Nic abruptly moved his hands to her shoulders, rolled away and pulled her on top of him. "There's something I want first," he said, close to her ear, "Like this, I can put both arms around you, I want you to feel just how precious you are, how beloved, belovable. I want all your weight on me, just allow it. You can be in charge."

"Captain, aren't you supposed to say 'You have control'?"

"Very well. You have control."

With a great sigh she relaxed onto him, kissed his neck, his chin and finally found his mouth. Just the tip of her tongue began to explore inside his lips but even that caused his whole body to tense and expel all his breath. With an effort he moved his mouth aside.

"Talk to me," he pleaded, gasping.

"Why? What's to say? What do you want?"

"Contact. Connection. If I come into you, it all moves down there, it takes over. I want to stay with you like this, just holding, being present. Loving. I want you to be sure of it. Putting my thing in your thing doesn't say that."

"Nic, for God's sake, there's nothing wrong with it."

"I know. But how much sweeter for you to be sure, if you can trust where it's coming from."

From past experience he thought it might be rejection-rage that made her arch above him but then she sat up, straddling his thighs. Her hands moved over his torso, lightly through his chest hair, softer still on his belly, then up over his shoulders and down his arms, all the way to his hands, entwining fingers, then up to his face and backwards over his temples, all smoothing. She said nothing but her touches conveyed all he wanted to know, that she had received the message ·
and there were no longer any limits. The front of his pants were soaked from both of them so he reached down and unbuckled. Anastasia put

her head on his chest to take some of her weight as she reached back to ease them down his legs. Restraining again, she moved herself down and gently massaged his thighs, smiling in the half light, not so much taunting as hesitant and respectful, her face utterly soft and radiant as she moved closer, then away again, then another agony of closer. She was so in tune by this time that his sensations seemed duplicate in her own thighs, both bodies gone critical-mass in mystical erogeny.

Both agreed later that the full interaction of joining was just a blur of overwhelming sensation as the parts obeyed their natural compulsions without technique or artifice, while the hearts seemed to pound as one, like two over-powered units seeking and finding each other as series of climaxes tried and failed to distract them.

Only gradually did the deafening in the ears give way to the soft pervading roar of their passage. Close to his ear, Anastasia was finally able to utter, "I was about to say something stupid, like, will it always be like this? And then I realized it will never be like this, it will always be different, because love abhors routine... Did you suffer little death, my love?"

Nic said nothing but she felt his head shake in sure denial and his arms moved to circle her more tightly. Bursting to express, she went on, "I never knew it could be like this, where the hell was education? I never met any woman who did, I never even read about it. I feel like I'm in a sanctuary and I am blessèd... It would take a lifetime to express the gratitude I feel... I completely forgot where we are, on some terrible aerial tightrope. How long have we got, before you must be about your manly duties, resume control and decide out destination? Or we could just lie here till the juice runs out. I don't care anymore, I could go anytime now."

Nic chuckled, groping around for his pants. "Well, luckily it's decided. We're going to Warsaw."

"But...I thought you had a better idea. They'll be waiting for you. Why are you putting those on?"

"I have no spare clothes. How else can I dry them?"

"I saw a uniform hanging in the crew-rest compartment."

"Hm...We're on a Flight Plan, see. If we don't show up, the owners get informed immediately. This leg is about five hours so hopefully we'll arrive just before our two guys wake up, so there'll be no alarm."

"I see…Tell me, how do you know you know what you're doing?"

Nic laughed. "How does anyone? How do you know how to make love perfectly?"

"Do you think so, really?"

"Yeah, but it's just an opinion."

She dug at his chest playfully. "Well, yours is the only one that counts and right now I can't get a second…Nic, do you ever write about it, you know, the graphics of lovemaking?"

"No, I don't think you can. Descriptions of plumbing can titillate but can't convey feelings. To me it's something so sacred, almost other-worldly, words could never convey. I mean, I get that knowledge is always subjective, but this I feel I *know*." He slipped his hand gently into her crotch.

Anastasia hesitated, finally prompting, "What do you know?"

"That this is the most sacred place in the Universe. And you are the shrine."

Anastasia gasped deeply several times while clinging to him with total ferocity, her legs around his, her strength astonishing. Eventually she calmed enough to say, "Are you the only guy who knows that? I have always known that… It will change the world when everyone knows…And do you think we'll ever be able to explain what we just did?"

"I'm not sure we did anything. I think we were done *through*. I don't think it can be explained, or even described. It can only be experienced. We were out of our minds—literally."

She sat up and clasped him. "I wish I could just stay there."

"Me too. I'm told it takes practice. Lots of practice."

"Lots and lots?"

"Sure, why not?"

"Nic, I just realized something—I don't know who you are. I've read some of your stuff but it's all fiction and conjecture, fantasy, if you like. So, who are you?"

"Me? I'm just a pseudonym."

"Really? Now that doesn't help."

He chuckled and kissed her eyes. "Well, Ok, I'm not anything you might want to categorize. Maybe that's a fatal flaw, I don't know. What would you like to be able to say? My lover is a stock-broker, an astronaut, a lawyer, a proctologist, some label? I don't have one. It's kind of ornery, I suppose, but every time I've looked like acquiring a label, I seem to veer off and do something else. Nothing you can be proud of. You might be uncomfortable with that."

"Hm…My lover is a dilettante, a dabbler, a will o' the wisp, a ne'er-do-well. A Jack-of-all. A factotum."

"Huh… but he's also your invention, your creation. Is that what you intended?"

"I never consciously intended anything—except revenge of course. Now that's gone, I suppose I don't know what I am either."

"You're a linguist, a Ph.D., you're Secret Service, an asset. Right now, you're a prison guard."

"Not true!" she squealed, "I'm the prisoner here. An asset? Is that a small ass? I know nothing of what I am."

"A pilot is nothing without a plane."

"And prison guards need prisoners. A proctologist is nothing without—oh, never mind!"

"Heh heh…I'll pass on that too. But lovers need beloveds."

"That's it! Thank you, Nic. My beloved is a lover. That works fine for me. Now, don't you think it's time you got back to being a skipper? This situation is kind of a nerve-wrack, don't you think?"

"Me, think?"

"Somebody should."

"Don't look at me," he said, "I am in post-coital total bliss-out. I don't think I could even crawl to the bows of the ship to throw out the anchor."

"Tell me what to do then."

"Oh, let's just lie here and simmer. Empty ocean below, empty sky above, Rolls and Royce a-roaring behind, aurora ahead—that means sunrise, did you know? Is this an imminent catastrophe or a happy memory in the making?"

"Either way, we'll never tell, it's just for us. We'd never find anyone who'd believe it. It was more like an NDE, near-death experience."

"It's not over yet."

"Oh, Lord, I'd completely forgotten I had a body. Hey, are you suggesting second-helpings?"

"Seems a shame not to, while we're here. Then you could get a second opinion. You know the Australian for foreplay?"

"No, I don't. But please, nothing earthy. Not here."

"You're right. Thanks for the reminder. My lover is a sky-high angel, with a pure and open heart."

Anastasia murmured into his neck. "Burst open. Shattered. Beyond repair. Good for nothing."

"*Au contraire, chérie.* I think it's doing what it does best. On autopilot."

CHAPTER 18

*When simply 'being' takes over, it is non-dual, and so duality
mind cannot handle or control it and simply, even gracefully,
gives up. When everything's let go, what remains?*

Nic Moncrieffe

In the darkening of evening, Rose and Igor, two misfits near the
back of a ramshackle bus, tried to ignore the stares and cackled
comments from the exclusively Mexican passengers, crowding
beyond capacity. The frequent stops offered no relief beyond the rise
and fall of decibels as locals recognized and greeted one another, and
most of the patois was unintelligible. Increasingly distressed, Rose
kept trying for a signal on her iPhone while Igor kept his hand lightly
on the back of her neck, attempting comfort.

"As soon as I can get a signal, we'll get off this jalopy," she said,
exasperation building.

Igor merely chuckled. "Let's imagine there's been catastrophe, a
tsunami or something, and we have the last seats on the last bus out
of danger zone."

Rose looked at him sharply, scowled, sneezed and finally smiled.
Then she kissed him heartily to a roar of oohs from surrounding
passengers. Some even stood for a better view and the questions
streamed: "*Ay, es vuestra luna de miel? Viaje de novios?*"

Disengaging from Igor, Rose grinned back at the faces. "*Si, hon-ee-
moon. En el mas bonito autobus en May-hee-co!*"

A gleeful woman screeched back,, "*Ee, estan fugandos, como Dusteen
Hoffman!*"

One elderly, black-clothed and almost toothless woman produced
a yellow rose from a huge cloth bag, broke the stem, leaned across and
pushed it gently into Rose's hair. Another, kneeling over the seat-back,
put a gaudy paper garland around Igor's neck. The first then picked

up Rose's left hand and asked pityingly why there was no ring. Rose explained that it was more fun pretending to be eloping *adulteros*, which was quickly spread and raised a great cheer as well as some doubtful scowls.

Discomfort forgotten in hilarity, the rest of the journey to Cananea seemed to pass in minutes and they left the bus almost reluctantly, chased by laughter and well-wishes. They quickly found a small hosteleria, ordered margaritas and Rose in triumph obtained a signal.

"Who were you trying to call?" Igor asked, sighing into the luxury of his drink.

"What I should have done and you wouldn't let me in Nogales, rustle up an air-taxi. We'd have saved—"

"*Querida*, it was not a good idea to stay there and get arrested."

"I know, I'm sorry."

"Well, we had a little adventure. May I use the phone please?"

Rose was about to ask why and had a sudden revelation which came in like a grace. The moment consumed her with affection and the astonishment showed in the softening of her features. Igor looked puzzled when he saw it, taking the phone and feeling a stroke of gentleness in the transfer.

"*Hola, Señor Larry?*" Igor spoke with heavy Spanish intonation. "This is Luis, airport maintenance in Nogales, May-hee-co. You L-*treinta nueve* came in here and pilot, he ask me to call you. He say he leave something under front seat, and tell you most sorry. You come soon and collect aircraft please. He say again, bi bi, sorry.....No, *Señor*, Aeroflot twin jet come after dark, take him away....*Si, Ruso*.....I no workin' *mañana*, but you come, is hokay, you airplane safe. *Adios Señor.*"

Eyebrows arching, Rose said nothing as he handed back the phone but there was no mistaking the affection in her smile.

"What happened, *mi Rosita?*"

"Something very significant, Narciso. I renounce bossiness in favor of respect. If I fail sometimes, it's just old habit. Chew gently on my ear if you ever have to remind me."

Igor said nothing for a full minute, watching her eyes, a smile flickering, sliding his fingers in and out of hers across the table, not entirely sure he understood.

"One more thing, *querida*. Can you send email from that?"

"*Si.*"

"Can you do it for me? My fingers are too big." He stood and asked the *patron* for pen and paper and carefully wrote in block letters. Rose thumbed them into the phone with a broadening smile.

DOBRAYA FEYA, BUD' GOTOVA. DRAKONCHIK SVOBODNY MEXIKANETS. DO SKOROGO! Email to elemosk at cs.ru.com

"You notice I haven't asked what it means?" Rose smiled, her thumb on the Send tab.

Igor grinned back. "I do. Send it please, and I will tell you."

Rose complied graciously. "There. 'Tis gone. So?"

"Thank you, dearest lady, it means a great deal. It says, 'Good Fairy, get yourselves ready. Little Dragon is a free Mexican. See you soon'."

"Little Dragon?"

"Yes, we had children's game. Only she will know whom it is from."

"That's funny, it's grammatically correct, yet we'd likely say, 'who from', which is incorrect. Am I confusing you? And I take it that the free Mexican is being unfaithful to me already?"

"Beloved, you have just given me a great idea. We could spend all our lives keeping each other guessing, what do you think?"

"Hm…I think everybody does that already, just not deliberately."

Igor gave his sandpaper chuckle. "Then me and you shall deliberate."

"You and I."

"I know, I just wanted to see if you would correct me."

Online with her IPad, Irina exclaimed, brightening, "Lenochka, reinforcements are coming! Kolya is on his way here, to Warsaw, can you believe it?"

Elena's eyes and mouth opened together and hung with wild speculation. "How did this happen, what did he say?"

"He just says he will come and find you."

"But how will he know me—oh, I think Igor said he would show him my photograph. But we will not know him. Can I check my emails on that?"

"Sure. Go ahead."

Elena signed in and in moments jumped and whirled. "Oh, oh. There is one here in English letters, I cannot read it."

Irina looked at the screen, frowning. "Who is Drakonchik?"

Elena jumped excitedly. "That is Igor, my dear, dear brother. It was a name I used to call him, when we were children. It means he knows our emails are being intercepted. What does he say?"

"You should get ready, he's in Mexico. He says, 'See you soon.'"

High fives and a little dance were interrupted by a knocking on the partition door. Irina put her finger to her lips and then pointed to herself. Moving next to the door, she spoke in refined English.

"Yes, who is it?"

"You are Elena?" the voice asked in Russian.

"No, certainly not. What do you want?"

"Hotel Security. I am checking on a guest."

"I don't see why. You should come to the main door so I can see you and your credentials."

"*Khorosho*—Ok."

Irina gripped Elena's arm. "Put your case in the closet. When he knocks, go out through his room. When I let him in here, go downstairs. I'll meet you in the piano bar."

Elena grinned mischievously, nervously, but did as she asked. When the knock came, she unbolted the adjoining door and slipped through, hearing it locked behind her.

Her nervousness allayed by hearing voices, she paused a moment and looked around. The bed was crumpled from a nap but a black lanyard protruded from under a pillow. She lifted the pillow and with a jolt recognized a squat black sidearm in a holster, a Russian PPS. Opposite the bed was a desk strewn with papers. There was also a yellow folder which she recognized. Quickly thumbing through it, her frown deepened; in the printed emails the only Russian texts were those between herself and Irina. The rest were in English. Boldly, she grabbed several of these, stuffed them into her blouse and exited with darting caution. From the passage she saw her own door was now closed, voices and obscenities raised beyond it. She heard Irina's exaggerated outrage when the door opened, just as she turned the corner and ran to the elevators.

When Irina joined her in the almost deserted bar a few minutes later, she found Elena white-faced and clutching the papers. The barman came to enquire and retreated to a shake of heads.

"Lenochka, what's the matter? I told him you had been sent to another hotel. It's all right."

"But these emails are in English. What goes on here?"

"Let me look." Irina quickly scanned the copies, frowning. "It seems they have a sent a Polish woman. She is coming here with Kolya. Her task is to isolate you and get the code system, at any cost, starting with your fingers. It's crazy, because it says it makes no difference if you won't give it, because Kolya will surely reveal it under, I quote, 'enhanced interrogation'. They are taking him to Egypt, he is not stopping here. But, it says if you will give it up it will be quicker and Egypt not necessary. Oh, but wait, here it also says if Ukraine woman gives up codes, operation is closed. Terminate the Englishman. Silence the Ukrainian using mother and child. Any doubts, terminate all three. Attached is a copy of a bank wire, $10,000 to an account in Turks and Caicos. It seems they know where you work and where you live."

Elena paled even further. "What about you, Irina? Do they mention you?"

"No. Perhaps they do not know I am here yet, but I did send Kolya an email to say I was coming, so they will know soon. The brute upstairs didn't seem to know. But the whole point is, he's getting his orders from United States, not Moscow. You're sure he's Russian?"

"Dead sure."

"Hm…Well, I told him I was a journalist from London covering the trade show, that your room had become free because you had left the hotel. He came and stood too close to me, that's when I started shouting."

The two stared at each other, checking speech several times. Gradually Elena relaxed, her color returning noticeably. Irina looked at her in puzzlement.

"What goes on, tell me?"

"I was going into a bad state, too many things, but then I remembered the letters with Kolya."

"What about them?"

"Fearlessness. You can only be fearless if there is nothing to fear. And there IS nothing to fear. The problem is in believing it. There is a trick for the mind—do you know what it is?"

"No, you better tell me and quick. I am getting very, very scared."

Elena put her hand on her heart. "It's here. All the answers."

"But, *Lyubimaya*, we have to think."

"No. Thinking is the problem."

"But fear is natural. It's even essential, like when you are face-to-face with a tiger."

"No…Irina, listen…I admit I have not fully proved this for myself but I am absolutely dying to believe it. I may *have* to die to believe it, but it is the only way out, I am sure. It is the only answer to all the woes of the world. I can feel it. When I go into my heart-space with no thoughts, a symphony begins, it is like a great knowing. It is not rational. It is cosmic, greater than this life, I swear, my heart is telling me, my heart cannot be lying." She pounded her ribcage. "In here is the truth, that all is well no matter how it seems."

Against Irina's pained expression, Elena's outburst dissolved into a slow intriguing smile. "I love it that you are here with me. I love you. Please try, *please*, see if you can join me. It's like a new game, play it with me. We'll call it the Heart Game. We let the Cosmos throw the dice while we just watch and see what happens. Can you do that?"

"No, not if I am afraid to lose you."

"What if you cannot lose me? I am here right now, that is all we know. The rest is fear and speculation about fearful things. Please Irishka, try this with me, I'm not sure to do it on my own."

"Well, dearest Lena, this is madness, you know that, don't you?"

"Yes, of course! It's called Divine Madness. Do you think God was scared when he pushed the button for the Big Bang?"

"I don't believe in God, Lena."

Elena laughed out loud. "Neither do I. So if there's no God, then there's definitely nothing to be afraid of, right?"

Irina gave a great sigh of resignation. "I'll have to think about it. Let's have a drink." She signaled to the barman who came eagerly.

"Good idea. But I do actually feel there is a Source of some kind, just not some crusty, bearded old fart with a ledger. An essence, if you like. Kolya calls it Godness… How's your Polish?"

"None. But the woman coming to dis-finger you, she's Polish."

"Oh. Then we will dis-arm her with our new system."

"What if she's a big bull dyke?"

"Mm…one of us will have to pretend a change of orientation. We'll toss for it."

"Were you ever curious?"

"No. That shit Leonid almost drove me that way, but I haven't given up yet. Let's drink up and get some sleep. We'll have to whisper in the room. Tomorrow might be interesting."

"When does the trade show start?"

"Day after. I don't think they even need me, they're just being nice."

"Really? I wonder why…?"

"I need to find my watch. Can you help me?" Nic asked, groping around in the half-dark of the cabin.

"No, I don't want you to go," Anastasia answered sleepily, pulling him tighter into the snuggle.

"We must be nearing the coast of Spain. If I don't call in they'll see us on radar and push the panic button."

"Then what?"

"Jet fighters, scramble."

"Sounds scary. Speaking of scramble, what's for breakfast?"

"You are."

"Ha. So how long have we got?"

"Ok, I found it." He peered at the luminous dial. "Two plus hours, roughly."

"But Nic, if you go with the Flight Plan, won't they be waiting for you?"

"We'll change it, honey. At the last minute."

"Oh… I was dreaming, or so I thought. I was in a space-ship on an endless voyage to meet my lover, it was all about longing. Then somebody woke me, still in the dream, and said, 'Wake up, we're here', so I did, and you were."

"So who was your lover in the dream?" Nic gripped her as if interrogating.

"Oh, he was formless, a myth, no, a pseudonym!"

"Speaking of lovers, at college I had a rowing coach called D-D-D-Denys. He had a terrible stutter, bit of a handicap for a coach but we loved him. I was in my first heartbreak and D-Denys was trying to comfort me. He said, "Nic, y'know, w-w-w-within reason, anyone'll do!"

"What? Like, anyone you fixate on?"

"No, anyone. He was trying to defuse idealism, the notion of specialness. The Course has a lot to say about notions of specialness." .

"I see. As in, all affairs become humdrum eventually?"

"It depends on attitude, I guess. It's in our very nature to be never satisfied. Being satisfied is like settling, giving up."

"There must be a way to bypass that, don't you think? If we could always be a mystery to each other, which we are of course if we choose to see it so. I mean, is it ever possible to know another completely? I don't think so. Igor told me you had a wife who changed teams— that must have been hard, to recognize that she must have had other longings all the time you were loving her, or rather loving who you thought she was."

"Yes, it was. So then it became a choice between bitterness and gratitude, which is like the difference between hate and love."

"I know which one you chose."

"Well, it took a while, the bruised ego bleating away. It helped that she stayed affectionate."

"Didn't the bruised ego resent the affection?"

"Very astute of you, Miss Annie. Yes it did for a while, until the choice became clear. Then it was gratitude for everything, even gratitude for her having the guts to leave if her feelings were elsewhere. Listen, I need to go check on things and call in. Come join me when you feel like it."

"What shall I wear?"

"Wear the space-suit you were born in, there's absolutely nothing wrong with it."

"Thank you, glad you like it. No remorse, no *tristesse?*"

"No, just eternal hunger."

"Till the fruit is but a husk?"

Nic sat up abruptly. "It scares you, doesn't it? You think you'll be discarded, abandoned?"

"It happens."

"Well, it's not happening now, is it? But fear can create it."

She didn't answer but he could feel her nodding into his chest. He eased his fingers into the mass of her hair, holding her skull gently, firmly, like a new-found treasure. He felt sure the clasp conveyed his feelings but how received was out of his control. Returning to the high-wire actuality of their situation, scorching through the upper atmosphere at near the speed of music, he shook his own head at the crazed unreality of it. He also realized that Anastasia's grasp of the situation must be far more tenuous, if not totally surreal.

He heard her murmur something into his chest. He lifted her head and asked, "I couldn't hear, what did you say?"

"I said, 'So far, so good'."

"How good are we talking?"

"Um...compared to what?"

Laughter broke the languid spell like an *allegro* third movement, following both as they leaped up and bounded naked to the cockpit. It ceased abruptly as they were met with beeps and lights flashing, for Anastasia a tocsin of fearful reality.

Warsaw. Meridien Hotel.

Close in the huge bed, Irina whispered, "So what do you think Igor can do for you?"

"I have no idea, but in Amerika he could do nothing, to not betray our existence. And Kolya once said, 'What can I do for you?' All I wanted to answer is a scream, Get us out of here! Ilya is not doing well and Mama is dying of sorrow, there is no hope for us there. But with the moment of Kolya's question it all changed, it is a mystery. Igor, believe me, he is one formidable guy. It must have been hell for him in Amerika, almost like a prisoner. But that was a lot better than what they would have done to him in Gulags."

"Yes, but now that he's out, what can he do?"

"Well, at least we can communicate. I am full of joy now and we can start to make a plan. He is so very loving, you know. He could have just forgotten us, much easier for him."

"And the cockroach next door, Sergei?"

"I think he must be a double. See the complication? If Americans find out that we are Igor's family, they will believe that he still works for Moscow, with us as the enforcement. If Moscow finds out, they will either kill us or use us to influence Igor. But this Sergei, I think he is not here for that reason. He is here because of letters between me and Kolya, so we are suspected spies. Or if Sergei is a double, he will have told Moscow... Irishka, it is all too complicated. I have to sleep and shut down my brain. And you are here, dearest, so all is well... Irina? Are you sleeping?...Irina?"

As Igor emerged from the shower in a grubby little *pension*, Rose switched off her phone and pulled the thinned-out sheet up to her chin. He saw that she was smiling happily.

"*Ay, Rosita, que pasa?*"

"We 'ave a Peepair, Narciso, coming in the *mañana.*"

"A peepair?"

"Is espanish for Piper. Twin engine Seneca, take us to paradise. Then you and I have three months to complete."

"What do you mean, *querida?*"

"Well, in the first flush you can't tell if you really like each other. There's a critical point, a glimpse of daylight reality, usually around three months when it can be seen as either love or infatuation. Does the notion scare you?"

"Rosita *mia*, I know that you are very likeable, quite apart from romance and desire. That doesn't worry me and I must trust that I will not bore you. But not knowing and suddenly discovering that you are wealthy…there we have a big disparity."

"I see…Whereas if the man is wealthy and the woman not, there is no problem?"

"So it would seem, yes."

"So the poor man's *machismo* is under threat?"

Igor leaned over the bed and took her head gently. "*Cariño,* do you remember the very first premise in Miracles."

She smiled knowingly. "Why don't you remind me?"

"'*Nothing real can be threatened. Nothing unreal exists. Herein lies the Peace.*' If my presence and my loving enhances your life the way yours does mine, there is nothing to worry about. My only thought regarding the wealth is to ask you for help for my sister and my mother who are trapped in poverty. If that is not something you wish to support, I will love you no less, but I will certainly find a way to rescue them. I am also saying that I have no interest or concern about what you do with your money, but then I must question myself—is that really true? It probably is not, because money does have huge potential for self-deception. I was speaking idealistically, I suppose. For myself, I would now be hitch-hiking to Cosumel, but you have summoned a Peeper."

"I just want you to enjoy it. Would it bother you if I asked you how much you left under the seat of the little jet?"

"Not at all. It was $5000. I spent $300 to get rid of my car and $170 on gasoline. I had saved this. I have not touched your $10,000."

Rose looked astonished. "I thought you said you had no money?"

He laughed. "Well, I certainly don't anymore! I had to be fair to Larry, big nuisance for him. So, did your money come from family?"

"No, not a cent. They cut me off when I was still a student. I went into real estate and I guess I just have the Midas touch. Unlike many realtors, I was carefree and joyful. I think it makes a huge difference if you're not greedy. Also, there's my songs, they've done very well… Narciso, I will be ecstatic if I can help your family, I hope you will allow it?"

"You are so kind. But first, let me see if I can do a deal with Portnikov."

"Who is that?"

"FSB, Moscow. Now that I have something to tell him."

"Really? Can you trust him?"

"No. Unless there's promise of more."

"And now you're out of the loop, where will you get that from?"

Igor shrugged. "We'll think of something."

"Oh, my God, Nic, what's happening, what's wrong?"

"Let's have a look," he answered with quiet calm, easing into the left seat. "It's Ok." He touched a button and the clamor ceased abruptly. "It's just a Selcall from Maastricht. Eurocontrol. Now we've answered, so they know where we are and going to plan."

"You never told me how you know all this stuff."

"I worked for a repo company, we had to know a lot of different types."

"How come we didn't know about it?"

"I worked under a different name, based in a different country. It wasn't exactly steady work. Some wicked stories, though."

"Like what?"

He shrugged and thought for a moment, refraining from being too scary. "Oh, like heisting a 747 with a dud engine under the guns of drug thugs... Right now, we're crossing the Coast of Spain. We have no conflicting traffic because of our altitude. Clear direct to Warsaw. ETA is 06.10 local. Late dinner just became breakfast. We're over the Bay of Biscay, just North of Bilbao. Dawn in about an hour. You want to go back to bed?"

"No, I want to dance in the aisle! Can we find some music?"

"Sure. There's a touchscreen in the galley. You want ballet, rock or ballroom?"

"I think I want Reggae."

"Go for it."

The stars began to blink out with approaching dawn, which due to their great height came far sooner than on the darkened terrain. Steel Pulse streamed from the audio player while France and then Germany streamed below as they breakfasted, danced, laughed and gallivanted, a deliberate toying with the seriousness of their situation.

Periodically, Nic checked in with Maastricht control until finally given clearance to begin their descent and switch to Warsaw approach. At 150 miles out they were cleared down to 25,000'. He reset the autopilot and emerged with a smile to find Anastasia still dancing, this time to Dvorak's Serenade for Strings.

"This is exquisite," she paused breathless, "Why was it never a ballet?"

"Time to get dressed, Pavlova."

"Why now? Do you think they'll care if they find me naked in the wreckage?"

Nic laughed and slid open the crew-rest door. "It's cold on the ground, sweets, and nothing but thick cloud cover. I just hope this guy's a good fit." He held up the blue Captain's uniform jacket against himself, seeing her look doubtful, and quickly dressed. The pants were wide in the waist and an inch short but there was a crisp and clean white shirt complete with gold epaulettes. There were no spare black shoes. He shrugged and retrieved the one anomaly, his worn brown Dockers.

"Come up and help me when you're dressed. It gets busy up there."

"Me help? I'd love to. Ten minutes?"

"Sooner."

"Roger, Captain. My, you do look smart. For a dilettante."

She ran back and began to dress hurriedly while Nic eased back into the cockpit. She joined him breathlessly a few minutes later, tousled but alight with excitement, wearing jeans and a pink cotton blouse.

"Roger, Gulfstream NG2587, this is Warsaw Chopin Approach. Be advised we have low visibility, less than 100 meters, in light fog, expect clear from the West within the hour. Airport closed till further notice. Do wish to divert, or do have enough reserve to hold?"

"Thank you Warsaw, we will divert. Canceling Flight Plan. Will advise. Over."

"Roger, 587, No other traffic this time."

Nic changed frequency to 124.5 and called several times, not expecting an answer. Anastasia, headphones in place, looked at him enquiringly.

"Talk to me, Captain."

"Aye aye. Warsaw is closed, fog. I wasn't going to go there anyway, obvious reasons like a cool welcome. Twenty miles to the Northwest is another airport called Modlin. It's not answering, so I assume it's also closed, which is just what we want. And it has an 8000-foot runway."

"But won't it be foggy as well?"

"More than likely. Doesn't matter, it's not too thick. With our EVS we could have gone into Warsaw, I just didn't tell them. Now, that big white knob in front of you, that's the landing gear. When I tell you, pull it out and push down, all the way and call the result. Should be three green lights. On your left, down here, flaps. I'll ask you first for 20 degrees, then 39. Slide it back to the indents. Don't be alarmed when you hear another voice, it calls out altitude below 500 feet. The center screen will show you what's happening. When I start bringing the throttles back, read me the airspeed figures from here, it says ASI."

"Is this an important job?"

"Yes. Very important."

He glanced across to see her smile vanish and her jaw set, betrayed at once by a mischievous twinkle. It made his heart swell even further. The sun had almost appeared in the brightening sky before their descent made it retreat again and a few minutes later they went into cloud, that eerie transition from visible surroundings to a different mind-set, an essential and absolute trust in instruments.

Anastasia was trying to take it all in, astonishment, delight and disbelief playing havoc with her senses. She reached across and grasped his forearm.

"Nic, I have to tell you, my system is barely coping. It's been over-stimulated or something. Whatever's happening now, I can't grasp it. I'm all jitters. Can you talk me through it?"

"Sure. Be easy. We are 65 miles out, descending through 8000 feet. What's our speed?"

"Er, 340."

"Right. We're heading 080 which is the same as the runway. It doesn't show on the display yet, we're not in range. This needle here shows Warsaw beacon at 088. I've given the computer the co-ordinates for Modlin and the autopilot is fixated on that. Cabin pressure is reducing automatically. 58 miles. We're doing about 5 miles a minute.

So, ten minutes to go. Up at altitude it all seems leisurely, but nearer the ground it gets suddenly fast."

"Needing nerves of steel?"

"Huh, blind faith more like. And precision. Ah, there we are, top of the Head-up display, Modlin airport. I'll try them again, hope they don't answer." He transmitted again several times without response and gave a smug thumbs-up, then reached out to reduce power. Anastasia saw the gesture and snapped eagerly into her role. Although he didn't need the information yet, he relished her co-operation.

"Airspeed 320...315...310......Oh. 280 already....255."

"That's Ok. Just tell me when we get to 160, then give me 20 degrees of flap."

"What do flaps do, and I don't mean the one I'm trying not to have?"

"They sort of make the wing bigger, more rounded, so we can fly slower."

"Ah...190...180...I'm ready...160. Now, flaps 20."

"Good...Now, gear down."

With obvious glee, Anastasia reached out to the white knob and depressed it firmly. The gear cycled audibly and she cried out, "There, three greens! Oops, sorry, Airspeed 135."

"Got it." Nic increased power to compensate for the extra drag. "Now then, flaps 39 degrees, please." He switched the landing picture on the HUD to the main screen on the panel. "See the runway on my display?"

"Wow, yes."

"I want you to keep looking outside. Tell me the moment you have runway visual."

"Still nothing but white. Are you scared Nic?"

"No, too busy."

"Is this what it's like in a simulator?"

"No. Simulator's much more scary."

The mechanical voice cut in abruptly, ominously. "*Five hundred.*"

"Speed is 130."

"*Four hundred.*"

"125."

"Three hundred...two hundred...one hundred."

"I see it, the runway! Speed 120."

"Thanks."

"Fifty...forty...thirty...twenty...."

Nic brought the throttles to idle as he clenched back on the yoke to flare and touched down with a slight bounce. With such a long runway, he let the speed bleed off by itself and the nose-wheel settle before applying brakes and spooling up reverse thrust. Glancing across he saw Anastasia's face looking at him radiantly. In fun, he barked at her, a peremptory order. "Flaps up!"

Without even looking down at the lever, she complied with a fierce smile. He needed no more convincing of her intunement. She pointed to the EVS screen as they reached the turn-off to the taxi-way.

"How do we know it's the real thing? Supposing the last four hours was just—" she stopped, her eyes alight and shining. "Just a practice run. A simulation?"

He looked up from the screen to the outside where there appeared ghostly airport buildings. "You mean it could get better? Welcome back to Poland, Countess, let's see if we can find a parking spot."

"Or a simulation of one?"

"Right. Then you can rustle us up a locksmith."

"Real or imaginary?"

"Let's see what shows up."

"Nic, why is it more scary in a simulator?"

"Oh, probably because there's an examiner breathing down your neck. After you crash and burn, you feel guilty and stupid and a failure."

"I see...And with the real thing?"

"Um, I dunno...Bunch of hooting hysterical angels, clapping your back and saying things like, 'I say, old boy, way-to-go-pile-up, wizard prang, what?'"

"British angels?"

"Well, naturally."

CHAPTER 19

For we wrestle not against flesh and blood but against Principalities and Powers, against the rulers of the darkness of this world, against spiritual wickedness in high places.

Ephesians 6.12

Marienbad, Czech Republic.

"Gentlemen, I regret to spoil your breakfast but something very odd has happened. The aircraft that was bringing our source from New Mexico has gone missing."

The tall gaunt Texan surveys the disappointed faces around the long table. Two of them ask the same question at once.

"You mean, crashed?"

"No, not as far as we know. It's a Gulfstream 5 from Fort Worth and Los Alamos. Put down in the Azores for a rest-break. Pilots came back to find the aircraft gone. It was on charter to the NSA. They'd already filed a flight plan to Warsaw but somebody snatched it while they were sleeping."

"Do we know where it went?"

"There's no word on that."

Querulous voices range around the table until an elderly figure taps his coffee cup. "Let's not speculate. We still have the woman from Ukraine."

"Not any more we don't," chimes another voice, his finger swiping his phone. "Our man there says she switched hotels and now he can't find her."

"So, get the cops on it, all the hotels have to report their guests."

"He did that already. There's no trace of her."

A stunned and angry silence follows the announcement. Faces contort and most of the thought patterns behind them are clearly congruent: We are busy people. We've come many thousands of miles for nothing.

"What was the range of the Gulfstream?"

"Pilots report they had taken on fuel for six hours, plus margin."

"Maybe they forgot to add Prist!"

Amid groans another asks, "When was it snatched?"

"We don't know. Early hours sometime. Lajes field was closed. Could have gone back to the States or on to Europe."

"Mexico?"

"No. Too far. Caribbean's another possibility, about five hours."

"What was the call sign?"

"NG2587."

While others murmur loudly, the Texan consults his phone and finally announces, "Shit, Henri, that's one of ours, from Minneapolis. Who insures it?"

"We do, of course," answers a suave English voice. "Lloyds, that is. You won't be covered for theft, though."

"Oh, why not?"

"Nobody steals 50 million dollar jets, old boy, it's unheard of."

"Stop quibbling, please. The point is, where is the passenger and the NSA escort? There's a team ready to meet them at Chopin Warsaw."

Blank, annoyed faces and shrugs meet the questioner, then another looks up from his phone, speaking with his mouthful. "Flight plan was followed to the letter, then cancelled at the last minute. Warsaw Chopin's in fog, plane was diverted. No further information."

"Very well. Looks like the intention was Warsaw so I suggest we go to plan. They say the fog is thinning out."

"Why can't we take our own aircraft, Henri?"

"We've been lucky here, we came from London well-spaced. The guards have seen no sign of photographers. If we all fly to Warsaw at the same time, the pinkos will be onto us like the cockroaches they are and the rumors will explode. Henry will remember what happened in Dublin. If they find out he's here…The anonymity advantage of private aircraft can work against us, fueled by manic jealousy and conspiracy nuts."

The young social-media mogul, pensive at the far end of the table, raises his hand.

"Yes, Jack?"

"I have to meet a Congressional committee tomorrow afternoon. If you don't mind I'll take my own aircraft. I can use another airfield if you're concerned."

"Well, I can't compel you to come with us."

"Good. That's settled then. I'll see you all at the Meridien. I'll go right away."

After he leaves, the Frenchman is heard to mutter, "Hm, I am sensing dissociation. He could be a mistake. We must be very discreet. The younger generation is not in tune with our thinking."

He nods to a burly figure in the doorway. "The cars are here. When you're ready, gentlemen."

The knocking became insistent. Irina finally roused herself from deep sleep, shucked on a robe and padded to the door. Through the peephole she saw distorted faces of Sergei and two other men behind him looking anxious. Irina had to speak loudly, in English, through the heavy door.

"What the hell do you want now?"

One of the others answered, thrusting himself to the forefront, an American accent. "Ma'am, you must help us find the lady who left this room. It's mighty important."

"Why?" Irina turned to see Elena shrinking inside the bedclothes, only her eyes showing. They widened in surprise as Irina pointed to the adjoining door. Elena sprang from the bed in a thin cotton nightgown and quickly let herself into the next room. Irina strode to the end table and grabbed her cell-phone.

Back at the door she heard a voice say urgently, "Ma'am, there's a delegation of very important people coming. They will pay her a lot of money for an interview. And yourself, if you can help us find her, tell us where she went."

"And if I refuse?"

She saw one of the magnified round faces nod to another. A key-card was inserted and the door opened violently, stopped by the entry-guard. Irina stood away just in time as a heavy boot tore the guard from the jamb. Tripping back caused her robe to open which caused a momentary pause and the needed surprise pose as she clicked her cell-camera, looked down, swiped and pressed Send. Four hands grabbed her roughly, ripped her robe down to her elbows and seized the phone. Sergei shut the door.

"Where did she send it?"

Another peered at the phone. "An address in the UK."

"It's earlier there. Get someone on it. Now, ma'am, we know you're a friend of hers. Where is she?"

"Hotel Security is on its way. You better leave."

"No, ma'am, they are not. We have already spoken to them. You are in a foreign country with no protection whatsoever."

Forced naked back on the bed, Irina tried to scream but rough hands covered her mouth and then quickly taped it. A thumb was forced into the side of her throat, the pain excruciating. An arm was raised to strike her.

A metallic click from the side door had all three men stiffen and start to turn. The thumb was suddenly released from Irina's throat when there came another sharp click and an almost silent, plosive pfft, followed by a terrible roaring groan. The man fell to the floor clutching his left buttock as the others turned to see a small figure in the doorway holding a short, black pistol. It swung to the other stranger who had reached into his jacket to draw his weapon.

Elena's voice was icy. "*Sleduyslchiy!*" (Next!), but the gun came out and he started to move towards her. So as not to miss, she too stepped forward and shot him in the right thigh from a range of less than 3 feet. The man dropped his gun, staggered and fell, his face rigid with shock, writhing and groaning incoherently. Both men appeared semiconscious, contorted with pain and pulsing blood onto the carpet. Sergei looked on, helpless with empty hands, his expression terminally desperate, like a man being pushed out without a parachute. Irina stared in horror, hands to her face, unable to speak.

"Get on the floor, Sergei, face down." Elena's voice grated in Russian, "Who are those men, why are they here?."

He knelt slowly and leaned forward on his arms. "They are advance guard for the delegation."

"How did you get a gun on the plane?"

"Diplomatic passport."

"I see. Well, you just used it to protect us from two terrorist intruders. We are most grateful. We will now trade rooms with you so you can clean up your mess."

Irina finally found her voice, rasping through the pain in her throat. "Lenochka, what have you *done*? Oh, my God!"

"What have I done? I give this Sergei animal a big problem, that is what I have done... Mr Animal, down and hands behind you... Ira, please check them for more weapons."

Nervous and very cautious, Irina relieved them of two 38's from hidden holsters. Both men seemed in-and-out of consciousness, the pain and shock precluding any resistance. Elena picked up the spool of tape and tossed it.

"Sergei's hands."

"Lena, have you thought this out?"

"Of course I have not! But I had a clarity that to these guys, the gunpoint is still playtime. They would never believe I would use it."

Irina said bitterly, still in shock, "Are you going to shoot Sergei as well?"

"No. This is his gun. Tape his hands, please." She moved close and looked directly into her friend's eyes. "Dearest, he's not dangerous now. These two, they were hurting you. How else to stop them? They're alive, aren't they?"

Though Sergei's hands were still not taped, she knelt down next to him. "Mr Animal, do you think you can sort this out or shall I just call the *stasi*?"

His head sideways on the carpet, his expression anguished, Sergei said quietly, "No cops. Take your things into my room. Get dressed and go down to breakfast. At 10 am go to the small conference room, the Moniuszko Salon. You will be quite safe there, I give you my word.

Take my room key."

"Who are these people coming, Sergei?"

"You will be warned not to tell. They want no publicity."

"Who are they?" Elena repeated, her voice hardening.

"No names, all right? They are the most powerful people in the world. Not the .1 per cent, not even .01, more like .0001."

Irina's alarm increased visibly. "You mean the Bil—?"

"Quiet! It's the steering committee of that group, the policy-makers. They're called the Masters of the Universe. They don't necessarily hold office but they decide who gets elected. And those they choose must obey them."

"I know who they are. But why do they want to meet Elena here?"

"I was not told this. Only to make sure she is there."

"I will go with her. Will it be safe?"

"Oh, certainly. They never do their own dirty work. Mostly they kill by the million. Three thousand is the usual minimum. You should go now. I must get help for these two idiots, get to hospital. And—oh, shit, they were supposed to go to the airport to meet another plane from the States. I'll have to do it myself...For this I will need my pistol."

Irina and Elena looked at each other in amazement. One laughed, the other shook her head in disbelief. Elena kept glancing at the two agonized and leaking figures and finally nodded with decision.

"Sergei, do not move until we are gone. Otherwise..."

She left the threat hanging but with no doubt in her voice. They gathered all their belongings and quickly moved into the next room, returning with all of Sergei's stuff except the papers and a spare clip. In silence, Irina placed their room key-card next to Sergei's hand. She was about to add something when Elena tugged at her urgently.

In the next room, they stared at each other for a long moment, both minds in ferment. Finally Irina asked,

"How did you know how to fire the gun?"

"My husband Leonid had one. It's called the PSS. It doesn't have silencer. The bullet is special, a silenced cartridge. It is an assassin's gun. We must get rid of it, and the other two."

"They will be able to tell that you fired it, not Sergei. From residue on your hands."

"No, not with this gun. All the gas is contained in the cartridge, so there is no trace."

"I am still shaking, Lenochka. What now?"

"We take a shower and go down to breakfast. Then we take a little walk to the river. Then we keep our appointment."

"I have to say I am completely shocked by you, your coolness. You were not afraid, were you?"

"No. It is a feeling I do not like and it has never been useful. I am giving it up."

"That sounds terrifying by itself!"

Laughter broke the tension and they sat on the bed, arms entwined. Elena stood suddenly, remembering.

"There was a woman in here. I shoo'ed her out. I was insulted. The Animal is not too discerning."

Irina also moved quickly away from the tangle of sheets, with a muttered *yerch* of disgust. "I think we should hurry. While the Animal is busy cleaning up, yes?"

"He'll have to bring a team, medics with stretchers. And all that blood on the carpet—"

"Not our problem. My God, if they ever needed any convincing you're a spy!"

"Hm. This committee thing, do you know anything about it?"

"Lena dear, I know everything about it. I've been researching it for years. I'll tell you at breakfast. Go take a shower, quick. I'll strip the bed and throw the sheets out."

"But we can't stay here!"

Irina shrugged. "Yes, you're right. I think we'd better pack our stuff. Who knows where we'll be this evening?"

Like the engines subsiding into silence, Nic and Anastasia slumped in their seats, staring ahead into the fog and then glancing at each other quizzically, she still in suspended disbelief.

"What now?" she asked eventually, "Why did you need a locksmith?"

"For the outside panel. We can raise and lower the stairs from inside but without a key we can't close it up and leave."

"There's a briefcase here, let me look...Ship's papers, a Shell fuel *Carnet*...and a key! Won't we have to clear Customs?"

"Only if they're here. Seems like no-one's about. Can you phone for a taxi?"

"I'm on it, boss."

"Re-phrase that, please."

"I'm on it, *naczelny wodz.*"

"Meaning?"

"Commander. In chief."

"Try again."

"*Umilowany.* That's Polish for 'beloved'."

"More like it, thanks. I suggest you be in charge now, you're on official business after all."

"And you're my prisoner?"

"No. He escapes. I am your pilot, respectful, humble and compliant."

"I see...And your name is?"

"Let's see....Kiddink. Captain Kiddink. I am Estonian."

"First name?"

"Yost."

Anastasia giggled. "Yost Kiddink! What happens when Uren discovers I let you escape?"

"Another heart attack, my guess. Did you find a number for a cab?"

Anastasia nodded and swiped on the number, then spoke rapidly in Polish. "He'll be outside the terminal in ten minutes. But what about formalities?"

"I guess everyone stayed in bed because of the fog. If the plane's parked here and locked, they'll assume it's legit. Let's get our stuff and go."

Nic retrieved the double chock from the rear compartment and with the steps down, the little key fitted the panel. He placed the chock astride the nose-wheels and waited for Anastasia to descend the steps, smiling as she played a regal role. When the stairway hissed back into the hull, he re-locked the panel and stood back, the pilot's jacket slung from his shoulder, casting his eye along the length of this astonishing machine, with its long and exquisitely-tapered wings. Anastasia stood next to him, holding her case and his small bundle with the passport on top.

"I still can't take it in," she breathed, "It's really huge, but beautiful. Our 55-million-dollar love-nest. Is there any way we can keep it?"

Her phone chirped, announcing the taxi's arrival, with an apology for the fog-delay but it took them several minutes before they found an unlocked door to the outside. In the cab, Anastasia had a short, heated exchange with the driver, after which he became sullen and silent. She smiled at Nic but before she could explain, her phone trilled again. Glaring at it, she muttered, "It's Frank Uren, from Los Alamos…." She held up her hand for silence. "Yes, boss?…No, all went to plan. What? No, a reserve pilot showed up and took us the rest of the way…No, I assumed the charter company had sent him… His name? I forget, he was Estonian. We had to divert, Warsaw was fogbound. We're headed there now, by car… Moncrieffe? No, he was no trouble, quite the opposite. He's here. Very good company…No, not a word on that. Oh, I see…Hold him here? I'll need more money, won't I?…Ok…What!?"

She listened for a long minute, her expression darkening with concern. When the call ended abruptly she turned to Nic to explain.

"I decided your escape could wait. He's getting prepped for surgery and he's frantic. They're down to one agent and he's real doubtful. Apparently the harmless secretary from Ukraine, little Miss Elena, shot and seriously wounded two of his agents, the ones who were supposed to pick you up."

"Holy Mo, this is getting out of hand."

"I think it's already got. Now we have to go to the Hotel Meridien, there's a bunch of VIP's coming to talk to my prisoner, that's you, and of course Elena, who now has an ally from London."

"Irina?"

"The same. Multi-lingual lady."

"Irina's a Russian. Elena doesn't speak English. Could get interesting."

Anastasia's frown slowly lightened into a sparkle of mischief. "And you, what shall you be?"

"Your pilot, naturally."

"And the prisoner?"

"Just say he'll be here any minute. Didn't Elena get arrested for the shooting?"

"No, they're keeping it quiet. Cleaners are coming in but Uren says they're fresh out of backup. He was a bit vague, he's on pre-meds. Anyway, he says it's all up to me now."

"Have you decided whose side you're on?"

She grinned at him slyly. "Ha. It's emotion versus profession. Nic, I hope you realize I was only following orders. Uren told me to seduce you, pump you and dump you. Now he's making me escort you, and I'm supposed to keep an eye on you until the water-boarders can take over. But he also said it again, Give us this Biggall and all is forgiven. Is Uren trustworthy? No, not even slightly. That's why I haven't bothered to ask you."

"I noticed. But if I told you, you'd be compromised."

"That wouldn't matter if it kept you from rendition."

"Beloved, there's a catch. If I don't follow through, this is all wasted, the most amazing opportunity. Do you know who the VIP's are?"

"Pretty much. I should tell you something else—this Irina from London is a human ferret, an expert researcher. Following her online searches shows an obsession with the, ah, let's call them The Overlords. She doesn't twit or tweet, she absorbs. She's a speed-reader with amazing recall and a passionately curious mind."

"And you know all this, how?"

"Need you ask?"

"Probably not!"

"So you see, Captain Beloved, we are venturing, no, wading into an estuary full of crocodiles, and an apparently innocent bystander has found a gun and shot two CIA agents."

"And your point is?"

"Hell, I can't remember. Let's go check it out. We must get you some black shoes but it's too early for shops."

"No-one will notice, not with you on my arm."

She made a gleeful sound and squeezed. "Hey, how about that? Pilot envy, right?"

"Yes, ma'am, you are beautiful enough to qualify. Listen, I have an idea…"

CHAPTER 20

"When asked if that's you, pretend it isn't and see what happens."

Winnie the Pooh

Once a late 19th Century cigar room, the Moniuszko Salon gleamed with polished paneling, crystal chandeliers and subdued lighting. A murmur of male voices reached Irina and Elena as they approached with some apprehension. Two bodyguards at the entrance frisked them perfunctorily and opened the ornate door. The murmur ceased abruptly as they entered, expectant patrician faces turning their way, mostly tanned heads expensively groomed over immaculate tailoring. The Frenchman stood abruptly and the others followed.

"Ladies, welcome. Please announce yourselves, and please describe yourselves. And thank you for coming."

Irina touched Elena's shoulder and whispered a translation. Elena looked at each man in turn, her expression calm and almost radiant. When she finally announced herself, in Russian, something in the high timbre of her voice caught everyone's attention. Irina translated as soon as she finished.

"She says she is Elena Knyazeva from Zaporozhye, Ukraine. She is 36 years old, a secretary in an engineering design company."

"Thank you. And yourself, Madame?"

Irina scanned the faces round the long table. "Thank you, Henri. It's Ma'amzelle. I am Irina Popova, originally from Moscow. I live in London. I am a professional translator. Elena and I have been friends since High School. We are both curious to know what you want from us."

Frowning, the Frenchman asked, "How do you know my name, Ma'amzelle?"

"The same way I know all of your names. The annual meeting, this time in Austria, there was much publicity. For once."

Frowns deepened to some muttering as she stepped forward and looked at each face in turn, reeling off first names, leaving out any titles: "Roger. Josef. Marcus. Philip. Franco. Ian. George. Étienne. Kenneth. Timothy, Robert, Henry, Tony, Klaus, Benjamin, Evelyn, Mario, another Henry, David." She left out several others and pointed to the younger man, the only one with a loose collar and no tie. "That one I do not know, is he new to your group?"

"Ma'amzelle, are you also a journalist?"

"No, I am not. I became interested in researching because of increasing worldwide focus on your activities, ever since the previous meeting in Watford, UK."

"I see. So you think you know exactly who we are?"

Before she could answer, the door opened and one of the guards put his head round it. "Sir, there are two more people here, they say they have business with you. A pilot and a woman. She has NSA credentials. We secured a service automatic from her handbag."

"Thank you. Send them in. Oh, and get some more chairs, please."

Anastasia strode in confidently followed by Nic, his Captain's jacket slung casually from finger over shoulder, his expression diffident as if not belonging.

"Good morning, gentlemen. I am Anastasia Wojerkowski. I work at Los Alamos in New Mexico. This is Captain Kiddink, my pilot. I'm sorry we are late, we were diverted."

"Were you not escorting someone?"

"Yes, but he has a stomach complaint. He had to run to the bathroom."

"Thank you. Tell us, Captain, how you came to take over a Gulfstream 5 in the Azores."

Nic spoke with the merest Slavic inflexion. "I vas on standby in Lajes and I receive call from Los Alamos, authorizing me to continue planned flight to Warsaw."

"On whose authority?"

"His name was Uren, Frank Uren. I believe he is Security Specialist at LANL."

The Frenchman turned to the table. "Check that, would you, someone. It doesn't make sense. I believe the Gulfstream requires at least two pilots."

Anastasia spoke up quickly. "Agent Uren gave him special clearance, sir, because of his experience. Uren is my immediate supervisor, but he's presently undergoing heart surgery, you won't be able to reach him for several hours."

"I see. Well, Captain, may I see your credentials?"

"I'm afraid I hef nothing with me. The order was top urgent and my gear was all locked up, including my shoes." Nic looked down shyly at his worn Dockers. "Lajes was officially closed, do you see? Uren said he would get me full clearance into Poland and out again. We are scheduled on to Egypt."

The Frenchman flapped his hand in annoyance. "This is hardly relevant. It is the passenger we wish to interview."

Anastasia pointed to the speaker system in the center of the table. "Does that have a phone number? Good, give it to me please."

She entered the number in her cell-phone and turned to Nic. "Captain, please take this to Mr Moncrieffe in the restroom and ask him to call us as soon as he is able."

"Yes, ma'am. It may be a little while, he vas in some distress." Nic took the phone, bowed respectfully and left the room.

"Now, Ms…"

"Popova, but please call me Irina."

"I prefer not. Ms Popova, and you, Ms, ah, Knyazeva, everything said in this room is strictly, and I mean strictly, confidential. Is that very clear? I have no wish to detail the consequences of a breach, let us just say it would be extremely prejudicial. If as you say, you know who we are, you will understand the severity of this stricture. It is absolute. Am I clear?"

"Yes, sir." Irina's nod was emphatic and serious but when she translated to Elena she saw only a contented smile. Turning back to the Frenchman she asked, "Can we expect complete frankness also?"

"You may, in fact it is essential. But we will not welcome any questions."

Irina turned to Elena and quickly translated. Elena said something in reply, as much as two long sentences, her smile still radiant.

"What did she say, please?" asked the Frenchman.

"She said, In that case she will not answer any."

"I see. There was more, I think?"

"Yes. She wants to ask what you would like to hear that would make you less afraid."

The Frenchman frowned, puzzled. "Afraid? I do not understand."

Before Irina could answer, Elena said something quickly and was translated at once.

"She says this whole room is full of fear. Except for the young one."

More chairs appeared and the three women sat down, the two Russians close together and Anastasia slightly separate. Their placing was awkward for some at the table who had to shift to face them.

"Of what does she think we are afraid?" The Frenchman asked with a faint smile.

After conferring, Irina translated, "She says you're afraid of whatever caused you to bring us here, or bring yourselves here."

"Listen to me," the Frenchman grated, "You are in a very dire position. We know that coded messages have passed between Knyazeva and this Moncrieffe and you in London are the go-between, an abortive and naïve cut-off attempt. The primary question is whether Ms Knyazeva passed any information to either Moscow or Beijing. Ask her that, would you?"

The table phone rang just as Irina was relaying the question to Elena. The Englishman tapped the answer button and said loudly, "Just a moment, please."

Irina translated the answer. "Sir, she says she has no knowledge of any codes."

"But the emails contained cryptics!" He turned to Anastasia. "You, ma'am, what did your people make of the encryptions?"

"It was assumed they were code but we were not able to crack it without a key."

The Frenchman was thoughtful for a moment, then said loudly, "Mr Moncrieffe, are you there?"

"I am," Nic answered in measured BBC English.

"I gather you have a gastric situation, are you alright?"

"Well, I dare not leave this stall just now, I'm sorry."

"I understand. Do you know who we are?"

"I have some ideas. What do you want?"

"Quite simply, we want your source."

"Source? Of what?"

"I warn you, sir, do not irritate. You know perfectly well, since you have been asked many times, for the source of your information about the additive in the jet fuel."

"I've answered that already. The name I heard was Biggall. I don't know where he hangs out, he never told me."

"A description then, what did he look like?"

"Well, it's hard to say. Chaps with beards tend to look alike, at least to me. I don't usually trust a man with a beard but there was something inspiring about this character."

"There must be more you can give us—it could save you much grief and an onward journey. Need I say more? How did this Biggall find out about the additive?"

"You mean it's true, what he said? Gosh, I was never able to verify it for myself but he seemed to know so much. And he knows all about you chaps."

"Explain, please."

"Golly, how long have we got? Er, just a moment..." There came a distant flushing noise over the speaker then Nic's voice came back after some sounds of distress. "Excuse me, I am not very well...Let me see, where to begin...First, I am not anti-Semitic, and neither is Biggall, that's for sure. There is a segment which has been referred to as the—"

"My friend, I advise you to be very cautious with your words."

"—who are not Israelis and are not even necessarily Jewish. They are, however, impregnable because of the Anti-Defamation League and the fearsome smear of anti-Semitism. If you wish me to guard my words, I need to know who is in the room. The pilot said he recognized a couple of you."

While the Frenchman hesitated for an answer, Irina spoke out quickly and clearly. "All are known to me. All except one are members of the Tri-Lateral Commission, most are members of the CFR, the Council on Foreign Relations. All except one have attended the last four Bilderberg meetings and all except one were invitees to Bohemian Grove in California."

"That's enough!" shouted the Frenchman.

"Why?" asked Irina bravely, "There's nothing wrong with all that, surely?"

Nic's voice cut in again, "Of course there isn't. But may I suggest we do not label them, simply to avoid a possible racial slur or accusations of bigotry...Let's simply suggest that there is a group or Cabal which is more powerful than any other on the planet. They own or control just about every facet of life in the Western world, starting of course with the money supply, the Federal Reserve, and from there the big corporations, the oil, the military and virtually every politician regardless of party. They also own or control virtually every media outlet with very few exceptions. Would you say there is some truth in this?"

"Just tell us what you know, or what this Biggall knows."

"Alright. To avoid the slur, let us call them the Overlords. In the interest of honesty I cannot pull any more punches. They have also been called the Corporate Goliath. Excuse me." Nic spluttered and made a few theatrical groans which made some of the listeners flinch in distaste. "Sorry about that. The old gut's playing up a bit...Biggall has attended your meetings and he is quite clear and emphatic. Are you sure you want me to go on?"

His question was met with a prolonged silence and there were nervous glances round the assembly.

"I take it that's a Yes," Nic continued, "Biggall told me that the Overlords have been responsible for every single war since the 1800's. In both World Wars they profited from both sides. They financed the Kaiser and Hitler, building ships, tanks and aircraft for both sides, not to mention arms. They knew in advance and enabled Pearl Harbor. They rigged the Gulf of Tonkin, the start of Vietnam, they colluded with 9/11—this is no longer deniable, gentlemen—they used it to attack Afghanistan and then quickly switched to Iraq which was provably unconnected with 9/11. Do you recall that the Vice-President at the time was quoted saying, on 9/12, 'Time to attack Iraq'? Before that, they instigated Saddam's invasion of Kuwait so they could have a noble rescue war and establish more influence in the Middle East mainly for the protection of Israel. The Israeli lobby is immensely powerful. But 9/11's other purpose was the creation in the United States of Homeland Security and the virtual crackdown of potential protest. They have power to imprison or liquidate anyone they choose, which is why I am threatened with rendition to Egypt or Djibouti. Finally, as your most senior member cannot deny since it's in his Manifesto, they are intent on establishing one World Government or New World Order, one currency, a decimated population and the complete electronic control of every citizen on the planet. To this end they have almost succeeded in unifying Europe, to be followed by a North American Union of Canada, USA and Mexico. They have enough power to quell all the Middle East factions but it is not yet in their interest. Miss Irina from London, I understand you have researched all this. Would you agree, or have anything to add?"

Irina hesitated, her nerves strung out. Finally she gathered herself bravely.

"Well, the rescue of Kuwait was to establish more control there. Afghanistan was thought to be about securing the oil and gas pipeline from the Caspian and Iraq was all about oil and minerals, but in reality the mainspring was Israel securing protection from the USA. Israel receives more foreign aid from the USA than any other country, more than $3 billion a year since 1949. Then there were of course the fortunes to be made from all the destruction and reconstruction. All of them together mark Middle East control. But, Mr Moncrieffe, none of this is why we're here, surely? These people want to know about the new chemtrails."

"Well, Ok," Nic answered hoarsely, "But he asked me what Biggall knew or had witnessed. Excuse me." He spoke in an aside, "Captain, could you get me some water please?"

They heard the Estonian answer "Jah," as if from a discreet remove.

"Mr Moncrieffe," said the Frenchman, "Are you on speaker? We don't wish to be overheard."

"Very well, but there's no-one else in here and the Captain went out...The chemtrails—well, all the evidence is writ large on the Internet, but Mr Joe Public has likely never heard of them because the media does not reference them, on orders from the Overlords. They also do not cover crop circles or alien incursions, and certainly not conspiracy quacks, except for outright mockery. They will not even investigate the more obvious anomalies such as the hole in the Pentagon being far too small for a 757 and no airplane parts. There were no aircraft parts in the hole in the field in Pennsylvania but wreckage was spread over 8 miles, indicating destruction at altitude. The World Trade Center, three buildings dropped in their footprints, which more than fifteen hundred architects and demolition experts declare impossible without weeks of careful preparation. Unmarked trucks arriving three weeks before 9/11, at 3am, after the janitors had left...Who was it, who bought and doubly re-insured the entire complex only two months before, said there was a fire on the top floor of building 7 so they decided to "pull" it. It cannot be done at less than many weeks lay-up of explosives, and jet fuel will not melt steel. There were puddles of molten steel and concrete pulverized to fine powder, implying Nano-Thermite...These are bare facts, not conspiracy theories...But back to the chemtrails— there is no way to find out beyond the obvious evidence contained in millions of pages on the Internet, because journalists and editors are controlled or forbidden—by the Overlords. I assume that what most interests you is the infusion of a psychedelic or mind-freeing chemical, spread all over the world unknowingly by high-flying aircraft."

"That is exactly why we are here. The rest is utter garbage. What else can you tell us about it?"

"Only what Biggall chose to let me know. I was skeptical at first and then all the tests they did on Prist proved negative for DMT. I'm now informed that the DMT is a result of the combustion of Prist and JP5, that's jet-kerosene, at high altitude, in ultra-low temperatures and virtual vacuum. Excuse me a moment."

There was extended murmuring around the table at this new information so Irina took the opportunity to brief Elena on what had been said. Even though she heard the name 'Kolya' mentioned twice, Anastasia listened stone-faced, quietly desperate not to betray her internal ferment and her terror that Nic's deception might be exposed, along with her own complicity. It was only too obvious that this group had the power and means to eliminate them all without compunction.

When the irritatingly hesitant and gravelly voice spoke out, the murmuring ceased abruptly. "Mr Moncrieffe, did this Biggall....did he give any opinion about the, ah, likely long-term effects of this chemical from the jet exhaust?"

"It was cryptic. He said the more people wake up to what is happening, the more they will wake up. In other words, it's exponential, like the Hundredth Monkey."

"I see. Did he suggest how the, er, Overlords as you call them, might try or be able to thwart it?"

"Yes, he did. He said they will start another war or cause another massive scare so that more controls can be imposed. The Overlords will only be safe when everyone is rendered powerless, by Martial Law or by being chipped. They would accomplish this gradually by advertising it as a safety device and the elimination of cash money. Once every transaction has to be made by chip, everyone will be in electronic shackles."

"And you think this is the intention of these so-called Overlords?"

There was a long pause and some coughing from the loud-speaker on the table. Finally Nic's voice emerged again, clearly distressed.

"Henry, I'm sure that is your name, right? Biggall tells me that of all the Overlords, you are the most craven. It does not suit me to converse with you."

The oldest man present leaned forward and thundered into the microphone. "You will guard your tongue, sir! You have no right to impugn an honored elder statesman."

"That I believe is the voice of David, am I correct, Ms. Popova?"

Irina's answer sounded emboldened. "That is correct, sir. Another famous statesman."

"Thank you. Referring to the former, I would say he has not been impugned enough, a sycophant who viewed the misery and death of millions as a necessary stepping stone to power, and who probably persuaded himself that power would enable him do some good in the world. That's quite apart from it being 'the greatest aphrodisiac'.

Fortunately he is near the end of his life, though not the end of the damage he has done. And nor could any retribution ever be appropriate."

There were loud murmurs of protest although the owner of the rasping voice sat toad-like and unblinking.

Nic's voice cut in again and all listened intently. "Just one example of many—Cambodia. That was your doing, Henry, and all in secret and illegal. More than a million Cambodians, and another 25,000 American soldiers, all down to you because you believed that America, and Henry, needed to save face. "

The Frenchman intervened with an outburst. "Mr Moncrieffe, I command you to silence—at least on this topic. The slur is unwarranted. Henry is—"

"—I know, Henri, he's just a pudgy, cuddly family man who wouldn't swat a fly. But he'd get someone else to do it for him. A mass-murderer who never held a pistol. Right now, I bet he wants your guards to come in and tear my limbs off. Well, you better give them respirators, it's pretty rough in here. The bottom just fell out of my world, or rather the other way round."

At this a number of heads glanced at each other, the topic too edgy for them to titter. Nic added, more gently, "But I thought you wanted to hear about what Biggall has to say."

"Thank you," the Frenchman answered, "The insults and implications are inappropriate and time wasting. We need to know what can be done about this new development, can you tell us that? We will of course reward you most handsomely for a solution, a pardon, multiple dollars, whatever you require."

The tension in the room seemed to evaporate with this manageable suggestion and more familiar ground. The Frenchman resumed his questioning.

"First we need to know if the jet-fuel information has been passed to Moscow. A Russian defector, known to you I believe, has since re-defected from Los Alamos. We do not know his whereabouts, but we know he had the information. We doubt if he would be well-received in Russia even though they offered amnesty to former defectors. I mean, who would ever trust them?"

"Henri," another voice spoke from the table, a former US Secretary of the Treasury. "If this stuff is doing its work, then Russia and China will be affected as the rest of the world. Admittedly they don't have the same amount of air-traffic as the West. But jets fly everywhere. Where are we going with this?"

The only answer was a low groan from Nic through the table speaker. The Frenchman raised his eyes in frustration and turned to Irina.

"Ms Popova, please ask the Ukrainian a question for us. Did she pass her information to anyone else—and do warn her that we have the means of extracting the truth. In fact—" He broke off and strode to the door, barking to one of the guards.

Irina spoke quickly to Elena, whose gentle smile was unwavering and again caught the attention of the whole group. One asked sourly, "What is she looking so smug about? Doesn't she realize what we can—"

His voice was shushed by several others before he could complete the threat. Anastasia had become increasingly tense while Nic was speaking, but now something in the very tone of Elena's replies had her relaxing in her chair.

"Mr Moncrieffe, are you still there?" the Frenchman asked, returning to his seat.

"I am, but I am rather sick. I think it's really serious, quite honestly. Food poisoning, I guess."

"Sorry to hear that. Did the captain bring you water?"

"He did, thanks."

"How did you know my name?"

"It was an educated guess. You are after all chairman of the Overlord's steering committee, right?"

Henri didn't answer the question but returned to topic. "What is suggested we do about this jet-trail question? That's why we are here. That is what you have to tell us, to avoid any unpleasantness."

"Oh, start another war, of course."

"But our researches tell us there have been too many wars recently, that there would be overwhelming protest. Personally I don't believe it. We have the West sown up and too comfortable to rise up significantly.

It is also believed that a crackdown on protest is expected and being prepared for, otherwise America could face a bloodbath. Another epidemic, on the other hand—"

"Henri, I was being sardonic."

"*Ah, Zut!...*" The Frenchman slumped and looked around the faces, most of them anxious or puzzled except for the young man at the end who cleared his throat pointedly.

"Why don't we ask the women what they think?"

Heads jerked aggressively towards him but he stood and spoke up strongly. "Have you guys noticed something? The little Russian is in a different space from the rest of you. I think she knows something we haven't heard yet."

Irina quickly translated to Elena who nodded affably, her smile deepening, and then answered at length. Her voice was strangely dulcet and almost detached. All waited till she finished and Irina stood ready to relay her remarks.

"I trust someone is recording here? This will not be verbatim but I will do my best. First of all she asks that each one of you think of someone you love, love like for a child, with no condition, not romantic or erotic. Then shrink that thought into a hand-clasp size and place it in front of your heart."

Only a few complied while the rest sat stone-faced but with their eyes fixed on Elena. Irina spoke quickly to her in Russian to clarify a point and had to wait for an answer. With the apparent serenity and engagement of Elena's smile, it seemed that something mysterious was happening in the room as more men were seen surreptitiously to close a hand in front of their chests. After a lengthy pause, Elena spoke again and Irina had to compose herself with an effort before translating from shorthand notes. Understanding the exchange, Anastasia too struggled to disguise emotion.

"The information and the codes you are all seeking, she says, are only available to those willing to see. It requires a shift in perspective, it requires willingness to conjure something you may never have imagined or entertained, yet it is closer than your breath. The power that you have sought and duly attained has its basis in fear. For some born to a race long-oppressed, that fear seems justified but there is an irony too massive to ignore. The race oppressed and decimated by Hitler had also produced men of exceptional cleverness who supported him, albeit through nominees. Their goal of course was not to have Hitler rule the world but to use him to rule it themselves. The price was some 80 million lives on all sides but since they also supported the Allies, it made no difference who won the war, they emerged the victors and finally attained wealth and power enough to make themselves impregnable."

"Ms Popova, the Ukrainian did not speak at such length, and we did not ask for your personal opinion."

"I apologize, and I will only translate verbatim. We have only spoken briefly since I arrived here but I can tell you that Elena has never heard of you as a group. But would you do us the favor of clasping a hand in front of your heart-space and hear us out?"

Irina spoke very gently and she waited quietly until curiosity won out and the Frenchman finally complied. Several others cautiously followed suit, all staring at her intently. Irina scanned the room again, her right hand clasped to her chest. Settling herself, she gestured to Elena to continue, watching her closely for cues to translate. Elena's gaze seemed to have gone glassy and unfocused.

"......She says there is a concentration of power in the hands of those who do not think like the rest of humanity.... Their wealth and position separate them and cause them to view the desperate masses as little more than ah, vermin.... They believe that unproductive vermin should be eliminated to make life better for everyone else.... Some of them are very high-minded and believe they are benign overlords striving for an end to war and a better world and that the better world can only be achieved if they control it.... They can't control it if the numbers are out of hand..."

Irina suddenly looked wide-eyed at what she had just relayed. She looked at Elena in astonishment but her surprise was unseen as the stream of Russian continued.

"....Communism as a political philosophy had its merits but it still had its privileged few to control it. It was therefore unfair and eventually rejected by the masses who were down-trodden and non-cooperative...Here and now, she says, is your chance to do something different."

At this, Elena's face brightened and she looked slowly round the room and then back to Irina, her expression switched from somber. The same smile with which Ekaterina Gordeeva, the gold-medal skater, had charmed the world, appeared to light up her face and remained luminous as she scanned the room, lingering on the younger man at the far end who seemed transfixed, his right hand pressed tightly to his open white shirt. She only said a few words and gestured to Irina to continue. Meanwhile Anastasia, fragile with emotion after her wild experience, had been resisting tears, but now gave up and silently let them stream.

Irina listened again and continued in a dulcet near-monotone. "… What is happening here is the exact opposite of all your intentions…. Blessedly you are too late with the chip because the joy coming from the airstreams will help the populace become free. If you stay in opposition to this… it could take a very long time, after much struggle and suffering, but the outcome is inevitable…. With you in support, it could happen very quickly."

A stern American voice from the table interrupted, to visible annoyance from others. "Excuse me, but what is it you are suggesting could happen?"

Irina turned to Elena and relayed the enquiry. Elena looked directly at the questioner, her radiance undiminished. He looked down but the prolonged silence forced him to look up again. Reluctantly and almost in slow motion, his hand clasped and settled on his chest, while his body visibly relaxed. Elena said nothing but with a simple gesture deferred to her friend who continued solemnly.

"Gentlemen, I have to tell you that something very strange is happening here. I have never heard her speak with such fluency and her voice has changed. There is something other-worldly about it. I will try to convey the tone but I am very puzzled."

She turned again to Elena who seemed to be looking in the far distance, speaking hollowly. "She says …It is as though your isolation has put you in opposition with those you control or wish to control… Whatever we oppose acknowledges it and gives it power—as in the saying, 'what you resist persists'… It works the other way as well—

those who wish to oppose and defeat you... do not know how to proceed beyond protest and reviling you and trying to expose you.... They too are fixed on opposition even though many of them are gentle, peace-loving souls merely seeking justice.... The likely outcome is an, ah, intensely bloody revolution and a complete re-set of the system..... In the process you will mostly all be crucified—that's not literal, by the way—along with your families.... Centuries of power-mongering will likely fizzle out....In the great scheme of things, none of this really matters, but you do have a choice in what to visualize as your legacy....

"....The faces we first saw at this table were not those of benign philanthropists.... Right now we are seeing changes and we will explain exactly why so that you are not suspicious of some chicanery.... She says she made a decision, very recently, to divest herself of fearful thinking ....There's a quotation from one of the so-called coded texts that she received: '*The ego is quite literally a fearful thought.*'

Irina held up her hand to pause the flow from Elena. "These are my words, for a moment, excuse me. It seems that divesting herself of it automatically shifted her awareness to her heart-space which, in case you were not aware, has the energetic power to calm all in its presence—a proven fact, believe us. And I'm sure you noticed that it is not oppositional, yes?"

Irina looked around the table and noticed several solemn nods. The Frenchman at the head now seemed to be transfixed, his expression rigid but with vivid high color in his cheeks. The young media-mogul was looking at Elena like the man who has seen true love across a proverbial crowded room and is in awestruck uncertainty of the outcome.

Irina went on. "Up to now, my researches into all of you have been for discovery of what we are up against which as was said, is simply oppositional, a recipe for a catastrophe which none of you or your heirs will survive..."

Irina paused for a moment and looked at Elena again, responding to the Gordeeva smile with a shy version of her own. "I have not seen Elena for years until yesterday. We are unrehearsed. I am not at the effect of some psychedelic, but I feel as though I am immersed in a warm sea of what I can only describe as heartfelt compassion...She is speaking again…I am to call Kolya."

Irina raised her voice for the microphone. "Moncrieffe, are you still there?"

Nic croaked his answer. "I am. Just. This is pretty bad."

The Frenchman called out, "Is there anything we can do to help?"

"No, thanks. Best stay away. I'll manage. Please go on."

The Frenchman shrugged and gestured Irina to continue. Elena took the cue as if she understood and continued in short sentences, Irina translating with palpable surprise at each one.

"…The reason we asked him is that he had many accusations and blame for past, er, discrepancies…. Only accident of birth seems to separate us but in truth, any of us could have been an appointed advisor to a crooked U.S. President…. just as any of us could have been Saul on the road to Damascus…. The ego-mind does not know anything of compassion or of forgiveness…. and cannot conceive of the notion contained in the texts that there is nothing to forgive…. Forgiveness is impossible without that notion…. just as fearlessness is impossible if you believe there is still something to fear. She wants to ask around the table, 'What do you still fear?' Henri?"

The Frenchman looked up from working his tablet. "*Moi?* Well, chaos, of course. Revolutionary chaos."

"Why, because the revolution would be against you?"

"Well, yes, I suppose that is so."

"Timothy, how about you?"

"Because of my sector, I fear monetary collapse. And I fear the Chinese."

"And you, Henry? You are shaking, are you alright?"

"Uh, well it is not like me to be unsure, but for once I am."

"But your fear is—?"

"Disgrace." The gravelly, hesitant voice was notably subdued, even pitiable. "Average people do not understand the incredible complexity of diplomacy. Sometimes you have to choose between several unwelcome scenarios."

"Thank you. And Kenneth?"

"My fear is of the world reduced to the lowest denominator. So many are completely ignorant."

"We understand, and yet you fear an educated populace?"

"Listen, there's about three billion humanoids who don't have the I.Q. or even the genes to BE educated!"

"Thank you. And the young man at the end, Jack is it? What do you fear?"

He smiled in some relief. "Well, I was beginning to feel that my only fear was of these people here, but from this compassionate space I find them all just fragile and human. Elena's radiance has me convinced. I confess I was afraid that if I did not fall in with them, they would have me eliminated or at least stripped of everything."

"Thank you for your honesty. Is that still the case?"

"No, it isn't. Somehow that fear has left me, just a few minutes ago, and I would be privileged to use my network to spread her message. Would you tell her that, please? I have many avenues available to me."

One man who had kept his back to the women stood abruptly and glared around the room. "This is frankly preposterous, pathetic, it's like mass hypnosis! We've come half across the globe to find a solution and you've all turned to putty. I will be informing all the members of your betrayal. I think we should get this Moncrieffe in here, and right now. I don't care if he shits on the floor!"

The outburst was followed by loud protests and shouts of "Sit down, Robert," which he ignored and turned to glare at Elena. She avoided his glance by looking down and closing her eyes, but her smile remained in a kind of ecstatic and winsome Cupid's bow. The man they called Robert continued to glare but then his posture visibly weakened, his furious expression turning first to a kind of despair and then to perplexity. Finally he sat down and turned his chair to face her, staring intently.

Nic's voice cut in over the speaker, "Gentlemen, have you decided where to go from here? I think I may have to get help. Definitely something wrong. I've asked the Captain to call a doctor. I don't know if I can be any further use to you."

The Frenchman stiffened and resumed his former posture. "With respect, sir, you haven't been any use at all. We never got to pin down this Biggall and you did not tell us anything about him, how to find him. I have looked in our database for one anonymous attendee who has been at the last four Bilderberg meetings, and it doesn't add up. He may even be a fiction, is what I'm thinking. In your favor you were instrumental in bringing to us Ms Knyazeva whose words we must rely on Ms Popova to translate or perhaps embellish, rather. We will have someone check the transcripts later. It only remains for one of you to give us the reference codes and frankly, I don't believe any one of us wishes to put pressure on the women ... Ms Popova, please ask Elena if she knows anything about this Biggall."

Irina relayed the question and Elena looked up for a moment. Her headshake began emphatically but then seemed to change to a thought as if ambivalent. Her beatific smile remained as if she was in a trance, then her eyes glazed and she spoke two sentences.

"What did she say, please?" asked the Chairman sharply.

"She says she will try to find him for you. He may be nearer than you think."

"What?! You mean he may be one of us?"

"She didn't say that...She said, 'These people don't give orders, do they? They simply make suggestions. They know everything that goes on in the world, they control it with suggestions.' Like Henry the Second and Becket: *'Will no-one rid me of this turbulent priest?'* So it was done. For myself, I ask, Is it true?"

"Well, ah, between us we certainly have great influence."

"And is it your intention to make the mass of men powerless?"

"Uh, I would say they are already powerless, don't you think? It's just a matter of degree. We cannot be attacked because we cannot be pinpointed. Listen, if you or she intend to ask me about the truth of 9/11 or any of Moncrieffe's strident accusations, I would ask a question in return: What does it matter what they believe if they are powerless?"

"Excuse me, sir, but from my researches it would appear that there are Ninja-type teams from Asia who have you already pin-pointed and simply await the word. They could in fact take you all out, right here, today even. Surely you must know this yourselves?"

The Frenchman looked suddenly confused, gripped by some internal dissension. His demeanor had hardened and softened again. His glance took in the two Russian women and then looked further as if for support, locking on to Anastasia whose tears had ceased though she still tightly clutched a soaked tissue.

The door opened and the uniformed pilot reappeared. "Excuse me, gentlemen, ladies. I thought best to call doctor for Moncrieffe. He takes one look and ordered an ambulance. I think it must be food poisoning. He will go to Emergency Room. He is far too sick to run."

"Someone should go with him! Which hospital?"

"They did not say, I'm sorry. I will try to find out."

An English voice spoke up. "God, this is a bloody shambles...Tell me, Captain, have you ever heard of Bilderberg?"

"No, sir. Where is it?"

"It's in Holland. I think it would be best if you waited outside."

Nic bowed out agreeably and shut the door. Outside he twinkled at the two guards and was stoically ignored so he retreated once more to the men's room. To his surprise and as if on cue, the siren of an approaching ambulance sounded clearly through the hushed surroundings.

CHAPTER 21

*"Some even believe we are part of a secret cabal working against the best interests of the United States, characterizing my family and me as 'internationalists' and of conspiring with others around the world to build a more integrated global political and economic structure--One World, if you will. **If that's the charge, I stand guilty, and I am proud of it.**"*

David Rockefeller, *Memoirs*

lena began speaking rapidly, animated, the corners of her mouth flickering upwards. Irina quickly signaled a request for pen and paper and began taking notes in her own personal shorthand. Her eyes were wide and increasingly astonished. Anastasia tried to look neutral, which became increasingly difficult as the information streamed and Elena's words in Russian held her transfixed. Having read all the correspondence between Nic in Santa Fe and the woman from Zaporozhye, an apparently simple and straightforward person, what she heard was astonishing. She found herself worrying about how the group would receive it when Irina was given a pause for translation.

"She was saying, 'Something is happening to her which she does not understand, she is receiving, not in words exactly but in groups of thought. She does not know the source... She says, Many of these people here are genuinely high-minded... and believe that they use their influence for the good of all humanity...aiming for a world that is properly controlled or controllable.... Unfortunately their great wealth and influence separates them to the extent... that they have forgotten who they are and what humanity in general is longing for, is craving.... It is quite within their power to give it but they are afraid to do so.... because of their scorn for the yearning millions... whom they regard as little more than factory workers or even farm animals....

The information they are seeking from Kolya... is being conveyed to all in varying degrees and its source is in the very environment.... We are integral with, and dependent on, our actual environment and it is now rapidly changing.... The one you seek knows all this and is simply watching developments.... He knows that you believe you are too powerful to be opposed... because you hold all the means to extinguish any revolution.... but your methods, which you have long been preparing.... will have to be drastic in the extreme and will lead to humanity's greatest disaster...We asked that you hold love in your hands, close to your hearts, for a reason."

As Irina stopped, Elena turned to her with a request. Her voice was markedly different, less grave and almost carefree. There was a pause as Irina translated and a glass of water was passed from the table. Elena drank deeply and took a long breath before continuing in the strange tone, taking pauses while Irina translated about a sentence behind, as if they had found a private rhythm.

"Thank you...I am hearing that the one you seek, the one called Big, cannot be found...I am not told why but he is like the many-headed hydra and can't be extinguished... There is very definitely something in the atmosphere which is changing all who breathe it and it cannot be avoided... Some even believe it is an influence from another world but at present there are very few who believe that such things are possible...Most of us do not have the capacity to believe that there are realms beyond our current understanding...and so we dismiss the rumors absolutely...One of those rumors is that on another level, not conscious of course, we are as interconnected as a forest of aspens...I do not know what that signifies in nature, only that it means we are all connected both to each other and to our very source...that no thought or deed is ever erased...The storage unit cannot be tracked because it is in the very fabric of what gives us life...It is integral, just like part of our environment...The old myths of some Deity with a ledger of our debits and credits had their origin in our intuition of this fact... but it is essentially something that is felt rather than intellectually perceived...The hand on the heart contains the key...At present, all your political systems are corrupt and counter-productive...because they are all being worked by selfish interests of one kind or another...

but you will have noticed the rapidly increasing numbers of those whose lives…whose lives and intentions are rooted in service to others, the only possibility of true happiness…Most of the people around this table are addicted to power and are not happy…They may be smug or satisfied and able to afford every luxury but these things…are simply a distraction from the truth, while the possession…the status of power requires others to hold power over…

"In the revolution which you all fear, many of those would be removed…by the violence of your fearful reaction and you would be left…with a populace in utter horror and revulsion at your methods…A manhunt would ensue, resulting in your complete extermination…but the world would be in devastation and this very civilization completely ended…This has happened before…But now, finally and starting right here in this room…you can prevent the re-occurrence of another Dark Age…But this time you do not have a choice because…7 billion people are gaining a new perspective and the clarity…to reject a system which has brought misery to countless millions for hundreds of years…you do not have a choice because you yourselves are also co-dependent on…inseparable from your environment…

"If every action, every thought, every initiative begins with the hand that holds that beloved child, next to the heart…"

Elena had stopped speaking and swallowed several times, her eyes brimming, *"U menya est rebionol...ya znayu shto eto znachit. U mnogikh iz vas est dieti i vnuki..."*

In the pause the Frenchman asked quietly, "What was the last thing she said?"

Irina translated, also with a catch in her voice. "She said, 'I have a child…so I know what this all means. Many of you have children and grandchildren…'"

She looked at Elena who had gone silent, though emotion had subsided and her smile returned. The Frenchman turned as the door opened and a white-coated technician pushed in a small trolley, plugged in an extension and waited deferentially. When the Frenchman pointed to the seated Elena, the technician approached her and held out his hand. He was tall and thin with a narrow pointed head, bald and shiny. Curiously, as if she knew his intention, she held out her own in submission, not to a handshake, and then complied with his directions. There was no sound or movement round the table, just the silence of the stunned. None of the faces seemed to look at each other, their eyes unfocused. Irina checked her notes and then turned to see Elena being hooked up with wires to the machine, her expression unperturbed even when her blouse was lifted.

"What is this, please?" Irina asked.

"It is a polygraph. We must ask her some questions and we require absolute truth. We would have preferred to question Moncrieffe but we assume he has told her everything. Is that not so, Ms Wojerkowski?"

Anastasia simply nodded in confirmation.

"Very well. Ask her, please, what is the first name of this Mr. Biggall?"

Irina translated and the answer came back promptly. "She says it is Biggall."

"I see! And his last name?"

"She was never told."

"But as far as you know, Moncrieffe got his information from this Biggall?"

"She asks, What information?"

"That there is, ah, DMT produced by the combustion of Prist at high altitude?"

"She knows nothing of this."

"I see." He turned to the technician. "Doctor, do you speak Russian?"

"Yes, I do."

"Then tell me is the translation accurate and are the replies truthful?"

"Yes, to both questions. I will let you know at once if there is an anomaly."

"Thank you. Please ask her now—ah, I understand that she has no political background—from where did she receive all the information contained in her lengthy deposition?"

On hearing the relayed question, Elena merely shrugged but answered promptly. The Doctor nodded to confirm truth and said, "She does not know."

The young man called Jack spoke from the far end of the table. "Ask her, please, is channeling a reality?"

The Doctor looked confused so Irina translated exactly, after explaining to the room that the word 'channeling' was the same in Russian. She was met with a puzzled silence from Elena, so she took several sentences to convey the meaning. Elena listened carefully, brightening and finally nodding before her answer.

"She says she has never heard the term but she understands it to mean that she hears communication in her head from an unknown or mysterious source."

The Doctor quickly intervened. "There was a slight anomaly on the read-out. I believe it was at the word '*neizvestnyy*', meaning 'unknown'."

"Thank you. Ms Popova, ask her what she thinks is the source."

The Doctor nodded confirmation as Elena's hesitant reply was translated by Irina. "She says she does not know for sure. It feels like the same source as Moncrieffe has, but she hesitates with a name."

"In other words, she is asking us to believe that it is this Biggall somebody who is communicating telepathically?"

"She says she feels that is correct but cannot be certain."

"Has she had such communication before?"

"She realizes she may have, but merely thought it intuition."

"Is the name Biggall a pseudonym?"

Irina interpreted, listened and said, "She says it's just a name given to her by Moncrieffe. She is not aware of a personality when she receives these blocks of thought…Mr. Chairman, I have to say that I know this lady very well and she is not given to lengthy diatribes and certainly never of a didactic nature. She is normally very humble and reserved. This is an entirely new side to her character. Also, when she was speaking it was not with her normal voice or inflexion. I am not able to explain this."

"Thank you. I suppose neither can we…Does she have any inkling of the last name of Biggall?"

Irina referred and gave the answer while the Doctor nodded approvingly. "She does not know exactly but she believes it means something of great power. She has never heard it spoken."

"I see. Thank you. Does she have anything else to impart, or indeed any questions for this gathering?"

In response to translation, Elena seemed suddenly as if lit from within. The whole room responded, intent on simply watching her very presence and not yet understanding, since the tone of her voice seemed to convey deep significance. Irina resumed her note-taking while the Doctor monitored the moving graphs. Elena began with a question for the Doctor which he cautiously answered, both speaking Russian.

Irina said, "She asked the Doctor if she heard an answer from the room that was untruthful, would it register on the machine? He answered that it probably would if she herself felt or intuited that it was untrue. Do you still welcome questions?"

There was murmuring from all round the table, the younger man notably grinning at this turn of events. The Frenchman, and others, looked disturbed, but he answered, "Well, because I asked, I do suppose the questions must be welcome."

As soon as this was translated, the Doctor raised his hand. "I must inform you, that reply registered as, ah, questionable."

To his credit the Frenchman shook his head ruefully and said with a smile, "I walked into that one, gentlemen. I apologize. We may have to take the Fifth."

This elicited some good-humored chuckling as well as some scowls. Still smiling herself, Elena spoke briefly and Irina forwarded the question. "She asks if you are able to dictate policy for the whole world?"

"Um, we are working on that. It has been problematic."

"Did you demand of the American leadership that they invade Iraq?"

"Tell her we take the Fifth Amendment on that."

Pause for translation. "She understands that means admission."

"Tell her this is not a court of law and neither is she the judge."

"She asks, Did you know about 9/11 long before it happened?"

"After Susan Lindauer's warnings, we would have to say we were informed, as the White House was informed. But of course we could not be certain that the information was correct."

The doctor's arm swung up but the Frenchman ignored him, pretending not to see. Irina listened and said, "She will not question you further on any past, er, machinations, because it is pointless. She is not here to accuse, and the truth is there for anyone who cares to look for it. She wishes to speak again, if that's alright?"

With obvious relief the chairman acquiesced and waited quietly. Once again all seemed to come under the spell of the quiet voice and a presence bordering on angelic.

"She says this morning she had to injure two men who were going to harm me…. She regrets that it seemed necessary and hopes they will recover…recover in good time and also that Kolya, that is Moncrieffe, is properly cared for and allowed to go free…. I have to say I do not know how she knows this, but she said there was an Act of Congress to do with patriotism which has actually destroyed all semblance of democracy in the USA and Britain…. It was many thousands of pages which were not read by the representatives but was signed in a panic….a panic which was induced by all of you…. You must have this law repealed as soon as possible because it is every bit as evil as the Third Reich…. Now that an increasing number of citizens know about you… because of their new connection to the environment… and your influence over every aspect of life in the West… it is time for you to reveal yourselves and show that your intentions are benign…. First there is in America a panel of nine of which more than half is corrupt…. It is not representative of justice and it has clearly been politically coerced…. which is why democracy no longer exists in that country… or any country where the information reaching the public is restricted and controlled…..But almost no-one in this room believes in democracy because they do not believe that any populace is intelligent enough to understand the issues."

Irina looked away from her and glanced around the room. "Gentlemen, she asked at this point that you again place hands in front of hearts…In this state you will note there is no call for regret, remorse or guilt, all of which imply fear of some kind, mainly of retribution. Excuse me."

"She says she is receiving direct thoughts again." She glanced down at Elena who continued to smile with notable calm, her eyes distant. The Doctor remained standing next to her, looking perplexed. "Since the doctor speaks Russian, he can confirm that I am not augmenting from my own knowledge. She says, Because of this new awareness which is permeating the planet, your choices are becoming more limited every day.... Are you alright, sir, the one called Henry?"

The elderly, white and frizzy-haired man facing her on the far side of the table appeared to have slumped, his head bowed, the hand on his chest clutching horn-rimmed glasses while his left hand mopped his face and eyes with a napkin. His only answer was a quick, repeated nod. Some turned to stare at him while others appeared to be wrestling with emotion.

"To continue... It was not perhaps to be expected that your accumulation of influence would have a purpose or outcome beyond your intentions.... Normally you would also have two very powerful women in this committee, neither of whom could attend. The three women here have no such influence and might be seen as on the other side of the fence, so to speak.... We wish you to understand that we are not in contention with you at this time... and we appreciate that many of your ideas have sprung from a genuine desire to bring order to a disordered world.... However, the actual flavor of this intention was based on an idea of separation and elitism.... whereas what you are feeling in your hearts, those that are open, is actually true compassion for all living beings...

"This moment is the gateway, the threshold of the most magnificent... the most significant moment in the history of *homo sapiens*... the opportunity to turn from what was fast becoming tyranny and fascism, which is always doomed... into benevolent guidance...

"You can retain your power...But it must be used only for altruistic purposes. You are currently able to end starvation, suffering and injustice on every level...throughout the world, not just in the West, and so go down in history... as saints and saviors...I am not receiving any information about any alternatives, in fact I am hearing that there are none except the unwelcome."

Irina stopped speaking and looked at Elena and then at Anastasia, who sat spellbound, her mouth slightly open and disguising its tendency to scowl, her tears once again brimming. Elena remained composed, smiling still and seeming unconcerned. Irina asked her in Russian if there was anything further, but she shook her head. The Doctor raised his arm immediately.

"I see an anomaly, gentlemen. I will ask again." When he did so, Elena looked suddenly startled, her smile vanishing to the rapid Russian speech. He then waited stiffly for the answers. There were none until he had the intuition to rephrase them, and to each she voiced a simple affirmative though her smile had vanished. "*Da.*" Her voice was formal and clipped. Hearing them, Irina's eyes widened and her body went rigid. Anastasia felt herself squirming in her seat with the effort to look neutral. The Doctor too had paled and seemed to shrink inside his lab-coat even as he watched the polygraph confirm truth at every sentence.

"What did she say, please?" the Frenchman asked but Elena interrupted, this time in her normal voice. Almost sick with terror, Irina used the moment to translate only the last request and the former exchange was glossed over. She trembled to think what would happen when the recording was transcribed and distributed, surely a death sentence for the doctor. But then again, she thought, calming herself, the truth is all over the Internet for anyone who is able to use it, as surely Goliath once thought he was impervious to a diminutive slingshot.

"She has something to ask but it is strictly personal and not part of her message to you. She has a request." Irina listened again and relayed the message in its entirety.

"She recognizes that this may be her only opportunity to beseech a personal favor, that she and her small family be given the means and opportunity to leave Zaporozhye in Ukraine so as to seek proper medical care for her child. She is hesitating about this because so many are suffering in far worse circumstances, but as some of you have recognized, the love and care in each mother for her child is paramount. She declares that she is innocent of any kind of espionage and this truth also applies to Kolya, known to you as Moncrieffe. That is all."

The Frenchman stood up slowly from his chair, his hand still firmly clenched on his chest. He looked straight at the Texan who'd claimed ownership of the Gulfstream.

"George?"

"Yeah, Henri?"

"Are you with us?"

The Texan stood and answered briskly, "Well, maybe I too got a bit choked up, but logic says this is nuts. You gotta know you're being taken here. Any more in that direction, it's a goddam hunting license. Truth in the media, we'll be run down like rats. The Asians....As it is, these people here cannot be allowed to—"

"George!"

The Texan stopped and checked himself with difficulty, finally speaking in measured tones. "Well there ya go. A purty smile is all it takes to make candy-asses of you Euro-peons. We didn't get where we are by chawin' on sentiment. That gal there," he pointed at Elena, who returned his glare with unperturbed expression, her hand clasped over her breast. The tall man stopped, flustered, and seemed to shrink into his suit. "Well, let's see what kinda consensus we got here."

He looked around the table for support, found none and repeated the round to make sure. "Well now, I guess I'll be lookin' fer a back channel ta check on how y'all *really* feel. But listen, if yer sayin' there's no hist'ry, just a whole new page, I could mebbe see a way to, hell, I dunno..." The Texan halted suddenly, looking thoughtful, perhaps even sly. Abruptly he added, "Ok, get that pilot feller in here, would ya?"

Anastasia stood and went to the door, spoke briefly to one of the guards outside. All waited a minute until Nic appeared, still with the ill-fitting jacket slung from his shoulder.

The Texan drawled, "Cap'n, seems we gotta change o' plan. You good to go?"

"Yes, sir. But I hef not received order from Los Alamos."

"Ya get 'em from me now, buddy. I own that ship, get me? Here's the deal. Get that baby back Stateside A-SAP, but on the way, you take this lady here to Zaporo-whatsit, pick up her folks and be on ya way. But ya need to get another pilot—Stateside and solo you're in the shit. I'll get you clearance over Kiev, and all points west, North Africa or South Europe, it's up to you. Guess you'll have to wait till that other guy is outta the hospital. I'll have my people clear the way for you. You gotta fuel card, right?"

"Yes, sir. Does that mean we no longer take prisoner to Egypt?"

"S'right. Tell him to call me when he gets home, we'll arrange some compensation for all the disturbance, plus a fat bonus if he can find us this Biggall friggin' ghost." He glared around the table. "You guys, tell me something—I think this jet additive's a hoax. If so, where do ya stand? Business as usual?"

As if the flavor of his words conveyed, Elena stood up suddenly, the wires dangling to the polygraph. The Doctor made to prevent accident but she didn't move beyond their scope. Her tiny figure was in vivid contrast to the Texan's 6'3", and after a lengthy pause she spoke quietly. Irina waited till she finished and then stood up again herself.

"Sir, she says you are still afraid, afraid that if you do the right thing, the wrong thing will result. You have been a fine warrior in your time but power has ah, estranged you. You have armored yourself with wealth and influence but the armor separates you not just from all that might harm you but also from your connection with all. She said actually, *Vsyo Suscheye*, meaning not just all of us but All-That-Is."

Irina listened and spoke again, both women still standing. "Change is difficult for the elderly but in time the truth will be exposed...There is still a presence of evil in this room...So now you have a choice for your legacy...It is earnestly to be wished that you will not be remorseful or seek forgiveness but will simply make amends while you still have breath and function...The heart speaks only truth...This is your moment. This. Now. There is nothing to be wary of."

The tall Texan's glare seemed to soften in the face of Elena's slightly saddened smile. He looked away in discomfort and then with a muster of his old courage, looked directly back at her eyes as if summoning defiance. It failed him almost immediately and he looked down, meeting no-one's eyes. Next to him the Englishman held up his hand as both women also sat.

"Er, if I may, could somebody explain what is happening here and also what is the nature of the chemical you mentioned?"

The Frenchman answered despairingly, "I wish I knew. Anybody?"

Anastasia held up her hand, then stood abruptly and drew everyone's attention. "Researches in Los Alamos and Albuquerque reveal that DMT is a natural substance produced in the body, by the pineal gland. It seems that people who are content with their existence produce more than the discontented. But when DMT is supplemented from outside, ratios change proportionately. Prior to recent developments, you would perhaps not have been able to hear what we have heard today because of contraction in thinking. DMT in supplement causes expansion of thinking, to be more inclusive than separate and the myths of the contracted mind seem to evaporate. All have been signally affected here this morning."

The Frenchman turned in his chair. "Are you saying that some such substance has been induced in this very room today?"

"Certainly not, no sir. You could verify this with Elena and the polygraph."

The Frenchman nodded to the Doctor and repeated the question. The Doctor relayed it in Russian and still smiling Elena shook her head, saying simply "*Niet.*" The Doctor looked up from the graph and nodded assurance.

"How is it we are allowing her to be some kind of oracle?"

Ignoring the Chairman's question and subsequent murmuring, Anastasia went on, "It seems that when confronted with fearlessness, a most enviable quality, we see something so exquisitely desirable that it fills us with good feelings and thus more DMT is produced. It is virtually instantaneous. In just the same way, and I'm sure you have all felt this, when a person smiles, genuinely and from the eyes, the body chemistry changes abruptly—in both parties. The same when they go to gratitude. It can actually be measured from the IG, that is Immuno-Globulin in your saliva.

"Conversely, when a person has a strong negative reaction such as guilt or grief or rage, IG is instantly reduced and the immune system collapses. Those who can see auras will pick it up immediately. It normally takes about 6 hours to recover homeostasis. It has also been shown that those near death produce large amounts of DMT, which accounts for some NDE's, that is Near-Death-Experiences, awareness of, even interaction with alien beings and other-worldly phenomena.

Normally we do not have the mental equipment to see beyond the third dimension. Thus the bigger picture which most of you have in mind in your plans for the world is still hopelessly limited by the third dimension which is intrinsically fearful or self-protective.

"You have witnessed something different today where minds can open to greater possibilities. It seems that fearlessness is the key to the Great Shift which is being much spoken of these days, leading to an overwhelm of beauty and exquisite experience quite beyond the possibility of description in our normal 3-D thinking, and thus an increase in the individual's DMT. You would expect a humble secretary from Ukraine to be terrified in the face of a roomful of fierce patrician potentates but when the opposite happened, you found yourselves profoundly affected. We have all glimpsed a new dimension and a new possibility and we have been in awe…

"You could have changed, or rather you still can change, the way the whole world is thinking. Regrettably you have shaped what it is now. With your great influence you could be preventing the racial, religious and fiscal upheavals which are plaguing so many nations, and which have actually been of your very choosing, for your fearsome purposes. This includes the virtual enslavement of all peoples, which has clearly been your intent, in fact your declared intent. The Great Shift is calling on you all, here and now. Forgive my presumption in saying all this, it seems I did not have a choice. I'm afraid that neither do you—correction, no, I am not afraid. Simply put, neither do you. And the choice itself is not fearful, it is one of limitless, joyful possibility, as you have seen. But some of you are still resisting, perhaps to the death."

In the ensuing pensive silence, the younger man stood up and waited easily. Finally he coughed for attention and said, "Mz Popova, Irina, would you please ask Elena where she wishes to go? I have a proposition for her."

Irina smiled and said with a bold smile, "Sir, there is a look in your eyes, are you sure you didn't mean proposal?"

She put the question to Elena during the cautious laughter round the table, and when it subsided, she relayed the answer. "She says it does not matter, but she would naturally prefer cleanliness and warmth, friendly neighbors and good food, and something useful to do, wherever it is to be found."

Still grinning, the young man said, "Thank you. I am very happily married, but I have full time employment, for both of you, and it can be anywhere in the world. I run a worldwide social media business and I am going to use it to spread what I have heard here this morning. I believe I know these people here and some are still in disagreement, so it is likely that they will try to have me, let's say, compromised. My aircraft is being checked for sabotage as we speak. Captain, I would strongly suggest you do the same."

There were loud murmurs of protest although the Texan remained silent, still looking down.

"Thank you, sir," Nic answered, "As far as can tell, they do not know where is the Gulfstream. But is not yours itself a fearful reaction?"

"You have a point," admitted the young man, surprised, "So let's just call it prudence. I want to take care of something very precious, for the good of all." In passing, he stopped in front of Elena, while deferring to Irina. "Here's my card. Please call me when you get to wherever you are going. And here's a credit card, for any moving expenses. It has no limit, I trust your discretion. And make sure that other guy is taken care of. Now I must go...After this, I'm wondering how I'm going to deal with Congressional committees, I guess we all know where their interests lie... Gentlemen, till next time."

CHAPTER 22

We are on the verge of global transformation. All we need is the right major crisis and the nations will accept the New World Order.

David Rockefeller

After the young man called Jack had left, there was a prolonged silence, most of the members looking down. Some still held hands to their chests. Finally the second Henry coughed, shook his head and asked,

"What the hell has happened here? Could someone explain it? I feel like I've been bamboozled."

Many voices erupted but one man stood up and tapped his water glass.

"To me, as a military strategist, it seems we've been handed an ultimatum. All the minds are being affected including, I presume, our own. How else to explain your reactions to this young woman here? We are told she is naïve and unschooled in politics yet she has, for the moment at least, attempted to undermine all our strategies. What is being suggested is a complete *volte face*, in which case all our previous plans, unwritten though they are, will be uncovered and there will be intense outrage—and all from people who don't know what's good for them."

Several voices began to respond but Irina held up her hand while she translated to Elena. The room quieted as she did so but became completely hushed when Elena answered. She spoke for several minutes and Irina didn't interrupt but took shorthand notes. Nic stayed in the room and perceived a glow emanating from Elena, whether from within or from the intense focus of more than a dozen pairs of eyes, he could not tell in his own astonishment. He also had to quell a loving strong desire to stand behind Anastasia and put his hands on her shoulders, while she sat still and upright and wide-eyed.

During a pause in the rapid Russian, Irina relayed from her notes. "She asks for hands on hearts again, please. Is this not how you take a pledge? We ask, Do you have the conviction to convey a new message to all your members, expanding down your pyramid, to all those in a position of influence and power?"

Irina looked up from her notes. "Gentlemen, please note that, as earlier, she has been saying 'we', as if what she is saying is coming from a collective. It is not meant to include myself. I'll continue with Elena's words.

"We know that all of you have made decisions in your time that took extraordinary courage and conviction. None of those compare with what you now face because it goes contrary to a philosophy and the habits of a lifetime. We note that you understand the love of family and children and that you yourselves are beloved by some also. We are not here to preach, we simply pose a question: Can you treat the family of man as you would your own family, with benign and loving guidance, and not as serfs and underlings? We emphasize that because of what is spreading all over the globe, you have only one choice, but you can make it willingly or reluctantly. The world will no longer tolerate secret agendas aimed at controlling, enslaving or decimating."

When Irina finished, Elena said one more sentence, but Irina had difficulty speaking with the emotion of the moment.

"If your choice is willing, you have nothing to fear and we will always be with you."

A voice from the table said, "Ask her please, who this 'we', who is speaking through her?"

Elena answered the relayed question without hesitation. Once again the room was rapt as they waited for her to finish and to hear the translation. "You do not have the capacity to see us, only hear us. We are in another dimension. We have been in the physical so we understand your difficulty with belief. Simply know that we care but that we do not wish to intervene. It is up to you to follow the heart signals, as mankind's most exquisite gift. No alternative is seen or offered. We speak through this dear one as an unobstructed channel."

Elena had slumped in her seat as if inspiration had deserted her. The Doctor, who had been standing rigidly alongside her, also relaxed and at a signal from the Chairman started to remove the electrodes.

"Wait!" the Frenchman said suddenly, "Ask her if they know how to find Biggall?"

Elena drew sharp attention by saying "*Niet*" even before Irina could relay the question, then she smiled up at the Doctor as a different person. The Chairman asked, "Doctor, were there any anomalies in what she has just told us?"

"No, sir, none whatever. It was all certifiable truth. Very impressive, if mystifying."

"Thank you." The Frenchman turned and said, "That will be all, ladies, and you Captain. Thank you for coming. We wish to confer among ourselves."

Elena looked up sharply and said, "*Pri zakrytykh dveryakh?*"

"What?"

The Doctor explained, "She questioned, Do you wish to speak in private?"

"Yes, we do."

Elena spoke once more and this time the Doctor translated. "She says she will leave the room but from now on, nothing that is said among you is private." Over a background of garbled outrage, he listened again and added, "Everything is heard and the world will be informed. There is no need or place for guarded words, nor even thoughts. If you ever have doubts about what is right, place hand on heart holding the beloved. When loving kindness is the intention, all else will follow....She says, *Dasvidania*, Good-bye."

As soon as she was disconnected, the three stood up and joined Nic by the door, though the fierce murmuring continued. They filed out past the guards and Anastasia was surprised to be handed back Uren's .38. Once out of earshot down the hall, Nic who was leading, turned and smiled. They all stopped and looked at each other repeatedly, a seethe of unspoken questions. Finally Nic spoke briskly.

"I think we should scram right away. Annie, see if you can contact the brother and ask Elena to call her mother. Irina, do you want to come with us or go back to London?"

"I'll come with you. Where are we going?" Her smile was light and carefree as if the answer didn't matter. With Anastasia's help, Elena was on the cell-phone in moments, though the effort to speak calmly was obvious in her posture. After listening intently, she slumped against the wall, shaking her head to an audible tirade from the phone.

Nic understood at once and spoke tersely. "Annie, please take over that call. Say you are Authority. Just give her mother some orders. She's to be at the airport in four hours' time, at the private terminal, with only essential belongings and a ten year old boy. Irina, you two go get your stuff. I'll meet you out front in five minutes."

Irina held up her hand. "Wait, Captain, what about Kolya, we can't—"

Nic flicked his fingers and smiled jauntily. "Don't worry about him, he'll manage."

Upstairs, Irina and Elena found a line of housekeeping carts and a great bustle of cleaners moving in and out of their first room. Sergei emerged suddenly just as they were unlocking his original door. He made an attempt to draw himself up aggressively then quickly changed his mind at the sight of their expressions. Stone-faced, Irina opened the door while Elena smiled pleasantly but stopped and turned at the threshold.

In Russian she asked him if his two colleagues were going to be alright. He nodded and shrugged dismissively, then again asked for the return of his prime possession, the silent PSS assassin's handgun.

"*V. reke,*" she answered simply.

In the river! Sergei's face furrowed in rage. He half-squatted and extracted a four-inch knife from an ankle sheath, stood and whipped it up under her chin, his other hand curled behind her neck to prevent retreat. To his surprise, she neither flinched nor strained away, simply looked into his eyes and slowly brought her hands up to his face. Very gently her two small thumbs soothed the pouches under his furious eyes which widened helplessly under her gaze. Her fingers moved up and smoothed the hair on his temples. In the room Irina had turned and stiffened in the same moments but then she relaxed at seeing the two figures motionless and silent in mysterious embrace. It seemed as if the power had drained from Sergei's right arm as it lowered and fell to his side. His fingers opened and the knife fell softly to the carpet. He brought his hands up to cover Elena's and his head moved forward as if seeking a kiss. Just the tiniest away-movement of her head was enough to indicate refusal. His expression marshmallow, he continued looking into her eyes as if to complete his capitulation.

One of the cleaners emerged from next door to ask him a question and stopped in surprise at the strange tableau. Sergei merely nodded once and then let his hands fall away, like one who has just been given an anesthetic and is feeling its first effects. Leaving the knife where it fell, he turned and walked slowly away as if in trance. Elena simply looked straight ahead and then surrendered to a prolonged hug from Irina behind her.

"Lena," she whispered, "Whatever it is you've discovered, I want it. I must have it. Not for the power. For the peace. For a state of grace."

Elena hugged the arms around her. "It is yours for the asking, dearest. Just be it. What happened downstairs, it was as if I could see into the minds, the motives. Of a sudden they had a picture of something they desperately wanted but didn't know they could have... And it seems so easy...But one, perhaps more than one, will not be complying. It is seen by him as a weakness...Are we ready to go? I can imagine my Mama right now, half panic, half doubt. What to tell Ilya when she pulls him out of school?"

"I'm worried about Kolya, we cannot leave without him. "Do you really think any of us will make it out of here? Those monsters—"

Elena turned out of the embrace and put a hush-finger on Irina's lips. "You're forgetting. We gave them a choice when they have no choice."

"Because of what is in the jet fuel?"

"No, because the hearts were softened. The tall one was barely touched but they will over-rule him. The young one holds the key because he is not afraid. He knows who he is."

Irina smiled. "But he's prudent?"

"Just so. Let us leave in prudence. And thank you so much for being here for me."

"For us."

"For all of us."

"What do you think they'll do now, all those big-wigs?"

"It's out of our hands, Irishka. Expect a miracle."

Irina giggled, "Another one? All in one day?"

"Yes! And it has only just begun. Let's go."

Down in the conference room there was a prolonged silence, so unusual that most of the members kept glancing at each other and looking down again. The Texan stood abruptly and left the room without a word. The Englishman started to speak, "If I may—" but the Chairman held up his hand to stall him. Then, quite deliberately, looking round the table to be sure of attention, he closed the hand and brought it to his chest. He nodded at each in turn as one by one they copied him. The most elderly, a fading but still powerful character in his nineties, was the last to comply and his hand was clearly twitching as if barely under control. On his right the first Henry had replaced his intimidating glasses but his perpetual glower had been replaced with a mixed expression of serenity and puzzlement. The doctor, who had remained standing by the polygraph cart, cleared his throat.

"Is there anything else you require from me, gentlemen, and to whom do I forward my invoice?"

The chairman ignored the questions. "Doctor, are you also psychiatrist?"

"Yes, I am. May I ask who you people are, or who you represent? Some faces are familiar, on the world stage."

"There are certain drugs, are there not, which can actually change one's perspective?"

"Indeed there are. But I am sensing that something of great importance has occurred here without the use of such."

"Thank you. So I wish to ask if one has been, let us say, bewitched or bamboozled into another perspective, how long-lasting might be the effects?"

"Ah, well, mind-altering substances naturally wear off but they can offer a glimpse of another way of looking at life which is retained in memory if not in mood. It can be acted upon or not, depending on one's conviction, and whether one wants to retain the memory of the altered state. To change the habitual programming of a lifetime requires a very significant jolt. The effects would not last a day unless the offered new perspective held something more desirable. In my experience, there is only one power that can do this."

"Just so, Doctor. We thank you for your services. Here is my card. You may submit your account if you wish or be given a cash settlement immediately."

"The latter, if you please. I would appreciate also contact with the young woman, Elena."

"Yes. In view of the intentions of the man who left early, I suspect she will soon be in contact with the whole world!"

"One last question, sir: If there is, let's say, a pyramid of power on earth, is this the apex of it, right here in this room?"

The Frenchman shook his head in self-deprecation and looked at all the faces in turn, lingering on the oldest man present. "A questionable presumption, Doctor. Any leadership that can be pin-pointed is necessarily vulnerable. No one here could be so labeled beyond their own sphere of influence. With voices in unison we can certainly effect changes. However, as with a super-tanker, changing course just a few degrees takes considerable time and great mechanical effort. Come to think of it, it's more like tacking a full-rigged, four-masted barque, it'll need everyone's co-operation, all hands on deck, so to speak. We can do it in dread and under duress as on a lee-shore or we can do it joyfully."

The Englishman cleared his throat pointedly, raised his left hand and asked, "Well, can we assume the ship is still under command?"

"I do believe so," the chairman answered, to palpable relief from round the table, "I don't see any reason to doubt it. In sailing terms, are we Ready About, man your sheets and guys? And yes, we do get to stay up on the bridge, out of the weather. Yes, David?"

"It is not a ship. Methinks it is a horse." To startled faces, the nonagenarian hauled slowly to his feet, stooping but still lordly. "I have been on the same course for a very long time, most of my life. I do not know how much I have left, either of time or energy but today I glimpsed a new vision and it feels different to anything I have ever experienced.

"I can see that we have schemed and struggled and strategized every day of our adult lives, always from the point of view that we are trying to keep a runaway horse under control. But if the horse is actually the Life-force itself and the Life-force is actually the very essence of love as felt in the heart-space, then we have truly been wasting our energy and our time—our incredibly precious time. As I see it now, the high fence is coming up, the horse is unstoppable, so free the reins and let the thoroughbred fly. It knows exactly what to do. Is this the so-called quantum shift that is coming up? We either go with it or we bale out and perish? I looked at the young lady and suddenly I am in love again. I thought it was long behind me... but this is not carnal. I was seeing utter simplicity and purity of heart speaking to my own."

The old man gulped down on built emotion. "Our belief in our aristocracy, by accident of birth, is frankly a ridiculous vanity. Yes, it is true that we have control of all the nations, but could it be that we have worked all our lives to gain command for a purpose we had never considered? The young lady was right in that we have tended to view the mass of mankind as a disposable nuisance, despicable even, and terribly threatening because of overwhelming numbers. I have been privileged and separate all my life but today I found union with a humble little Russian lady and my heart feels ready to burst open." He looked around and grinned frailly. "I trust it will not make a big mess if it does!"

With a great sigh, he waited for some strained laughter to subside and said solemnly, "Very well, gentlemen, let's go to work. This is my, I beg your pardon—this is to be *our* legacy. Henri, I trust your plane has been well-guarded? This is a lot of expensive eggs in one basket, eh? I nearly said Egos! Is our entire reality changing, our vision, and our perspective? If so, we are going to have to come up with a new model—and a very clear one—if we are to avoid chaos or collapse, and our think-tanks will require a completely new hypothesis. This is our challenge. Right action will follow right thought...I can't really believe I am saying all this. Could we have a show of hands that we are all in accord? Left hands, please, let's keep the right where it was."

In a ragged sequence, all the arms went up. The Chairman watched, nodded ponderously and turned to his left, to the empty chair. "We do not know where George stands on all this, but for sure he was resisting…I know we don't take oaths here but our word must be our bond. My team will produce some guidelines. There will be opportunity for queries and modifications but the principle remains. There can be no withdrawals or subtle compromises. I trust that is clear? Very well, to the airways, and thank you all for being here."

Just then the door opened and the Texan strode back in, raising his voice as he approached the table. "Listen here, gennelmen! Do you realize we must have a Judas? How can she say that nothing we have to say will be secret? We haven't been predictable, so she can't be talking about bugs in here, surely? Ya know, I don't think it's a good idea to keep them around. If they talk.…"

He glared around the table but most of the eyes were cast down and not meeting his. Clearly, for most, the old habits were clashing frantically with the new ideas. The Irishman spoke again.

"Well, frankly, with such a radical change of direction, who's going to be able to keep quiet?"

"Hm…Tell me, Henri," asked the former Treasury Secretary, "Do you use Prist in your 737?"

"I have no idea. What's your point?"

"Oh, nothing, just wondered."

In the ensuing laughter, the Doctor wheeled his cart to the door, not understanding the joke but busily filing in his acute memory for faces. Back in the era that was just passing, this memory would have cost him his life. He scanned the faces once again, lingering on the Texan but without changing expression and said quietly, "Good day, gentlemen."

As he left he heard a final query, the voice with a very slight Irish lilt. "Henri, just to be clear, would we be responding to a carrot or a stick?"

The door closed before he could hear the answer.

A threatening wind had cleared the early fog as they put the bags in the trunk. The cabbie readily agreed to accept dollars and then opened the passenger door with a sweeping invitation. None of the four moved to take it and all shook their heads. The cabbie shrugged and they all squeezed into the back. In the center, Irina offered her knee to Elena who took it readily but then lay back across all three of them, her eyes closed over a smile of tired contentment.

On the right, Nic was cradling her head and Anastasia spoke to her in Russian from the left, taking off her shoes and soothing her feet. "We haven't been introduced, Elena Knyazeva. I am Anastasia Wojerkowski and this man, finally, is Kolya."

Irina looked astonished but Elena simply nodded and widened her smile. "Yes, I know."

"How did you know?"

Elena giggled, "I do not know. But a word popped in my left ear so it must be he."

"What word?"

"The very first he used for me, *Vozlyublennyy*."

Irina visibly relaxed, her own smile broadening and she held out her hand to Nic. In exaggerated English she said, "I am Irina Popova from London. How do you do, Captain Vozlyublennyy?"

"Very well, thank you. What did you just call me?"

"The word means 'beloved', do you remember? I believe it changed her life. It was impulsive and could have got us all killed, or worse. It was also fearless. I too wish to be fearless, but I fear that such fearlessness might be simply because I am with you, Captain Dreadnought."

Nic and Irina laughed while Anastasia translated for Elena and added in Russian, "It doesn't matter how you achieve it as long as it's not dependent on something or someone else."

Irina said, "We didn't know you spoke Russian. So you understood all that was said?"

"Yes, I did. I can't get my mind round the possible consequences."

Nic asked, "What d'you mean, Annie?"

"About what she said when the doctor asked questions. They didn't get translated."

"And?"

"Nic, it's almost as if repeating it implies a death sentence. Are you sure you want to know?"

"Of course. Shoot."

"Very well. The doctor was so bold. He asked who was behind 9/11, all the Kennedys, Oklahoma City. She didn't answer until he changed the questions: Did it involve a Middle-eastern Secret Service? She answered *Yes*. Was there collusion from the Overlords? *Yes*. And who is behind them, is it these people here? *Yes*."

Irina chimed in, "But surely, everyone knows this? The evidence is overwhelming on the Web. The regular media don't touch it since the same people own the media. Internet rumors abound, even plenty of proof but nothing could ever come of that because it is also riddled with lies and inventions. Just google anywhere, Bilderberg. Illuminati, CFR, Tri-Lateral Commission. But say anything against them and AIPAC and the Anti-Defamation League'll have you for breakfast. It's a shield used just as effectively by many non-Jews."

"I agree," Nic answered, "That's why the only possible solution was presented this morning, but what they do with it is out of our hands."

The taxi, clearing the Zoliborz suburbs out towards Route 7 was rocked by a vicious gust of wind and Nic frowned. "We may have a problem. Looks like a big Westerly coming in. Our steed is parked facing East."

"So what's the problem?" Anastasia's voice sounded carefree and confident.

"Well, you can't get steam up if there's a half a gale from behind. Anyway, could you do a search for a caterer in Zaporozhye, rustle up some gourmet meals? Say six meals for six people, plus snacks, drinks and ice. Deliver to the GA terminal. Oh, and did you get anything from our escapee?"

He glanced pointedly down at Elena, indicating discretion. Irina's eyes were closed as if she were overloaded with straying thoughts but Anastasia caught on almost at once. "Who? Oh, no, not yet. What did you want to say."

"A rendezvous. Surprise."

"There's a message from Uren. He's about to go under. He wants to know what we've done to his people and what's going on."

"Did you answer?"

"Not yet. I wonder what would have happened if he'd been here with us?"

"Huh, heart attack, probably." They both chuckled but with a hint of remorse, while the two Russian women opened their eyes and looked at them quizzically. Irina was frowning but Elena still had her smile of seeming beatitude. Nic, still cradling her head, reached across for Anastasia's hand. She took it but nodded easily as if to convey she felt no need or doubt.

Nic said, "Annie, would you ask the driver to divert around a couple of blocks, to see if we're being followed?"

The cabbie complied with her request in Polish as if accustomed to a natural precaution. She said, "It's like they do this a lot. Are you scared, Nic?"

"Uh-huh, just prudent," he grinned.

"Do you really think they—"

"I've no idea. But it did seem like someone had different ideas and saw no choice." He looked down in his lap. "And then there was this astonishing little presence. She had them folded up like crêpes."

The cabbie completed a deft slalom round two blocks and pronounced loudly, "*Wszystko jasne!*"

Anastasia answered, "*Dziekuje.* He says it's all clear." She got busy with her tablet and searched in silence, deciding that Elena would be no help in the catering category. Before she found a connection, the cabbie spoke again, his voice low and menacing. "*Zwolenniczka!*"

Anastasia listened to some more phrases before explaining. "He now says we *are* being followed. Black embassy car. He thinks it's Russian, a Moskvitch."

Nic thought for a moment and said, "Ask him to pull a U-ey, go back to the hotel—no, to Warsaw-Chopin. General Aviation terminal."

"What for?"

"Let's see how powerful these people really are."

She translated and resumed her Web search while the cabbie found a slot in the oncoming and made a violent maneuver. She was unfazed and simply adjusted in her seat, noticing herself in extreme euphoria as well as urgent sensuality. The black Moskvitch swept on by, unable to follow.

"I don't see much in the way of caterers. There's a wedding and banquet outfit. I'll try it. Looks expensive, though."

"That's a good sign. Go for it."

Irina chuckled and then abruptly leaned forward, taking Elena's hand and speaking rapidly. There was a long pause before any answer came. In response to Nic's questioning look, Anastasia translated behind Irina's head.

"She asked her, How was she able to say that nothing is private for the Overlords from now on, and she answered that the guides or the voices told her this. They explained that with the hearts open, this suggestion is planted in the DNA and they would feel compelled, no, actually delighted to reveal...Because of the new perspective... Because the heart-mind cannot lie, cannot hold sinister secrets...Oh, and she says the guides were very amused by your strategy, pretending sickness."

"Hm...I'm glad they didn't call it deceit."

"They couldn't, really, since they put the idea in your head!"

"*What?* But didn't they say they do not intervene?"

She put the question to Elena for a prompt answer. "She says they simply make suggestions, just like the Overlords. You just tuned in and responded. As you have been for a week or more."

Nic looked across at her in quiet amazement and the space between them seemed to crackle. Irina leaned back at that moment and was jolted from interrupting the line-of-sight. She leaned forward again and looked at each in turn but then Elena, still with her eyes closed, said something too quiet for Anastasia to hear.

Irina translated. "She said 'It is sealed between these two. I let him go, though he is my beloved forever'."

Dismay flared briefly when they reached the Warsaw GA terminal and found it almost deserted, but within minutes a cavalcade of limousines swept up and disgorged the entire committee. Anastasia got out and almost lost control of the door as the wind tore at it. Clutching hair and clothes, she waited by the taxi until the Chairman saw and approached her. She had to shout to be heard.

"Sir, we're a little concerned about being followed, and we wondered if something could prevent us from leaving?"

The Frenchman promptly produced his phone, scrolled for contacts and swept a number. The wind whipped his jacket open and he beckoned her inside the terminal, the others crowding behind them.

Anastasia heard him say, "Aleksandr, it's Henri. I'm in Warsaw... You knew that? Of course you did!" He laughed and moved out of earshot, speaking for several minutes, his face crinkling with amusement. Finally he came over, saying "Someone to speak to you."

He handed her the phone while beckoning the others past him to the boarding gate and the 727 waiting outside. "It's Portnikov, head of FSB Moscow. Tell him what you told me."

With some astonishment, Anastasia spoke briefly in Russian, no more than three sentences, listened for a moment and looked aback when the call was cut off. The Frenchman raised an enquiring eyebrow.

"Thank you, sir." She handed him the phone. "He just said 'Leave it with me. You are free to go to Zaporozhye and then out of Ukraine airspace.' Does he always do what you tell him?"

The Frenchman smiled and shrugged modestly. "On principle, no. In effect, mostly yes. Did you find your informant, the one who was sick?"

"No, not yet."

"Well, it seems he didn't get to any hospital. Portnikov's boys wanted to have a word with him. But then, if he didn't make it, the ambulance might have taken him straight to the morgue. Did you and the pilot eat the same food?"

"I—I think so, yes."

"Very odd. I wonder if the Russians—well, never mind. I don't suppose he matters now. Moscow knows about the Prist."

"Oh...so they're on the same page? How did they find out? Are we safe from them? And I don't see the Texas gentleman with you."

"You can never be sure, frankly. Be on guard. I think it was your Russian defector from New Mexico, Knyazev. He was trying to do a deal. Look, when you're settled we'll arrange a meeting with them. Portnikov, Putin and three beautiful women...Hm. Oh, by the way, if Frank Uren doesn't make it, do you want his job?"

Anastasia was so startled that her jaw dropped and she jokingly attempted to push it back up with her hand. The Frenchman grinned with satisfaction.

"Well, you think about it. It's yours for the asking. And the two Russian ladies, I have a feeling we are going to be needing them, for reinforcement. Here's my card. Stay in touch. I'd like you to sound them out and let me know, alright? Well, *bon jour,* safe flight and *au revoir.*"

CHAPTER 23

"It would have been impossible for us to develop our plan for the world if we had been subjected to the lights of publicity during those years. But, the world is more sophisticated and prepared to march towards a world government. The supranational sovereignty of an intellectual elite and world bankers is surely preferable to the national auto-determination practiced in past centuries."

David Rockefeller, at the June, 1991 Bilderberg meeting
in Baden, Germany.

"**P**onownie, *Moskvitch*," the taxi driver muttered, pointedly adjusting his mirror as they headed Northwest on H.7.

Anastasia relayed, "The Russians are back. That's if they're Russian. They're not supposed to be following."

Nic shrugged. "Ignore. Maybe they didn't get the recall yet."

"The Frenchman thinks that Igor tried to do a deal, for a family that he's not supposed to have. Moscow is not going to like that."

The Moskvitch followed all the way to Modlin, stopping a hundred yards away in the almost deserted car park. Wind-gusts shook the cab as Anastasia paid the fare and they exited cautiously. The same door gave them access to the GA terminal where a large solitary maintenance man in the cafeteria pointedly ignored them. Locking it from the inside, Nic crossed the lounge and peered through the window where the G5's long wings twitched warningly. He had the same feeling as going down to the harbor and finding conditions too high for sailing.

"Ok look, ladies, that bird weighs about 25 tons," he said, "Somehow we have to turn her." To unspoken questions he explained, "You can't start the engines if there's more than a breeze from behind. It turns the fans the wrong way. Feeling strong?"

The three looked at him anxiously. "Ok. Give me your bags. I'll go out and get the brakes off. When I signal, you all come out and push. Two on the front wheels, two on the port main gear, Ok?"

He opened the boarding gate to a rush of wind and approached the aircraft, unlocking the little panel. As the steps miraculously unfolded, he went up them and disappeared. Anastasia had been glancing anxiously out of the other window.

"The Moskvitch's gone," she said, sounding relieved, "But where's everyone else?" She came over and looked first at Irina who seemed only slightly anxious and then at Elena who still had an easy smile of contentment. She found her attention on her own face in comparison, starkly aware of the corners of her mouth pulled down by long-habitual attitude. Elena locked eyes with her and held out a hand but there seemed to be an exchange on another level, as jolting as a slap in the face. Thoughts tumbled wildly, all that had just happened, their geographic location, the uncertainty, unknown danger. All of a sudden in her mind, precarious switched to hilarious, the sheer improbability of it all overwhelming. She pulled an unresisting Elena into her arms, both of them laughing gently. Irina called from the window.

"He's coming back down. We should go now."

Outside, Nic pulled the chocks from the nose-wheels and pointed to their positions, finally shouting "1..2..3..Heave!" but no amount of straining produced any movement. Finally, Anastasia went back into the building and spoke quickly in Polish to the maintenance man. He looked startled and shook his head but after a further plea changed his mind. He put down the wrench he'd been using, grabbed his coat and hurried outside, their figures heeling against the wind.

The maintenance man stood baffled as they strained against the G5's resistance, finally catching on and leaning his main strength to the port main gear. Inchingly and with much help from the gale, the aircraft began to move and as soon as there was enough momentum, Nic ran to the steps and bounded up them. In a few moments the nose-wheel inched to starboard and the inertia completed the quarter-turn. A touch of the brakes was the only signal they needed and they scrambled for the steps. Anastasia gave a silent, deep-bowed thank-you to the man who stood there scratching his head and grinning. He shouted something about a jump-start which made Anastasia laugh, then he turned startled as the APU began to roar behind him. He ran inside the building and peered wide-eyed from the window but they could no longer see him as Anastasia touched the switch. The stairway folded up with a solid clunk, shutting out the wind-roar.

Inside she found Irina and Elena looking round in amazement at the luxurious interior. "Have a seat, ladies," she said in Russian. "I will be up front, very important job. See you later." Grinning and leaving them bewildered, she ducked into the cockpit where Nic had left the door wedged open. His hands were busy as he also transmitted to ATC but again received no reply. He soon had both engines running and they began to move, following the eastbound taxiway past several commercial airliners on the ramps, huge and still.

It was only an old discipline that made him turn left onto the runway and back-track to the very threshold, when with high wind and over 8000' feet available this extra increment was unnecessary, especially so lightly loaded. He completed the U-turn back to the westbound runway 26, methodically checking his instruments when Anastasia, looking out through the windshield, suddenly exclaimed.

"The Moskvitch, coming from the right!"

Nic looked up to see the black sedan approaching the runway from the next turn-off. It stopped short and then slowly moved across until it was straddling the centerline, headlights beamed up towards them. He stiffened at the sight and then seemed to switch to another mode, coldly muttering aloud at the airfield diagram screen, then to the left screen for the Flight Management Computer.

"That turn-off is at 1620 feet. I need 1500. Gross weight is 58,560 pounds. Computer says V1, abort limit, 114knots, Vr-rotate 117 knots. Major headwind at 43 knots. Is the car moving?"

"No. Just sitting. What are you thinking, Nic?" Her voice was clearly strained.

"It's tight. Give me flaps 20. Read the airspeed, middle screen."

"Got it. Flaps 20. Windspeed 44 knots."

Nic glanced out briefly at the car, his gaze narrowing. His feet hard on the brakes, he disengaged the tiller steering and pushed the throttles right forward, over-ruling the automatic slow advance, watching till both RPM's reached 104%. The aircraft squirmed in protest until he released his foot pressure and let it surge into the wind. Within seconds Anastasia began calling figures, "55, 60, 70, 80..."

"Still not moving?" he asked tersely.

"No. 85, 90, 103 –"

"Put your hand on the white gear knob. Be ready."

"Got it. 110, 115, it says V1. Car's moving, THIS WAY!"

"FULL FLAP!"

The black Moskvitch loomed hugely on his airfield screen, the flaps extending too slowly for much effect. He forced himself not to look outside, steeled to the last second then hauled back viciously on the yoke. The G5 leaped off the runway with the stall-warning klaxon braying frantically. There came a distinct thump from below as the port main wheels contacted the roof of the car, shattering its windshield. The Gulfstream jerked to starboard and then dumped heavily back on the tarmac. The starboard wing-tip struck the ground with a stream of sparks but then the landing gear jolted the aircraft level just before it could tumble them to disaster. With the nose-wheel still in air Nic had to use rudder strenuously to bring them back on centerline, slewing violently. The nose-wheel settled again and the stall warning silenced.

"Speed 110," Anastasia called, her heart seeming to choke her breath. Forcing calm, she continued, "115, gaining."

"Ok. Flaps back to 20. ....Rotating!"

The rumbling ceased as he lifted off and called for gear up, tense with the thought of possible damage. The pause on yellow seemed to take forever but the three green lights blinked in unison. They looked at each other and let out long breaths. She put a hand on his where it still gripped the two throttles. The aircraft rocked in the gusting wind but surged massively into a safe climb-out at 150 knots, nose high at 25°.

"Flaps up."

As she looked down at the flap lever, her peripheral vision took in the cockpit door and two anxious faces peering in. She realized that none of them had fastened any straps, not that they would have done much good in a high speed catastrophe. She grinned back smugly and gave a cheeky thumbs-up, but then she looked across at Nic and gratitude overwhelmed her. His face was set in concentration so she had no idea what he was feeling which, he told her later, was actually a surge of belated fury. For a moment he'd seriously considered pulling up into a wing-over and diving in a triumphant blast over the Russian Moskvitch. It subsided slowly under pressure from both reason and gratitude. Just a couple of feet closer or 2 knots less wind and it would all have been over. The underarms of his stiff new shirt were soaked and he felt trickles down his sides. He called Warsaw approach, announcing his departure and entering his flight plan for Zaporozhye, Ukraine. In still air, he had enough fuel for the leg plus a half hour, but the high quartering wind gave him an extra margin. The air-traffic controller seemed unusually polite, offering clear passage to 40,000' and no conflicting. Sunlight suddenly filled the cockpit as they emerged above cloud but it took him most of the climb to complete his calming, despite excited chatter from the cabin. Anastasia crabbed out of her seat, touched his shoulder gently and went aft into the embrace of the two Russian women.

"Ladies, let us find some refreshment and then I'll show you around." Her self-mocking proprietary manner delighted them. From the fridge she extracted a gleaming frosty bottle of Louis Roederer Cristal 2004. "Last one. Let's have some music."

The galley screen came alive to her touch and she quickly selected Spirits (Having Flown) by the BeeGees, cranking up the volume.

> *I never fell in love so easily.*
> *Where the four winds blow I carry on.*
> *I'd like to take you where my spirit flies:*
> *Through the empty skies.*
> *We go alone,*
> *Never before having flown.*
> *Faster than lightning is this heart of mine.*
> *In the face of time I carry on.*
> *I'd like to take you where my rainbow ends.*
> *Be my lover, friend. We go alone,*
> *Never before having flown....*
> *I am your hurricane, your fire in the sun,*
> *How long must I live in the air?...*

As its magical crescendo filled the cabin, she popped the cork with a quiet *Phut.* The others watched reverently as the smoky waft crept out of the bottle.

"That's the genie, we get three wishes" she said and translated for Elena. "*Tri zhelania!*" She filled three glasses and they all sat sipping in luxurious blonde leather and total disbelief, swamped by the music. Elena, long sequestered from any form of luxury, stared into her glass as if trying to fathom some eternal enigma. Anastasia drew her tablet from her shoulder-bag and switched it on.

Nic was quietly reflecting on the bizarre events of the day when Anastasia slipped behind him with her tablet and nuzzled his neck. Refusing her offer of a glass of champagne felt soothingly protective.

"I know you can't drink and fly, Dreadnought, but I insist you have a sip. Guess what? I have an email from a man in Mexico, his name is Narciso. He says he safely ejected. He asks, How about you?"

Nic turned and put his lips to her glass, his grin broadening. "Tell him, Yes and thanks. Don't know about the word 'safely'. Can he meet us in, um, Gibraltar, tomorrow evening? Tell him to bone up on G550. If he can't afford the ticket, pay it with the card."

Anastasia grinned delightedly. "Got it. And Rose Madder sends her love…Well now, what did you think of my beloved Poland?"

"Not a lot. Foggy and windy. How about you, how was your visit back to the motherland?"

"Too brief to tell. I think I was ejected also. Let's go back to the sunshine. We have unfinished business, Nic. Life could always be shorter, um?"

"I guess. But then you'd never know, would you?"

Her nervous laughter stifled as she turned back to the main cabin and two questioning faces. She tried to explain to them that they were actually in a simulator and the real thing was yet to come. Considering all the implications brought increasing and champagne-fueled hilarity but the three women kept stopping and looking at each other in amazement and disbelief before erupting again. Up in the cockpit, Nic listened and basked in protective calm, avoiding future thoughts as much as possible. When the song ended, there was a short pause and then the cabin filled with the joyous strains of Handel's Arrival of the

Queen of Sheba. Nic felt he'd drunk the whole bottle by himself, the ultimate mellow high. He set the auto-pilot and climbed aft, seating himself next to Anastasia and facing the others across the table. He took both her hands and then kissed her long and gently while the Russians looked on, glancing in alarm at the empty cockpit. Locked in the kiss, Anastasia swiveled her eyes hugely at them, confirming their disbelief. Elena said something, so Anastasia pulled back to translate.

"She's wondering how she will recognize reality when it comes back."

"Hm. First we'd have to define reality," he answered with a grin. "I thought I knew. Now I'm not so sure. Ask her what she sees out of the window."

Elena said something else and looked rueful. "She says reality will be when she gets her mother on board and shows her the credit card."

"Huh. Did you guess that this Narciso is her brother?

"*What*? You mean Ig—" She stopped herself before completing his name. She closed her eyes as she considered all the implications, finally shaking her head in disbelief.

Nic asked, "Did that wedding outfit confirm our supplies?"

"They did. Nearly 3000 bucks! Better be good, eh?"

"Hm."

The caterers' truck was waiting as they pulled up to the GA terminal, a rudimentary building which also served the helipad. Pre-ordered from the air, the re-fueling bowser and waste handling also showed up as soon as the engines shut down, then the caterers arrived but there was no sign of Elena's family. There was a brisk wind from the northwest but the forecast front hadn't yet arrived. The women busied themselves for an hour sorting through mouth-watering gourmet supplies and planning meals while Nic went over to the Flight Center to file a formal plan. It was almost suspicious to be treated there like royalty.

When he got back to the private terminal he found an official behind a desk who looked up but said nothing, just waved his hand in a *carte blanche*. The street door opened for a small boy carrying two boxes; behind him came a tall, mean-looking man who then placed another box on the top. The boy started weaving erratically behind a pile higher than his head, while the man went back out. There came raised voices from outside as the door opened again. Nic took the pile from the surprised child, grinned and jerked his head towards the boarding gate.

"Ilya?" he questioned and the boy nodded as he held the door open, stiffly polite. Outside, Nic again signaled with his head towards the G5. The boy's expression was unforgettable as he caught on, ran to the stairs, hesitated and turned back for confirmation. A cry from inside was all he needed as Elena appeared in the opening and held out her arms to engulf him.

Nic put down the boxes on the bottom step and turned back into the building. An elderly woman all in black, handsome but greying and disheveled, was trying to maneuver three cardboard suitcases and looking around frantically for her grandson. The taxi driver was calling to her angrily from the street doorway but she had no focus left for him. Nic beckoned him inside and made a placating gesture, then turned to the woman with a bow and tried to take two of the cases. He was stumped to find the handles missing and his smile was greeted with suspicion until Elena burst in and ran to her, crying *Mama!* and causing an eruption of tears. Anastasia appeared behind her, took in the scene and placated the hostile driver with a $50 bill, over the grandmother's shrill protests.

His eyes privately to heaven, Nic ignored the wild chatter and hefted the cases one by one. As he did so, he was quietly moved by a wave of compassion for an older woman suddenly uprooted. He hoped the surprise in store, reunion with her exiled son, would go some way to compensate. He put the cases at the top of the steps and asked Irina to take them to the rear compartment, then he went back down and shepherded the mother to the steps as Elena held her arm and chattered brightly. When she looked up at the aircraft, the mother's confusion was almost total and Nic thought she might faint. He and Elena took her arms at the stairway but after two steps she firmly elbowed them away, stood up straight and completed her entrance with exaggerated dignity. Inside, Ilya was darting and exclaiming to

Irina. His grandmother was about to chide him but instead she found a smile of greeting as they introduced themselves. Irina steered her to a seat where she sat poised and rigid, clutching a bulging plastic purse and speaking tersely.

"Captain," Irina translated with a grin, "The dowager demands to know where we are going?"

Nic shrugged and smiled. "Ask her where she wants to go."

She relayed the question in Russian and got no answer but pursed lips. Tears brimmed the old lady's eyes. Elena answered for her with a tolerant smile.

Anastasia explained, "She just wants to find her son. But God help him when she does!"

Nic suppressed a knowing grin and triggered the stairway closed. "To your seats, folks. Westward Ho. Tell her we'll be spending the night in Rome. Annie love, would you find us a nice hotel?"

"Yessir! How many stars would you like?"

"*Cinque.*"

"*Solo il meglio, Commandante mio,*" Only the best. Grinning, she picked up her tablet and after a few prompts exclaimed, "There's an email from the Frenchman. He says Portnikov in Moscow says it wasn't Russians in the Moskvitch, My God…. It was the Chinese!"

Nic stood frozen in the cockpit doorway, his thoughts tumbling like shards in a kaleidoscope trying to find a pattern. Finally he grinned at her and shook his head.

"Do you believe that?"

"No," she answered, "Not for a minute. Anyway, what difference does it make? I assume somebody wanted to know what went on with that committee, someone who doesn't have an inside track or someone who wants to take counter-measures. Did you know there are only four countries in the world whose central banks are NOT run by the Overlords? Iran, North Korea and Cuba. Hungary just got rid of them, or so they think."

"You're kidding, right? They don't own them all, surely?"

"Not directly, but they do control them, and thus the Governments and everything else, starting with the US Fed. Back in 2000 there were also Iraq, Afghanistan, Sudan and Libya that they didn't own.

Look what happened to them. Taken over. Get the picture?"

Nic nodded thoughtfully. "So they really can change everything? Damn, I just had an idea, Annie. They all knew we were coming to Zaporozhye and why. Could you go back and look through the new luggage, very carefully?"

Anastasia stared and stiffened then moved quickly toward the rear without a word. Nic entered the cockpit to go through check-list and start-up and was just about to call ATC for taxi clearance when she appeared quietly and tapped him on the shoulder. He turned to see her holding out a padded package, much too carefully wrapped and taped for a hasty departure.

"Ask the mother if it's—"

"I already did. She said she's never seen it, it's not hers. It's quite heavy. Shall I open it?"

"NO!"

"Just kidding. Got a plan?"

Nic had already frozen in thought as he took the package from her to assess its weight. He found his mind going hazy with the mental tussle. She stood behind him in silence for long seconds, her own thoughts clamoring.

"Right," he said, "Four or five pounds. Don't know what it is. Assume explosive. So…Is it altitude triggered, is it timed, or is it set off by remote?"

Decisively he shut down the mains, leaving the APU running and eased out of his seat. He said coldly, "First thing is to get it away from us. That solves one and two. For three, remote—let's see if that cab's still there. Come to think of it, he was weird, doing a fair bit of distracting. Hang in here."

He eased out, collected his jacket from the crew-rest cubicle and was about to trigger the stairway when he realized it was in direct view of the building's windows. He strode past puzzled stares to the rear and slid open the baggage door a few inches, peering through the crack to see if any eyes were watching. Seeing none, he opened it just enough to exit and jump down, reaching up to collect his jacket with the package rolled inside. Back inside the terminal, the official looked up questioningly, nodding with indifference when he received a just-a-moment hand signal.

Separate from the half-dozen cars parked outside, Nic saw a grey taxi on its own some fifty yards distant. He strode towards it, opened the rear door and barked a good-afternoon. The driver looked up from his cell-phone with a firm headshake, "*Ya zakonchil smenu.* Off duty."

Half in the seat, recognizing in the mirror the driver who had overloaded the boy, Nic made a typical impatient sound but said "Ok, chum." He got out, dropped his jacket, bent to retrieve it and slid the package under the rear of the car. Striding quickly through the terminal past a nonchalant hand-sweep from the official, he saw Anastasia's anxious face at the Gulfstream's oval window. He pointed to the steps and she promptly triggered them down.

"What did you do with it?" she asked, "Flushed it down the loo?"

He grinned and kissed her quickly without answering, then went aft and closed the baggage door before resuming his pre-flight routine.

They got their taxi instructions right away and take-off clearance even before the holding point. Anastasia slipped into the right hand seat, reporting everyone strapped in and within 20 seconds they were lined up, accelerating and airborne to some squeals of excitement from the cabin. Anastasia took fierce delight in watching the speeds, announcing gear and flaps up without any command.

Nic just smiled and then banked the aircraft in a small turn to starboard. "Is there a grey taxi still there, can you see?"

Anastasia looked out of her side window, nodded and then yelled, "Oh my God! Look!"

"What's up?" he asked, trying to see past her.

"You mean, what blew up?" she shrieked. "In the car park, can you see?"

He banked further and after a few moments saw past her head, the remains of a fireball, a black mushroom of smoke and dwindling flames beneath. A figure ran frantically from the wreckage, tripped, fell, and stumbled on again. Nic turned back on climbing course with a taut expression.

Neither said a word for a full minute until Anastasia muttered in French. "*Il est pris à son propre piège.*"

"Meaning?"

"Like in Shakespeare: 'Hoist with his own petard.'"

Nic shook his head grimly and after a long pause said, "I have a quote."

"Tell me, do."

"'Wasn't me. I didn't do it.'"

"Oh? And who said that?"

"Bart Simpson."

She tried to smile but found herself taking long deep breaths instead. Finally she squeezed out of her seat. "I'll go and organize the trough. Then I'm going to come back and quiz you about all the other things you didn't do."

"Like what?"

"Like telling the truth about psychedelics in the jet fuel. They never asked Elena about that, did they?"

"That's because you swamped them with facts about DMT. That was brilliant."

"Thank you. How about you spirited away their prime witness and had him griping and moaning in the men's room? They'll be able to compare voice-prints, y'know, with recordings we made at the lab. Then they'll—"

She stopped abruptly and giggled. "Then they'll know it was you! And then you vanished. What happens when you turn up again?" She looked across at him but he just shrugged and didn't answer.

She touched his sleeve. "If this is a big mess, can your Biggall get us out of it?"

"I dunno. I'd say he got us into it."

"How come?"

Nic put his finger to his lips and said quietly, "Put the idea in my head, after seeing the chem-trails."

"About Prist? And you really don't know his last name?"

"Elena came close, she said it was something powerful."

"So what is it?"

"It was hippie-speak for The Boss, from the Sixties. It's actually two words, Big Al."

She drew back with her hands clenched. "Last name?"

Nic turned in his seat and beckoned her close to whisper.

Astonishment blazed in her face as she repeated in disbelief. "Mighty? Al-mighty? Big Al for short?"

"You got it, sister. Keep it to yourself, won't you?"

"Hm. If I say yes, how shall we seal the deal?"

"Tonight. When in Rome, do as the Romans do…"

"Worship at shrines?"

"Or roll over." Nic's answer came with a sly smile as he sneakily disengaged the autopilot, pushed forward on the yoke, banked to port and eased it firmly back, easing forward during inversion. The Gulfstream arced through a perfect barrel-roll, maintaining 1G all the way round. No-one would have even noticed unless they were looking outside. Still holding her tablet, Anastasia had seen the initial movement and gripped the seat-back and was then astonished to find herself standing firmly on the deck but rolled through 360°. A spate of Russian came from the main cabin, followed by whoops and nervous laughter.

As the aircraft came level she let out a long breath and said, "Kindly notice, I did not squeal."

Nic chuckled saucily. "Ah, but you will!"

"Promise?"

EPILOGUE

*"... Narcissism...indicates an excessive love for oneself and....
can produce serious damage not only to the soul of those affected
but also in relationship with others, with the society in which
one lives. The real trouble is that **those most affected by this**—
which is actually a kind of mental disorder— **are people who
have a lot of power.**"*

Pope Francis 1

D earest Jamie,
Since my last note a few things have happened, so here's
an update. We're tramping South between islands where the
easterly trade-winds kick up some mighty moguls but the wind is
warm and the sea color deep as midnight, with white tops frothing
joyfully. The monohulls plunge and heave and bury their lee-rails,
drenching everyone on deck but this 50 foot Catamaran takes it all in
stride, forging through the mêlée at a steady 15 knots without spilling
a drink! The aesthetic is very different—the sloops and ketches show
character with slanting and vigorous movement but the cat is kinda
blah, it's like standing on a pier with the water running underneath
except that some of the wave-tops crash up under the bridge-deck
like explosions. It's a new experience for me and almost guiltily
comfortable and it kept Rose from sea-sickness. On the (big) plus
side, you can pull right up to the beach without worrying about going
aground and it doesn't roll in a swell at anchor. With an engine in
each hull you can spin it in its own length and including the net
there's about 1000 square feet of deck space so the different language
classes don't clash. (Just kidding!). But it's hard to think of it as a 'she'.
Most nights we are tucked in the lee of an island, in delicious hush
and flat water. When the sea's quiet you can see the bottom at 70 feet!

We stayed an extra day in Rome because Igor and Rose couldn't get to Spain in time. The girls all went shopping, a lot! From there we planned for Casablanca but diverted to Madrid, to mislead any further interference. Igor was so changed, his grey complexion gone and a spring in his stride. You can imagine the pandemonium of reunion for the Knyazev clan, in a great huddle and torrent of Russian and tears. Astonishing are the linguists, Annie and Irina rattling away in Italian and then Spanish, relaying in Russian and badgering Svetlana (Elena's mom) to give up wearing black. Her entire demeanor changed when she finally caved. More shopping, (moving expenses!). I have a gallery tolerance of about 20 minutes but I spent 7 hours in the Prado, mesmerized by Rubens and Velasquez and Goya and all.

We flight-planned to Miami and diverted to Tortola. Igor and Ilya couldn't be dragged from the cockpit until they were starving and it was a wrench to let the Gulfstream go—sorry you missed that but there'll be others…I got hold of Captain Piston and told him where to pick it up, then we scuttled off to sea. Your ticket's waiting as soon as school's out. Your Mom and Karen are welcome too, if they want, we're going to explore islands until hurricane season. Annie is my new lady love and is ready to teach you French, German, Polish, Russian, Spanish and Italian! She is currently studying Mandarin, glug. Her former boss, Frank Uren, did not do well after his operation and was retired but she hasn't decided yet about her job. She thinks of all those secrets she might have but she says she's too busy rehearsing for her honeymoon! If she takes the job I can presumably get my house back!

As for the big picture, it's too early to tell. We left Svetlana, Elena, Irina and Ilya in a villa in St Lucia—I think the sea-life overwhelmed them after all the other changes. Elena and son are doing a crash course in English and she and Irina are in almost daily contact with the tattle-man called Jack. He's even been down to visit. He's kind, clever and sincere. His outpourings about the Overlords (collectively he calls them Goliath) and their intentions are causing ever-greater scrutiny and some serious re-direction. There had to have been a maverick, a dangerous dissenter in the Warsaw committee but we don't see it any longer as a threat since Jack's revelations. So intriguing—they invited him to get him on their side and—BACKFIRE!

Some of this you may not understand but I'm putting it down for my own clarity. No doubt you've heard all about the end of the Mayan 26,000 year calendar—the good news, IT'S OVER!! And a new one has begun and you are alive in the most amazing time that's ever been in humanity's history. Well, someone had to be! This is our privilege and there's a new vision of an emerging world completely transforming itself. It will surely take time but Time itself seems to be speeding up. Since it's a human invention I suppose we can do anything we like with it!

I think of evolution as an unstoppable force and therefore any plans to enslave under a one-world government must ultimately fail—but as Elena said, the Overlords will come willingly or unwillingly. When they examine the choice, they'll see it's a no-brainer. Humanity is waking up from what will be seen as the very darkest of Dark Ages but now there is no excuse, such as ignorance.

As for Dark Forces and aliens and reptilians you mentioned—there's a million notes on the web but I have no clear idea. Some people do, but anything we can't understand from them we tend to label as crank. Quantum physics has thrown a wrench into conventional thinking by showing that everything is simply energy in one form or another, including the very energy of a thought. We cannot see it, we can only see its results and there've undoubtedly been evil forces at work—quite logical because this duality we inhabit must contain everything imaginable AND its opposite. The only thing 'wrong' is that we forget who we really are, remember?—the joyful and fearless Cosmic Super-voyagers exploring Eden/Gaia and all the things that intrigue them which also means deciding on all the things that don't—and some of those we even see as fearful! Some are addictions, some simply diversions from the truth. I am SO hyped at your existence at this time and I smile inside whenever I think of you, which is often.

We've a Yamaha keyboard in the saloon for your Mom as well as me, while Rose Madder plays guitar and writes songs—we discovered that's where most of her wealth comes from—royalties. She has half a dozen major hits but she shies away from saying what they are. She wrote this one with Igor and they seem quite delighted with each other and there's so much laughter. He has a huge bass voice. He's never been sailing before and is mesmerized, like he's enchanted. In Antigua we got invited for a day-sail aboard the most exquisite 80' schooner called *Lelantina,* so exciting that Rose forgot to get seasick! Together they came up with:

Caribbean Dream

> *A schooner swoons on a sapphire sea,*
> > *Eager the look in your eye,*
> *She leans to the wind as you lean to me,*
> > *There are no dark clouds in the sky,*
> *Oh, the easy breezes gentling skin,*
> > *Tomorrow moves like the horizon,*
> *The warm deep blue invites you in,*
> > *And your beauty fills my eyes. On*
> *The helm your hand and the other in mine,*
> > *I see your gaze full of wonder,*
> *Neath swelling sails she heaves so fine,*
> > *You ask me, Where do we wander?*
> *There's an island new for you every day,*
> > *There's coves and reefs for exploring,*
> *The under-scenes take our breath away,*
> > *There's peace with every mooring.*
> *There's a warm wind waiting to take us there,*
> > *The pliant palms are beckoning,*
> *Their blessing for lovers everywhere,*
> > *And the end of old dead reckoning.*
> *If cosmic voyages have no end,*
> > *And we set sail together,*
> *If you're my love and, too, my friend,*
> > *Then this must be forever…*

As for Elena, words aren't enough. She does look a lot like that famous skater, Gordeeva. (see pic). Here is someone who has emerged from a stretch of poverty and poisonous discomfort and she is clearly transfigured and has affected everyone, but one in particular, her mother! From translation by Annie, I gather that any hint of complaint or censure is promptly neutralized by that sublime smile or some affectionate gesture. In the attached pics you'll see Svetlana's posture and expression in the G5's cockpit with her hero son Igor in the left seat completely in command and showing her all the baffling technologies. Nobility has been restored. At one point he got up and left her sitting there alone and then stuck Ilya in the left seat, first with tears of joy, then grinning like a big puppy. And Ilya's physical problems have apparently vanished. And Anastasia smiles constantly and seems lit from within. She says she will change her face if she has to grin for 30 years. Fine with me! And Irina is bonded to Elena like a limpet and writes everything down. They're planning a book together...

Elena seems to understand her discovery of herself but there's no hint of vanity, just delight in being alive, sentient, conscious. Everyone just LOVES being around her! She encapsulates the secret of existence. She rivets us all and sometimes we sit in a circle while she gazes at each of us in turn, says almost nothing and seems to transmit a mysterious grace.

So....Instead of going South all the way to Trinidad or Venezuela, we keep turning back to St Lucia to see them again! That's when the speed of this great beast is useful...We've even had visitors aboard who have eagerly joined in and when Jack came here with his wife, Elena blew them away and started her channeling again. She began by saying that one word changed her life, can you guess what that was? I thought it was just a careless throw-off yet it had to be inspiration and makes me want to contradict an established saying: 'Be care*less* what you *don't know* you wish for', because, and far more thoroughly than any NSA spying, the Universe is listening, and unlike the Internet, it can't be shut down! It's there for the asking, loaded with blessings, and it knows who you are and what is your yearning. It can take a while to discover this power, and there's no hurry. All is well....*Panta rhei*, said Heraclitus, an ancient Greek—Everything is in flux. Everything. That's quantum. I wonder how he knew? Must've been channeling! *Just delight in how you are with whatever shows up...Delight produces DMT!*

Love always, see you as soon as you report for duty, First Officer James Moncrieffe,
Dad. xoxox

In the end, only kindness matters. *Jewel*, Singer/songwriter.

Previous work by Christopher Murphy, also on Kindle

- Scream at the Sea
- The Jericho Rumble
- Dance for a Diamond
- Dance on Wild Ice
- Emerald Passage
- How to Startle Yourself--A Self-Help book about why Self-Help books don't help!

Made in the USA
Lexington, KY
09 December 2019

58321749R00188